I hope you enjoy The Cast Net!

Millie West

The Cast Net

by

Millie West

BQB

Alpharetta, Georgia

The Cast Net
Original edition © 2012 Millie West
Revised edition © 2013 Millie West
All Rights Reserved.
www.milliewestauthor.com

No part of this book may be reproduced in any form or by any means, electronic, mechanical, digital, photocopying, or recording, except for the inclusion in a review, without permission in writing from the publisher.

This is a work of fiction. All of the characters, names, incidents, organizations, and dialogue in this novel are either the products of the author's imagination or are used fictitiously.

Published in the United States by BQB Publishing
(Boutique of Quality Books Publishing)
www.bqbpublishing.com

Revised edition.

ISBN 978-1-939371-12-6 (p)
ISBN 978-1-939371-13-3 (e)

Library of Congress Control Number: 2012931891

Cover painting by Rick Reinert, www.rickreinert.com
Interior by Robin Krauss, Linden Design, www.lindendesign.biz

Dedication

This book is for Tony, Whitney, and Micah. Thank you for your love and support. And it is also for my late mother, Edna, who believed in me with unfaltering love.

Acknowledgments

I would like to thank the following people who helped bring *The Cast Net* to life: Terri, Lisa, Jeff, Robin, Lori, Katy, Julie, Heidi, and the highly talented team at Boutique of Quality Books Publishing Company. I am grateful to you for giving me a chance and allowing the message of my novel to be heard!

My editors, Eve Paludan and Megan Miller, for their countless hours helping me with my work, giving excellent advice, and strengthening my novel. Their patience and brilliant suggestions will forever be appreciated!

My favorite artist, Rick Reinert, of Charleston, South Carolina, for allowing me to use his beautiful painting, *September Marsh*, as the cover for my novel. Besides being a phenomenally talented artist, he is an extremely gracious man who helped bring my vision to completion.

Felix Kirszenbaum for allowing me to use his likeness as the talented contractor, Fritz Zimmermann. I have been fortunate to learn from this exceptional thinker, and he really does speak seven languages!

Attorney Gary Pickren for allowing me to use his humorous flower mix-up tale; Danny Brown for his Georgia ghost story; Kristen Emptage, FNP, and Dr. Danielle Bernth for sharing their medical knowledge; and attorney Smokey Brown for his legal advice.

Several people who helped shape *The Cast Net,* and whose assistance I will always appreciate: Vicki Haren Dwan, Gayle and Lou Chiasson, Charles and Sharon Weber, Dottie Ellett, Sheri Martin, Mary Emmerling, Sheri Ross, Sara Clary, and Betty Lanier. I could not have managed without the assistance of my daughter, Whitney, my husband, Tony, and son, Micah.

Last, but certainly not least, I want to thank the Chapin Writer's group, whose many excellent suggestions helped bring *The Cast Net* to completion. Elaine Allcut, Cathy Fitzgerald, Vonnie Fulmer, Ellen Menzo, Madelyn Serina, Charlotte Blackstone, Jim and Sallie Peters, Lauren Dunn, Edith Hawkins, Jessica Morris, Sue Cryer . . . to all of you, I say, thank you!

CHAPTER 1

Discovery – December, 1988

Mills jumped back toward the curb as a speeding taxi ran a red light and came within inches of hitting her. Losing her balance, she slipped on slush from yesterday's snow storm. It had been the first snow in December and had caught most of New York City by surprise.

As she fell, Mills lost hold of her briefcase and landed on her hands and knees. She heard a man with a Bronx accent yell at the taxi driver. "Hey, look where ya goin—"

The morning rush-hour crowd pushed by her to cross the street, and she couldn't get to her feet before a man and two women stepped over her. She crawled out of the street back onto the sidewalk, but her path was blocked by a pair of worn brown work boots caked in salty grime. The next thing she knew, Mills was on her feet being supported by a burly construction worker—he was wearing a metal safety hat on his head.

"Hey, you okay, lady? That cabby almost run you over."

Mills's knees were shaking from the fall, and she stammered, "Yes—thank you for your help."

He bent over, picked up her briefcase, and handed it to her. "Now watch these New York cabbies," he said with a smile. Before she could say another word, he turned and crossed the street with the light. Mills brushed the wet snow from her pants, took a deep breath, and crossed Sixth Avenue. As she reached her office building on West 57th, a strong gust of wind whipped between the buildings, blowing snow from window ledges into the air. The powder descended to the ground as twinkling ice crystals, glittering in the early morning sunlight. When the air cleared from the blowing snow, Mills saw the red flashing lights of an ambulance that was underneath the front portico of her building. She froze in place.

Paramedics briskly pushed a stretcher out to the ambulance from inside the building. Mills watched as a man with an oxygen mask on his face was placed inside the vehicle. She was mesmerized by the flashing red lights and the siren as the ambulance pulled away. A tug on her coat sleeve by the security guard, Claude Glenville, gained her attention. "Miss Taylor, are you okay?"

"Yes, Mr. Glenville—I think so. I slipped on the snow on my way to work. Who's in the ambulance?"

"Mr. Wilcox—he's a lawyer with Jacobs and Sons on the fifth floor. He was having chest pains. I hope he'll be okay."

"Yes—I do too."

"Let me get the door for you—it's supposed to warm up this afternoon, so most of the snow should be gone later today." He went ahead of her, opening the glass door.

"Thank you," Mills said as she passed him.

"Have a good day now," he said as she entered the foyer on her way to the elevator. Mills smiled at him and waved before pushing the up button. By the time the elevator arrived, a small crowd had formed and went in with her. When the doors closed, she asked a man at the front to press the button for the tenth floor. Then her thoughts went back to the man on the stretcher, the red lights and siren of the ambulance, and the sparkling crystals of the blowing snow in the sunlight. As the elevator doors opened on her floor, she took a deep breath and went to her boss's office.

Knocking on the oak door, she waited until her boss Harry called out, "Come in."

She opened the door and entered his office. He turned and studied her appearance for just a moment, his eyes lingering on the wet marks on her knees. "What happened to you?"

"I was almost run over by a taxi this morning on my way to work."

"Are you all right?"

"Yes, just a little flustered from the experience."

"Well I guess so—catch your breath and when you're ready, let's take a look at the advertisements you did for the Roberts's account."

She inhaled and then removed several sketches from her portfolio spreading them out on his desk.

He studied her work before saying, "Mills, this is excellent. I believe that Roberts will be very happy with what you've done."

"Thank you."

As Harry continued to look over sketches, Mills noticed a newspaper article from *The New York Times* on his desk, neatly folded to display the photograph of a man. The date on the article: November 12, 1988. The caption read: "Cooper Heath, of Heath Brothers Shipping, Newark, NJ, and Charleston, SC." Mills thought him very handsome with dark, wavy hair and well dressed in a business suit.

"Who is this man in the newspaper photograph?"

"He's an old friend of mine. We attended the Air Force Academy together." Mills picked up the paper and scanned the article. Apparently Heath was a shipping executive from Charleston, South Carolina, and his wife had been missing since August. "Why was this reported in *The New York Times*?"

"My friend is from an old Southern family, and aside from his family's assets, he's done well for himself. His family owns a global shipping firm. I guess *The New York Times* picked up the story."

Mills nodded.

Harry continued, "He phoned me several days ago, seeking a director for an educational foundation that he operates. I thought about recommending a couple of people out of our Boston office."

"Please tell me more about this foundation."

"The scholarship program is for low-income youths who maintain good grades and stay out of trouble. His mother started the program before her death and Cooper wants to get more of the community involved. He said that with his job and farm responsibilities, he doesn't have the time to properly run the foundation."

"Farm responsibilities?"

"Yes, he maintains a large farm on the Edisto River near Charleston. He uses much of the profits from the farm production to fund the scholarships. Cooper was one year behind me at the Air Force Academy; I tease him that he turned in his F-4 for a John Deere."

"I don't understand."

"He traded in his jet fighter for a tractor—Cooper is a conservationist. Dating to the late 1600s, his ancestors on his mother's side were merchants and planters in the Charleston area. They came to South Carolina from Barbados to make money, and that's what they did—it seems to be a family trait."

"Sounds interesting," Mills added.

Harry sat back in his chair. Mills noticed a puzzled expression on his face. "What are you thinking?"

"I went to school on a scholarship."

"And?"

"I could help others get ahead—like I was helped."

A frown crossed Harry's brow. "Is what happened to you this morning causing you to think about leaving? You do a nice job here, and I don't want to lose you."

Almost getting killed by a taxi does give me cause to pause and think. "Harry—I nearly got injured this morning—I'd just like to read the job description."

"Fair enough—you can take the file on the Heath Foundation home with you tonight."

"Thank you; do the authorities have any idea about what happened to his wife?"

"No, they haven't been able to get a lead. Cooper's been beside himself. The police, Cooper, his friends, and members of the community searched all of the roadways in the Edisto area, the waterways, you name it. Missing person posters were put up all over the Low Country. She vanished without a trace."

"It must be awful not knowing what happened to her."

"Yes. Elise Heath is a charming woman. Her disappearance is a terrible tragedy."

That evening Mills pored over the information in the Heath Scholarship file and found herself once again staring at the photograph of Cooper Heath in *The New York Times* article. The foundation's address was in Alston Station, South Carolina—a small community near Charleston. The more she looked over the file, the more impressed she was about the positive impact that his program had on young people.

When one of her roommates, Amber, came home that evening, Mills handed her the information on the Heath Foundation, including the newspaper article on Cooper Heath. "I think I might have a job opportunity in Charleston, South Carolina."

"Are you serious?" Amber replied in astonishment.

"Yes, I am—I would be the director of an education foundation that was started by the late Julia M. Heath. I read the file—she was involved in charities in the Charleston area. She wanted to help families get out of poverty, so she started a scholarship program for young people. I think I'd like to be involved."

Amber looked at the newspaper photo before she glanced up at Mills. "Nice looking man."

As she began to read the article, her expression changed to a frown. "It says here that his wife has been missing for several months—she disappeared without a trace. What do you know about Cooper Heath?"

"He's a friend of my boss's, and Harry says he's one of the finest people he's ever known."

"People change. Even sophisticated, wealthy people commit crimes of passion. I've never known you to take risks, and I'd say that you could be living dangerously. What's wrong with your job here in New York? You've done very well."

"I want a change." *I almost died on the way to work this morning.*

"Please make sure that this is the change you should make. I'm sure there are plenty of opportunities for a smart girl like you."

"Thank you, Amber." Mills smiled at her friend, but her mind was already moving ahead with her plans.

The next morning, Mills knocked on the door of Harry's office as soon as she arrived at work. After a moment, Harry called out to her, "Come in and have a seat, Mills. Did you think about the Heath Foundation last night?"

"Yes, I did. I decided that I would like to speak with Mr. Heath before I make a decision."

"All right—he did tell me that he would be at the Newark office of Heath Brothers next week. Perhaps you can meet with him then. I haven't seen him in months—I'll go with you."

Harry had made arrangements for them to meet with Cooper Heath at Antoine's on Madison. Christmas was less than two weeks away and the storefronts were handsomely decorated with red bows, wreaths, and garlands of green. It was the coldest day of December so far and the sky was cloudless and a brilliant shade of blue.

When Mills and Harry entered Antoine's, a tall, well-dressed man stood up at a corner table in the rear of the restaurant and smiled at them. "There's Cooper." Harry smiled back in recognition.

They joined him at his table, and the two men embraced each other in a hug. "God, it's good to see you," Harry said. "Cooper, this is Mills Taylor. She's interested in the director's job for your educational foundation. Of course, I've tried to talk her out of it for purely selfish reasons—I don't want to lose her."

He took Mills's hand to shake it, and she noticed how warm his hands were. "I confess I recognized you from a newspaper photograph that Harry had of you."

He did not respond to her comment, and Harry quickly added, "Cooper, how are things going with your company's contract negotiations?"

"I'm meeting with a representative of Perret International of Le Havre, France, Henri Duchard. If talks work out, we should increase our shipping with France and bring more jobs to Charleston and Newark."

Mills studied Cooper's appearance and she thought him attractive, with an excellent complexion and an athletic build. His blue eyes exuded brightness and warmth when he smiled.

"Mills, thank you for your interest in the directorship," he said.

"Yes sir. I went to school on a scholarship, and I believe I'd like to help. I'd think of it as a way I can pay back those who assisted me." *He only has a slight Southern accent, and his voice is confident and calming.*

They discussed the foundation until their lunch arrived, and then the subject changed to current Broadway plays. "I'm a big fan of theater, especially musicals," Mills said.

"The oldest designed theater in the United States, the Dock Street Theatre, is in Charleston. Many performances are still held there," Cooper added.

"Speaking of performances, Mills, you should hear Cooper play the piano," Harry said.

"What type of music do you like to play?" she asked.

"Mostly classical."

"He writes his own songs—simply amazing."

"I'd like to hear you perform."

"I'll be glad to play for you some time," Cooper responded.

Harry was especially jovial around his friend, and Mills concluded that he attempted to brighten Cooper's spirits. After they finished eating, Harry told Cooper, "I think Mills brought her portfolio to show you examples of her work."

"Yes, by all means—please do," Cooper said.

She placed her portfolio on the table and removed its contents. The case contained magazine promotions, news releases, original art, and several business plans that were executed when she'd assisted companies as a public relations advisor. There was also a photo of her wearing her dark brown hair at shoulder length with a brief biography. She handed the photo to Cooper.

"I see you finished the University of Virginia with degrees in journalism and art." Cooper nodded his head as he read her biography.

"Yes sir. I've been with Harry's agency for the last four years."

"Very good," Cooper said as he continued to look over her creations. When he finished, he looked up and their eyes locked. "Mills, I think your work is excellent. You've shown clever ingenuity on your projects."

"Thank you, Mr. Heath."

They spent more than two hours at lunch, but before they finished, Cooper told Harry that he would like him to attend his annual oyster roast, which would be held the first Saturday in February. "I had considered not having it this year, but so many people inquired that I decided to go forward with it. After all, the donations from the oyster roast do fund scholarships."

Harry looked at his watch before saying, "Thank you for the invitation, Cooper. Unfortunately, I have an appointment in an hour. I must go."

As they retrieved their coats, Cooper told Mills, "I have some time before my next meeting. Would you like to take a walk?"

Mills nodded, and Harry embraced his friend saying, "Please know that I've been praying for you and Elise."

"Thank you, Harry," Cooper quietly responded before Harry departed.

Even though she wore high heels and a fitted business suit, Mills wanted to know more about him and decided to join him for a walk. Cooper helped with her overcoat before putting on his, and they left the restaurant.

Madison Avenue bustled with holiday shoppers and they stopped in front of a jewelry store that displayed an extravagant collection of diamonds in the window. Inside the business, they saw a couple looking at rings. The woman held her hand out in front of her, admiring a ring that her companion had placed on her finger, and then she leaped into his arms. He held her tightly as they slowly rotated together.

"Looks like someone's just been made very happy," Cooper observed.

"Yes, it certainly looked that way to me too," Mills commented as they resumed their walk.

They stopped for a cup of coffee at a vendor's cart near Central Park, and Cooper removed his Wayfarer sunglasses and looked attentively into her eyes. "What was the newspaper article about where you saw my picture?"

"It was an article in *The New York Times* about you and your missing wife."

"There have been many newspaper articles about me in recent months, but I'm not familiar with that one."

"Mr. Heath, I—"

"No, it's okay, Mills, a number of people have passed judgment on me. They believe that I am involved in my wife's disappearance. I promise you, I did not harm her."

"I have not judged you, but why are you hiring a director for your educational foundation from outside the Charleston area? I'm sure there are qualified candidates in South Carolina."

He was quiet for a moment. "I wanted to work with an individual who would not judge me on the negative information that has been in the regional news for the last several months."

"I see—anyway, Harry vouched for you."

He gazed at her briefly and then signaled for a taxi. "I'm sorry, but I must go. Please think over what we've discussed. I'll be in Charleston next week, and I hope to hear from you. Where would you like to go now?"

"I'd like to return to my office."

Cooper gave instructions to the driver and before she left, he warmly shook her hand. When the taxi reached her destination, she asked the driver what she owed. He replied, "Miss, your companion already paid me. Thank you, and have a good afternoon."

When she entered the office, Harry asked, "How did you like Cooper?"

"I thought he was candid and very charming. Harry, I don't think I've ever seen you smile as much as you did at lunch today."

"Cooper won't show it, but I know he has been very depressed. I just want to cheer him up, if that's possible—have you decided what you're going to do?"

"Yes, I'd like to accept the position with the Heath Foundation. Mr. Heath asked me to call him next week."

Harry's expression was unreadable. "Just remember—you always have a job here if things don't work out."

"Thank you, Harry."

Mills accepted the position with the Heath Foundation the following week. She had familiarized herself with the job expectations from the foundation file, and she and Cooper worked out final details over the phone. The job offer included free lodging at a townhome Cooper owned in downtown Charleston, but he explained there was also a cottage on the Heath Farm where she could reside—it was her choice.

Mills spent Christmas at her mother's house in Virginia and she had a difficult time convincing her mother and sister that her decision to accept the job with the Heath Foundation was a sound one. She reminded both of them that Cooper was not under arrest. Inquiries into what Mills thought of Cooper led her to describe him as sincere and charming. Her sister, Vivien, who was two years older than Mills, reminded her that Ted Bundy had lured his victims with charm. Based on Harry Foster's judgment, her mother, Rebecca, eventually agreed with Mills's decision to move to Charleston. She believed that Harry possessed a high moral character; his unwavering confidence in his friend was the persuading factor in her decision.

On the day after New Year's, before 6 a.m., Mills began her drive from Virginia to South Carolina. When she turned on her car radio, the first song that played was "Cast Your Fate to the Wind."

As she drove south, the day was stunningly clear. The weather was similar to the day when she had met Cooper in New York. As she thought of the events of the last few weeks, Harry's gentle warnings came to mind. "Mills, while Cooper is a straight arrow, I'm afraid you might encounter some people in his social circle who don't share his moral convictions. I don't want you to go down there and get involved with . . ." She had been tickled by his fatherly advice.

Lastly, he'd said, "I just want you to be the success that I know you can be—don't ever forget that."

Harry had been fair with her, but Mills thought she was about to accept a worthwhile challenge that could help other people. She understood the importance of scholarship programs for people who lacked the financial resources to attend college—she had attended college on an academic scholarship while working part-time in one of the school's cafeterias.

Her thoughts wandered to her own father who had died at age forty-two, following a massive coronary. He had not been overweight, but lean and fit, which made his life-ending heart attack harder to understand. Both of his daughters had inherited tall, slender frames from his side of the family, but resembled their mother, Rebecca, with large, dark eyes and thick, brunette hair that curled into waves when allowed to dry naturally.

Mills did not want to disappoint her mother. She was the kind of woman who had made sacrifices in order to ensure her daughters received the best education and had every opportunity for success. Rebecca had grown up during the Depression, which caused her to exercise caution in money matters. However, she generously tried to give the best to her daughters. She always told Mills and Vivien, "The first part of achieving your goals is to see yourself there. If there's anything you want in life, you'd better go and get it."

Out of respect for their mother, both Mills and her sister strived to do their best in school and were not the type to misbehave. Mills loved a challenge and was always the top fundraiser for school projects and charities. She felt that the directorship for the Heath Foundation was a natural fit for her and that it was her opportunity to help others succeed. It helped that Cooper had been intent on hiring her after he learned of her educational background.

By the middle of the afternoon, she had reached Alston Station, located in the western portion of Charleston County. As she neared the community, she noted the surroundings were sparsely developed with numerous waterways and marsh areas. Her first impression was that it was more of a village than a town, with a mercantile named Dawkins Market, a post office, a couple of antique stores, and several lovely houses built along the Edisto River. Enormous live oaks, drenched in Spanish moss, lined the sandy streets and filled the yards. Several brick buildings no longer housed businesses, but Mills thought that they must have been used as warehouses during the days of cotton production. Cooper had explained that the town was named after a prominent Southern family, which included a former governor, and was used as a loading post on the Edisto for rice and later cotton. These staples, which produced Southern wealth, were shipped to Charleston and then to the north or overseas.

Mills drove down a sandy lane to Cooper's property. His farm bordered the south branch of the Edisto River and she found that the low terrain was thickly overgrown with scrub palms. She passed over a bridge with a plaque that read "Simmons Creek," but it was hard to tell that a creek was there, as the entire area looked more like a dark-colored marsh.

She continued driving down the lane and a large area of fenced-in land appeared on either side of the road. Part of the property was a pasture, but a large portion had been plowed and appeared to be set aside for crops. When she reached Cooper's address, she turned her Volkswagen down a tree-lined drive where she saw an old barn and a stately horse stable. At the end of the lane, surrounded by live oak trees, was a raised cottage with a muted silver-colored roof. In front of the home, a courtyard displayed a fountain with a cherub holding a torch. Water cascaded out of the torch into a lower brick fountain base, which was surrounded by miniature boxwoods.

Parking her car in front of the courtyard, Mills climbed the steps to his front door. She felt nervous for the first time and took a deep breath. Wind chimes on the porch sounded a gentle resonance of blended tones in the breeze. In fact, the only sounds she could hear were the harmonious tones of the chimes and the water cascading from the fountain.

Old gas lanterns were situated on either side of the double doors. She took another deep breath and rang the doorbell. Within a few moments, Mills heard the footfalls of someone approaching the doorway. When the door opened, an older woman with a round face, graying hair, and a radiant smile appeared in the threshold. Her face showed few wrinkles and Mills knew immediately that she was Cooper's housekeeper, Marian. During one of her conversations with Cooper, he had mentioned Marian and her son, Charles, who managed his farm.

"Are you Miss Taylor?"

"Yes, ma'am."

"I'm Marian Sullivan. We've been expecting you. Please come inside."

In the foyer, Mills glanced around appreciatively at the opulent setting.

In the center of the room was a stunning, antique mahogany table; on it, a delicate glass hurricane lamp engraved with tropical birds and foliage took center stage. And above this was an ornate crystal chandelier hanging from a decorated plaster ceiling.

"Let me take your coat," said Marian. "Cooper is out on the farm this afternoon doing repair work to some damaged fence wire. Why don't you come into the kitchen and I'll fix you some tea—oh, forgive me, do you need to freshen up first?"

"No, ma'am, I'm fine."

Mills followed her into the kitchen, looking into the rooms as she passed. Most of the decorating was done in a West Indies furniture style that complemented the design of the home.

"Mr. Heath's home is lovely."

"I agree. I'd show you around but I'm sure he'd like to do that himself." Marian put on the tea kettle and offered Mills a seat at the kitchen island.

She smiled again before asking, "How was your trip from Virginia?"

"The driving conditions were good, but it's been extremely cold."

"Down here too."

When the tea was ready, Marian poured the steaming water over the tea bags and handed Mills a cup. Within a few moments, the front door opened and Marian called out, "Cooper, Miss Taylor and I are in the kitchen."

"Please call me Mills," she told Marian.

Cooper entered the kitchen and extended his right hand for a handshake. "Welcome Mills. I apologize that I was not here to greet you in person, but I see that you and Marian had the chance to meet."

"Cooper, would you like some hot tea?" Marian interjected.

"Thank you, Marian. I'm going to show Mills into the study. Would you bring the tea in there, please?"

"I'd be glad to."

Cooper helped Mills with a chair in the study and then sat down behind his desk. He looked at her warmly, studying her face. "I hope your trip from New York was a pleasant one."

"Yes, it was. I visited with my mother and sister in Virginia over Christmas. It was nice to see them."

Marian brought in a cup of tea for Cooper and he thanked her as she left the room. "What would you like to do first, see the cottage or discuss business?"

"Let's first go over business."

He handed her a file that had "Oyster Roast Fundraiser" written on it.

"This is the invitation list for the oyster roast and I'm afraid that I'm behind this year. Information on the printing company that I use for the invitations is in here. Don't worry. I've already made arrangements with White Point Catering to handle the oyster roast, and I've written the contact name inside the file." He sat silently for a moment. "I really didn't want to hold the oyster roast this year, without Elise, but donations from guests to the scholarship fund have proved very helpful in the past."

Mills nodded sympathetically. As he spoke to her, Mills noticed the photograph of a beautiful woman with wavy, golden hair on the shelf behind him. She knew immediately the photo was of Elise Heath, but her attention was quickly drawn back to Cooper.

"This file contains the names of students who are actively involved in the scholarship program, a list of possible donors, and contact information on Dr. Frances Warren with the Charleston County school system. Her assistance has proved to be invaluable, and I believe you'll enjoy working with her."

Mills glanced back at the photo of the lovely woman on the shelf behind Cooper's desk, and he seemed to notice the photograph had captivated Mills's eyes. He picked up the frame and said quietly, "This is Elise."

"She's very beautiful."

He appeared tense as he placed the photograph back on the shelf. "Thank you." Rising from behind his desk, Cooper helped Mills with her chair and said, "Please allow me to show you around."

Walking back into the foyer, he began to tell her about the house. "My parents purchased this property in the 1950s. As far as we know, the house was built in the 1870s by a northern investor named Samuel Atkinson. When my parents bought the property, the house was in disrepair and it took several years to restore it. I spent most of my summers here as a boy."

On the living room walls were several gorgeous paintings of Low Country scenes. "Your paintings are lovely."

"Thank you. All of the artwork was done locally. There are very talented artists in Charleston."

Beside the fireplace was a carved wooden cane leaning against a corner. The top of the staff was carved in the shape of an African woman's face, her hair flowing back to form the handle.

"What an exceptional piece of woodwork. Would it be all right if I held the cane?" Mills asked.

"Yes, go right ahead. It was carved by a past relative of mine."

Mills studied the carved handle with care before remarking, "Her features are so delicate."

"George Camp was the craftsman, and he possessed a rare talent. He carved this piece during the American Civil War."

As Mills returned the cane to its resting place, she glanced up at a painting above the fireplace. "Who is the lady in the portrait?"

"Julia, my mother."

"She was an elegant woman."

"Thank you. She was very ill during the last few years of her life. I still miss her."

A magnificent baby grand piano graced the living room and Mills noticed the intricate carving on the legs of the instrument. "Don't forget . . . you said you'd play the piano for me."

"I won't forget."

She ran her fingers across the back of a mahogany chair. "Where did your furniture come from?"

"Years ago, my parents purchased most of it from an estate in Barbados. When the elderly owner passed away, the heirs weren't interested in retaining the furniture."

Before going outside, he showed her one last room, which he called his hunting room. "This is my favorite room."

On the walls were numerous hunting trophies, family photographs, ocean charts, and what looked to be aviation charts.

"What type of map is this?"

"That chart is done by Jeppesen. They print aviation charts for pilots."

"Do you still fly? Harry told me you were an Air Force fighter pilot."

"Yes, I own an airplane that I keep at the John's Island Airport. I don't fly it as much as I'd like."

Mills looked around the room. She glanced inside a glass gun cabinet, which held several shotguns and rifles; on the wall beside the gun cabinet, a photograph caught her attention. "Is this you, and who is this with you? He favors you a great deal."

Cooper looked at the photo. "That's a picture of me with my brother, Beau. He passed away some years ago."

"Mr. Heath, I'm sorry, I didn't mean to bring up—"

"It's all right. It was a long time ago. Did Marian put your coat in the closet?"

"Yes, she did."

Cooper returned with her coat and they exited the house into a rear courtyard. A large yellow Labrador sunbathed on the brick patio. He rose to his feet as soon as he saw Cooper.

Petting the dog on the head, Cooper said, "This is my dog, Sam. He's quite the bird hunter."

Mills gave the dog a pat. An outdoor fireplace was located at the back of the courtyard and near it was a large red-colored handle on what appeared to be a water pump. "What type of handle is that?"

"I'll show you."

Taking the handle in his right hand, he pushed it back and forth several times, and water began to flow out of a nozzle. "It's a manual well pump; it comes in handy when the electricity is off."

Azalea bushes lined a sandy lane from the courtyard and, beyond the pathway, numerous live oaks and palmetto trees turned the terrain lush and wild. "I'm going to show you the river," Cooper said as they continued to walk. The Edisto River came into view, prompting Mills to ask, "Why is the house such a distance from the river?"

"The builder of the home must have been knowledgeable of hurricanes and flooding. The storm surge that comes ashore with a hurricane can rise twenty feet high or more. It's doubtful that we could get anything that catastrophic, but it could rise several feet in severe conditions. When my parents renovated our house, the construction workers found that the fireplaces are built many feet into the ground to anchor the home in high wind and flooding situations."

"That's very interesting," Mills responded.

When they reached the waterfront, she gazed at the river and the marshlands before saying, "It's beautiful here—so peaceful."

"I think so too. Come this way—I'd like to show you the boathouse," Cooper said, motioning for her to follow him to a small building at the edge of the waterway. He opened the door, showing her inside. The front of the boathouse had a den area with a table and chairs in the center; mounted on the walls were numerous pieces of fishing equipment. Two kayaks rested in one corner of the building.

He pointed to the kayaks. "You're welcome to use the kayaks any time you want."

"Thank you, Mr. Heath."

"Come—I'll show you the dock." They left the boathouse and walked toward the river.

Two fishing boats were on boatlifts. Cooper explained that the smaller of the two was a flats boat used for fishing and hunting in the marsh. The larger craft was a Boston Whaler, named the *Miss Elise*, and underneath the name was Charleston, SC.

"What makes the river so dark?" Mills asked.

"The color is caused by the tannic acid in the leaves of cypress trees and other waterfront trees that line the river. As the leaves break down, they dye the water a dark, amber brown."

They walked back toward Cooper's home, and he led her through a row of mature camellia bushes to a privately situated swimming pool.

"This is beautiful; did you put the pool in?"

"Yes, my wife and I did."

They continued their walk. About fifty feet down a pathway from the swimming pool, a small cottage presented itself. Like the larger house on the property, it had a raised foundation with a lengthy set of steps that led to a porch.

"If you want, you can live here."

"Oh, it's beautiful." *I love it*. She climbed the stairs and opened the screen door to the porch. Her eyes focused on a set of French doors. She crossed the porch and opened the double doors. Stepping inside, Mills glanced up at exposed beams that spanned either side of a cathedral ceiling. Upholstered furniture was casually arranged around the fireplace. At the rear of the cottage was a door that opened to the bedroom, and inside was a four poster wooden bed with mosquito netting over the top of a canopy.

When she went back into the living area, Cooper was waiting beside the French doors. "What did you use the cottage for?"

"My mother lived here before she became too ill. Later, my wife used it for entertaining her friends. It hasn't been used lately."

"I think this cottage is wonderful. I'll be able to do most of my work right here in the living area."

"So it's no to the townhouse in Charleston? You haven't seen it yet," he said, raising his eyebrows.

"I think I'll be happy here."

"Okay, I'm glad you like it. Can I help you move anything inside?"

"Yes. I gave my furniture to my roommates in New York, so I just have my clothes, personal items, and some of my artwork. I'll move my car!"

Cooper waited for her outside the cottage while she drove her Beetle from the main house. Together, they unloaded her possessions, which included an extensive shoe collection. When they finished, Cooper told her that a friend of his would be joining him for dinner that evening, and he invited her to join them. "You were on the road most of the day. Please join us at seven."

"Thank you, I'll see you then, Mr. Heath."

"Oh, and Mills, I'd like for you to call me Cooper."

"Yes, sir," she said with a smile.

When she entered his house for dinner, there was a recording of Billie Holiday's poignant rendition of "Solitude" playing in the kitchen. Mills thought, *does his choice of music reflect his frame of mind?*

Three people in the kitchen waited to greet her, and Cooper turned off the music. "Mills, I'd like for you to meet Charles Sullivan, and his wife, Elizabeth." As she shook their hands, an attractive, dark-haired man, standing at the rear of the kitchen, stepped forward to meet her. "Mills, this is my friend, Britton Smith." Britton smiled and extended his right hand to her.

Cooper continued, "Charles manages my farm and Elizabeth also wanted to meet you."

Cooper watched as they exchanged greetings. *Charles is taller and more muscular than Cooper and has a serious scar on his forehead.* Taking her hand for a hand shake, Charles said, "Miss Mills, I look forward to working with you." Elizabeth then shook her hand smiling broadly as she did. "We need to be heading on. See you tomorrow," Charles said as he put his arm around his wife's shoulder. *Nice couple—probably in their mid-fifties.* Then he and Elizabeth said good night and left through the kitchen door.

As she spoke with Britton, Mills noticed a collection of sweetgrass baskets displayed on bookshelves along the wall. A door leading to a pantry was open, an abundant collection of homemade canned items crowding its shelves. The pantry was orderly, though, with sections set aside for tomatoes, jams, and other canned goods. In fact, she had never seen such detailed organization in a pantry.

Cooper motioned to them. "Please sit down; we'll be ready to eat in a few minutes."

He placed a salad and a baked potato on each of the plates before opening the kitchen door. "I'm going to take the steaks off the grill. Have some wine if you'd like." When he returned, he put fillets on their plates and joined them at the table.

"Mills, Britton is a harbor pilot in Charleston."

"What does a harbor pilot do?" she asked.

"I assist in the navigation of commercial ships traveling in and out of the Port of Charleston."

"Do you assist ships for Heath Brothers?"

"Yes, ma'am, occasionally."

She noticed that Britton seemed shy around her and that he said very little unless he was asked a question.

"Mills—tomorrow morning, Britton and I are going duck hunting."

"What time do you start?"

"We'll rise at four to get out on the river," Cooper said.

During the meal, they discussed the oyster roast and Cooper's foundation. When they finished dinner, Mills told him how much she had enjoyed the steak.

"I'm glad you liked it. I shot that deer just a few months ago."

"That was venison?"

"Yes—I'll play the piano for you if you'd still like to hear a few songs."

"I'd like to, very much," she responded as they rose from the table and walked into the living room. Britton sat on the sofa across the room while Mills sat in a chair beside the piano to watch Cooper. She noticed that he had attractive hands; Cooper wore a gold wedding band on his left ring finger, and he wore an unassuming wristwatch, a Timex.

He introduced the first song as the "Love Theme" from the movie *Spartacus*, and his rendition was hauntingly beautiful. *I feel like I'm listening to a reading of fine prose. He's so passionate in his playing.*

His voice regained her attention. "Okay, this play is currently running on Broadway."

He began the song and she recognized it immediately: "Memory" from *Cats*. The next composition was from *The Phantom of the Opera*, and she easily identified "The Music of the Night."

"Mills, I'm sorry, but since we're rising early, this is the last song. This composition is by an artist who composed the music for a play written by DuBose Heyward, who was a Charleston resident."

He had to only play a few bars and she exclaimed, "'Summertime,' by George Gershwin, from *Porgy and Bess*."

"That's right. When DuBose Heyward and George Gershwin worked on the musical in the 1930s, they drove around the Sea Islands to listen to the singing in black churches."

"You remembered that I like Broadway musicals."

Cooper smiled at her and said, "I did. Thank you for joining us for dinner."

"I had a nice time—Britton, I enjoyed meeting you."

"You as well."

Cooper rose to his feet and shook her hand. His smile was gentle and his warm hands held hers, but only for a moment.

"I'm going to walk Mills to her cottage," he said to Britton.

After Cooper retrieved her coat from the closet, they left by the front door. The nighttime air was frigid and their breaths formed clouds of vapor as they walked to her cottage. When they reached the steps of her new home, he said, "When you're trying to promote the scholarship program, it is possible that you could meet with some resistance because of my personal situation. Please don't trouble yourself if that happens."

"Thank you for telling me," she said softly.

He paused. "If you like to ride horses, I'll show you the ruins of an old plantation house that's on this property. I could meet you at the stables at three o'clock Sunday afternoon."

"I'd like to, but I don't have any experience riding horses."

"You can ride Ginger. She's a docile animal; you just have to point her toward the trail."

"Yes—I'd like to try."

"I'll see you Sunday then."

"Goodnight," she said as she climbed the stairs to her cottage and then waved from the top step. She watched him until he disappeared from view beyond the camellias.

Her last thoughts before falling asleep were that she would design the invitations to the oyster roast herself; she wanted to surprise Cooper.

CHAPTER 2

Old Acquaintances

Saturday morning, frost lay on the pathway as Mills made her way to the riverfront with her sketchbook in hand. She wrapped her scarf tightly around her neck and sat down in an Adirondack chair to watch seagulls dive into the water after baitfish. The air was filled with the smell of the marsh and pluff mud, and she inhaled deeply, holding her breath before releasing it.

As she began to sketch a palmetto tree situated along the shore, she noticed two boys fishing from a dented johnboat and floating in her direction with the current. They methodically cast their fly rod lines back and forth into clock positions, from ten o'clock to two o'clock. Their fishing lines sailed through the air with a metronome-like rhythm, until one of them snagged a medium-sized fish not far from where she sat. The younger of the two boys suddenly noticed her, tipped his hat to her, and said, "Good morning, ma'am."

She acknowledged them and included them in her sketch. The boys' boat continued to move with the current, and they were around a bend in the river within a few moments. Mills included the fly-fishing duo in her sketch and finished the drawing before returning to her cottage.

That afternoon, she drove into Charleston and spent a number of hours exploring the downtown streets and sketching churches, sweetgrass basket weavers at the market, and the bandstand at White Point Gardens. She was not far from the corner of Queen and King Streets when she noticed a wrought iron gate leading to a pathway for the Unitarian Church. She went down the lane and entered one of the most fascinating churchyards she'd ever seen. Many of the graves were covered with paper whites, making some of the markers unreadable. The first grave marker she could make out was from the nineteenth century.

A man wearing a charming tweed blazer and beret came past her on the pathway. She thought he might have been a college professor from his sophisticated attire. He looked at her, and Mills met his gaze with a smile.

"What a nice smile," he commented.

"Thank you," she responded.

As she departed the churchyard, she noticed that he had turned and glanced at her, as though he suddenly recognized her.

When she left Charleston in the direction of Edisto, she decided to explore several nearby islands and ended up at a quaint village named Rockville, at the end of a roadway on Wadmalaw Island.

She parked her Volkswagen at a small church named Grace Chapel and was captivated by the fascinating community of waterfront homes. At the end of a sandy lane was an attractive white-boarded building, the Sea Island Yacht Club. As she stood in the sandy lot near the club, a man who was about to launch a powerboat noticed her presence and called out, "Young lady, can I help you?"

"I was exploring. I've just moved to Charleston."

"I'm Joshua White. Welcome."

He offered her a Coke from his cooler, which she gladly accepted. Joshua appeared to be a man of about forty-five with dark, tanned skin and graying temples.

"Would you like to see the interior of the yacht club?"

She nodded, and he politely showed her the building, which was classically designed with hardwood floors and fireplaces on either side of the expansive meeting room. Ceiling beams spanned the width of the building.

"I apologize to you, but I have a guest waiting for me." He took a business card from his wallet and gave it to her. "Call me—I'll take you to lunch."

She thanked him for his kindness and watched as he joined a young woman with blond hair and lovely features. Joshua waved to her as the boat traveled into what Mills thought was a river. Looking at his business card, she read that he was an attorney in Charleston. As she began walking back to Grace Chapel, she encountered several well-behaved Labrador retrievers and decided that the Lab must be the pedigree of choice for Rockville's residents.

Mills returned to the chapel where a gray-haired gentleman was standing near the front steps. He smiled as she approached. "I hope you don't mind that I parked my car here. I was exploring."

"That's quite all right. I'm making sure that we have heat on in the building tonight. It's going to be cold, and we don't want burst water pipes. I'm Ed Seaborne, and you are?"

"My name is Mills Taylor. I've just moved to Charleston."

"Where are you from?"

"Originally, from Virginia."

"Mills Taylor, it's a pleasure to make your acquaintance. I'm going inside the church. Would you like to join me?"

"Yes, sir."

"So, this is your first time to visit Rockville?"

She smiled and nodded.

As he opened the doors, he volunteered, "This community was originally started as an escape for planters during the summer season to avoid fever-producing mosquitos. For many years, there was an annual reunion of Civil War veterans at Rockville until their numbers dwindled. That reunion was replaced by an annual regatta that is held on the first weekend in August. You'll have to join us. It has become quite a celebration."

He opened the door to the chapel and Mills was impressed by the beauty of the house of God. The pews were of dark-stained wood, as were the walls and ceiling. At the back of the church was a beautiful stained-glass window of Christ.

"Miss Mills, if you would like to walk along the waterfront, it will be all right. No one will mind, I assure you." He closed the doors of the chapel and they walked through his own yard to the waterway.

"When South Carolina was under exploration, Captain Robert Sandford and the crew of the Berkeley Bay claimed this area referred to as 'The Rocks,' for England and the Lord's Proprietor. Deposits of iron ore run underneath Wadmalaw, and if you look closely, you can see the rocks cropping out into the water, hence, present-day Rockville."

"I see them in the river," she responded.

"Believe it or not, this is actually a creek, Bohicket Creek. It just looks like a river." He took her hand and shook it. "Now don't forget about the Rockville Regatta—it's the first weekend in August."

Mills thanked Mr. Seaborne for his kindness, and then taking his recommendation, she walked in front of the waterfront homes, enjoying every moment of the experience. Most of the dwellings were historic masterpieces. The last remains of daylight approached and she made her way back to Grace Chapel, where her car was parked.

As she returned to Edisto, she saw a sign for the Angel Oak Tree. Curious, she exited off the paved road onto a sandy lane that led to the massive tree. The limbs of the live oak were, themselves, as large as trunks of most other trees. Some of the branches rested on the ground, spreading many feet from the main trunk. Reading a plaque about the tree, Mills marveled at the ancient oak, which was thought to be the oldest living tree east of the Rocky Mountains. The canopy of the massive branches stood majestically against the waning light of day, and she thought of the tree's survival through hurricanes, natural phenomena, and human interference. *It was a gift from God*, she thought.

Mills arrived home at dusk. Cooper's dog, Sam, came to greet her. Together, they walked down to the marsh front. The scene was beautiful, the last light of a cold winter's day, red sky, and a few clouds making their way across the heavens. Church bells from Alston Station sounded in the distance, and as they started back up the darkened lane, Sam's ears perked up.

Crossing their path, about fifty feet in front of them, were five deer. Sam took off to pursue the deer and disappeared into a thicket. Mills called the dog for some time before he returned, still panting from the chase.

"Why don't you come inside, Sam? We can keep each other company for a while."

She reviewed her sketches, and the first drawing she had done, the one of the palmetto tree and the two fly fishermen, appealed to her the most. That evening, she worked on variations of the sketch to show to Cooper the next afternoon.

On Sunday morning, she drove to Alston Station to begin her search for a church where she could share her Christian faith. She drove past the two closest churches and continued to one that was a few miles away. The look of the church was old and attractive, like several she had seen in downtown Charleston. Situated in the shadows of live oak trees were a number of ancient gravestones. Mills entered the church and took a seat in one of the rear pews. The sanctuary was not large, but it was lovely, with intricate woodwork and brightly illuminated chandeliers.

A few people smiled and greeted her during the service. After church, a gray-haired woman approached and introduced herself as Christina Shell. "Are you visiting our community?"

"No, ma'am; I've moved here to be the director of an educational foundation."

"What organization will you be working with?"

"The Julia Heath Foundation."

"Oh, you're employed by Cooper. I knew his mother. She was a tireless worker with her charities—we have all prayed for Cooper and his wife." Christina looked closely at Mills.

"Yes, I pray that there will be a positive resolution to her disappearance."

"We all do—please come back and join us whenever you'd like."

Before three o'clock, Mills walked to the stables and found Cooper already there and the horses saddled. Ginger was a light palomino mare; she stood taller than the magnificent black stallion that Cooper would ride.

"What's your horse's name?" she asked.

"Mephisto."

"Did you name him?"

"No, ma'am. I thought about changing his name, but he already answered to it. When I first brought him here, he was aggressive; it took a year of working with him to calm him down." He paused as he patted the horse's neck and then said, "At one point, this property was a profitable rice plantation, and later, Sea Island cotton was grown here. The ruins of an antebellum home and buildings are near the river. First, we'll cross the green before entering the pasture. The horses know the way."

"What's the green?"

"It's the front yard, but I call it the green."

Cooper helped Mills mount Ginger and handed her the reins. "Don't be nervous; she's very gentle. You won't need to hold the reins too tightly."

As Mills watched Cooper astride Mephisto, she said quietly, "That is a gorgeous creature."

The riders crossed the green and Mills understood the reason for the name. The green was a manicured lawn almost the size of a football field surrounded by live oak trees. On the other side of the green, the horses followed a sandy lane that ran into the pasture, and their pace quickened as they descended toward the river, through high grasses that resembled fields of gold. The pasture gave way to a forested area with live oaks and scrub palms; shade covered the narrow pathway.

They must have been riding for twenty minutes when Mills noticed an old brick entranceway. Ivy grew on the columns, and Cooper slowed his horse, with Ginger automatically following suit. Ahead were the ruins of the home surrounded by live oak trees. The brick columns were still in place, with five across the front.

Cooper dismounted Mephisto and tied the reins to a tree limb before assisting Mills with her dismount from Ginger.

"Come this way," he said. "Carefully."

There was a set of brick steps leading up to what would have been a front entrance, but the steps led to nothing. The inside of the old mansion was filled with resurrection ferns and old bricks that had collapsed into the interior of the structure. Mills could see the river from this portion of the ruin; there was a clear alleyway from the back of the structure to the waterway.

"What happened to this home?"

"It was burned by Union soldiers when they occupied the Edisto area. Today, less than a handful of antebellum homes survive in this area."

Mills stood on the highpoint of the foundation and studied the scene around her. "This is amazing," she observed.

He assisted her through the uneven bricks of the collapsed structure, and they took a path toward the river. Passing canals with dykes to control water flow, Cooper said, "Charles and I have been clearing this area, but there's still a great deal of work to do. These canals were flooded for rice production. It was quite profitable before the planter system collapsed."

"What caused the collapse?"

"The end of the plantation system, the end of slavery—at the time of the plantation system it was acceptable to hold other human beings as slaves. We now recognize that the system was brutal, whether to Native Americans or Africans who were forced into slavery—terrible business."

They maneuvered down an embankment toward the river, and Mills noticed a deteriorated dock extending out into the river. Cooper cautioned her, "I don't think we should tempt the dock. I haven't replaced it, because I don't want the location of this ruin to be noticeable from the water—I have something else to show you."

For just a moment, she studied the surroundings of the riverfront before following Cooper up the embankment toward a clearing. There were paper whites blooming in the opening, and she noticed early sprouts of daffodils.

"The daffodils are amazing when they're in bloom. You can't begin to count them all."

At the edge of the clearing were numerous small structures that were in a state of collapse. "These cabins are the remains of slave dwellings. If you come down here in the warmer months, I want you to be especially careful around these buildings. The foundations are inhabited by a number of snakes, some of which are poisonous."

Mills walked closer to one of the cabins, which was in better condition than the others. On the exterior was a rosebush; it had proliferated itself over the front of the structure and onto the roof. Although the growth pattern was wild, the bush appeared extremely healthy.

Noticing her interest in the rosebush, Cooper remarked, "The blossoms are a brilliant white, and it starts to bud in the early spring and will have flowers all summer long. The roses are a beautiful sight among these ruins."

Near the end of the row of cabins was a large bell that stood about six feet off the ground on a metal pole. Mills rang the bell and, though it was rusty, it gave a loud clang.

"Amazing that it still works."

"I have one more item of history to show you."

They walked toward the location of the old mansion and came upon a churchyard and the walls of a decaying building. "This was the chapel for the plantation owner's usage."

There were a number of deteriorated and broken grave markers, but the legible stones dated back to the eighteenth century. She paused as she looked over the names and dates on the markers before turning her attention back to Cooper.

"Are you ready to ride back up to the stables?" he inquired.

"Yes, I've enjoyed exploring."

"You should come back when the daffodils start to bloom."

Mounting their horses, they rode back to the stables and tended to the animals after their workout. While they groomed the horses, Mills mentioned that she had created a sketch that she'd like to use for the invitations to his oyster roast.

"I'd like to see what you've done," he responded, smiling.

Meeting him in the rear courtyard of his home, Mills brought her sketchbook and showed him the drawings that she had made during Saturday's exploration. He immediately focused on the drawing that she had done of the two fishermen and the palmetto tree. "I like this one the most."

"That's my favorite drawing as well. Tomorrow I'll visit the printer and get the invitations started."

Before he said good night to her, Cooper told her that he would be hunting in the morning with two friends and that they would try not to disturb her.

That evening, she worked on the sketch until she was completely happy with the drawing. When she finished, she went out onto her screened porch to sit. The sound of piano music came from the main house. While his music was captivating, there was a common element to his songs; they all sounded melancholy. *What he must have gone through, not knowing what had happened to his wife.* The music stopped, and Mills sat for a few more minutes before she went inside.

Excited about her first day of work for the foundation, Mills woke early and dressed in her favorite navy blue suit. She decided to say hello to Marian before departing for the day. She walked to Cooper's house and, as she knocked at the kitchen door, Mills could hear Marian's footfalls moving in her direction, and her kind voice invited her inside.

"Now, you do look pretty this morning," she told Mills. "Would you like a cup of coffee?"

"Thank you, Marian, but I've already had breakfast. I just wanted to say good morning. I'm going to see potential donors after I stop by the printer."

"You're going to be a great success! I hope you had a nice weekend."

"Yes, ma'am, I did. I explored Charleston, and yesterday, I rode horses with Cooper down to the old house ruins."

"What did you think of the place?"

"I found the ruins to be extraordinary and captivating."

"I don't like to go down there. Something about the place bothers me—people say it's haunted. Cooper and Charles laugh at me when I say that, but I have my own thoughts."

Glancing down at Mills's high-heeled shoes, Marian recommended, "You might want to take a pair of low-heeled shoes to wear when you walk around downtown Charleston and change into your dress shoes before your appointments. The sidewalk pavers are uneven in some locations, and I don't want you to have a fall."

"Thank you for your suggestion," Mills responded, as she checked the time on her watch. "I should leave now."

Marian walked her to the kitchen door and then waved goodbye through the window. As she walked to the edge of the courtyard, Mills was unable to see down the lane because of a camellia bush, and she walked right into a man who approached from the boat dock. He wore hip waders and camouflage, and carried several ducks and a shotgun.

"I was looking for Cooper, but I think I'd rather find you." Mills thought him intensely handsome with muscular features and clear, blue-green eyes. His blond hair was disheveled from wearing a hunting hat. *Study at arm's length—he could be dangerous.* "You must be Mills—I'm Jeff, Cooper's first cousin."

Cooper and Britton appeared on the pathway coming from the direction of her cottage, both dressed in hip waders.

"I see you've met my cousin, Jeff," Cooper said. "We were just looking for you at your cottage."

"Yes, we were just making each other's acquaintance—did you have a successful hunt?"

"Cooper did," Jeff responded.

"I just had more shots than they did."

"We still had a good time though. Hard not to," Jeff added.

"Mills have you ever been bird hunting?" Cooper asked.

"No, I've never fired a shotgun. I don't know how."

"Well, if you'd like, I'll teach you how sometime," Cooper said.

"Yes. I'd like to learn."

Cooper changed the subject. "Jeff owns a real estate company named Radcliffe Real Estate and Development in Charleston. Are you on your way out?"

"Yes, I have an appointment at Collins Printing at eleven. I planned to leave early, just in case I got lost."

"You'll be fine," Cooper said.

She said goodbye to them and started down the lane to her cottage. As she turned to go down the pathway between the camellia bushes, she glanced back and found they had not taken their eyes off of her.

Mills entered the printer's office at eleven, and a man came out from behind the counter to greet her. "You must be Mills Taylor. I can tell that you're an associate of Cooper's—you are on time for your appointment. I'm James Collins."

Mills shook his hand and then showed him the drawing she wanted to use for the invitations and media items. He looked at her artwork for a few moments before saying, "This is quite good, and I believe we'll have no trouble getting this scaled for the invitations and anything else you'd like to do. Cooper mentioned that he'd like for us to do a business card for you. Also, if you'd like, we can do a few larger displays."

Mills showed him a write-up she had done concerning the Heath Foundation, and Mr. Collins said he'd immediately start work on it.

"I know that Cooper needs the invitations quickly, so I'll have a preliminary example by tomorrow afternoon. Come by at three o'clock."

After departing the printer's shop, her first stop was the Low Country Gourmet, the flagship store of a chain of gourmet stores in the southeast. Cooper had told her that the owners, Ford Butler and his wife Melea, were active philanthropists in the Charleston community and should be interested in helping the Heath Foundation.

As she entered the store, she inhaled the aromas of fresh ground coffee and baked bread. *Smells wonderful.* She asked to speak to Mr. and Mrs. Butler, and a tall man with deep brown skin emerged from the rear of the store, accompanied by his wife. Mills introduced herself and explained that she worked for an educational foundation to help disadvantaged youths in the Charleston area.

"How can we help you?" he asked.

"I would like to place a display about the foundation in your local stores to give exposure to the scholarship program."

"Miss Taylor, we'll be happy to help you. I believe in helping others as much as I can. I think we can arrange a donation for you too. When you have the display ready, bring it by the store and I'll take a look at it."

He accompanied her to the front of the business and introduced her to a slight-framed man with thinning, sandy-colored hair.

"Miss Taylor, I'd like to introduce you to the manager of this store, Paul Westmore."

Paul took her hand and smiled. "Oh, my God, Audrey Hepburn, it's a pleasure to meet you."

Mills felt her face flush with his comment and she shook his hand enthusiastically while Mr. Butler explained to him that she represented an educational foundation. Before she left the store, both men told her to come back as soon as she had her display ready.

Uplifted by her first experience, she went to the next business on her list, which was a law firm with the contact name of Hamilton Bentley. Mills asked the receptionist if she could make an appointment, but after the receptionist called his office, she was informed that he would see her immediately.

When Mr. Bentley came downstairs, Mills saw that he was in his late thirties with a trim build, wearing a tailored and probably very expensive business suit. They exchanged greetings and Mills told him who she was and why she had come to see him.

Mr. Bentley waggled a finger at her. "Miss Taylor, we have a no-solicitation policy at this firm. Didn't you see the sign on the door?"

Taken aback, Mills began to stammer a polite apology, but Mr. Bentley interrupted her.

"So, you're working with Cooper Heath. What do you know about him anyway? I watch the property transfers, and I know he's accumulating significant land holdings in the Low Country. Tell that land baron to take the funding for his educational foundation out of his own bank account!"

That was enough for Mills and she stood up to leave. "Mr. Heath is a generous person, and I think very highly of him."

Mr. Bentley gave out a hearty laugh and gestured for her to remain.

"Miss Taylor, please sit down, I'm just giving you the run around. I'm an old acquaintance of the Heath family and I'd like to hear about your program— I'll tell you what, if you've got time, I was just about to walk down the street for lunch. If you'll accompany me, I'd like to hear about the foundation."

Mills laughed, mostly in relief, but also in wondering if he pulled these pranks in the courtroom. She agreed to accompany him to the restaurant. After she gave details about the educational program, he asked, "May I call you Mills?"

"Yes, you may."

"Call me Hamilton. Now, I went to school with Cooper, his brother Beau, his cousin Jeff, and their friend, Britton Smith. Have you met Jeff and Britton?"

"Yes, I have."

"I was in the same class with Beau and Britton. Beau . . . tragic thing about him and his father; both of them drowned."

Shocked, she admitted, "I didn't know that. I only knew that Beau had passed away a long time ago."

"It was the summer right after we graduated from high school. Beau had been accepted to the United States Naval Academy and, for a graduation present, Mr. Heath took Cooper, Beau, and Jeff to the Caribbean to go sailing. While they were off Eleuthera, a terrific storm came up. Their sailboat capsized in high waves, and Jeff was swept overboard without a life jacket. Cooper saved his life; he was only fifteen at the time but was already a strong athlete. Sadly, Mr. Heath and Beau were inside the cabin and could not be saved—terrible shame. After Cooper finished at the Air Force Academy, he was in the military for several years. He is a fine person, if he's anything like he was at our college prep school, Porter-Gaud."

He paused for just a moment and then emphatically stated, "I don't believe he had anything to do with his wife's disappearance. This is the first time I've been contacted about the foundation, but I know that Cooper has an oyster roast at his Edisto property each February. It has turned into quite a social event and my partners and I would like to attend. If you'll get us invitations to the oyster roast, I'll work on getting a donation for your charity. It would be nice to see Cooper again. These days, I only read about him in the newspaper."

Cooper's father and brother killed in a boating accident. He didn't let on about their deaths. Terrible tragedy.

After lunch, Mills made several more introductory business calls. Her last stop was at the Charleston daily newspaper, the *Charleston Dispatch*. Introducing herself to the receptionist, she explained that she was the director of the Heath Foundation and that she'd like to submit press releases on a regular basis to acquaint the public with their efforts to fund scholarships.

"Miss Taylor, have a seat and I'll call Mitch Key; he's the editor of the Metropolitan section of the newspaper."

After several minutes, Mr. Key emerged from the newsroom, introduced himself, and invited her into his office. She walked through an area of desks to a private office and handed him a copy of a news release, which introduced herself as the new director of the foundation.

After he read the document, he glanced up. "I'm familiar with Mr. Heath. Miss Taylor, I think you've covered what you needed to in the release, and I'll be glad to help you. I went to college on an academic scholarship, so I know how important it is to have an opportunity to attend college, especially when one can't afford it."

He placed her article on his desk and then acknowledged a tall, blond young man standing outside his door, dressed impeccably in a navy suit and red bow tie. Mr. Key motioned for him to come inside, and upon entering, the young man said, "Mr. Key, I've got the story on the Webb Pharmacy robbery—there's quite a twist." Suddenly noticing that his editor was not alone, he said, "I'm sorry, I didn't mean to interrupt you."

"That's okay. Miss Taylor and I were almost finished with business. Miss Taylor, this is Lee Mencken. He's one of our reporters and he does an outstanding job of uncovering the truth. Miss Taylor has just taken the directorship of the Heath Foundation—you know, headed by Cooper Heath."

Lee appeared to be about her age and he firmly shook her hand saying, "Yes, sir, I did know that Mr. Heath was funding scholarships for disadvantaged youths." Looking curiously at Mills, he said, "I've become acquainted with Mr. Heath during the last six months. I hope that all goes well with your cause."

As Mills rose to leave, Mr. Key said, "Miss Taylor, stop by any time you have a news release for the *Charleston Dispatch*, and best of luck with the foundation."

As she left the newsroom, she noticed a pair of double doors outside the lobby labeled "Archives." Mills approached the receptionist, asking her permission to look at past newspaper articles. After showing her how to access the microfilm, the receptionist left the room and Mills removed copies of the newspaper from the previous August at the time of Elise Heath's disappearance. The first articles written about the case concentrated on the missing woman and efforts to find her. Within several days, however, there was a series of reports that detailed police searches at the properties of Cooper Heath. There was even a suggestion by one columnist that Cooper was out of jail due to his family's wealth and influence. After two weeks, reports on the disappearance vanished from the front page and follow-up reporting on the case appeared in the midsection of the Metropolitan news. The last article that Mills read quoted Lieutenant Nathan Barnes with the Charleston County Police Department as saying, "The investigation is far from over."

There was one more event that Mills wanted to investigate. Returning the first set of microfilm to its archives, Mills found the records from the summer of 1969. She had calculated that would be the time of the boating accident off Eleuthera. As she scrolled through the microfilm, she came to the report on the deadly event. The report had originated from Nassau, Bahamas, and the caption read, "Boating Accident Claims Life of Charleston Shipping Executive." Mills began to softly read out loud, "A series of freak waves struck the sailboat operated by Phillip B. Heath, Chief Executive Officer of Heath Brothers Shipping of Charleston, SC. Killed were Heath, 49, and son, Beau, 17—a younger son, Cooper Heath, 15, and relative, Jeff Radcliffe, 16, survived the accident. Cooper Heath is credited with saving the life of his cousin, Jeff Radcliffe, after the first catastrophic wave struck the sailboat." Mills went on to review all of the continuing articles written about the accident. *My God—what Cooper's been through.* She left the newspaper office stunned.

Mills drove home to Edisto and walked to the riverfront, thinking of what she had learned during the day. There was no one at home but Cooper's dog, Sam, who joined her. The evening sky had a beautiful red tint, and she stood at the dock, studying the marsh and wildlife until she felt chilled. Sam walked with her. Near her cottage, he abruptly stopped, ears perked up. Toward the end of the darkened lane near Cooper's house, Mills saw a shape go around the corner of a group of camellia bushes. Sam started to bark and wanted to charge in the direction of the figure, but Mills grabbed his collar and kept him with her.

"Stay with me Sam. I think you'd be a good protector."

She coaxed Sam into her cottage and locked her doors. She left the lights off inside her cottage and looked out the windows around the perimeter of her home, but she did not see anything else.

Picking up the telephone, she called Cooper's house. The phone rang, but the answering machine picked up. Sitting down on her bed, she took several breaths to calm herself. *Probably someone finishing work on the farm.*

The following morning, when Mills picked up the *Charleston Dispatch*, she turned to the Metropolitan section of the paper. The section's headline read, "Webb Pharmacy Robberies: Pharmacist to Face Charges."

As she read the article, written by the journalist she'd been introduced to, Lee Mencken, Mills was amazed to learn that the head pharmacist's lover—they were gay—was blackmailing him over their relationship. The robberies had been staged to obtain opiate drugs.

On the last page of the Metro section, she found the article about the Heath Foundation. Her release had been printed exactly as she had drafted it. Under her photograph was the caption, "Mills Taylor, Director of the Julia Heath Foundation."

At three o'clock, she stopped by Collins Printing; the proofs were ready for the invitations. The sketch had been reproduced flawlessly.

"I'm going to be a little longer on the business cards, but here is an example of a larger display board." He placed the exhibit on the counter and they both studied the work-up.

Pleased with the results, Mills responded, "I'll have Cooper take a look at this before you print the invitations."

"Just call me when you're ready."

Mills left the print shop and made one more professional call downtown to deliver the display about the foundation to the Low Country Gourmet. As soon as she entered the shop, Paul called out to her, "Audrey, what do you have for me this afternoon?"

Mills brought the board to him and Paul read over the information on the Heath Foundation. He placed her exhibit near the front counter. "There—that ought to get you noticed."

"Thank you, Paul."

"We told you we'd be glad to help. The Butlers aren't here this afternoon, but I'll show them this in the morning."

After leaving the Low Country Gourmet, she took a walk through the downtown and came upon a salmon-pink hotel on Meeting Street. It shared her name: The Mills House. Throughout the hotel lobby, she found the decorations to be quite elegant. At the rear of the lobby was a piano bar named The Barbadoes Room. The name seemed appropriate to her, as many of the original Charleston settlers had come from Barbados. She admired the exquisite furnishings and antique maps that adorned the lobby.

When she exited the hotel onto Meeting Street, she found herself within a group of pedestrians preparing to cross the street. From about a half-block away, a voice called out to her, "Miss Taylor!"

Turning to see who had called her, she recognized the man she had recently met at the Sea Island Yacht Club. He came forward and shook her hand. "Miss Taylor, I hope you remember me. I'm Joshua White. I've been in court, and I must have timed my departure perfectly as I've run into you. How about afternoon tea? I know just the place."

She agreed, and they walked to the Ocean Place Hotel. Entering an elegant tea room located in the hotel lobby, Joshua helped Mills with her chair, saying, "Have a seat, young lady. I want you to tell me about the job you've just started."

"I'm the director of the Julia Heath Foundation." Noticing his frown, Mills asked, "Is something wrong?"

"I know that you and I don't know one another, but how much do you know about your employer, Cooper Heath? That's who you're working for, isn't it?"

"Yes, and I think very highly of him."

"His wife disappeared without a trace about six months ago. I know that every law enforcement agency, including the South Carolina State Law Enforcement Division, has been investigating her disappearance. He's been taken in multiple times for questioning. He's the prime suspect—I think his family's influence has been able to keep him out of jail. I hate to see you involved with a potentially dangerous individual. He's highly intelligent, and from what I've been told, a very cool customer. There hasn't been an arrest— mainly, because the police haven't been able to recover her body."

"Mr. White, I don't believe he's guilty of anything."

"Please, call me Joshua, and I don't want to see you get hurt. If you find that your job isn't working out as you'd like, I hope you'll tell me. I have many contacts in the legal field that are always looking for hard-working individuals ... I'll stop, I see I'm ruining your tea. Tell me where you're from and where you've been living."

When she returned home, Cooper was out in the fields on his tractor; he didn't seem to notice her as she drove by. At dusk, she heard the tractor shut down, and she went to the rear courtyard of his home to wait for him. Several minutes later, he came up the lane toward home, with Sam right behind him.

She called out to him, "Good evening, Cooper. I was hoping to show you the invitation to the oyster roast."

He slapped his pants and dust came off his thighs before he took a seat across from her.

"I met with the owners of the Low Country Gourmet, Ford and Melea Butler, and they're open to helping us. The manager of the King Street store, Paul, he's a little different. He calls me Audrey Hepburn."

Cooper smiled at her. "I'm glad that you're having success. I knew you would."

"I also went by one of the law firms that you had on the business contact list, and I met with Hamilton Bentley. He said that he had grown up with you and your brother."

"That's true, but I haven't seen him for years."

"He said that he would help work on a donation to the foundation and he wanted invitations to the oyster roast. Is that all right with you?"

"You're running this operation. I'll leave that up to you."

"I also saw someone today that I met at the yacht club at Rockville. His name is Joshua White; he's an attorney."

Cooper paused, "Yes, I know to whom you're referring; he's a criminal defense attorney and a very good one—let me see the invitation."

She showed him the invitation, wondering why he had changed the subject.

"This is excellent, Mills. I like what you've created."

He carefully read the inside of the card. "I think this is perfect." As he handed the invitation back to her, she asked, "Are you going duck hunting tomorrow?"

"Yes, very early. I take time off during this time of the year to duck hunt."

"I'd like to take you up on your offer to teach me how to shoot a shotgun and hunt birds."

"I'll be glad to. First, I'll need to check you out on the shotgun and give you some lessons, especially on gun safety. You can get your hunting license at Dawkins's Market. I'll take off from work early tomorrow and we'll get started."

"Thank you, Cooper. There's one more thing I'd like to show you. I went by the *Charleston Dispatch*, and they ran a press release in today's paper about the foundation. I plan to submit news releases on a regular basis about our progress."

She handed him a copy of the paper and he read the article before commenting, "Well done, Mills."

"I hope people read it and don't stop at the article on the Webb Pharmacy robberies."

Cooper turned to the front page. "By Lee Mencken—I've become acquainted with that young man in recent months."

"That's what he said about you."

"You met him?"

"Yes, he was turning in the article on the Webb robberies when I was in the Metro office."

"A persistent young man."

"That's what his editor said about him."

Cooper read through the article on the robberies and said, "Whew, I see I'm not the only one with problems."

When he finished reading, Cooper rose from his seat and handed the newspaper back to her. "I'll walk you to your cottage."

As they neared the row of camellias near her home, Cooper stopped her. "Be quiet for just a minute. I thought I heard a noise." They stood motionless, but there was only silence.

Mills remembered what she'd seen last night. "Cooper, last evening, as I was walking up from the river, I thought I saw a darkened shape near your house. You weren't home, and Sam stayed with me."

He looked at her with a concerned expression. "If you ever see, or hear anything unusual, please let me know. I don't want you to be afraid."

She nodded and he responded, "Good night, then." Cooper walked down the path and disappeared outside the bushes. Watching for several minutes, she eventually saw him pass down the lane on the return to his house.

CHAPTER 3

The Duck Hunt

Mills ordered the invitations and thanked Mr. Collins for his prompt attention to the print project. Before leaving for appointments in Charleston, she stopped at Dawkins's Market to buy her hunting license. The man at the counter smiled at her when she tried to explain what she was attempting to purchase. "You're going to need the federal and state duck stamp if you're going to duck hunt. You don't want an unpleasant visit with the game warden. Are you Miss Taylor?"

"Yes, sir. How did you know?"

"I recognized you from your description that the ladies at church gave me. They said that Cooper had hired a young lady from Virginia to assist him with his mother's foundation. My name is James Dawkins, and I'm pleased to make your acquaintance. I think you're going to enjoy working with Cooper." He helped her with the paperwork. "This is what you're going to need—this hunting license is good for both hunting and fishing."

The rest of the day was spent making calls for the foundation and, while she had not yet received a financial commitment from anyone, she felt positive about her prospects. At four o'clock, Mills waited for Cooper in the rear courtyard. He came down the driveway in his Suburban and parked in the lane adjacent to the house. Quickly getting out of the car, he walked in her direction and apologized for his tardiness.

"Don't worry—you're two minutes late."

"I don't like to be late for appointments."

Wearing a dark suit and tie, he looked professional and handsome. "I've picked out a twenty-gauge Remington for you to shoot this afternoon."

He took off his Wayfarers and invited her inside while he changed clothes. Waiting for him in the kitchen, she noticed that the door was open to his hunting room, and she went inside to look at his photographs. There was a photo of Cooper with a military haircut. He stood beside a jet fighter—on the fuselage was the inscription, "Captain Cooper Heath." A nearby photo caught her eye: Cooper, Jeff, and Elise were together in a fishing photo. They were a striking trio.

"Where are you, Mills?" Cooper called to her from the kitchen.

"I'm in the hunting room. I'm looking at your photos. I especially like the one of you beside the jet fighter."

"Thank you."

Cooper now wore blue jeans and a dark green Barbour hunting coat. He joined her in the hunting room and removed a shotgun from the gun case, then picked up a couple of boxes of shotshell before handing her a headset. "Here's your ear protection. Are you ready to go?"

"Yes, sir."

They got in his Suburban and drove down into the pasture. On their way, Cooper explained that a section of the pasture was set up to shoot sporting clays. He parked his vehicle near a skeet machine. "Mills, the most important thing about using a firearm is situational awareness. Know where you are, who and what's around you, and if you're not shooting the gun, the safety should be on. Always treat the gun as if it's loaded, and never point it toward anyone."

He showed her the position of the safety on the shotgun, "Push it forward and it's off, pull it back and it's on. Here, you hold the gun and get a feel for it." She placed the stock firmly against her shoulder. Then she held up the gun, trying to keep the barrel ahead of a bird that she saw flying through the pasture. Cooper came behind her and put his arms snugly around her, helping her hold the gun and aim at the target. After a few minutes, he abruptly stopped and sat down on the hood of the Suburban.

Mills lowered her gun and turned to face him. "Are you okay? You have an odd look on your face."

"Yes, you go ahead and continue to practice."

After several minutes had passed, he got up from the hood and walked toward her.

"Mills, I'm going to help you learn to shoot with the skeet machine. I want you to place the stock of the gun on your shoulder, resting against your cheek.

Position your lead foot in the same direction that the bird is traveling. When you're ready, say 'pull.'"

She followed his instructions. "Pull!"

Cooper released the clay bird and Mills fired the shotgun, but missed the target. They continued to practice until Cooper told her, "Now, I want to see you load the gun without me."

She put the shot in by herself and yelled, "Pull!"

Another bird was released, and Mills fired, smashing the target to pieces.

Cooper congratulated her, "Well done, Mills Taylor, or should I call you Annie Oakley?"

She smiled at the compliment, and they continued to practice until dusk. When they returned to his house, he went into his hunting room and returned with a pair of hip waders and a Filson hat and coat. He held the hunting attire in front of her to judge the size and said, "These should work, they belong to my cousin, Blair, and I'm certain he won't mind if you wear his clothes. I'll see you in my kitchen at four-thirty tomorrow morning."

"Four-thirty!"

"That's late—I'm going to take you to a nearby location."

"Four-thirty it is."

The morning air was frigid as Cooper's boat traveled in the darkness toward their destination. Tears formed in her eyes from the cold wind in her face, and within twenty minutes they had reached an island in the river. Familiar with the location, Sam jumped out of the boat and disappeared into the night.

Cooper helped her out of the boat, handing her a thermos, and then lifted two gun cases and a shell bag onto shore. She watched as he covered the boat with a camouflage net and then she followed him to the duck blind. There was camouflage netting pulled over walls constructed of straw and bamboo. Upon reaching it, Cooper pulled out a large net bag from inside and placed the duck decoys into the water. He softly said, "Winds are out of the northeast."

Pouring her a cup of coffee, he asked, "Are you cold?"

"I was while we were on the river, but I'm warming up."

"Good, it's just a few minutes before legal light. While the temperatures are below freezing, we probably won't see any alligators, but as spring arrives, they'll be prevalent. I don't let Sam go into the water at that point. I've never had a problem with an alligator, but be aware, they are present. Never feed them."

As they sat quietly in the blind, Mills began to hear a whistling noise.

Cooper explained to her that the whistle was ducks flying by, and created by the primary feathers on the wing sliding through the air.

Cooper uncased both shotguns and loaded them. "It will be legal light shortly," he said rubbing his hands together.

"What does that mean?"

"The Department of Natural Resources puts out a timetable that states when it's legal to begin the hunt."

"I see."

Cooper placed a lanyard around his neck. "This is a teal whistle. I use it to call in ducks."

He looked at his watch. "It's legal light." He put the whistle to his lips and it made a peep-peep whistle sound.

The birds were still darkened shapes in the dim light, but to Mills, they sounded like jet airplanes coming in to land.

"Here's your shot."

She came out of the blind, put the gun up to her shoulder, aimed and fired at one of the ducks, but missed.

She was disappointed with her inaccuracy, but Cooper interjected, "That was a good try. Have patience."

After a few minutes passed, Cooper blew the teal whistle, and ducks began to fly near the decoys again.

"Mills, I'm going to take this shot."

Cooper fired his shotgun and a duck fell into the water with Sam immediately retrieving the bird.

"The next shot is yours," Cooper quietly told her.

Continuing to use the teal whistle, Cooper pointed out three ducks that were flying toward the decoys. Mills fired at one of the birds, but only wounded it. The duck went under the surface, and Sam dove under the water to retrieve it.

Exhilarated by the hunt, Mills stepped out of the blind to shoot again and struck another bird. Sam retrieved the duck for her and as she walked back toward the blind in knee deep water, an underwater limb snagged her foot. She fell backward into the river and frigid water rushed into her waders. Although breathless from the shock, she still managed to hold the gun out of the water.

Cooper charged into the river to help her, took her gun, and pulled her up. She gasped as the icy water settled into the bottom of her waders. "I'm freezing, but I didn't lose the bird," she said in a quivering voice.

Mills knew the duck hunt was over when Cooper quickly gathered the decoys and put them inside the blind. "I've got a wool blanket in the boat, but I'm afraid the ride back home is going to be cold."

He wrapped the blanket around her, then pushed the boat away from the island and started the motor. She huddled inside the craft and pulled her hat down low onto her head. By the time they arrived at his dock, she felt frozen and waddled back to her cottage in the soaked waders.

Cooper accompanied her up the lane and before entering her home, she asked, "Are my lips blue?"

He looked at her carefully before responding, "No, not yet—are you all right?"

"I'll be okay after I get the waders off."

"Please put them on your porch and I'll come by to get them. You did well today. Don't let the fall discourage you. That can happen to anyone."

She managed a smile and said, "Thank you for taking me hunting."

She left the soaked waders on the porch, then stood in a warm shower to unfreeze her limbs. After she dressed, Mills noted that the waders had been removed and an invitation to dinner had been left for her. Teal was on the menu.

She called Cooper's house to accept the invitation but had to leave a message on his answering machine when no one picked up the phone. As soon as she hung up her receiver, Collins Printing phoned to tell her the oyster roast invitations were ready. She dressed and drove to the print shop. When she arrived, Mr. Collins placed a large box on the table and showed her the invitations.

"I'll have your business card ready next week. Let Cooper know I'll send him a bill."

"Thank you, Mr. Collins."

That evening, Mills arrived at Cooper's house at seven-thirty and was greeted in the kitchen. "Did you get thawed out?"

"Yes, but it took a while."

"I haven't picked out a bottle of wine yet, would you like to go with me to the wine cellar to choose a bottle?"

"Wine cellar? I didn't realize you had one."

He led her to a door off of the kitchen, and they descended the stairwell into the cellar. Amazed by his wine collection, Mills took several bottles down from brick holding bins and read their labels. The lights in the room were dim, and she had to look closely as he explained that he had sorted his collection by countries and regions. He picked out a California Petite Syrah to accompany their meal and handed the bottle to Mills so she could read the label.

Suddenly, the door at the top of the stairs slammed shut, and she almost dropped the bottle to the brick floor. Cooper quickly explained, "I'm sorry, but that door slams shut sometimes. I hope you're not frightened."

"No, I'm not afraid. It was just the noise that startled me."

Cooper ascended the stairs ahead of Mills and held the door to the kitchen open for her. Mills was glad to return to the brightly lit kitchen.

Cooper opened the wine. "For your dinner tonight, I'm preparing the ducks that you shot. Why don't you help me?"

He removed a large skillet from the pan rack above the island, and together, they seared the breasts in olive oil. Mills watched him carefully as she served as his sous chef. When they finished preparing the duck breasts, Cooper added mashed potatoes and a wine sauce to the meal.

She sampled his delicious creation. "This is wonderful. How did you learn to cook like this?"

He poured Mills a glass of wine and handed it to her. "Thank you, Mills. My mom taught Beau and me how to cook."

"I picked up the invitations to the oyster roast this afternoon and I plan to get them in tomorrow's mail." She took one out of her handbag and showed him how nicely they had turned out.

"This is excellent. Thank you for your hard work."

He handed the invitation back to her and there was silence between them for a moment. There was a question that had been on Mills's mind ever since she had met Charles. "Cooper, how did Charles get that scar on his face?"

"Charles was a career military man, and he retired as a sergeant-major after thirty years in the US Army. During one of his tours in Vietnam, the Vietcong overran his platoon, and there was considerable loss of life on both sides. He doesn't discuss his military experiences often, but a bayonet caused the scar. Charles killed his attacker with his bare hands. When he retired, he came home to Charleston to run the farm. I'm fortunate to have him here."

"Charles and Marian have been very nice to me."

"They're two of my best friends."

She studied his face for a moment and asked, "Cooper, where do you go to church?"

"I don't attend church."

"I went to a church a few miles from here last Sunday, but I'd like to find a church that has a more contemporary service."

"I'm sorry; I can't be of help to you."

"The church I attended last Sunday was very nice. After the service, a lady greeted me and when I told her I was working with you, she said your mother had been very involved with charity work."

"My mother spent a lot of her time trying to help the poor and less fortunate; the educational foundation was founded with her own funds. She also helped start a medical clinic out here in this rural part of Charleston County. I broke my arm when I was twelve years old, and my parents took me to Charleston to have the arm attended to. The emergency room doctor, Williston Devereux, impressed my mother. Julia was able to convince her to move out here and start a medical clinic. That was back in the 1960s. In those days, this was a sparsely populated area."

"This is still a rural area."

"Not like it used to be. Later this week, I'm going to Williston's clinic to donate blood. I count her as one of my best friends, and I'd like for you to get to know her. Would you like to go with me to donate blood Friday morning?"

"Yes, but I've never given blood before."

"Look at all the firsts you're experiencing. You help someone else when you donate blood." There was a pause, and then Cooper asked, "What happened to your father?"

"He had a massive coronary and died in his early forties. It was his first heart attack, and it was unexpected, because he was young and fit. I suppose these things can happen to anyone."

"I'm afraid so."

After dinner, Cooper walked Mills to her cottage explaining that he had to be in Charleston early the next morning. "My cousins, Anne, Blair, and Zack, are going to come out this weekend to hunt. Anne is Jeff's sister. Please join us over the weekend if you don't have plans."

"I'd love to join you and meet your cousins."

He said good night and walked down the row of camellias back to his home.

Before bed, Mills walked to the riverfront to listen to the sounds of the night and the flowing waters of the Edisto. On her way back to her cottage, she could hear Cooper playing the piano. She stopped to watch him through the window.

Eventually, he stopped playing the song and sat at the piano bench, wiping tears from his face. For a few moments, Mills could not take her eyes off of him as she observed his heart-wrenching solitude, but then he rose from the piano, closed the keyboard cover, and left the room.

She slowly walked back to her cottage, saddened by what she had witnessed.

The next morning, Mills prepared the invitations for mailing, but before going to the post office, she stopped by the kitchen to speak with Marian.

Marian made Mills a cup of hot tea and they began to talk. "I've got the invitations to Cooper's oyster roast finished, and I'm going to Alston Station to mail them. I noticed that a number of his guests had titles—like 'the honorable Mr. Smith'—before their names."

"Cooper knows lots of folks from all sorts of backgrounds. He took over where Miss Julia left off."

"What happened to Cooper's mother?"

"Cooper retired from the Air Force and accepted a job as an airline pilot. The company went out of business, but during that time period, Miss Julia started to become forgetful. Miss Jenny, her sister, eventually told Cooper about her problem. I'm afraid that memory loss issues struck her aggressively."

"How sad," Mills said.

"Cooper came back here with Elise, and for the next three years, he devoted a great deal of his time to taking care of his mother. It was the saddest thing to see. Her personality changed; she wasn't the same woman. The way a man takes care of his mother says a lot about his character. The doctors said that she suffered from a type of dementia—if you have not seen for yourself what it can do to a person, you really have no idea how horrible the disease is. Cooper, bless his heart, did everything he could for her."

"Cooper didn't say anything about her illness to me."

"He rarely discusses his problems. In fact, I can't remember seeing him get angry about anything. The Lord must have given him the strength to bear hardship, because he has been through enough of it."

The telephone rang and after Marian answered it, she let Mills know that she was going to be preoccupied for a while. Mills waved to her as she departed for Alston Station.

Housed in a small cottage-style building, the post office had light-blue shutters and a metal roof. A middle-aged postal worker with sandy hair pinned on top of her head greeted Mills as soon as she entered the building. "I see that it's time for the oyster roast. You must be the young lady Cooper hired to help him with Miss Julia's foundation. I'm Caroline Cummings."

"I'm Mills Taylor, and I'm pleased to meet you."

"Miss Taylor, I'll make sure the invitations go out in today's mail, and I'll look forward to seeing you at the oyster roast."

While she spoke with Ms. Cummings, an elderly lady—in what looked to be a Ford Model T—pulled up in front of the post office. The vehicle was in impeccable condition and could have just come from the dealership. Mills opened the door for the woman as she came inside.

"Thank you, dear," the woman told her. "Caroline, I have two letters that I'd like to purchase postage for." She smiled at Mills and asked, "Are you a visitor to our community?"

"No, ma'am. I've taken a job as the director of the Heath Foundation."

"Julia Heath, a lovely woman. She was very active in our community and has been greatly missed. Please allow me to introduce myself; my name is Miss India Lefaye Tate." Mills introduced herself, and then Miss Tate said, "I wish you great success in your endeavors and please give my regards to Cooper."

When she left the post office, Ms. Cummings told Mills, "Miss Tate's family roots in the Charleston area go back as far as Cooper's."

"How has she maintained that automobile all these years?"

"Miss Tate's Model T? Her father gave her that car decades ago. I know a number of collectors who would like to get their hands on her automobile, but she'll never sell it. Back in the 1960s, she purchased a Thunderbird, but she said she didn't like the way it handled, so she gave it to a relative." The telephone rang in the back of the post office. "Got to go—Miss Taylor, I'll take care of your invitations!"

CHAPTER 4

Guardian Angel

The medical clinic at Alston Station was in a brick-sided building with dark-green shutters at the windows. It was situated in front of the boughs of a live oak tree that shaded the rear of the structure.

When Cooper and Mills arrived at the clinic to donate blood, there was a Red Cross vehicle parked near the entrance. Cooper held the door for Mills, and as they entered, a middle-aged woman with graying hair came out from an examination room.

"Cooper, I was wondering when you'd be out. You must be Mills Taylor. Cooper has told me so much about you. I'm Williston Devereux and you can call me Dr. Will if you'd like. I think it's easier." Williston smiled brightly as she extended her right hand. "Cooper tells me that you've never given blood before. Do you know what your blood type is?"

"No, Dr. Will, I don't know."

"We'll find out, and you'll get a card in the mail from the Red Cross telling you your blood type."

Mills sat down in a chair and a Red Cross nurse asked her questions about her health. As she answered, Mills noticed a woman with three young children enter the building. Their clothes were soiled and only one of the children was wearing shoes. The woman looked pale and unhealthy and there was a bruise around her right eye. She was holding the smallest of the children on her lap, a little girl who appeared to be about two years old. Mills watched until she realized she was staring at them. Williston went over to the woman and began to talk to her before they entered an examination room. When she came out, the woman was in tears and she held the youngest child close to her.

Cooper had finished donating blood, and Mills watched as Williston spoke to him in the front of the clinic. He then went over and began to talk to the woman. Mills could not hear what they said, but eventually, Cooper ended up on one knee while he spoke to her. Patting her on the hand, Cooper returned to Williston and engaged in a conversation for several more minutes. Eventually, the woman rose from her seat, carrying the little girl while holding the hand of the middle child. The oldest child walked in front of his mother, and they went out the clinic door.

The Red Cross nurse thanked them for donating blood, and Williston told her how much she had enjoyed meeting her. As Cooper was driving Mills home, they passed the woman on the road—she walked with her children on the sandy shoulder.

"Couldn't we offer them a ride? They look so pitiful."

"I offered them a ride home, and she said she couldn't accept it. That poor woman—Eula Mullinax," he said, while shaking his head.

"What's wrong with her?"

"Poverty is one of her problems, but she has others. Do you mind if we make one more stop before we go home?"

"No, that's okay."

Cooper stopped at one of the two churches located near his house. When she had attended church on her first Sunday in Alston Station, Mills passed by those two churches, feeling like she would not belong. The sign outside the church read, "Edisto All Saints A.M.E. Church." Cooper went in the front door and was inside for more than fifteen minutes. When he came out, there was a man with him, slight in build and several inches shorter than Cooper.

He walked to the Suburban and introduced himself. "Miss Taylor, I'm Reverend Smalls. Cooper has told me so much about you, and thank you for continuing the work of Miss Julia. I know you'll be very successful."

He paused and then looked at Cooper, "I'll see what I can do, and I'll let Williston know as soon as I find someone to help. Good to see you, Cooper, and a pleasure to meet you, Miss Taylor. I'm sure that I'll be seeing more of you." He turned and walked back into the church.

By the evening, Mills was weary from donating blood and she fell asleep in front of her fireplace. She never made it off the couch and into bed, but instead rested near the warmth of the fire.

Morning sunlight filtered into her cottage through the French doors when Mills awakened to the sound of knocking. She made her way to the front of the cottage and standing on the front steps was a lovely, sandy-haired woman dressed in riding attire.

"Good morning, Miss Taylor, I'm Anne Jefferson—Jeff's sister. I wanted to see if you'd like to go horseback riding with me. Cooper has taken my boys hunting." She extended her right hand for a handshake. "Oh, I received my invitation to the oyster roast, thank you! My husband and I will attend."

"Yes, thank you, Anne. I need just a few minutes to get dressed."

"Take your time. I'll see you shortly."

When Mills arrived at the stables, Charles had saddled both horses and explained that he had come to see Anne and her children. "Enjoy your ride," he told them as he gave Mills a foot up into the stirrup.

When Anne mounted Mephisto, the horse reared slightly, but she patted him on the neck to calm him. "Cooper said that he showed you the ruins of the old plantation. Would you like to ride down there?"

"That would be fine."

Mephisto took the lead as they neared the pasture and both horses began to canter through the field. As they got closer, they saw the ruins enshrouded in a mist that was heavier along the river. Anne held the horse's reins tightly, bringing him to a stop, and Ginger followed suit.

"Anne, you ride well," Mills complimented her.

"You should have seen Mephisto when Cooper first brought him here. He was aggressive, but Cooper worked with him, and he's a different animal. What do you think of this place?"

"I find the ruin amazing. Marian told me that she believes it's haunted."

"There are all kinds of tales about this property. Did you know that this land was owned by some of our ancestors and was sold after the Civil War to satisfy debts? A few years ago, Cooper bought this part of the property. It was not part of the original tract that his parents purchased in the 1950s. He seems to be on a quest to regain properties that our family lost, and I tease him by calling him an empire builder. Jeff, of course, tries to talk him into developing the tracts, but Cooper will hear nothing of it. He's going to be one of the largest landholders in the Low Country."

They walked around the perimeter of the old house ruins, and Mills noticed multitudes of paper whites in early bloom, along with a few daffodils.

"Wait until you see this meadow when the daffodils are in full bloom. It's like a sea of flowers."

She looked at her watch. "I expect that Cooper will be back with the boys any time now. We should probably start back to the house."

When they returned to the stables, Charles insisted that he would take care of the horses. "Miss Anne, you don't get to see Cooper too often, so please let me be of help. You too, Miss Mills."

They both thanked Charles and walked toward Cooper's home. As they got closer, they could hear the boys talking behind the home in the courtyard. "Mom, come and look at what we did. I shot four birds and Zack got three. You should have seen the retrieves that Sam made—he even dove under water to retrieve a bird."

"Blair and Zack, this is Miss Taylor, she's helping Cooper with his educational foundation."

Both boys removed their hats and gloves and shook her hand. "We're pleased to meet you, Miss Taylor."

Putting their hunting hats back on, they told Anne, "Cooper shot a limit. He always does."

"Are we going to prepare these birds for supper tonight?"

"That would be great," the boys responded.

That afternoon, Mills met the group on the green. She joined Anne in a seating area under a live oak tree.

"How do you like it here, so far?"

"I'm enjoying my work, and I like Charleston."

"Cooper is a wonderful person. He's a hero to my boys. I think you're going to like working for him. The past six months have been difficult for him, but he always seems able to handle adversity. The ordinary person would be crippled with the pressures he controls so well. So, you must know about Elise?"

"Yes, I was very sorry to hear about her disappearance."

"I wish we knew what happened. Cooper says she left home one morning last August driving her red Mercedes convertible and didn't come back. The car's never been located. After her disappearance, he was put through a nightmare by some members of law enforcement. They searched his cars, his boats, his homes—multiple times. I'm not sure how many times he was taken in for questioning. I know Cooper though, and I know he would not have done anything to hurt her."

"What was she like?"

"Elise was probably the prettiest woman I've ever known. She was in my sorority at Carolina. Every boy at the university was in love with her—she was so beautiful. One weekend, she came home with me and met Cooper. She couldn't take her eyes off of him, and the attraction was mutual. Her senior year, she was the homecoming queen and Cooper was just starting pilot training. They stayed in touch and saw each other as much as possible. After a year, he asked her to marry him. I think they were happy for years, but I'm not sure why they didn't have children. It's a shame, because Cooper would have been a wonderful father. A few years ago, there seemed to be a strain on their marriage during the time that Cooper's mother was ill, and in recent times, they didn't seem to be as close . . . I'm talking out of turn. It's none of my business."

The football landed at their feet, and Mills got up and threw the ball back to the boys.

"Wow, how'd you learn to throw a spiral?" Blair asked her, excitement in his voice.

"Playing on the neighborhood football team every Sunday afternoon," she responded.

After they went back to playing football, Anne looked at Mills and said, "Cooper has really missed her. I'm afraid I fear the worst."

The football came back in the direction of Mills, and as she returned it to Blair, he asked, "Mills, why don't you come and play? You and I can be on a team, and we'll play Cooper and Zack."

"Anne, do you mind if I join them?"

"No, by all means, go right ahead."

They played tag football on the lawn for over an hour, and Mills threw the ball to Blair for several touchdowns.

"I never saw a girl throw a football like that," he exclaimed.

"Years of practice," she responded with a smile.

Mills joined the group for dinner at seven o'clock, and Cooper was outside grilling the duck breasts from the morning hunt. Anne poured Mills a glass of wine and told her, "I hate that Jeff could not come; he seems to always be working. I wish that he would spend more time with my boys. Bless Cooper, he always takes the time to entertain them. I used to enjoy coming here when I was a child. Cooper, Jeff, Beau, and me—we ran all over this place. Beau was so handsome and smart. Do you know about Beau and Mr. Heath?"

"Yes, I know they passed away in a boating accident."

"Terrible misfortune. Mr. Heath took Jeff, Cooper, and Beau on a trip to the Caribbean to go sailing. It was a graduation present to Beau. He had been accepted to the United States Naval Academy in the fall. A squall came up while they were off Eleuthera, and the boat capsized in high waves. Cooper saved my brother's life, but they were in the water beside the overturned boat for hours before they were rescued. Poor Cooper—he couldn't get to his father and brother. I hate to think about it."

She stopped speaking for a moment and then continued, "When we were kids, we spent many happy hours out here. Jeff was a scrawny little guy and I could beat him up—he was almost in his twenties before he filled out. Cooper and Beau were always athletic and they never excluded me from exploring. We'd heard that pirates came up into the rivers to hide their booty, and we must have dug a thousand holes looking for it. When I was about thirteen, I had a crush on Cooper. Imagine my disappointment when I found out that it was no longer acceptable to marry your first cousin." She started to laugh and poured them more wine. "Let's get the salads on the table."

That evening, after a delicious duck dinner, the group went out onto the green to stargaze with a telescope. With no interference from sources of light produced by humans, the nighttime sky was brilliant. They took turns looking at the moon, star systems, and the planets, huddling around the telescope in the frigid night air. On the far end of the green, a group of deer, illuminated by the moonlight, hurried into the woodland shadows, their silhouettes disappearing into the darkness.

Cooper pointed out the Big Dipper and the North Star. "Do you know who Harriet Tubman was?"

"Yes," Blair responded. "She was a leader in the Underground Railroad that helped escaped slaves from the south flee to freedom in the north."

"That's right, Blair. She was very brave. I want both of you boys to look at Polaris, also known as the North Star. It's the first star in the handle of the Little Dipper."

The boys both gazed into the telescope and then stepped back from it. Cooper continued his story as he pointed out the stars. "Slaves were permitted to sing so they often hid messages in their songs. There was a song about the

Big Dipper called, 'Follow the Drinking Gourd.' Escaped slaves traveled by night so that they would not be apprehended, and if you draw a line from the two pointer stars of the Big Dipper to Polaris, the line points to the north and that meant freedom for escaped slaves."

"Wow, let me see that again," Zack exclaimed.

Admiring Cooper's attentiveness to his cousins, Mills listened carefully to his story. When he finished, Anne said to her, "I'm glad I've had an opportunity to spend some time with you. I wonder if you would mind if I gave Jeff your phone number. I would like for you to get to know him."

"That's fine. Thank you, Anne."

Mills noticed in the moonlight that Cooper stopped looking through the telescope and glanced at them. It was as though he wanted to speak, but refrained. He went back to talking with the boys and discussing Orion's Belt.

On Sunday, Mills decided to visit a West Ashley church she had seen on her drive between Edisto and Charleston. On its marquee was a notice that a contemporary service was held at eleven each Sunday. Taking a seat midway in the sanctuary, she found the congregation to be a mixture of races, young and old. The music was led by a Christian rock band and the people sang and rejoiced in a relaxed style of worship. Feeling comfortable among these people, she especially enjoyed the sermon by Joseph Rose, the pastor. She found him charismatic and he also possessed a sense of humor. When the service was complete, she felt energized, happy, and hoped she had found her place of worship.

After church, she stopped by the Low Country Gourmet and found Paul at work and in his usual high spirits. "Greetings, Audrey, how are you this afternoon? As always, you look fabulous. What are you up to?"

"I went to a church where I really felt comfortable, and I thought I might explore the downtown area this afternoon."

"Just wait another couple of months and the trees and azaleas will be in blossom. Charleston is a treat in the spring. I have had several inquiries about your scholarship program. Have you had any phone calls?"

"Not yet. I'll bring some business cards to you this week."

Paul rearranged a display of chocolates that was on the counter and asked, "How do you like working for Cooper Heath? I've seen his photos in the newspaper. He's quite handsome and apparently very intelligent as well. There have been several articles in the *Charleston Dispatch* about his accomplishments in the shipping business, and then there were the unfortunate stories about him, and his beautiful, but probably very dead wife. Aren't you afraid to be around him?"

"No, Paul, I feel very comfortable with him, and I sense only sincerity in his personality."

"Well, I have to admit, I wondered."

A man came in the front door and exchanged greetings with Paul before going to the gourmet coffee section. Looking at the man for a few moments, Mills thought he looked familiar, and when he returned to the counter, he stared at her with a strange recognition, "Young lady, I believe we recently exchanged greetings in the Unitarian churchyard."

Recalling the man who had looked at her with great curiosity, she responded, "Yes, I remember. My name is Mills Taylor."

"Miss Taylor, my name is Piet van der Wolf. I am pleased to make your acquaintance."

"Piet, Mills is working with the Julia Heath Foundation in fundraising for educational opportunities for youths in the Charleston area."

"Yes, I have heard of this organization."

Mills showed him the foundation's display in the gourmet shop, and then he thanked Paul and paid for his coffee. Turning to Mills, he said, "Miss Taylor, I'll look forward to seeing you in the near future."

After he left, Paul said, "Piet is an old acquaintance. Fabulously wealthy. His ancestors moved to the Charleston area after the Civil War. Poor fellow, he lost his daughter in an automobile accident years ago. His wife was confined to a wheelchair for the rest of her life from her injuries in the wreck, and she passed away a few years ago. You should see his mansion on Wentworth."

After saying goodbye to Paul, Mills explored the side streets and alleyways of the downtown, impressed by the number of elaborate gardens that were hidden off the main thoroughfares. When she returned home, Cooper was fly fishing from a kayak. The marsh was quiet except for the sounds of bird calls and the current of the Edisto gently flowing with the outgoing tide. Sitting down in an Adirondack chair, she watched his smooth technique; as the line sailed back and forth through the air, it appeared to have a life of its own.

That night, while preparing a list of businesses that she would call on during the week, Mills began to hear the faint sound of piano music. Stepping out onto her porch, she could hear Cooper playing the piano fast and furiously.

Wrapping a blanket around her shoulders, she sat down in one of her wicker chairs to listen. He played with a profound intensity, as though he was trying to divest himself of some inner turmoil. She listened to the piano until the music stopped and the lights went off in the living room.

Cooper stopped by her cottage early on Monday morning. He was dressed in a business suit and carrying a suitcase and a briefcase. "I'll be in Newark for the next several days. If you need to get in touch with me, please call the local office of Heath Brothers. I hope you have a successful week. In case you don't have plans for the weekend, I'm going to have several friends over to shoot sporting clays on Saturday. On Sunday afternoon, I'm going to join some local volunteers who are restoring an old schoolhouse near Alston Station. I thought you'd like to join us and meet some of my neighbors."

"I look forward to it."

He smiled at her as he departed down the row of camellias, and as she went back into her cottage, the phone began to ring. A man who identified himself as Joseph Cook was on the line. "Miss Taylor, I am Piet van der Wolf's personal assistant. He asked me to phone you to arrange an appointment in regard to the Heath Foundation, this Tuesday at two in the afternoon."

Writing down the address, Mills responded, "Mr. Cook, I'll look forward to the appointment."

Before she could pick up her briefcase to leave, the phone rang again, and she thought the voice sounded like Cooper's. "Mills, I hope you're having great success in the foundation business." There was a bit of teasing in his voice. "This is Jeff Radcliffe. I met you after a duck hunt recently. Do you remember me?"

"Yes, of course."

"My sister, Anne, says that you're adorable, and I should ask you for a date. How about this Thursday? I'm going sailing with some friends, and I'd like for you to join us. I know that Cooper will let you get away for one afternoon."

"Yes, thank you. I'll see you on Thursday."

"Meet me at the City Marina at one o'clock, and wear warm clothes and nonskid shoes."

Elated by his invitation, she drove into town to pick up her business cards from Collins Printing, and then stopped by Joshua White's law office to personally invite him to the oyster roast. The office manager, Sophia, asked Mills to wait in the conference room and she sat down at a long mahogany table that was surrounded by ten chairs. Within a few minutes, the door opened and Joshua White entered the room.

"My goodness, I was afraid I wasn't going to hear from you again. I want to apologize for my criticisms of Cooper Heath on the afternoon we had tea together. I hope there are no hard feelings."

"No, there are not, and I'm here to personally invite you to his oyster roast." She handed him the invitation, and he smiled broadly as he opened it.

"Mills, I must explain something to you. My wife—rather, my ex-wife—has an attachment of sorts to Cooper Heath's first cousin, Jeff Radcliffe. They are often partners on real estate development projects and I'm afraid they have shared a deeper connection. What I'm trying to say is—I don't like to be around Jeff Radcliffe. I'll come to the oyster roast, but I could lose my manners if I'm near him. I'd like to stay as far away from him as possible. Is that okay?"

"Yes, that will be fine."

"Are you going to be my date?"

"No, I'm in charge of the oyster roast, so please bring a guest."

"All right, it's just about lunch time. Please allow me to take you out." Mills nodded, and Joshua opened the door for her. "After you, my dear."

CHAPTER 5

Resemblances

Mills rang the doorbell at the home of Piet van der Wolf at her appointment time on Tuesday. The home was an imposing structure with a mansard roof and a full three stories. The grounds were flawless and three fountains were visible from the front entrance. The door opened and a tall man with thinning black hair greeted her: "Miss Taylor, I'm Joseph Cook, welcome to the van der Wolf residence."

She stood in the foyer and marveled at the stunning décor of rich mahogany. After taking her coat, Mr. Cook showed her into the drawing room. As she entered through the double doors, Mr. van der Wolf rose from his desk and came forward to greet her, "How nice of you to come. Please sit down."

Motioning for her to have a seat in a chair that was opposite to him, he said, "I'm having tea prepared, and I hope you'll join me."

Within a few minutes, a woman wearing a black skirt, a white blouse, and a white apron brought in a magnificent tea service and placed it on the table. This was the first time in her life that Mills had seen a housekeeper dressed formally in a private residence. He introduced his housekeeper, Anna, to Mills, and Anna began to serve the tea. Mills noticed that Anna looked at her intently while she poured the refreshments and had a kind smile for her as she finished.

"Would you care for anything else?" she asked.

"Thank you, Anna—that will be all."

As they sipped their tea, Mills explained the goals of the Heath Foundation to him, and he listened intently to her presentation, occasionally asking questions.

"Miss Taylor, you are well spoken. I have a donation for your foundation, but I was wondering if I could show you my house and gardens. I rarely have guests, and it would be a pleasure for me to show you my home."

She agreed to the tour, and he bowed when she stood up. He motioned for her to follow him through the double doors of the drawing room, and he led her to the outside through a side entrance. "Most of the statuary was imported from Italy by one of my ancestors." The marbles were of museum quality, were classical in nature, and accentuated the geometrical design of the garden.

"A genius must have designed your garden."

He smiled at her words, and responded, "Mills, it was designed many years ago, before my birth—please come inside. I'll show you the interior."

They entered through a rear door that went to the kitchen and he introduced her to the staff of two women who worked at the stove. The older of the two women, Anna, whom she had already met, smiled at her again, and then looked at Mr. van der Wolf with a hard stare.

He did not seem to notice her intent look as he continued to show Mills around his home.

Upstairs, there was a large two-story ballroom with hardwood floors and exquisite detail work. The room was painted green and the ceiling was hand painted in a classical depiction of a hunting scene.

"This is lovely. You must have wonderful parties here."

"Not for a long time, Mills." He suddenly had a sad expression on his face, but as he looked back at her, he smiled and said, "I have one more room to show you."

Returning to the downstairs, he led her into the most exquisitely decorated living room she had ever seen. There were a number of portraits on the walls, mostly of men. Noticing her interest in the paintings, he remarked, "Most of these individuals are my ancestors."

"Some of them look like they could have been painted by the Dutch Masters."

He laughed at her comment and then opened French doors that led to an outside garden room with a fountain. There was a wall around this portion of the garden, making it intimate and private with only one exit door, which was painted a deep shade of green.

"This is my favorite part of the property. When my wife and daughter were alive, we spent countless hours of pleasure in this garden room. I'm glad that I was able to show it to you."

As they walked back into the living room, Mills noticed the portraits of a lovely young woman who resembled the middle-aged woman in the other painting. "Who are the ladies in the portraits?"

"That's my late wife and daughter. My daughter was killed just before her twenty-fifth birthday in an automobile accident, and my wife suffered injuries that left her paralyzed for the rest of her life. Several years ago, she passed away."

"I'm sorry about your wife and daughter."

"I am, too, but it was a long time ago."

As Mills walked closer to the portraits, she began to realize an uncanny resemblance between herself and Mr. van der Wolf's daughter. They had similar features: wavy dark brown hair and the same hazel-colored eyes.

"What was your daughter's name?"

"Lydia. I can still hear her voice, see her smile."

He gazed at her, and then said, "I have a donation for the Heath Foundation. Please accompany me back into the drawing room."

Following him into the room, he handed her an envelope. "This is to help with scholarships, and it should make Mr. Heath very happy. It has been a pleasure having you in my home this afternoon and I hope to see you again."

She placed the envelope in her purse and shook his hand while thanking him. "Mr. Heath is going to have an oyster roast at his farm the first Saturday in February, and I'm sure that he'd like for you to attend."

"Thank you for the generous offer, but I'm afraid I don't get out too often—Miss Taylor, don't be a stranger."

He pushed a button on his desk, and Mr. Cook reappeared, leading her to the front of the house. Opening the door for her, he said, "Have a nice afternoon, Miss Taylor, and we hope to see you again soon."

Walking a short distance on Wentworth Street before opening the envelope, she was stunned to find a check to the Julia Heath Foundation for $25,000.

That evening, Mills penned a thank you note to Mr. van der Wolf, acknowledging his generous gift. She had reached one conclusion about him: he suffered from the unfortunate human condition known as loneliness.

Admittedly, she was eager to meet Jeff Radcliffe on Thursday. Mills had never been sailing, and she awaited their date with great anticipation. Cooper and Anne were even-keeled, so she expected Jeff to be like them.

Just before one in the afternoon, Mills arrived at the city marina. Jeff had not shown up yet, so she waited for him in the lobby. At least fifteen minutes passed before she saw a silver Yukon pull into the parking lot. Jeff hastily exited the car. When he entered the building, he immediately came in her direction. "Mills, I'm sorry I'm late. I hope that you'll forgive me."

He took her hands in his and smiled broadly. *His blue-green eyes seem to pierce right through me.*

"I had a real estate closing to attend and the attorney received some of the mortgage documents late, which caused a delay. Can I get you something to drink while we wait on my friends? They're going to be late."

"Some friends of yours are joining us?"

"Yes, I hope you don't mind. I sail with them often."

"No, of course I don't mind—and I'd love some hot tea."

"Coming right up."

Entering the Marina's Club Quarters, Jeff ordered hot tea and a scotch and soda, and they sat down at a table in front of the boat slips. There was a large array of watercraft moored at the docking system, from Sunfish boats to transatlantic yachts. A waitress brought their drinks, and Jeff asked, "How did Cooper find such a lovely, talented young woman to help him with his foundation?"

"Thank you, Jeff. Cooper and my former employer are old friends from the Air Force Academy, and Cooper asked Harry to find a director to run the foundation."

"Ah, someone from the outside, someone who wouldn't judge Cooper on the negative information that's been in the media for the last six months. I can't blame him—you know he's very private and rarely discusses his business. I suppose that's how he's made himself so wealthy. If he ever discloses any investment strategies, I want you to share them with me. We'll both make money." He smiled as he sipped his drink. "How's the endowment business going?"

"I'm very excited. This week, we had a substantial donation from a local businessman."

"Who was that?"

"Piet van der Wolf."

"Piet van der Wolf," he said slowly. "Does Cooper know about his gesture?"

"No, I thought I would tell him in person when he returns from Newark." Jeff appeared to be deep in thought with her mention of Piet van der Wolf, but then he turned to her and said, "I'm glad that you could meet me here today." As he placed his glass on the table, she noticed his wristwatch, an impressive Rolex Presidential. *Cooper wears a Timex.*

A couple entered the Club Quarters, and Jeff raised his arm up to signal his friends. As they approached, Jeff stood and introduced Mills to Abigail and Irving Sellers.

"Sorry we're late," Irving responded, shaking Jeff's hand. "Well, are we ready to launch?"

As they walked on the boardwalk, Jeff pointed out his boat to her, a sleek Hunter model. The Sellers were familiar with his sailboat, and Jeff started the motor, moving the vessel away from the slip. Once they were a comfortable distance from other watercraft, Jeff and Irving rigged the sails and maneuvered through Charleston Harbor. The afternoon winds were brisk and cold, but the smell of salt air invigorated her. Mills watched as they trimmed the sails and steered the craft. *Wow, they're excellent sailors.*

Abigail went below into the cabin and returned with four shot glasses of bourbon, passing them out to each person. "Here's to Mills, welcome to Charleston, and to great success with the education foundation!" They raised their glasses, toasted her, and then downed their bourbon immediately, except for Mills, who found the alcohol too strong to drink all at once.

"Jeff, how about something a little stronger?" Abigail suggested.

"Mills, here's your first sailing lesson," Jeff said smiling at her. "The winds are steady. Come up here and steer the boat. I'm going in the cabin for a few minutes. Irving—give her a hand if she needs it."

"Aye-aye, sir," Irving responded.

She walked to the helm and took the wheel.

"You see that structure off in the distance? That's Fort Sumter. There's not another boat out here. Just steer for the fort and you'll be fine."

Jeff and Abigail descended into the cabin and when she returned, she was smiling and laughing. Without any discussion, Irving went into the cabin, and, like Abigail, he was below for a few minutes before returning to the deck.

"Jeff is waiting for you," he told her, as he offered to steer the craft.

As she descended into the cabin, she noticed lines of cocaine set out on a table. Jeff came behind her and gathered her hair to hold it back.

"I wanted to offer you some of our coke."

I can't believe they're doing drugs and operating a sailboat! "Jeff, I don't want to. Bourbon is strong enough for me."

He released her hair and arranged it for her. "If you change your mind, there's plenty left." He then put his arm around her, kissing her on the cheek. "Okay, Captain Taylor, you can return to the deck and keep us from hitting The Battery." Once on deck, Jeff told Irving, "Mills is going to skipper."

"I don't know about this," Mills said. She realized her hands were shaking.

"I'll help you," Jeff responded.

"Are you sure you're able to help me?"

Jeff laughed. "Come on Mills—I'm fine."

She went to the helm and sat down on the seat beside Jeff. Over an hour went by as Mills commanded the boat, receiving instructions from Jeff. Jeff looked at his watch. "Okay, folks, I've got an appointment in Mount Pleasant later this afternoon, so let's take her in."

When they returned to the marina, Jeff easily maneuvered the sailboat into the slip. He took Mills aside and thanked her for joining him, then added that she should shoot sporting clays with them on Saturday afternoon.

"Thank you for asking me, but Cooper has already issued an invitation."

"Then I'll look forward to seeing you on Saturday."

Jeff is nothing like Cooper . . .

Saturday morning, Mills knocked on Cooper's kitchen door before ten in the morning. He had returned from New York and after a few moments, he answered the door. "Greetings, Mills, I was just about to have coffee. Why don't you join me?"

The aroma of fresh-brewed coffee lingered in the air and she breathed in the rich scent. As he poured a cup of coffee for her, he asked, "How was your week?"

"I received the first donation to the foundation and I've been excited to tell you about it." Eager to see his reaction, she put an envelope on the table that contained the van der Wolf gift.

"Wonderful, Mills," he told her, as he opened the envelope.

Watching his face with anticipation, she was astonished when he did not smile, but slowly said, "Piet van der Wolf."

"Is there something wrong?"

Quickly changing his demeanor, he smiled as he looked into her eyes. "I'm sorry, please forgive my reaction. Your work is excellent, and I'm proud of what you've accomplished." Rising from his chair, he gave her a pat on the shoulder before reminding her, "Don't forget about shooting with us this afternoon. Jeff, Britton, and my attorney, Murphy Black, will be here after lunch."

At two, Mills walked toward Cooper's house, and she could hear voices from the front porch. Standing beside Cooper was a man dressed in shooting attire; looking serious and intellectual, he wore oval glasses and his thick, sandy-brown hair was parted to the side.

Cooper called out to her, "Please join us on the porch. I'd like for you to meet my attorney, Murphy."

Mills walked up onto the porch and shook his hand. "Miss Taylor, I've heard so much about you, and I am pleased to make your acquaintance. I enjoyed the artwork on the invitation to the oyster roast, and yes, I will be attending." He had a southern drawl that sounded sophisticated. *I bet he wears a seersucker suit with a bowtie when he appears in court.*

After Britton arrived, they went inside the house to the kitchen; Cooper asked Mills to join him in the hunting room. "This is the shotgun that you used when we went duck hunting, and I think this shooting vest will fit you."

The fit was perfect, and she returned to the kitchen with Cooper, her shotgun case in hand.

Just as they were about to leave the house, Jeff appeared at the kitchen door and apologized for his lateness. "I had an appointment to show a house to a client, but he was late. Sorry, folks." As soon as he saw Mills in the room, Jeff smiled and said, "I'm glad that you could shoot with us."

"I don't know if I can hit anything, but I'll try."

"You don't need to worry about hitting the sporting clays. We've been taking Murphy hunting for years, and he still can't hit a thing. We haven't kicked him out yet."

"Thanks for the encouragement, Jeff."

"Oh, you're welcome, Murphy."

Jeff opened the kitchen door for them to leave when the doorbell rang. Cooper excused himself and went to the front of the house. Upon returning, he took Murphy aside and asked Jeff to take his Suburban and drive Mills and Britton to the shooting range.

"Who is it, Cooper?" Jeff asked.

"It's Lieutenant Barnes with the Charleston County Police Department." Mills looked toward the foyer and a well-built man with a receding hairline stood in the doorway of the kitchen. He was grinning at them with a look of curiosity on his face. While he was dressed in a dark business suit, a policeman's badge graced the front of his coat.

"Well, it's the trust account boys getting ready to shoot—a sport for the rich and infamous—Cooper, you must introduce me to the young lady who is joining you. Miss Taylor?"

He already knew her name and walked forward to shake her hand. Cooper introduced them to one another, and Lieutenant Barnes added, "Miss Taylor, I wish you great success in your endeavors."

Cooper is handling this with a cool head, but Jeff looks angry.

"Lieutenant, Murphy and I are going to join you in the study. I believe you know where it is."

"Sorry, Cooper, I didn't mean to spoil the party."

"Jeff, I'll see you in a few minutes," Cooper said, nodding for him to leave. As Jeff motioned for Mills to join him, she looked back with concern toward Cooper; noticing her expression, he calmed her by saying, "It's okay—I'll join you shortly."

When the trio reached the sporting clay range, Mills was invited to shoot first and the two men helped her with her technique. Britton's shyness was diminished as he gave her advice. As Jeff launched one bird after another, her shooting improved to the point where she began to hit most of the targets.

The sound of an unusual combustion engine was coming in their direction, and an old Land Rover appeared in the pasture. When the vehicle came to a stop, Cooper and Murphy got out of the vehicle with their gun cases.

"Where did you get that?" Mills asked.

"I had it delivered from England last year. I keep it stored in the equipment shed. It's not licensed to drive on the highways, so I drive it around the farm."

"Have you ever seen the movie, *The Gods Must Be Crazy*?"

"No, I don't believe so."

"There's a vehicle in that movie called the 'Anti-Christ.' It looks just like your Land Rover—that's my favorite movie."

"I'll have to watch it sometime."

"Everything all right?" Britton inquired.

"Yes, I've already answered the questions that he asked today."

For the next couple of hours, they took turns at shooting sporting clays, and while Britton and Cooper were talented marksmen, she noticed that Jeff was an expert, not missing one shot.

Mills leaned against Cooper's Land Rover, and Murphy joined her. "Well, Mills, I think you're a better shot than me, and you just started. Maybe I should get my eyes evaluated," he chuckled.

They watched Britton as he fired his gun, and she asked, "Is Cooper okay? He doesn't seem to be upset by the policeman's visit."

"If he was, you'd never know it. He's one of those people who has the rare talent of maintaining composure under pressure. He always has."

Jeff called out to Murphy and Mills, "I think we're finished shooting."

"Is it time for a porch party?" Murphy asked.

"What does that mean?" Mills inquired.

"You'll see."

"Cooper, can I drive the Land Rover back to your house?" Mills asked.

"You do use a clutch in that Beetle, don't you? Well, get in, and I'll check you out."

The Land Rover had a right-side steering wheel, and Mills found it difficult to put the old machine in first gear. When she released the clutch, the vehicle lurched forward, and she didn't fare much better with second gear.

"I'm embarrassed. This is more challenging than I thought it would be."

"You're doing fine. Just park the 'Anti-Christ' in front of the house."

When they reached the front courtyard, Mills parked the Land Rover and asked, "Did I beat you to death?"

"No, you just need a little practice on changing the gears. Drive it anytime you want. I leave the keys in it."

As she started to return her shooting vest to him, he told her, "That's yours. I bought it for you while I was in New York last week."

"Thank you, but I really shouldn't accept it."

"Mills, it's just a hunting vest. It's yours."

"All right—but how did you know my size?"

"I described you to the sales clerk at Holland and Holland. She suggested this vest."

"You must have given her an accurate description. It fits perfectly."

"Please join us on the porch. We're going to have drinks and talk."

"I'm not sure I should be joining you and your friends for drinks."

"Mills—I don't know what customs you're used to, but please set aside any misgivings. I would consider myself rude for excluding you." She nodded and joined him on the porch. Mills quickly discovered that the porch party was a friendly forum to discuss current events. Cooper poured her a glass of wine while the others drank beer or bourbon.

The conversation centered on a residential development project on a pristine section of the Edisto River. "Cooper, I heard that you and your neighbors are trying to block the development of the old Youngblood tract," Jeff said.

"We're attempting to get information on the development at this point, but I don't think this area is in need of a seven-hundred-lot development. The building of new homes results in runoff from fertilizers, which will foul the waterways."

"Cooper, I hate to tell you this, but sooner or later, development is coming. You can't stop it, and you can't purchase every tract."

"No, but I can take a stand against poorly planned expansion. Growth doesn't always mean progress."

Britton joined the conversation, "Jeff, I think you would even cut down the Angel Oak if you could make enough money from developing the land around it."

"Even I'm not that greedy."

"One day, someone will be that greedy."

"Speaking of greed, Mills got a substantial donation for Cooper's foundation from Piet van der Wolf."

"Piet van der Wolf," Murphy repeated the name. "Cooper, what are you doing letting her take a donation from that reclusive old vulture?"

"How can I forgive the actions of my own family if I can't forgive Piet?"

"That's different," Murphy interjected.

"Is it really?"

"Cooper, let's not discuss our ancestors today. You know that I'm not apologetic like you," Jeff said.

"You brought up Piet."

"Okay, Cooper, where are they?" Jeff inquired.

"In the usual place."

Jeff went into the house and returned with four cigars. "Mills, you don't look like a cigar smoker, so I didn't get you one."

Even in the open air, the cigar smoke was overly pungent to Mills, and she stepped to one end of the porch. The conversation evolved to a discussion on the excavation of a ship that had gone down in a hurricane off the coast of the Carolinas in the 1850s and the rights of the recovery team versus the government and insurance companies.

Mills remembered that she needed to visit Dawkins's Market for a few items, so she thanked the group for including her in their party. Cooper followed her to the bottom of the steps and said, "Don't let them upset you about Piet van der Wolf. I'll explain about him tomorrow."

When she reached Dawkins's Market, church bells tolled the hour and Mr. Dawkins greeted her by name. She smiled and went toward the bread aisle, almost colliding with a child who was racing through the store. Mills stepped aside quickly, but the boy continued on his path without a word. She recognized him as the eldest of the three children she had seen at Dr. Will's clinic on the day she had donated blood. Her eyes followed him until he joined his mother and two siblings. They all appeared to be in better condition than when she had last seen them; their clothing was clean and well fitting, and they all wore shoes. *They must have met their guardian angel.*

After selecting a loaf of bread, Mills passed by the group on her way through the market. The woman smiled at her, revealing the poor condition of her teeth, and wished Mills a pleasant evening. Mills wished her the same and continued to shop.

When she finished, she went to the checkout aisle. Several cartons of eggs were stacked on the counter, and Mr. Dawkins said, "I get these eggs from a local farmer, and I think you should try a dozen." He opened a carton, showing her the eggs, which were brown and of various sizes.

She paid for her items, which included a dozen eggs, and thanked Mr. Dawkins as she picked up her grocery bags. He went ahead of her, opening the door. As she left, he thanked her for the invitation to the oyster roast, "I wouldn't miss it for the world."

The evening turned to dusk as Mills drove back toward Cooper's property.

In the dim light, Mills passed the mother and her three children who walked on the side of the sandy road. She stopped her Volkswagen after passing them and called out to the woman, "It's getting dark, can I give you a ride home?"

The group neared the vehicle and Mills noticed a sad and lost look in the children's eyes as they huddled near the side of her car.

"Thank you for offering, but we don't live far from here, and we don't mind the walk," the woman responded.

"Well, good night," Mills said as she drove away from the group, leaving them beside the sandy roadway in Alston Station.

After church on Sunday, at one-thirty, Mills knocked on Cooper's door to accompany him to the Freedom Road Schoolhouse. Curious to hear the explanation as to why Murphy referred to Piet van der Wolf as a reclusive vulture, she readily took a seat in his study after she was welcomed inside.

"I told you I would explain about Piet and the past. First of all, Piet is a highly successful businessman. Like his forefathers before him, a great deal of his wealth has been accrued through speculative business dealings, many of which have been in real estate." He paused before continuing. "This history goes back to a time when many people in the south were thrust into poverty. Piet's ancestors were adventurers from the north who became wealthy on land investments and, later, in the phosphate business."

"Why did you say that if you could not forgive Piet, then how could you forgive the actions of your own family?"

"My ancestors in my mother's family were some of the first settlers who helped colonize Charleston. They arrived from Barbados in the late 1600s and were successful merchants, which provided them with the capital to become planters. Acquiring substantial land holdings in the Low Country, they first planted indigo and rice, and later, cotton. Do you remember who Henry Laurens was?"

"I think so. He was a Revolutionary War patriot from South Carolina."

"Yes, that's true—he was also one of the most profitable slave brokers in eighteenth-century America. My family made some of their money in the same way. While many of the companies that engaged in the slave trade were based in Liverpool, England, or Boston, they had local brokers with whom they dealt in the Charleston area. Thousands of slaves entered America at Sullivan's Island and were auctioned off to the highest bidder. Some of Jeff's and my ancestors were brokers in 'Black Ivory,' and they made a fortune off the horrendous acts of selling human beings. They were industrious individuals, some of the richest in colonial America, owning several plantations and hundreds of slaves. I think the institution of slavery was this country's anathema."

"I think so too," Mills responded.

He paused for a moment, "It's true that my family lost almost everything they had after the Civil War, but that's over and done with. We're all here together, and we should try to look out for one another. While I can't apologize to people who died hundreds of years ago, I can help now. That's the reason for the educational foundation."

"Why are Jeff and Murphy hostile toward Piet?"

"I think it's because, at times, he has conducted his business dealings in a morally questionable manner. He is a land speculator and has made large profits at the expense of other people. I know that some people consider Piet a smart business man, and perhaps some of the things he's accused of are simply untrue. I can understand that, as well."

"You mean he has a reputation for being ruthless in business."

"Yes ma'am. Mills, there is one policy I'd like for us to observe in the future: let's keep the names of our donors to ourselves. I know that you didn't mean any harm discussing Piet van der Wolf with Jeff. He is, after all, a member of my family, but I think we should keep their identities private."

"I'm sorry; I didn't mean to cause a problem."

"It's all right. I didn't give you any guidelines on this issue, but I think we should observe that policy from now on."

She nodded in agreement but felt embarrassed that he had corrected her.

"Are you ready to go work on the schoolhouse?" Cooper asked.

"Yes, I am."

CHAPTER 6

Hope

The schoolhouse, surrounded by a grove of live oak trees and the thick vegetation of scrub palms, was situated on a rural sandy lane. A sign—"Freedom Road Schoolhouse Restoration in Progress"—stood in front of a small, white building that was in poor condition, with broken windows and rot damage to its fragile frame. The double doors of the building stood open and stacks of fresh lumber were in the schoolyard.

In front of a roaring campfire, an old white-haired gentleman stooped, his back bent over as he warmed his hands near the flames. A group of young children played near the fire and Mills heard the sound of hammers echo from inside the building.

As soon as the man noticed Cooper, the ancient wrinkles on his face transformed into a beaming smile. "Cooper, it's been months since I laid eyes on you. Who is this young lady?"

"Mr. Camp, this is Mills Taylor. She's the director of the Heath Foundation."

Cooper introduced them, and Mr. Camp added, "Cooper is a fine judge of character, so I know that you'll do a fine job for Miss Julia. Cooper, where have you been keeping yourself?"

"I've been busy with work at Heath Brothers."

"You have to get away from there sometimes. I think you're the hardest working young man I know."

"Thank you, Mr. Camp."

"Edmund is in the building with the others. My arthritis is so bad these days that I can't use a hammer, but I brought Edmund with me to help. I decided to sit by the fire with the young folks while y'all work. It helps to get out sometimes—well, I know you want to get started—we'll talk after a while."

Cooper shook his hand before turning toward the building. He asked Mills, "How old do you think he is?"

"Maybe eighty-five."

"On his last birthday, he turned one hundred and five years of age. He's the son of former slaves and a walking history book. His son, Edmund, is in his seventies, but he looks much younger."

They stopped and looked at the building before entering. "This schoolhouse was abandoned in the 1950s and fell into near ruin, but the people in our area want to restore it and make it a community center for young people."

"I think that's a great idea."

When they climbed the steps to the entrance of the building, the workers inside enthusiastically greeted Cooper and Mills. Introductions proceeded and Mills met about a dozen of Cooper's friends and neighbors. The pastor she had met from the Edisto All Saints A.M.E. Church, Reverend Smalls, came forward to greet her, accompanied by another local minister, Reverend Johnson. Charles and his wife, Elizabeth, replaced rotten wood on a windowsill, but they stopped their work to greet Cooper and Mills.

One of Cooper's neighbors, Joe Caldwell, called to them, "I could use some help with these floorboards."

As Cooper and Mills helped him pry up damaged flooring, Mr. Caldwell observed, "It looks like termites did some hefty damage to the flooring in this area, including the sill."

The flooring was heart pine, and Mills noticed that the workers attempted to match the planks with similar wood. After a few minutes, Mr. Caldwell's daughter, Susan, who was about the same age as Mills, joined them. She said, "We're Cooper's closest neighbors to the north side of his property—we're looking forward to the oyster roast. It's become quite a social event."

Mr. Caldwell changed the subject back to the renovation, adding, "You know, so far we must have removed thirty birds' nests and a family of raccoons from this building. I'm afraid to see what kind of snakes come out of the woodwork as it begins to get warm."

When the workers took a break for refreshments, Mills spoke with Edmund Camp by the campfire and, just as Cooper had told her, he appeared young for his age.

The elder Mr. Camp asked, "Well, how is it going?"

"We've made progress, but we have a long way to go," his son replied.

"Edmund, can you remember what it was like to go to school here?"

"Just like it was yesterday. We all tried to contribute—even if it was just gathering firewood for the next day. Our books were used ones, but we were just thankful for the opportunity to learn. Pops, there's just a little more light left in the day—I'm going to work for a while longer, and then I'll take you home."

As the sun began to set, the warm glow of the embers from the dying campfire cast shadows against the old building and the volunteers began to pack their tools. Mills stood beside Susan Caldwell as they both warmed their hands above the fire. She found Susan to be friendly and very excited about her upcoming nuptials, which would take place in April. Cooper joined them at the fire and after Edmund secured the front doors of the building, he walked toward the group. Mills loved the smell of the fire and she breathed deeply, inhaling the light wood smoke that rose from the embers.

The elder Mr. Camp volunteered, "Cooper, we'll be at your oyster roast, but I won't be able to stay very late. Edmund's wife makes me go to bed early. She says that I'm ornery if I don't get a good night's sleep." He chuckled. "I think it's wonderful that this building is undergoing restoration."

"So do I," Mills replied.

Edmund added, "I hope that when we finish, the youths in this area take advantage of the opportunity to use this building for worthwhile activities, the way we did when we went to school here. We're planting seeds; may they grow and be nurtured."

Edmund drowned the fire before helping his father into their Ford pickup. As he sat down in the cab, the elder Mr. Camp said, "Cooper, do you remember this truck? I drove it to your place when it belonged to your parents. It's a bit rusty, but it keeps on running—just like me. You know, I can still remember teaching you and Beau to throw a cast net . . . didn't take either one of you too long to catch on. That summer, you must have been twelve or thirteen. I'm proud of you. You sure did grow into a fine young man."

"Thank you, Mr. Camp."

Mr. Camp gestured to Mills to move close to the car window, telling her, "Young lady, I enjoyed meeting you today, and I want to tell you something: Cooper Heath is one of the finest men I've ever known. Don't let anybody tell you different. Oh, and mighty fine artwork on the oyster invitation. Good night."

On the drive home that evening, Cooper asked her to make an appointment for both of them to visit Piet van der Wolf to thank him for his generous gift to the Heath Foundation.

Before they turned down his driveway, Mills added, "I invited Joshua White to the oyster roast. I think I know why you changed the subject the last time we discussed him."

"You noticed that—Jeff and Joshua White's former wife are partners on real estate development projects, but their friendship goes deeper than that. I'm not sure that I understand their relationship."

"Yes, he explained about them."

"I told you before that you're in charge of this operation, and that includes guest geography."

Mills approached the front gate of the Heath Brothers parking lot just before two o'clock on Wednesday afternoon. The Heath Brothers building was in a remodeled warehouse near the Columbus Street Shipping Terminal. Container cranes towered above the waterfront and the building and the adjoining parking lot were surrounded by a high metal fence. When she reached the security house, the guard opened the door for her and, with an enthusiastic voice said, "I think you must be Miss Taylor, but per company rules, I need to see a photo ID."

Mills removed her driver's license from her wallet and showed it to him. Looking at it carefully, he said, "I'd like to introduce myself. I'm Bob Eastman, Director of Security for Heath Brothers." He pointed to an exterior door, and said, "If you'll take that door, the staircase will lead you to the second floor, and Cooper's office is the first one on the right—it's a pleasure to meet you, Miss Taylor."

As Mills entered the second-floor hallway, she could see Cooper at his desk, talking on the telephone. As soon as he noticed her, he motioned for her to come in and sit down. When Cooper finished the conversation, he rose from his chair and greeted her, "Good afternoon, Mills."

Cooper introduced her to all the staff members and she marveled at the large central room with several clocks that displayed the time in London,

Cairo, Singapore, San Francisco, and Charleston. Everyone greeted her with enthusiasm and wished her great success with the foundation. Cooper went to a closed door and knocked. After a few moments, a good-looking man answered the door. He was probably in his sixties with tanned skin and dark hair with some gray mixed in; he immediately reminded Mills of Cary Grant.

As soon as he saw her, he gave her a beautiful smile. "Miss Taylor, I'm Cooper's uncle, Ian Heath, and I'm thrilled to meet you."

His British accent added to his sophistication as he took her hand in his, saying, "Cooper speaks very highly of you. I'm surprised that he's just now bringing you around to meet me."

Cooper looked at his watch before telling his uncle, "Mills and I have an appointment; we need to leave."

"Daniel," Ian said as he looked directly at Cooper, "I want to speak with you about the *Madame Talvande*; and Miss Taylor," he smiled at Mills, "I look forward to seeing more of you—for certain, at the oyster roast."

As Cooper entered his uncle's office, he said to Mills, "I'll be back in just a moment."

Walking around the office, she studied the artwork and old maps that hung on the walls. The charts depicted the seas and oceans of the world, and glass cases displayed antique maritime artifacts and replicas of ships from the past. Above one of the compartments was a framed display with medals mounted on the inside. An inscription underneath the medals stated that the honors were bestowed on Phillip B. Heath in 1945. As she read the details about each award, she saw that one of the medals was the Victoria Cross.

As she gazed at the medals, she realized that someone had walked up behind her. Startled, she turned to find Cooper standing right behind her.

Taking a breath, she confessed, "You were so quiet, I didn't hear you walk up."

His lips quirked up into a slight smile, and he said, "Are you ready to go?"

"Were these medals awarded to your father?"

"Yes, they were."

She pointed to the Victoria Cross, and he explained, "That medal is the highest honor for valor that can be awarded to military personnel of the United Kingdom. It's the equivalent of the Congressional Medal of Honor. I'll tell you about it sometime, but we'd better leave if we're going to be on time at Piet van der Wolf's home."

As they left the building, Mills looked thoughtfully at Cooper before saying, "Daniel?"

"That's my first name, and my uncle calls me that when he's perplexed about a problem."

"And who is Madame Talvande?"

"She's not a person, she's one of our container ships named after the headmistress of a Charleston finishing school for young ladies, prior to the Civil War."

"I see," Mills nodded.

Welcomed by Mr. Cook into the van der Wolf home, Cooper and Mills were shown into the living room. Piet rose from a chair to greet them.

"Mr. Heath, I'm glad to meet you. I've read about your contributions to the shipping industry in the *Charleston Dispatch*, and what an exceptional negotiator you are."

"Mr. van der Wolf, thank you for your contribution to the Julia Heath Foundation."

"Miss Taylor wisely articulated your goals for the foundation and I thought I'd like to help. You should give her the credit for the donation."

He smiled at Mills before continuing, "I hope you both have time for tea." Cooper accepted his invitation, and Mr. van der Wolf replied, "Please make yourselves at home. I'm going to notify the kitchen staff."

When he left, Cooper looked around the room before saying, "Piet lives in quite a mansion, doesn't he?"

"Yes."

Watching Cooper's face as he studied the room, Mills noticed his eyes linger on the Steinway grand piano and then move upward, resting on the portraits of Piet's wife and daughter. He turned to Mills and intently gazed into her eyes before speaking. "That young woman in the portrait could be your twin. Who is she?"

"I asked Mr. van der Wolf about her when I last visited here. That portrait is of his daughter, Lydia; she was killed in an automobile accident a number of years ago. The other painting is of his wife; she was an invalid after the wreck and died a few years ago."

Cooper was quiet for a few moments before adding, "I do seem to remember something about that, but I was very young when it happened."

Mr. van der Wolf returned with Anna, the elder member of the kitchen staff, who carried an exquisite silver tea service. She poured each person a cup of tea, offered them biscuits, and then smiled at Mills before excusing herself from the room.

When they finished their refreshments, Cooper thanked Piet for his hospitality and again for his generous gift to the Heath Foundation. When they prepared to leave, Piet said to Cooper, "Mr. Heath, I've heard that you are a talented pianist. I would love to hear you play sometime."

"Thank you, Mr. van der Wolf," Cooper replied, but did not offer to play for him.

As they descended the front steps of the home, Cooper asked Mills to accompany him to a nearby park. A large three-tiered fountain was at the center of the diminutive square, and an abundance of water cascaded into the brick base. Cooper asked her to sit down on a bench.

"You bear an amazing resemblance to Piet's daughter. Does it make you uncomfortable that you look so much like her?"

"When I first saw the portrait, I was astounded by my likeness to her."

"Mills, I don't want you to feel uneasy, not ever."

"I'm not afraid of him."

Cooper sat quietly for a moment staring at the water fountain, and then turned to her saying, "I'd prefer that you invite him out to lunch if he wants to see you again, but until you know him better, for your sake, please meet him in public."

"I think he's just lonely, but I'll do as you ask."

"There's one more stop I'd like to make with you. I'd like to thank Ford Butler and his wife at the Low Country Gourmet for helping the foundation."

That afternoon, Mr. Butler, his wife, Melea, and Paul were all at the shop on King Street. Cooper thanked each individual for his or her assistance before engaging in a conversation with Ford Butler. Paul motioned for Mills to join him at the counter. "He's even more attractive in person than in the newspaper photos. I'm glad I got to meet him and see how nice he really is."

CHAPTER 7

The Oyster Roast

For a couple of days prior to the oyster roast, young men from White Point Catering set up tables and lighting around the green at the Heath farm. Mills had received most of the RSVP replies to Cooper's mailed invitations; the vast majority of those invited would attend. There was one response that shocked her: "Instead of shucking oysters for the so-called underprivileged, you should be out looking for my daughter, you son-of-a-bitch." When she showed the response to Cooper, he calmly said, "I'm sorry you saw that, Mills. Carlton Monroe is my father-in-law; he always has a way with words."

Just after sunrise on Saturday morning, the caterers began their final preparations for the oyster roast. Not only were oysters on the menu, but several pigs were roasting, along with the preparation of a stew called "chicken bog." The caterers lit bonfires around the green; the aroma of the pork roasting and the wood smoke from the burning logs was splendid.

Before the first guests arrived, a jazz ensemble from the College of Charleston set up and began to play. As the afternoon turned into evening, lanterns were lit around the green, supplementing the light from the bonfires.

Charles, Marian, and Elizabeth arrived before the start of festivities and offered to help, but Cooper quickly told them to simply enjoy themselves. Among the other early arrivals were Dr. Will, the Camps, and Paul and the Butlers from the Low Country Gourmet.

Cadets from The Citadel had been engaged to handle the parking and, after sunset, guests began to steadily arrive. While most of the guests were dressed casually, Mills saw Jeff arrive with two women who wore mink coats.

Cooper brought a couple for Mills to meet; they were Jeff's parents, Cooper's Aunt Jennifer and Uncle Robert. There was a close resemblance between his aunt and the portrait of Cooper's mother displayed in his living room. Not far behind them were Anne and her husband, David.

Anne informed her, "Blair has a tremendous crush on you and he hasn't stopped talking about you since we visited Cooper."

"Thank you, Anne. That's sweet."

As they went to the oyster tables, Reverend Smalls stopped by to congratulate her on the outstanding job that she had done on the festivities. "Mills, I'm thankful to see such a good turnout. I consider this a good show of support for Cooper."

"I agree," she said with a smile.

Mills did not participate in the feast. She was determined that every aspect of the oyster roast would be a success and she gave her full attention to ensuring that the food and drink tents stayed supplied.

She discovered that a popular subject of discussion by Edisto-area landowners was conservation easements and the need to control the rapid flow of development into the area. There was an older gentleman, Longstreet, with his two sons—Cooper told her that they were leaders in the Edisto conservation movement. When introduced to father and sons, they told Mills that, so far, this year's oyster roast was the best effort they'd seen.

Joshua White arrived and introduced Mills to the lovely blond who had been with him on the day that Mills had met him at the Sea Island Yacht Club. She kept in mind that Joshua White and Jeff Radcliffe were not on fond terms and she directed the couple to one end of the oyster tables, as far away from Jeff as possible.

"Hot basket—comin' through," was the call of the caterers as they went from one stand to another, dumping mounds of steaming hot oysters on the tables in front of the guests.

Jeff and Britton suddenly appeared at her side, and taking her by the hand, Jeff said, "Don't you think you could stop working long enough to enjoy some oysters?"

"I want to make sure that all aspects of the party are handled properly."

"Stop worrying, you've done a great job—come on over here."

They led her to one of the tables and began to shuck oysters for her. Britton went to the wine tent and brought back a glass of sparkling wine for her.

"How am I going to learn to shuck oysters?"

"We don't want you to learn—that makes you dependent on us," Jeff laughed. *He's in a great mood—so handsome when he smiles.* While Mills enjoyed the oysters, the two women in mink coats who had arrived with Jeff came over to their table.

"Mills, these ladies are my partners, Cassandra White and Madge Sinclair." He introduced them to one another, and added, "Mills has recently become the director of the Heath Foundation, and I believe you know Britton."

Madge Sinclair stepped toward Mills. "I'd offer to shake hands, but we're sticky with oyster juice. Jeff, let's go up to Cooper's house for a while. I need to get warm. Nice to meet you, Miss Taylor."

Mills realized that Cassandra was Joshua White's former wife and she watched the three walk toward Cooper's house. Suddenly overcome by shyness again, Britton became quiet, but clearing his throat, he asked, "Mills, can I get you another glass of wine?"

Before she could respond, Cooper called out to her, "Mills, I could use your help for a few minutes."

She thanked Britton for his kind gesture and joined Cooper, away from the oyster tables. "We're almost out of the Schramsberg. Could you help me carry the wine?"

"I'll be glad to help."

On their way to the house, they ran into Ian and Celeste, Cooper's uncle and aunt. Cooper introduced her to his aunt, who raved about how wonderful the party was. She was an attractive woman. Mills thought that at one time she must have been a beauty. Like her husband, a refined British accent added to her sophistication.

After they left his aunt and uncle, Cooper explained that his aunt was from Bermuda and he had two married first cousins, Ian and Celeste's daughters. As they lived in England, he rarely saw them.

When they arrived at the house, the gas lanterns cast warm light on the front porch. As Cooper opened the front door, the heat from inside welcomed them. They entered the kitchen, and the door to the hunting room was closed. Cooper knocked once before opening the door. The threesome of Jeff, Cassandra, and Madge sat at a card table, inhaling lines of cocaine.

Mills was stunned and exchanged glances with Cooper. His face darkened as he viewed the threesome.

"Cooper, come in and join us. We'd love to share with you," Madge said in a seductive voice.

"I would appreciate it if you three would not do this at my home," he responded.

"Cooper, you're so predictable," Jeff said.

"That's enough. What you do is your business, but you're not going to do that here."

"Okay, ladies—the boss has spoken. I'm going to visit the boy's room, and we'll go back to the oyster roast—excuse me."

As he came through the kitchen, Jeff saw Mills and kissed her on the forehead. "You're beautiful," he said, then continued toward the foyer.

Mills peeped into the room and heard Madge tell Cooper, "As many times as I've been to your house, I don't recall ever coming into this room. Did you shoot all these trophies?"

"Most of them, but some of the trophies are Beau's."

"Cooper, you're a violent man."

"I'm actually very gentle."

There was a pause while Madge gazed at Cooper. "Why don't you show Cassie and me just how gentle you are? I believe Jeff has other plans for the evening and we'd like to get to know you better."

"I'm married."

"I hate to tell you this, because I was fond of Elise, but she's been missing for over six months. You are married to a memory, and you've been alone for a long time."

"Madge, I'll try to overlook your comments. I intend to remain faithful. I have not given up hope." Mills noticed Cooper's brow grow tight with a deep frown. *My goodness—he looks mad.*

"If you change your mind, you know where to find us."

"I need to return to the rest of my guests."

Jeff winked at Mills as he returned to the hunting room and picked up a small bag of white powder in a plastic bag from the table. He was immediately engaged by Madge to open more oysters for her and Cassie. As Madge passed by Cooper, she kissed him on the cheek and said, "The party is simply wonderful."

When the three passed by Mills in the kitchen, the two women seemed unconcerned that she might have heard the conversation and nodded at her with a smile.

Cooper removed a case and a half of sparkling wine from the refrigerator.

"I'm sorry to have kept you waiting—Jeff and his friends really try my patience."

"Yes, I understand why." Their eyes met.

"Can you carry the half case?"

She lifted the bottles. "Sure, it's not very heavy."

On the front porch, he stopped her and said, "I'm proud of your work, and Julia would be proud of you too." The happiness in his face, and the smile that he gave her, were unforgettable.

As they returned to the gathering, Cooper nodded to Dr. Warren, the advisor on his scholarship program with the Charleston County school system. He waved to her as he approached and introduced the women to one another.

Dr. Warren volunteered, "Miss Taylor, it's my pleasure to meet you. Cooper tells me that you are working very hard for the foundation, and I admire both of you for what you're doing. I hope that the two of you will come to the junior and senior high schools in the next few weeks to discuss the scholarship program with the students."

"We'd be glad to," Cooper responded.

"Fine, Cooper, I'll phone you with some dates and times."

After a long conversation, Dr. Warren excused herself to return to her companion at one of the tables. The caterers flagged down Cooper and told him that they were running low on oysters; he told them to bring the next batch to their table.

"Hot oysters—comin' through," the man called out, as he made his way through the crowd and poured the steaming oysters onto the table in front of them. Cooper handed her a glove and an oyster knife. "I want you to slow down and enjoy yourself."

The first oyster that Mills picked up was so hot that she could barely hold it, even while wearing a glove. As she pried the shell open at the hinge, scalding hot oyster juice flowed out and burned her hand. She waited for the oyster to cool down, then dipped it in cocktail sauce before eating it.

When she was unable to open the next oyster, Cooper took the knife from her and opened the shell at the hinge. As quickly as she ate them, he opened oysters for her. Mills glanced at a nearby table, and she noticed Jeff with a beautiful girl. Jeff opened oysters for her and put his arm around her.

Madge and Cassandra joined Cooper and Mills at their table. "You lucky girl, but Cooper, you'd better watch yourself—remember what you told me a few minutes ago. I hope you went light on the oysters," Madge paused a moment and gave Cooper a teasing smile before continuing, "We've had a lovely time, but we're heading back to Charleston. You can count on Cassie and me for a donation to your foundation." She kissed him on the cheek and said good night. Mills glanced in Jeff's direction, only to see him leave with the young woman for whom he had opened oysters.

As the crowd dwindled, Mills started to assist the caterers with the cleanup, but Cooper put a hand on her arm. "You don't need to do that. The caterers will be back in the morning to complete the cleanup. Come up to the house and have a glass of wine with Britton and me. We ought to celebrate the success of the oyster roast." He paused. "Great job, Mills."

She blushed.

Mills and Cooper spent Sunday afternoon at the Freedom School, working on the restoration. There were even more people on the grounds that afternoon and Mills met Susan Caldwell's fiancé. Mills believed that she and Susan were becoming friends and they often worked together on repairs.

There was a noticeable improvement in the appearance of the building. Most of the exterior wood damage had been repaired, but the fresh wood siding still remained unpainted—the siding awaited the finishing touches.

That afternoon, Susan told Mills that she would like her to attend her wedding, saying, "I invited Cooper some time ago, but I'd love for you to attend too. Please look for an invitation in the mail."

On their way back home, Cooper and Mills stopped at Dawkins's Market for Cokes. The mother and three children from Dr. Will's clinic were at the front counter, purchasing eggs and a loaf of bread. As soon as the mother saw Cooper, she smiled at him and then put her hand up over her mouth before she spoke, "Mr. Heath, how nice to see you."

"Eula, I hope things are going well for you."

Excitedly, she told him, "Oh, Mr. Heath, I was able to start night school and my children are getting the care they need. Thank you so much for your help."

"You're welcome. Just keep up the good work. Reverend Smalls says that you're doing well, and I'm glad for you and your children. It's just about dark, can Miss Taylor and I give you a ride home?"

"Oh, no, sir, we'll be just fine."

On the drive home, Mills told Cooper, "That's the second time I've seen her since the day we donated blood, and she and her children are in so much better condition. Why did she thank you?"

"Reverend Smalls and some of his church members have been helping her with food, clothing, and sitting services so that she could attend school and work. I'm glad to see her life turning around. Sometimes people just need an opportunity and they can achieve success themselves. I believe that such is the case with Eula."

Mills noticed that Cooper didn't fully answer her question as to why Eula had thanked him, so she decided that she should not press him further.

When they returned to Cooper's property, the green had been cleaned up and, except for the marks left by the bonfires, she could not tell that a party had taken place the night before. As Cooper walked Mills to her cottage, he told her that he would be in New York for the next several days.

When she entered her cottage, she felt a slight chill and she turned on the gas logs. As the evening went on, she felt cold and fell asleep on the couch in front of the fireplace.

The next morning, she took her temperature. The thermometer read 101 degrees. She called Marian to tell her she was ill, and shortly after Mills made the phone call, Cooper knocked on the door of her cottage. She invited him inside and he sat down beside her and felt her forehead.

He was professionally attired in a dark business suit for his trip to New York. With a concerned expression on his face, he said, "You're burning up with a fever. Marian will bring you aspirin in a few minutes and I'll ask Williston to check on you today. Is there anything that I can get you?"

"A drink of water—there's a pitcher of water in the refrigerator."

He poured a glass of water for her. "Why don't you go back to bed? Several of my appointments in New York are with French government and shipping officials. If they weren't already scheduled, I would stay and take you to see Williston."

Before he left her cottage, he said he would call her from New York.

Marian arrived in a few minutes with a bottle of aspirin and several pink camellias in a glass vase. "Oh, my goodness, I'm sorry you're sick. Cooper picked these for you before he left and asked me to bring them to you. Here, honey—take the aspirin. How high of a fever do you have?"

"A hundred and one degrees."

"That's high. Hopefully, this will bring it down. Do you need for me to call anyone and let them know that you can't make it today?"

"Thank you, Marian. My agenda is in the living room on the coffee table. Thank you for helping me."

"I'm going to take the book up to Cooper's to make the phone calls. I've got something on the stove, and I'll be back in a little while."

When she woke up, it was after noon, and Marian was knocking on her cottage door. She had a tray of food for her and she put it down on the table beside the bed.

"This is chicken soup that I made for you—the best food to eat when you feel low." There was a glass of iced tea on the tray and Marian put pillows behind Mills's back before placing the tray in her lap.

"Do you need anything else?"

"No, ma'am. Thank you for this."

"Oh, honey, I'm glad to do it," Marian said, as she left the cottage.

In the early afternoon, Dr. Will came to the cottage and knocked while calling her name. Mills told her to come in and Williston approached her bedside. "Cooper called me this morning and asked me to look in on you. He said that you were running a fever."

She took Mills's temperature, which was still a hundred degrees. "What are your symptoms?"

"My head and my back ache, and I have a runny nose."

"Sounds like a case of the flu. I've seen several cases in my office in the last several days, but hopefully, yours will be a mild case. I'm going to have Marian bring you some aspirin and I'd like for you to stay in bed and rest. I'll check on you tomorrow, and I'm sorry that you're sick. You did a beautiful job on the oyster roast. I know that Cooper was proud of you. He told me so."

That afternoon, a rainstorm moved in and, except for occasional thunder, the sound of the rain on the metal roof lulled her to sleep. Late in the afternoon, Marian returned with her dinner. Wearing galoshes and a raincoat, she put the food on the night table and turned on the television in the bedroom. "I'm getting ready to go home for the evening. Is there anything I can get for you before I go?"

"No, ma'am. Tomorrow, will you please call my appointments and let them know I'm sick?"

"Yes, I'll be glad to. Good night. I hope you feel better."

On the local evening news, Mills was surprised to see that the lead story addressed the negotiations of Heath Brothers in New York. Both Cooper and his uncle were featured in the segment, which stated that there was hope that an agreement between the parties was imminent.

She fell asleep after the news but was awakened by the ringing telephone. Still half-asleep when she answered it, Mills found the voice on the other end to be soothing and calm.

"This is Cooper. I wanted to see how you're feeling."

"Terrible—but I saw you and your uncle on the evening news. I hope that everything works out with the negotiations."

"I do too. Quite a few hours have been spent negotiating this agreement. Dear, I hope you feel better soon."

After a little more discussion, Cooper told her to sleep well and wished her a good night. Before she fell back asleep, she thought of him calling her "dear."

The next morning began like the day before. Her fever was still over one hundred degrees—a visit from Dr. Will confirmed that the flu was circulating through the community, as she had seen five additional cases on the previous day. Her advice was to stay in bed and continue to drink fluids.

When Marian brought in her lunch, Mills asked, "Did you see Cooper and his uncle on the local news last night?"

"No, I missed it. I'll watch tonight and see if they're on again. I'm so proud of him, and I'm glad to see him in better spirits. I've been worried about him. At Christmastime, he wouldn't allow me to decorate, not even a wreath on the front of the house. Last fall was such a difficult time for him. I couldn't begin to count the hours that Cooper, Charles, and Britton spent searching for Elise. Sometimes Jeff accompanied them, but mostly it was those three."

"What was Elise like?"

"She was beautiful. Miss Elise dressed impeccably, but with her own kind of flair. I'd say she had her own style, just like you. The last several years that she and Cooper were together, there was added pressure on their marriage. Cooper took good care of his mother, but taking care of a person with Alzheimer's can be very demanding."

"I can imagine it is very hard to see a parent slipping away like that," Mills said.

"It was a terrible thing to see the degeneration of a smart and vibrant person like Miss Julia. At times, she became violent. To tell you the truth, she became violent with Elise one day. Cooper was not at home and Elise was trying to feed her lunch. Miss Julia threw the plate into a window, breaking it and the plate. I think Elise tried to calm her, but her reasoning capabilities were gone, and she grabbed Elise by the hand, trying to break her fingers. I had to pull Miss Julia off of Elise. Thank God I was home."

"My goodness."

"After that, Cooper hired health care professionals to come to the house, but Elise seemed to have had all she could stand. She spent more and more time away from home, and Elise and Cooper seemed to grow apart. Eventually, Cooper had to place Miss Julia in a health care facility and it broke his heart. He never complained, but I know the situation took a toll on him too."

"I'm sorry for the family. How long was she in the facility before she passed away?"

"Miss Julia passed away from heart failure, but the last six months were very difficult. Most of the time, she didn't know Cooper, or she thought that he was Mr. Phillip, Cooper's father. I still miss the woman that Miss Julia had been. And Elise–she began to spend a lot of time with those two real estate women, Madge Sinclair and Cassandra White. The day that Julia attacked Elise, she left the house and didn't come back until late that evening. Cooper was so worried about her. She never really explained where she was, and I didn't think she was the same with Cooper after that day. One thing is for certain: Cooper had nothing to do with her disappearance. I know Cooper well enough to know that. Well, Miss Mills, I'd better get back to my work. Can I get you anything before I go?"

"No, ma'am. Thank you for bringing me the soup."

"Sleep well."

After finishing her lunch, Mills rested on her pillows, thinking of what Marian had told her. *How sad—not even a wreath on the front of the house at Christmastime.*

When Marian came back with her supper and turned on the evening news, the contract negotiations between Heath Brothers and Perret International was again one of the lead stories.

Marian spoke while watching the television: "Just let Cooper do the negotiating and they'll work something out. I wish his parents could see him. Miss Julia was grooming both of those boys to be the president of the United States. They both learned to play the piano. Cooper really excelled at that; I can't imagine how many thousands of hours he practiced. He had a full scholarship to the Juilliard School, but he wanted to be a pilot instead. Both of those boys mastered their dance lessons and became fluent in both French and Spanish. They had such a wonderful education, so well mannered, and just brilliant. It breaks my heart." She stopped and looked at Mills. "My goodness, it's getting late. Elizabeth is going to be looking for me in a few minutes. Can I get you anything else?"

"Marian, there was a mean-spirited rejection to the oyster roast invitation from Elise's father."

"Try not to pay that man any mind. He blames Cooper for Elise's disappearance and has made more than one threat."

CHAPTER 8

A Host of Golden Daffodils

By Friday afternoon, Mills felt much better. Her fever broke and she sat in her living area with the gas fire logs for warmth. There was a knock on the door. Thinking that Marian was bringing her dinner, Mills called for her to enter. Instead of Marian, Cooper stood in her doorway with a tray of food.

"I–I thought you were Marian."

"I told her she could go home, and I thought I would bring your food tray. May I come in?"

She smiled at him. "Please do."

He placed her tray on the coffee table in front of her. "I have good news. I went by the post office box for the foundation and we have received a number of donations to the scholarship fund; some of them are substantial. I credit this influx of donations to your efforts."

"Thank you. Did you reach an agreement with Perret International?"

"No. I'm flying to France next week. Hopefully, we'll work out the final details."

On Sunday afternoon, Mills accompanied Cooper to the Freedom School to help with the renovations. The building began to take on a freshened appearance with new windows and hurricane shutters, which were painted a shade of bluish-green. Inside the building, workers were painting the walls. *I can't stay in here; the smell of the paint is making me feel light-headed.*

Mills walked outside and noticed that Mr. Camp sat in his usual place beside a fire, and she joined him. "May I sit with you?"

"Miss Mills, absolutely."

She pulled up a chair and began to warm her hands over the fire. "Mr. Camp, have you always lived in the Edisto area?"

"Yes, my entire life—the property that Cooper bought a few years ago with the old house ruins was called The Orchards because of the abundance of fruit trees that were grown on the land. That same property is where some of my ancestors lived and worked.

"The Orchards? I didn't realize it had a name."

"Yes ma'am—though the fruit trees died out years ago. Before that, I can track my ancestors to an area along the Cooper River. My grandmother was sold from a plantation to the owner of The Orchards—that owner was an ancestor of Cooper's and Jeffrey's."

Mills nodded, waiting for him to continue.

"Like a lot of southerners, those folks fell on real hard times after the Civil War, and their land was sold out of their family. The new owner of The Orchards allowed former slaves to live there after the war. Some left and moved north, but a fair number remained. I was told I was born in one of the slave cabins; it had a white rosebush on the front of the house. The last time I was down there, that bush was still alive; in fact, it was thriving."

"Yes, I know the rosebush. It's still magnificent."

"Cooper told me I could come back and visit any time I wanted, but I'm just getting so old. Marian and Charles are related to me. They are descended from my first cousin. My uncle, George Camp, and Cooper's ancestor, Grey Camp, were true friends and under the circumstances, I'd say their friendship was extraordinary."

"Mr. Camp, I'm confused. I saw a hand-carved walking cane beside the fireplace in Cooper's living room. I thought Cooper said that his relative George Camp had carved the cane."

"I'd prefer that Cooper explains that ancient history to you."

Cooper joined them at the fire, and Mr. Camp said, "I was just telling Mills about some of our local history. Did your parents ever tell you that during World War II, we had to adhere to a strict blackout policy? At night, we had to turn off the lights so the Germans couldn't locate targets. Work was in full swing at the Charleston Naval Yard—that was the thing that brought Charleston out of the cycle of poverty that it had been in since the Civil War. Who would have thought that it would take another war to help the citizens of this state recover from one that took place eighty years before? You know, I think I may have seen a German submarine down at the mouth of the Edisto while a group of us were fishing. I guess we weren't worth bothering with, because they didn't blow us out of the water."

"Cooper, you never told me about how your father was awarded the Victoria Cross and the other medals on display at the Heath Brothers office."

"My father and uncle served in the Royal Navy during World War II. The Heath family had been in the shipping business for many years prior to the war, and my father and uncle were often dispatched to the United States to supervise the transportation of war materials to Great Britain. On one occasion, a convoy of Allied cargo ships was en route to Plymouth, England, and the lead ship was torpedoed by a German submarine. An American destroyer accompanied the convoy, and while it released depth charges, sailors from the other transports saved as many men as possible from the sinking ship. My father told me he couldn't remember how many times he went into the water to rescue men. What made matters worse—as soon as blood went into the water, the sharks showed up."

"Oh, no," Mills gasped.

"The convoy was not far from Bermuda, and they were able to make it into port without a further encounter with the Germans. There was great loss of life from the torpedoed transport, but many men survived, because of the heroism of men like my father. That's why he was awarded the Victoria Cross."

"He was very brave."

"Indeed he was."

That afternoon, on the drive home, Mills inquired, "When I was talking with Mr. Camp beside the fire, he told me that George Camp was his uncle. I thought you said that the man who carved the cane was related to you. He told me to ask you about him and then changed the subject to World War II."

"Mr. Camp and I share a common ancestor, Amos Camp. I'm afraid that miscegenation was not uncommon during the years of slavery. The slave owner had power over his slaves to do with as he pleased."

"That's awful."

"Yes, I agree."

Early Monday morning, Cooper departed for Paris to meet with Perret International executives and hopefully complete the details of the shipping agreement. Having missed the previous work week due to her illness, Mills attempted to reschedule as many business meetings as possible. For the first time, she received a blatant rejection from the President of Crimson Label Clothing Company; she was told that a donation would not be made to a cause where the head of the foundation was a suspect in the disappearance of his wife. Mills was quick to defend Cooper, but the woman responded, "You've just started to work for him—you can't be sure of anything. Can you?"

As disappointed as she was by the ugliness of the woman's accusation, Mills remembered what Cooper had told her the first night that she was in town: ". . . it is possible that you could meet with some resistance because of my personal situation. Please don't trouble yourself if that happens."

An invitation to Susan Caldwell's April wedding arrived in the mail, which lifted her spirits. On Tuesday afternoon, there was a message on her telephone answering machine from Price's Chevrolet to get in touch with the owner, Steven Price, at her convenience. When Mills returned the phone call, Mr. Price asked her to stop by his dealership to pick up a donation for the Heath Foundation. He confessed that he had not paid close enough attention to who Mills worked for when she made a professional call at his business for the foundation. "Miss Taylor, my wife has reminded me that Mr. Heath has, on numerous occasions, donated his flying skills to help with a charity that I am involved with called 'Mercy Flights.' We help the injured and sick get to hospitals across the United States for the treatment they need. My wife said that we had met Mr. Heath on several occasions and wanted me to explain how I could forget that . . . she said that meeting your employer was something she would never forget."

When Mills picked up the gift from the Prices, she was excited to see a donation of $5,000. Included in the envelope was a note from Mrs. Price stating, "I don't think this donation can begin to make up for the time that Mr. Heath has spent helping 'Mercy Flights,' but please let him know that we are grateful for his help. Elaine Price."

The Charleston area was exceedingly warm that week of February, and Mills took advantage of the pleasant temperature to take long walks around Cooper's property. On the first afternoon walk, she found herself returning to the ruin of the old mansion and the grounds that surrounded it. Long before she reached the meadow near the slave cabins, the rich fragrance of daffodils filled the afternoon breeze. And then she saw them—a sea of daffodils.

Just as Cooper and Anne had assured her, the meadow was filled with an abundance of daffodils; so many in fact, that she could not begin to count them all. The scene reminded her of a poem, "Daffodils," that her mother used to read to her:

> I wander'd lonely as a cloud
> That floats on high o'er vales and hills,
> When all at once I saw a crowd,
> A host of golden daffodils;
> Beside the lake, beneath the trees,
> Fluttering and dancing in the breeze . . .

Captivated by the scene, she thought of her desire to paint again; for the next several afternoons, she sought the beauty of the meadow to create an everlasting memory through her art.

In the Friday edition of the *Charleston Dispatch*, file photos of Cooper and his uncle appeared with a business article that Heath Brothers was very close to working out a shipping agreement with Perret International. Henri Duchard was quoted as saying, "Due to Cooper Heath's in-depth knowledge of the shipping industry, international maritime law, and French language and culture, the negotiations have been professional and productive."

The article further stated that Cooper was one of the youngest people to ever be nominated to the State Ports Authority Board, but the nomination had been indefinitely suspended until the disappearance of Elise Heath, wife of Cooper Heath, was solved. The article was written by Charleston journalist, Lee Mencken, with Pierre Beauville of the French publication *Le Monde* contributing.

On Sunday morning, when Mills rose for church, there was a note on her door: "I got in late last night and I'd like for you to join me for breakfast. The kitchen door will be open. Cooper."

Instead of dressing in her Sunday best, Mills showered and slipped on her blue jeans to join Cooper. She quickly knocked on the kitchen door, and he turned, motioning for her to come into the house. "I'm glad that you could join me. We're having shrimp and grits for breakfast. How about some hot tea?"

"Love some. Did you reach an agreement with Perret International?"

"Yes, we did. Due to the increase in shipping, over the next several months, we'll begin hiring people for jobs. My uncle was very pleased."

"I have some good news too." She handed him the check from the Prices, and he smiled as he looked at it. "Well done, Mills."

"I don't think this donation had anything to do with me. Elaine Price arranged for this donation. She said that you had contributed your flying skills to their organization called Mercy Flights."

"Yes, I help them when I can."

"She said that she'd never forget you."

Mills sipped her tea and added, "There was an article about you and the negotiations in Friday's paper. The author said that you were one of the youngest people ever nominated to the State Ports Authority Board."

"Yes, but the nomination was suspended."

"What does the board do?"

"It's a private organization that facilitates growth and development of the Charleston shipping trade. I would have been honored to have been on the board, but I suppose it's not meant to be, at least, not yet."

"I think you've been unfairly treated."

"I appreciate your faith in me."

"I do believe in you, Cooper—you're my friend. Just don't get discouraged." Hearing her words, he smiled and then served the shrimp and grits.

"This is delicious."

"I'm glad that you like it."

The afternoon was spent with the continued renovation efforts of the Freedom School and the volunteers came close to completing their work. The schoolhouse had been afforded a new life and it displayed a youthful charm that had probably not existed even when the structure was new.

That evening, as they said good night, Cooper walked Mills to the row of camellias in front of her cottage before saying, "Tomorrow morning, Murphy is coming by with some legal documents that need to be witnessed. He has an appointment in Beaufort, and he said that he would be here around eight. I hope that you will be able to witness the documents for me."

"I'll be glad to help."

"Thank you. I'll have breakfast ready for you."

CHAPTER 9

Lee Roy

The next morning, the aroma of fresh bread and coffee enriched the air when Mills entered Cooper's house. "Biscuits are coming out of the oven—help yourself to some coffee. You know where the cups are kept."

She poured her coffee, and the rich chocolaty flavor of the beverage lingered on her palate. Glancing at the front page of the morning newspaper, she saw another article about the trade agreement, with a photo of Cooper shaking the hand of Henri Duchard of Perret International.

The headline stated, "Heath Brothers to Bring Jobs to Charleston," and the article gave credit to Cooper and Henri for successfully negotiating the agreement, which would be a lucrative contract for both parties.

"Cooper, this is wonderful. The article is written by the same journalist I met at the *Charleston Dispatch* office about a month ago—Lee Mencken."

"Yes—Lee's been very attentive to the disappearance of my wife, and I tease him, at times, by calling him H.L."

"H.L. Mencken?"

"He seems to like that nickname—he's a very tenacious young man."

A knock at the front door interrupted their conversation. Cooper left the kitchen, but returned with Murphy. He poured coffee for himself and said, "Mills, it's nice to see you again."

"You, as well."

For a few minutes, they talked in the kitchen while eating biscuits, until Murphy asked, "Cooper, are you ready to sign these papers?"

"Yes, Mills is going to witness the documents."

"I'd like to talk over something with you first. It will only take a few minutes."

Mills remained in the kitchen while they went into the study. As she poured herself another cup of coffee, Marian and Charles entered the house through the kitchen door.

"Good morning. What brings you to the house so early?"

"Cooper asked me to witness some legal documents; he's in his study with Murphy."

Charles poured himself a cup of coffee and said to the two women, "Time to get to work," and he exited out the kitchen door.

Marian became committed to a task, and Mills slowly walked into the foyer, studying the intricate moldings that bordered the ceiling. Classical figures graced the center of the ceiling, and Mills wondered how someone could design plasterwork with such perfect mastery.

Inside the study, the volume of Murphy's voice raised as he told Cooper, "I think you should start investing with Jeff and me."

"You know I don't purchase property with partners."

"You're one of my most independently wealthy clients, and I think you could gain substantially from investing with us."

"To what type of investments are you referring?"

"Mostly short term. We're purchasing properties and then reselling them at a profit to investors, sometimes substantial profits."

"Does this involve heirs' property?" Cooper asked in a concerned voice.

"No, it doesn't."

"Then, you're just flipping properties."

"I guess that's one term for it."

"You buy the property from owners who don't realize the value of their land, or else they're desperate to sell it."

"Don't you think that it's the responsibility of owners to know the value of their property?"

"I hope these investments don't involve the elderly."

Murphy paused for a moment. "Just think about it—Jeff and I are currently working on a transaction that we'll make a large profit on. With you involved, we could purchase the entire tract."

"Don't tell me any more. I don't want to know what you're doing and, as I told you, I won't buy property with a partner—what was the term that you used to describe Piet van der Wolf?"

Murphy did not respond, but Cooper continued, "I remember—you called him a vulture. How is what you're doing any different than what he's done throughout his business career?"

"I think you're too hard on me."

"I don't think so."

There was silence in the room for a moment. Then, Murphy said, "I have an update on the property you're purchasing on the Ashley River. I heard from one of the sellers' attorneys last week. After your family sold the land to Manson Cusworth, he left the property to his son, James, who agreed to your offer. Unfortunately, he died intestate before your contract could be closed. There are several heirs, all nephews, in dispute over the division of assets, and I think they'd rather fight each other than reach an agreement. This attorney told me that he is no closer to reaching a settlement among the heirs than he was months ago, but he said the parties would sign another contract extension with you."

"Why don't we close on the tract, and their proceeds could be held in escrow until they reach an agreement?"

"I suggested that, but one of the heirs won't agree to it. He wants the division of assets settled beforehand."

"Did you bring the extension agreement with you?"

"Yes, I have it with these other documents."

"Why don't you get out all the documents that I need to sign? Mills may have an appointment."

Mills heard Murphy open his briefcase and the sound of pages turning on the desk.

"Mills, could you come in, please?" Cooper called.

When she entered the study, Cooper rose from his seat and helped her with a chair near the side of the desk. He began to sign the papers and when he finished, Murphy asked her to sign her name as the witness. When she completed signing the last document, they heard the sound of a vehicle pull up in front of Cooper's home.

The car horn blew loudly and a man yelled out, "Cooper Heath, I want to talk to you!"

Cooper rose from his chair and went to the front window, adjusting the shutters so that he could see outside. The man yelled even more loudly, "Cooper Heath, I want to talk to you!" Mills couldn't place his accent—but it wasn't local.

"It sounds like I'm being called out."

"You're not going out there? Call the police!" Murphy exclaimed.

"It will take forty-five minutes for the police to get here—you know I'm careful."

Cooper sat back down at his desk and opened the top drawer, removing a large black handgun. Sliding the chamber back, he placed the gun in the waistband of his pants behind his back. Mills gasped softly.

"Mills, I want you to stay inside."

"Cooper, dueling is illegal, even in South Carolina!"

"Come on Murphy—I'm not planning to shoot anyone."

Cooper walked out onto the front porch of his home, leaving the front door open. "I'm Cooper Heath. What do you want?"

Peering out the window of the study, Mills could see the man had stubble on his face and was wearing a tank shirt with another shirt on top of it. His face was contorted with anger, and he appeared to be dressed for a construction job.

"Come down here; I want to talk to you."

"Go ahead and say what you've got to say. From there."

"I'm Lee Roy Mullinax, you blue-blooded son-of-a-bitch. What are you doing interfering with my woman?"

"I don't know who you're referring to."

"My woman—Eula, Eula Mullinax!"

Cooper paused for a moment and then said, "I am helping her, along with others in our community, so that she can go to school and work."

"That's not all you done. You know what I mean—and you know how I know it? I beat it out of her. What are you doing interfering with my woman, when you don't even know where your own woman is—or maybe you do? And what in the hell are you doing arranging for niggers to come inside my house?"

Mills's breath hitched as she listened to the man. Murphy left the study and within a few moments, returned with a shotgun—Marian was right behind him. She briefly studied the situation and then hurried to the back of the house. Murphy stood behind the front door and without thinking, Mills walked into the foyer.

The man narrowed his eyes at her from the base of the front steps and started to put his foot on the stairs. "Well, now, who's this? She is mighty pretty. Is this your new woman?"

Cooper glanced over his shoulder at Mills and gave her a warning look. "That's far enough, Mullinax."

"What are you going to do—shoot me?"

"Are you sure you want to find out?"

Charles walked up behind Mills in the foyer and said, "Excuse me, Miss Mills, but I need to come around you." He continued out onto the porch and stood beside Cooper.

"You know, I believe you would shoot me," Lee Roy said, withdrawing his foot from the bottom step. "But—let me tell you something. I ain't afraid of you, or your big driver—and you stay the hell away from my woman. You and that goddamn woman doctor—you two mind your own business!"

He shook his finger at Cooper and then climbed back into an old Chevrolet, flooring the gas pedal and scattering dust as he left.

Cooper looked at Charles. "Thank you for joining me on the porch."

"You're welcome—I didn't care for his behavior."

"I'm going to call Williston to make sure she's all right."

When Cooper entered the house, he looked directly at Mills and said, "I wish that Lee Roy hadn't seen you. He's trouble."

"I'm sorry—I just stepped to the door without thinking."

Looking into her eyes for a moment, he responded, "It's okay."

Cooper turned around and addressed Murphy, who still stood behind the door. "Murphy, you're very frightening, hiding behind the door with an unloaded shotgun."

"How did you know that I didn't load it?"

"You left the chamber open."

"Uh oh. I didn't have time to load it." He took three shells out of his coat pocket and placed them on the table in the foyer.

"How about closing the chamber for me? You'll wear out the spring if you leave it open."

Murphy and Mills followed him into the study, and Cooper phoned Williston, allowing it to ring for some time. When she did not answer, Cooper said, "I'm going to ride over to Williston's and make sure she's all right."

"Why are you wasting your time on people of that caliber?"

"What am I supposed to do, Murphy? Tell Eula that I couldn't help her—go see her church outreach ministry? She asked for help, and I gave it to her."

"Yes, but this particular experiment with poverty has a big problem named Lee Roy."

"I didn't think of my assistance to Eula as an experiment—she's a human being with hopes and dreams, just like you and me. Lee Roy is the problem that holds Eula back from the success that I think she can be—she just needs a chance to prove herself."

"Lee Roy is the kind of guy who will show up at your property at three in the morning with a gas can and burn your house down—with you in it."

Mills shuddered.

"Murphy, guys like you and Jeff—you well-educated charlatans—worry me as much as Lee Roy. Thank you for coming by with the legal documents. I'll see you later. Mills, thank you for your help."

Cooper left the room with the gun still in his hand. He stepped back onto the porch to speak with Charles. Mills ran out the door and stopped him as he descended the staircase.

"I'd like to go with you. Lee Roy said that he beat Eula—her children might also need aid. Please let me help."

"I think it's a bad idea. There's no way to know what we're going to find."

"Please."

He stopped abruptly and said, "All right, Mills, but if I tell you to go sit in the Suburban, please listen to me."

When they reached Williston's clinic, she was sitting at her front desk and Cooper told her, "I just had a visit from Lee Roy Mullinax, and I was worried, because I couldn't get you on the phone."

"Mr. Mullinax has just left here after spewing filth. I've called the police, and they're going to meet me at Eula's. Would you like to drive me?"

"Yes, let's go."

Williston directed Cooper to where Eula lived with her children. There was a group of mobile homes that barely looked habitable. Dr. Will directed him to park in front of one of them. When there was no answer at the door, Williston called out, "It's Dr. Will. Please open the door for me."

Within a few seconds, the door slowly opened. The oldest of Eula's children stood before them.

"Billy, where's your mother?"

"She's on the bed. She's not feeling too good this morning."

"Show me where she is."

The boy led them through the musty, dark trailer to one of the bedrooms where Eula sat on the edge of the bed. Her clothes had been ripped down the front and her right eye was swollen shut.

When she saw Dr. Will, she began to cry while attempting to speak. "Lee Roy got mad at me, and he's taken off again."

"Eula, Lee Roy has hurt you many times. Don't you think that you should put a stop to this kind of treatment? You don't deserve it—I'd like to call an ambulance for you."

"No, ma'am, I don't want to go to no hospital."

Dr. Will pushed her hair back and started to examine her bruises. "Eula, I called the police, and they should be here any time now."

"Oh, no. I don't want the police to come here. Lee Roy won't like it."

"You need to stop worrying about what Lee Roy wants and think about your welfare and your children. Reverend Smalls has told me that you're doing well with your classes and your work. We can help you get a lawyer, and a judge will issue a restraining order."

"All due respect to you, Dr. Will, but ain't no restrainin' order gonna stop Lee Roy if he wants to get near me."

"Don't you have somewhere you can go live, perhaps with relatives?"

"My sister lives in Tennessee, and she really ain't got room for us. Lee Roy's parents? They're lint heads—that's where Lee Roy learned about beatings. His pa would come home from the mill and drink, and then beat Lee Roy and his mother. I can't go live with them. My own folks are dead. We ended up here near Charleston when the mill closed in our town. Lee Roy works construction jobs and we been livin' hand to mouth—he's all right until he starts drinking."

Cooper spoke up, "Eula, I'm sure that we can help you leave here if you'd like. I can help you financially, and you can pay me back when you get the job that you're training for."

"Mr. Heath, you've already been generous with me. I can't take any more of your money. I didn't want to tell him how I use your financial help, but he choked me and hit me with his fists—I'm so sorry. I hope I haven't caused you trouble."

"Eula, he choked you?"

"Yes."

"That worries me a great deal. Why don't you let us take you to a women's shelter? You can get help in Charleston. Please file a police report and have Lee Roy arrested."

Eula's baby daughter started to cry from the next room and Mills went to check on her. Wearing a soiled diaper that sagged on her slight frame, she continued to cry after Mills picked her up. *What do I do now?* She was thankful when Cooper joined her in the bedroom. His eyes scanned the room, and he retrieved a box of diapers from a corner of the room. "Lay her on the bed, and we'll change her."

When the little girl wore a fresh diaper, Cooper handed her back to Mills, but once again, she began to cry. Someone knocked at the front of the mobile home, and Williston passed by to answer the door.

"Cooper, what am I doing wrong with her?"

"Nothing, she's probably just hungry. I'll hold her and you see if you can find some food in the kitchen."

As soon as Mills handed him the little girl, she stopped crying and began to touch Cooper's face. In a soothing voice he said, "Now, now, you're all right. You're all right." He lightly bounced her in his arms and joined Mills in the kitchen.

A sheriff's deputy entered the home and joined Williston as she directed him to where Eula rested. Mills found packages of macaroni and cheese in the kitchen and began to prepare food for the children. She watched as Cooper talked to Eula's children in a calm voice, while the youngest child ran her fingers through his hair. After Mills placed bowls of macaroni and cheese on the table with glasses of milk, she went into their bedrooms to look for clean clothes. She heard Billy tell Cooper, "We hate to see him comin' through the door, 'cause we know what's gonna happen."

When the sheriff's deputy finished talking with Eula, Cooper drove the group to Dr. Will's clinic and checked the premises before he and Mills continued home.

"Williston is going to take them to a women's shelter this afternoon. I'm afraid that Eula feels trapped."

"What was the secret that Eula was keeping from Lee Roy that would have caused him to beat her?"

He looked at her before responding, "I have every confidence in you. Reverend Smalls arranged for women in his congregation to stay with Eula's children, so that she could work and go to night school. I helped with a financial commitment to pay the sitters, her tuition, books—the church helped with food and clothes. The women who assisted with her children are all black women who attend his church. The one thing that Eula was the most upset about . . ." he paused, gathering his thoughts to explain. "Do you remember the day we gave blood, and she was in Williston's clinic and in tears?"

Mills nodded. Cooper continued, "Eula had just found out that she was pregnant again, and she was upset by the thought of having another child that she could not afford, or was physically unable to carry. Williston said that she shouldn't have had the last child. Lee Roy had forced sex with her."

"He raped her?"

"Yes, she has said that. She took some of my financial assistance and terminated her pregnancy. I certainly would not judge her because of her decision. Lee Roy beat her because of her choice—she needs to get away from him."

"Cooper, that's terrible."

"I agree."

The next morning, on her way to appointments, Mills noticed Charles and Cooper near the old barn at the entrance to his property. Written on the side of the barn that faced the road was the word, "Merderer," spray-painted in red. Cooper and Charles surveyed the situation, and Mills parked her Volkswagen, entering the pasture through an open gate.

She joined Cooper and he said, "It looks like Lee Roy paid me a visit last night—he spelled most of it right."

"I'm worried about this man."

"He does get your attention, doesn't he?"

Charles began to paint over the graffiti with an off-white color, and Cooper added, "I'm afraid he paid Williston a visit as well. She has 'Baby Killer,' painted on the side of her clinic. As soon as we get this painted over, we're going to see her." He paused for a moment and then looked intently into her eyes. "I'm sorry that you've been subjected to these events. I hope you'll bear with me."

"You have my support," she responded and patted him on the back. That was the way he expressed friendliness toward her, so she thought it would be all right.

When she arrived in Alston Station, Reverend Smalls and several local residents were already painting over the words scrawled on the side of the clinic; written in red were the words, "Baby Kiler."

Mills parked her car and asked Williston if she could help, but she responded, "I think the folks who are here will take care of this, but thank you for asking. I was able to convince Eula to go to the women's shelter. She's been encouraged to relocate and I told the staff that she has financial assistance available to her. Let's hope for the best. I'll talk to you later, there's a patient waiting for me inside the clinic."

Her first stop of the day was at the Low Country Gourmet and, as Mills entered the business, she saw Melea Butler at the front counter. "Greetings, Miss Mills," she called out as soon as she noticed her. "I have written down the names and contact information for several people who asked about your educational foundation." She handed Mills the list, and continued, "I hope that everyone on the list will become a donor."

"Thank you. Where is Paul today?"

"He is with a friend who, I fear, is very ill. I think you can reach him at home."

While they talked, several customers entered the store and Mrs. Butler excused herself to serve them.

The day turned out to be a warm one, and that afternoon, as she returned to Edisto, Mills let down the roof on her Volkswagen and tied her hair back, allowing the wind and sun to come in around her. As she passed the side of Cooper's house, he came out through the screen door, dressed in a black tux. He walked toward his Suburban.

Stopping her Beetle, she said, "Wow, where are you going?"

"I'm attending a function for the Society of St. John's Parish. My ancestors were members that date back to the early 1700s. Jeff and I make a date of it," he said with a smile. "Oh, I almost forgot—Dr. Warren made appointments for us to speak at several schools on Thursday. How about meeting me in my kitchen at seven-thirty, and we'll go together?"

"Sounds good—have a wonderful time tonight."

He smiled and waved goodbye as she continued to her cottage.

That evening, Joshua White phoned Mills from Washington, DC, where he was engaged in taking depositions for an upcoming court case. "I'm going to be up here for several weeks, but I know I'll be in Charleston this weekend—how about dinner on Saturday evening?"

"Where would you like for me to meet you?"

"Come to my office at six, and I'll show you our rooftop."

"What's up there?"

"Let it be a surprise—listen, I have to go. See you on Saturday."

CHAPTER 10

Lantern Lights

On Thursday, Mills and Cooper visited four middle schools and two high schools in the area. Cooper addressed each assembly and told the students how important it was to finish high school and earn a higher education degree. He explained the terms of the Heath Scholarship award, and Mills spoke to the students about why she had wanted to become the director of the Heath Foundation. She discussed how fortunate she was to attend college on an academic scholarship and how she wanted to help other people succeed. Dr. Warren and Mills handed out brochures to the young people who were interested and planned to follow up with each child and his or her parents. *Cooper's speeches are so inspiring.*

While at some of the schools, Mills discovered the buildings were of varying advanced ages. Some of the buildings had water stains on the ceilings and were in need of renovations.

After the last assembly, Mills said to Dr. Warren, "I noticed that some of the schools we visited are in need of repair."

"This is rural South Carolina. Some school districts are more financially capable than others. The buildings in this area aren't as bad as some I've seen."

"But why isn't something done about it?"

"In order to conquer problems with public education, there has to be enough concern in the state's leadership." Dr. Warren paused before continuing, "It takes generations to overcome the effects of poverty—I'm afraid the water is still wide."

After they parted ways with Dr. Warren, Cooper invited Mills to join him for a late lunch. "I know a wonderful Mexican restaurant near Walterboro."

She accepted his invitation and they drove to the restaurant on the outskirts of town. The building was constructed of concrete block and had brown leather booths and tables in the middle. Fans slowly rotated from the ceiling, and a waiter seated them in a rear booth. "Mr. Heath, I'm so glad to see you again. It's been months since you've been in. What can I get you to drink? Margaritas?"

"No, thank you, just iced tea for me."

"I'll have the same," Cooper added.

While the waiter went to get their drinks, Cooper told her, "I think you'll really enjoy their food. The chef is from Cuba and the owner is from Mexico." Cooper was right. The dishes were spicy and delicious. She could have spent the rest of the day with him, but after they finished dining, he took her back to Edisto. Before she got out of the car, he told her, "Thank you for your help today. I think there were a number of students who were very interested in our scholarship program."

"You mean, your program."

"No, Mills, I mean it is our scholarship program." She felt a blush spread over her face.

Friday afternoon, while Mills read on her screened porch, Cooper came by to see her. He was nicely dressed in dark khakis and a white linen shirt. "I wanted to see you before I left. Are you going to the Freedom School with me on Sunday?"

"Yes, where are you off to?"

"My aunts and uncles want to take me out this weekend."

"Are you celebrating a special occasion?"

"Yes, Saturday is my birthday, and they wanted to take turns treating me to dinner."

"I wish I'd known. How old will you be?"

"I'll be thirty-five."

She rose from her chair and kissed him on the cheek. "Happy birthday. I hope you have a wonderful weekend."

He looked down into her eyes. His face was so handsome and he had such a calm look in his sapphire-blue eyes. "Thank you, Mills, and I hope you have a nice weekend as well."

Cooper continued to stand near her, and then, it was as though he felt that he had lingered too long. "I'd better go. See you on Sunday."

He left her cottage and walked to the end of the row of camellias before he turned and waved. She felt terrible that she had not known that Saturday was his birthday. She wondered what she should give him. She went into her cottage and began to think of a gift she could purchase in Charleston before she joined Joshua White for dinner the next evening. As she stood in her living area, her eyes focused on her recently completed painting of the field of daffodils near the old slave row. She was very proud of her artwork and she immediately realized that she'd like Cooper to have her painting. That evening, she signed the back of the canvas and entitled the painting, *A Host of Golden Daffodils*, as a tribute to the Wordsworth poem she had enjoyed so much as a child. She also wrote the inscription, "For my dear friend, Cooper, on the occasion of his thirty-fifth birthday."

Mills knocked on the glass doors of Joshua White's office at six on Saturday evening. He was promptly at the door with a set of keys to let her inside the building. As soon as she entered, he put his arm around her and gave her a quick kiss on the lips. "I'm glad you could join me this evening. Now, here's my treat—I'm about to show you one of the best views of Charleston's harbor." They took the lift to the rooftop, which had a beautifully designed sitting area. As a large container ship entered the harbor, Joshua commented, "That's one of your employer's ships—see on the side, 'Heath Brothers.' They have quite a fleet."

"Yes, I see the words now. That ship is enormous."

"I've seen larger ones come into port. Has Cooper given you a tour of one of their ships?"

"Not yet."

"What would you like to drink?"

"White wine would be fine. Thank you."

He returned with a glass of chardonnay for her, while he sipped a martini. They talked for over an hour, admiring the harbor at twilight, then Joshua looked at his watch and said, "Our dinner reservation is at eight at Carolina's—we should probably get going."

When they reached the restaurant, their table wasn't quite ready and they took a seat in the bar. Within a few minutes, Mills noticed a party of four following the maître d' to a table in the back of the restaurant. The group consisted of Cooper, his aunt and uncle, and Jeff.

"Well, speak of the devil," Joshua said.

"It's Cooper's birthday."

As soon as he noticed Mills, Cooper stopped to say hello, and he reintroduced his aunt and uncle. Jeff smiled and winked at her. "Joshua, it's nice to see you again," Cooper told him.

"Mills has told me that you're celebrating your birthday—so, happy birthday."

"Thank you, and I hope you and Mills have a nice evening."

Cooper smiled again and then continued with his party to their table. After a few more minutes, Mills and Joshua were seated in a location in the dining area that gave them a view of the table where Cooper sat.

Joshua helped Mills with her chair and then sat in a seat that placed his back to Cooper's family. "I'm going to sit in this direction, so that I don't have to look at Jeff Radcliffe all evening," he said with a wry smile.

Twice, Mills glanced in Cooper's direction and found him looking at her. He would smile and then return to the conversation at his own table.

After dinner, Mills and Joshua walked around the downtown. Nighttime in the city was almost as beautiful as in the daytime because of the thoughtfully placed lighting on the homes. They found themselves in front of a house on Church Street with a plaque inscribed with the details of its haunting by the ghost of a long-dead physician. "Did you know that there are a number of haunted houses downtown?"

"Yes, I have heard this. I've also been told that the old plantation ruin on Cooper's property is haunted."

"Generations ago, that property was in Cooper's family. He might know who's rumored to have not rested in peace—I'm only kidding you." He pulled her close to him and gave her a lengthy kiss on the mouth. *Whoa—I'm not ready for this.* "I have to catch a flight tomorrow morning back to Washington, and I'm probably going to be up there for the next several weeks. I'd like for you to spend the night with me at my townhouse. It's a long drive to Edisto."

"Joshua, I'm not ready for a commitment."

"Baby, I'm not asking you for a commitment. I do care about you, and I think we could give each other pleasure."

"No, we barely know each other—please walk me back to my car."

"I'm disappointed that you won't stay with me tonight, but come on—we're just a few blocks away from my office."

He walked her back to her car and then gave her another passionate kiss on the mouth.

"Want to change your mind?"

"Joshua—no."

"All right, honey. Good night and drive safely."

He closed the car door and stood in the parking lot until she drove away. He was very nice to her, but she was not in love with him and she didn't want to be involved in a relationship that was based on sex.

As she neared Alston Station, several wild animals crossed the road in front of her, their eyes glowing red in the headlights. Just before she reached Cooper's driveway, she noticed lights, white and not very bright, deep in the woods near the direction of the old mansion ruin. For a moment, the lights appeared to move about, but as she pulled the car to the side of the road for a closer look, there was nothing, only darkness. *What was that?* She waited and watched, but there was only the blackness of night. As she drove down the sandy lane to Cooper's house, she caught sight of the light on her porch, welcoming her home.

When she woke the next morning, Mills made coffee and then put on her jeans and barn coat for an early morning walk to the river. There was a mist in the air. As she got closer to the water, the fog became so dense that she could only see a few feet in front of her. The air grew cold as she neared the river, and she pulled her coat tightly around her. A light shone inside the boathouse. She walked to a window and peered inside. Someone sat at the table in the center of the room. She wiped moisture from the glass. *My God, it's Cooper. What's he doing out here?* He stared out of the front window toward the river, and she thought that he spoke, but it was inaudible, except for the words, "in her sepulcher there by the sea."

When he stopped talking, he stared at an old lantern on the table in front of him. Concerned for his welfare, Mills knocked on the door of the boathouse. At first, he did not acknowledge her, but as she knocked louder, he looked in her direction and told her to enter. He appeared to be exhausted and he did not smile. His white shirt was open to his chest and his shirttail hung outside of his slacks.

"Hello, Mills, what brings you out so early?"

"I wanted to get some fresh air before I got dressed for church. Cooper, is there something wrong?"

"I had a bad dream and I'm afraid I couldn't sleep after it."

"Why are you down here?"

"I like listening to the sound of the river."

She touched his hand and found that he was very cold. "Can I help you?"

He didn't say anything for a moment, and then, as if he had been somewhere far away, he turned and faced her. "I'm sorry, dear. What did you say?"

"Cooper, why don't you come with me to my cottage? I have hot coffee and I think you need to get out of the cold."

He slowly seemed to realize what she had said. He rose from the table and accompanied her back to her home. She fixed him a large mug of coffee and he wearily sat in one of her armchairs, his face drained of emotion. As Mills turned on the fire logs, she inquired, "Is there anything you'd like to talk about?"

He stared into the fire, before responding, "No, but thank you for helping me."

"I thought I heard you talking when I came to the boathouse."

"I don't remember."

He seemed as if he was in shock as he sat in silence in her living area. Worried about his state of mind, she attempted to comfort him by gaining his attention.

"Cooper, how was your birthday celebration?"

"What? Oh, it was very nice."

"I thought you planned to stay in Charleston until today."

"I wanted to come home."

Mills observed him in silence for a few moments and then went to retrieve her painting, *A Host of Golden Daffodils*, which was in her bedroom. She placed the neatly wrapped present in his lap. "This is my gift to you—happy belated birthday!"

Her kind gesture seemed to take his mind off of what troubled him, and he looked up into her eyes. "Thank you, Mills. Should I open it now?"

"Yes, absolutely!"

As he removed the gift wrap from the painting, Mills stood by his side and watched his expression warm up with a smile as he studied the artwork. "This is beautiful. You painted this from the daffodils in the meadow?"

"Yes, I did."

Cooper rose from his chair and put his arms around her. "Thank you for such a lovely, thoughtful gift."

The embrace lasted for just a moment, and then he took a deep breath and noticed that his shirttail was out of his pants. "What I must look like."

"Cooper, please let me help you."

He took another deep breath before responding, "Mills, I had a bad dream, but that's all it was, a bad dream."

"I, too, have bad dreams sometimes."

He lifted the painting again to admire his gift. "Does the painting have a title?"

"Yes, it's entitled *A Host of Golden Daffodils*, after a Wordsworth poem that my mother read to Vivien and me when we were young."

"I'll treasure it."

He glanced at his watch. "I'm holding you up. I know you'd like to dress for church."

"I'll stay with you if you need me."

"No—no, I'm all right now. I'll see you this afternoon."

CHAPTER 11

"Annabel Lee"

During church services, Mills could not stop thinking about Cooper and his troubles. She repeatedly offered her prayers to God for his well-being. The phrase that she had heard him say in the boathouse went through her mind repeatedly, ". . . in her sepulcher there by the sea . . ." *Where have I heard that phrase before? A story, a poem?* She recognized that she was being allowed a glimpse into his innermost frailties—perhaps the first person permitted to do so. When the services were over, she realized that she had not paid attention to the sermon as thoughts of Cooper had predominated. Mills rushed home from West Ashley, changed into work clothes, and went to Cooper's house.

He answered the door and welcomed her inside. They stood together in the foyer before he said, "I hope you will excuse my behavior this morning. I wasn't myself."

"Cooper, we're good friends, and friends look out for one another."

Her response brought a smile to his face. "I have something to show you." He led her into his living room. Her painting was on the wall near the piano.

"I can admire the daffodils while I play. It's lovely."

"I'm so glad that you're pleased."

When they reached the Freedom School, a large group of volunteers was working busily on the restoration. Finishing touches were under way and several people were painting the wooden siding and the hurricane shutters.

Mr. Camp sat in front of a fire and he motioned for Cooper and Mills to join him. "Cooper, I believe that yesterday was your birthday. I know that I'm a day late, but happy belated birthday. Did you enjoy yourself?"

"Yes, sir. My aunts and uncles and Jeff took me out to celebrate."

"Mr. Jeffrey, how is he? I haven't seen him in a while."

"He's well, but seems to be working most of the time."

"I see." Mr. Camp looked at the schoolhouse. "I declare, this old building never looked so good, even when it was new."

After they spoke to Mr. Camp, Mills and Cooper began to help plant shrubbery around the school. "The next several weeks are going to be beautiful as the trees bud and the flowers bloom. April is one of my favorite months in Charleston," Cooper told her.

"Would it be all right if I plant some flowers around my cottage?"

"Purchase whatever you want and I'll reimburse you."

When they were finished with their work, Mills joined Mr. Camp by his fire.

"Mr. Camp, can I ask you about something?" Mills asked.

"Sure, what is it?"

"On my way home last night, I saw some dim lights in the woods near the old house ruin that's on Cooper's property. Since the leaves aren't out on the trees, I could see soft lights moving about. When I stopped the car to get a better look, the lights had vanished."

"Strange thing, these lights," Mr. Camp said.

"Have you ever seen them?"

"Yes, I have—I've heard stories about the lights all my life, but you have to remember, I grew up on that property and I don't recall anyone being terrified of them. Some folks think the lights warn of a tragic event. I've also heard tell that place is haunted by the ghosts of lantern-bearing slaves. You have to remember that slaves buried their dead at night because they had to work all day. I can tell you this for certain—the appearance of the lights has been associated with extreme weather phenomena. In 1959, I was on the river fishing with two other men. We were in the bend of the river near the old house ruins when we saw what appeared to be lanterns moving about near the old slave row. We must have watched them for ten or fifteen minutes—about scared one of those boys to death—he almost turned white. Then they just disappeared. A few weeks later, Hurricane Gracie came ashore between here and Beaufort and just about demolished the Low Country. I know of several other instances where the lights have been seen. Cooper has seen them. Ask him what he thinks."

"Thank you, Mr. Camp. I will."

On their drive home from the schoolhouse, Mills said, "Cooper, on my way home last night, I saw some lights that resembled lanterns in the woods near the old house ruins."

He turned and looked at her, but quickly returned his eyes to the road.

"I asked Mr. Camp about them, and he shared a supernatural explanation for them. He said that you had seen the lights before. What do you think causes them?"

"Mills, there has to be scientific justification for the lights, perhaps a reflection."

"They were moving about and I was frightened."

"Don't allow the lights to scare you."

Monday morning there was a phone call from Joseph Cook, Piet van der Wolf's assistant. He explained that Mr. van der Wolf would like to invite her to tea at his home on Thursday afternoon.

"Mr. Cook, instead of my coming to Mr. van der Wolf's home for tea, I would like to invite him to lunch on Thursday. Would you please ask him if he will meet me at 82 Queen at noon?"

"I'll have to ask him and call you back."

Mr. Cook called back within a few moments and said that Mr. van der Wolf would be honored to join her for lunch.

As Mills prepared to leave for the day, Cooper came by to request her assistance on several matters. He asked her to keep her schedule open on certain days and explained that they would be very busy for the next few weeks. The grand opening of the Freedom School had been arranged and there was an annual event that hosted children from the Charleston Children's Hospital for horseback rides. Cooper and two of his neighbors were the hosts and, this year, the event would be held at the Heath farm.

Mills was also invited to a dinner party by Ian, Cooper's uncle, to celebrate the arrival of his daughter Margaret and her husband Andrew from England.

They planned to visit for a week before traveling with his Aunt Celeste to Bermuda and then London.

Before he left, Cooper asked her to ride horses with him on Wednesday, admitting that he would like to have her company.

Mills agreed to meet him at the stables at three and then explained that Piet van der Wolf would be meeting her for lunch at 82 Queen on Thursday. "Good, Mills," he replied with a smile.

On Wednesday, Cooper waited for Mills at the stables. When she arrived, the horses were saddled and tied to a post outside the stalls. Mills attempted to engage him in conversation, but Cooper seemed to be distracted by his thoughts. They mounted the horses and headed toward the pasture. As they crossed the drive to Cooper's house, a car came down the lane and pulled to the side.

Cooper recognized the driver. "Lieutenant Barnes—Mills, I'll be back in a few minutes. Would you like to dismount while I speak with him?"

"No, I'll wait for you here."

Cooper joined Lieutenant Barnes beside his vehicle. They spoke for several minutes and then the police officer walked to where Mills was sitting on Ginger.

"Miss Taylor, how are you this afternoon?"

"I'm well, Lieutenant Barnes."

"You look like an experienced horsewoman."

"Honestly, Cooper just recently taught me how to ride."

Lieutenant Barnes walked to Mephisto and patted him on the neck. "Beautiful animal, Cooper—is he an Arabian?"

"Yes."

"What's his name?"

"Mephisto."

Lieutenant Barnes paused for a moment and smiled slightly at Cooper. "That's an appropriate name for a horse you would own, Cooper—Mephisto. Or Mephistopheles."

He continued to grin at Cooper, seeming to want to provoke a reaction. "I recall that in Faustian legend, Mephistopheles was a prince of the underworld who gathered the souls of those who had already been damned."

Cooper did not flinch. "Lieutenant, the horse was named that when I brought him here. Is there anything else you'd like to ask me?"

"No, that will be all, for now. Have a nice ride, Gretchen, I mean, Miss Taylor. Good afternoon, Cooper." *Gretchen?*

As Lieutenant Barnes departed, Mills noticed Cooper's frown. "Mills, I'll lead the way."

When they reached the old house ruins, Cooper dismounted Mephisto and then assisted her on the dismount from Ginger's back. Cooper was quiet as they walked toward the ruins.

"Why did the lieutenant call me Gretchen?"

"In the old German legend of Faust, a brilliant scholar makes a deal with the devil—his soul in exchange for worldly pleasures and knowledge. Gretchen is an innocent young woman who is seduced by Faust, and she and her family are ruined because of him. Mephistopheles is the agent of Satan who assists Faust with his wishes. Lieutenant Barnes tries his best to get my ire up."

As they walked the perimeter of the old house ruin, Cooper said, "I want to show you something."

He led her to the cabin with the magnificent rosebush, which had been severely pruned. "I had Charles come down and cut the bush back. It will now bloom more abundantly. Will you walk with me to the old chapel?"

She agreed and together they walked to the churchyard. Cooper went to a mausoleum tomb that was in the midst of other graves. "I think you are my friend and I need to confide in you. I have been suffering from a nightmare about my wife—I'm afraid she's not coming back."

Anxiety coursed through her limbs as he made this confession. "Cooper, shouldn't you speak with a professional who can help you interpret the dreams?"

"I want to talk to you. Please listen. In the dream, I can see Elise surrounded by darkness. I can hear the sound of flowing water, and I can hear her calling my name from the depths of a black abyss. When I reach for her in the chasm, her face turns to a fleshless skull. In the dream, I hear phrases from a poem, ". . . in her sepulcher there by the sea."

"I heard you say that phrase in the boathouse. Do you know where it comes from?"

"A poem called 'Annabel Lee.'"

"In a kingdom by the sea . . ." Mills recalled the poem and said the line automatically. She knew that the poem was written about the loss of a beautiful woman. "I've never attempted to interpret dreams, but we'll work on this together."

After they finished riding and grooming the horses, Mills asked Cooper to accompany her to her cottage. Edgar Allen Poe's poem was included in a collection of short stories and poems that was on the bookshelf in her cottage. Mills retrieved the book, and they read it together. Mills read aloud the last stanza of the poem that held the verse that haunted him:

> For the moon never beams without bringing me dreams
> Of the beautiful Annabel Lee;
> And the stars never rise but I feel the bright eyes
> Of the beautiful Annabel Lee;
> And so, all the night-tide, I lie down by the side
> Of my darling—my darling—my life and my bride
> In her sepulcher there by the sea,
> In her tomb by the side of the sea.

She closed the book and looked at Cooper. "In your dream, you envision Elise in a darkened chasm where the sound of flowing water is nearby. Perhaps the darkened chasm is some type of tomb—a sepulcher. That would account for the phrase that troubles you." *I shouldn't have said that.*

She realized she had just delivered a chilling interpretation of his dream and regretted doing so. "It's just a dream. You must remember that, and stop torturing yourself."

"There's something you don't know about me. This isn't the first time that I've suffered from tragic premonitions. I envisioned the deaths of my brother and father in a series of dreams before it came true."

Mills already knew about the boating accident that killed his father and brother, but she chose not to inquire further into his version of the incident. She concluded that he would open up to her if he desired.

Cooper's face was completely pale and he sat quietly on her porch. "I'm very worried about this. Please keep this confidential."

"Cooper, you have my word."

CHAPTER 12

Porch Party

On Thursday, Piet van der Wolf met Mills for lunch at 82 Queen. Before their lunch arrived at the table, Piet said, "Mills, I trust you are having success with the foundation work."

"We had a number of donations that resulted from the oyster roast."

"I'm glad to hear that."

The waitress brought out iced teas for both of them, and Piet thanked her for her service. "I presume Mr. Heath was happy about the donations. How is he?"

"He's well."

Piet was silent for a moment as he studied her face. "Mills, please ask him not to judge me in my loneliness; I do not judge him in his. Let your young man know that I am completely harmless, and that you are safe when you come to my home."

"Mr. van der Wolf, Cooper is my employer, not my young man."

"Yes, he is, Mills. He just hasn't realized it yet."

Saturday afternoon arrived and Mills drove into town for the Heath family's dinner party to celebrate the arrival of family from England. She wore her favorite black dress and styled her hair to fall in waves down her back. Cooper's aunt met her at the door, wearing an apricot linen dress.

"I believe that's your color," Mills told her, admiring her outfit.

The compliment pleased Mrs. Heath, and she smiled warmly. "Cooper and Jeff are in the rear garden." She showed her to the French doors that led to the rear patio and said, "I'm so happy that you could join us."

As soon as Mills entered the rear garden, Cooper came over to greet her. "I'm glad to see you," he said with a smile. "What would you like to drink?"

"White wine would be nice."

He left her to get her drink and his uncle came over and gave her a hug. "We're glad you could come. Is Cooper getting you something to drink?"

"Yes, sir."

"Have you ever had a Dark and Stormy? It's quite famous and very popular in Bermuda."

"No, sir, I've never tried it."

"Cooper, hang on. I'm going to get Mills a Dark and Stormy."

A bartender in a white coat prepared the drink and Mr. Heath retrieved it. "Here you are. I hope you like it."

"Thank you, Mr. Heath."

"Please make yourself at home. Daniel, could I speak to you for a moment?"

He called Cooper by his first name—Daniel. There must be a problem to solve.

The two of them entered the house through the open French doors.

She turned to admire the garden and ran right into Jeff, almost spilling her drink. "Seems like we're always running into each other." He smiled and gave her a kiss on the cheek. "I apologize for not having phoned you recently, but I've been very busy on a development project. Next Saturday night I'm going to have a party at my townhouse on Chalmers Street, and I'd like for you to come."

"I'm not sure I should. Is Cooper coming?"

"Cooper declines my invitations. He's too uptight to relax with my crowd." He paused and smiled at her. "Have you ever looked inside his pantry?"

"Cooper's just well organized."

"Anal retentive is a better description. I'm only teasing—I love him. He's my favorite Eagle Scout—will you be able to come?"

"Yes, I think so." *I'll stay for a while and see how it goes.*

He winked at her and then said, "I haven't had a chance to greet the Brits yet, but why don't we get out of here together after we say hello?"

"Jeff, I feel honored to have been invited. That would be rude."

"These are Cooper's cousins, and I told him that I could only stay for a cocktail. Margaret is all right until she gets to her third drink and then she becomes the life of the party."

Cooper rejoined them just as Jeff kissed Mills on the cheek. He cleared his throat and said, "I think Margaret and Andrew are finished talking to my uncle's neighbor."

Cooper introduced Mills to his first cousin and her husband and they both spoke with sophisticated British accents. "My dear, Father has told me so much about you. He says that you're doing an excellent job for Cooper's foundation."

Margaret's husband, Andrew, shook her hand. "Brava, Miss Taylor, I'm so pleased to meet you."

They then turned to Jeff, who stood beside Cooper. "Jeffrey, how marvelous to see you again," Margaret cooed.

Jeff kissed Margaret's hand, and she looked like she was about to swoon. "Maggie, Andy, how are you? It's been a while since we've seen one another."

"Jeffrey, too long, absolutely too long."

Margaret has a crush on Jeff; he really is attractive.

Andrew spoke up, "Cooper, are you still shooting those sporting clays at your place on the Edisto?"

"Yes, I am, Andrew."

Then motioning toward Mills, Cooper continued, "Mills has been shooting the clays and has become quite a good markswoman. She even shot ducks on her first hunt."

"That's outstanding, Miss Taylor. Cooper, I was wondering if Margaret and I might have a go of it out at your place tomorrow. I think Ian would like to join us as well."

"That's fine; tomorrow afternoon, around two?"

"Perfect, I don't want to get up too early while I'm on holiday. Miss Taylor, you must shoot with us."

"I'd love to, and please call me Mills."

"Very well," Andrew responded with a smile.

"Jeffrey, you will join us, won't you?" Margaret asked.

"I wouldn't miss it," he responded.

Margaret's face blushed to the color of deep rose as she stood beside him. When dinner was about to be served, Margaret searched the garden for Jeff, but he had already departed. Mills heard her ask Cooper about Jeff's whereabouts and Cooper explained that he had a prior commitment. *She looks like she just lost her best friend.* During dinner, Mills sat between Margaret and Andrew. As

Margaret continued to partake of spirits, her personality became quite lively, just as Jeff had predicted.

"Miss Taylor, I mean, Mills. How do you like living in the wilderness on Cooper's property? Father says that you live in Aunt Julia's cottage."

"Yes, I do, and I enjoy living there very much."

"Well, it must be very different after living in New York."

"It has been a big change."

"Mother says that you are a talented artist. She showed me a copy of the artwork you did on the oyster roast invitation. Did you know that she framed it?"

"Thank you for sharing that with me."

Margaret was quiet for a moment before saying, "I've been so concerned about Cooper. I know he has almost worried himself to death about Elise. We all have."

She sipped more of her wine and added, "When I was in my early twenties, I had a terrible crush on Jeffrey. I thought I would die if he didn't notice me. I practically threw myself at him."

You still have a crush on Jeff.

Mills noticed that Andrew was engaged in a conversation with Cooper, and Margaret continued her confessional. "Jeffrey is such a playboy. One summer, I went out to Cooper's property, but Aunt Julia owned it then. I'm sure that Beau and Mr. Brown had already passed away."

"Mr. Brown?"

"Yes, my father always called Cooper's father by his middle name, Brown. Besides Father, he was one of the most charming men I've ever known—and poor Beau. Cooper and Beau were supposed to manage Heath Brothers when my father and Brown retired. I suspect you already know about Beau."

Mills nodded, and Margaret continued, "Beau and Uncle Brown perished before their time and Cooper almost didn't come back to Charleston. My sister and I never wanted to get involved in the management part of the company, but we're well provided for—Cooper makes sure of it."

"Cooper does?"

"Yes, of course; Cooper makes most of the decisions for Heath Brothers now. Father prefers it that way. In fact, I believe that Father would adopt Cooper if he wasn't already related to him. As long as Cooper is in charge, and he will be in charge, we will be provided for. Cooper wouldn't have it any other way—my goodness, I lost my train of thought."

"You were speaking of Cooper's property when Julia owned it."

"Thank you. I was. Years ago, I went out to Aunt Julia's property to learn how to fly fish. Cooper and Jeffrey were in their early twenties and they had been working on a sailboat that Jeffrey's father had purchased. They both had their shirts off, and every time I cast the fly rod, I ended up getting the line stuck in a tree. I was too busy looking at them. The two of them have done nothing but improve with age."

A chocolate torte was on the dessert menu and Mills was served a large slice. Margaret looked at her thin physique before commenting, "That dessert should be named 'Death by Chocolate.' How do you manage to stay so thin?"

Andrew rejoined their conversation and he interjected, "My dear, it's known as being twenty-five years of age."

While the guests mingled after dinner, Cooper took Mills aside. "When you get tired, I'd like to walk you to my townhouse on Tradd Street. I don't want you driving back to the country alone this late in the evening. You'll have privacy there, and I'll sleep on the couch in my uncle's study."

"I don't want to displace you."

"I just want to know that you're safe."

When the party ended, Mills thanked the Heaths for the wonderful invitation and told Margaret and Andrew how much she had enjoyed meeting them. Andrew told her, "I'll look forward to seeing you for the clays tomorrow." Cooper told his uncle that he was going to walk Mills to his townhouse and that he'd return in a few minutes. Once they were outside, Mills felt chilled by the evening air.

"Would you like to put my coat around your shoulders?"

"Yes, thank you."

Cooper took off his blazer and placed it over her shoulders. She pulled it close to her, and they walked the few blocks to his townhome. Even in the shadows of the lamplights, she knew that she liked the street. When they reached his residence, he opened the door and handed her the keys. A lamp illuminated the foyer, and Mills turned to Cooper, giving him back his blazer.

"I had a wonderful time with your family tonight. Thank you for including me."

"The whole family wanted you to attend. I'm glad you had a nice time."

He handed her a slip of paper, which had his uncle's phone number written on it. "If you need anything, I'm just a few blocks away. Now, lock up."

As she closed the door, he waved goodbye from the base of the steps and turned to walk back to his uncle's. She watched from the window, but as he went out of sight, a man came out of the shadows and quickly followed in Cooper's direction. *Who is that?* Anxiety overcame her, and she took several deep breaths. After waiting several minutes to give Cooper time to get back to his uncle's home, she dialed the phone number. He was just coming into the house when his aunt answered and summoned him to the phone.

"Mills, is there something wrong?" Cooper asked.

"I saw a man come out of the shadows and follow you down the street."

"I didn't see anyone. Perhaps he was out for a walk."

"I–I don't know. I'm just glad that you're all right."

"Are you going to be okay?"

"Yes."

"Then, I'll see you tomorrow."

When she laid down the receiver, she looked around the townhouse. The home was richly furnished, and she turned on the lights in each room, admiring the décor before retiring for the evening.

Sunday, when Mills arrived home, she changed her clothes to shoot sporting clays. The last item she donned was the handsome vest that Cooper had brought her from New York. As she admired the vest in the mirror, the phone rang. Her sister, Vivien, was calling from Virginia, and she was in a highly jovial mood. "I know that you've got a birthday coming up soon, and I wanted to see if I could come to Charleston to celebrate with you."

"Yes, that sounds wonderful. I'll have to ask Cooper for some time off so I can show you around."

"I have two surprises for you, but I want to tell you about them in person."

"How about a hint?"

"No hints. I'll call you after I check on airline reservations. Is everything still going well?"

"Yes, absolutely."

"When I come to visit, I would like to explore."

"I'll look forward to it," Mills responded. *I can't wait to see her!*

The shooting group met at Cooper's home at two. Cooper's neighbors, Mr. Littlejohn and Mr. Caldwell, were participating, as well as Britton. Cooper had the Land Rover parked in front of the house to drive to the range.

As soon as Margaret saw it, she asked, "Where on earth did you dig up this old relic?"

"I had it shipped from England. Before that, it had been in Kenya."

"Good heavens, Cooper, that thing will beat you to death." She paused for a moment and then asked, "Have you heard from Jeffrey?"

"No, I haven't."

Everyone took their turn at shooting and Britton joined Mills to give advice on her technique. He was more talkative than usual and seemed to be overcoming the nervousness that he usually displayed in her presence. As they were about to finish, Jeff's Yukon descended into the pasture. He parked the vehicle, got out, and apologized to the group for being late. "I had an issue that had to be resolved with a client, and it took about three times as long as it should have."

"I'm glad you could come," Cooper told him.

Margaret beamed a radiant smile in his direction, and when he shot his gun, he displayed flawless accuracy. Without a doubt, he was the most talented marksman in the group.

Mr. Caldwell observed, "Jeff, I think you should go on the shooting circuit. You're talented enough to become the national champion."

"Thank you, Mr. Caldwell, but I think I'd better stick with my day job. The pay is better."

When the group finished shooting, they retired to Cooper's back porch to socialize. Mills joined Margaret and said, "Last night, you mentioned that Cooper and Jeff were avid sailors. I haven't seen Cooper sail since I've been here."

"Oh, yes, Cooper and Jeffery won most of the regattas in this area, as well as races up and down the east coast. They aren't as involved with racing anymore because it takes a great deal of time and commitment. Cooper was one of the youngest commodores of the Charleston Yacht Club."

Margaret frowned. "I hate to say this, but Cooper has become withdrawn since all this started with Elise. His reputation was damaged by individuals who don't even know him. I'm not sure how he does it, but somehow he stays calm and internalizes the pain."

I worry about him too.

Unlike the porch party that Mills had attended, social issues and politics were not discussed that afternoon. Andrew repeatedly sought investment advice from Cooper, and Margaret cornered Jeff on one end of the porch. When he left her side for a few minutes, he went inside Cooper's house and returned with a handful of cigars.

As Jeff began to pass them out to the men, Margaret held her hand out. "Give me one of those."

"Are you sure you want this?"

"Yes, I haven't had one since I was last in the States."

Ian grimaced at his daughter, and she responded by saying, "Oh, come now, Father. It's not like I do this every day."

Mills watched as Margaret motioned for Jeff to join her in Cooper's garden, and they disappeared in the direction of the river. *I wonder what they're up to.* Suddenly aware that someone had come up behind her, Mills turned to see that Britton had joined her on the porch. He cleared his throat before asking, "Mills, can I get you a glass of wine?"

"I'm fine, but thank you for offering."

He stared at the porch floor before he told her, "I confess, I've been nervous about asking you for a date, but I was wondering if I could take you to lunch. I won't be working on Wednesday, and I was hoping we could meet somewhere downtown."

"Britton, that sounds very nice. I look forward to it."

As the party began to wind down, Andrew began to look around for his wife, but she had not returned. At least thirty more minutes passed before Margaret and Jeff emerged from the garden.

Andrew glared at Margaret, and Margaret returned the look. *If looks could kill.*

"Jeffrey wanted to show me Cooper's Boston Whaler, the *Miss Elise*. I don't believe I've seen it before."

Cooper responded, "I purchased it since you were last here."

"Lovely craft. I admire the shade of red you painted it."

When the party was over, Mills approached Cooper about having time off to spend with her sister during her birthday. He responded that she could take several days off to visit with Vivien, but he added, "Would it be all right if I entertain both of you during her visit?"

She quickly responded, "Yes, that sounds wonderful. Vivien said that she'd like to explore." *I'm thrilled!*

He paused for a moment, then thoughtfully said, "Let me think about this."

That evening, Mills sat on her porch and listened to him play the piano. He worked on different chord combinations and it sounded like he was composing. What especially pleased her was that the music was inspiring, not melancholic.

CHAPTER 13

Death on the Edisto

Mills stopped by Dawkins's Market on her way into Charleston on Monday morning. Huddled around the counter were several local farmers that supplied Mr. Dawkins with fresh produce, poultry, and meats. She could hear their conversation as she passed them and it concerned a fatal accident that had occurred on the river the night before. Two couples from out of state were boating after sunset on the waterway and, unfamiliar with the river, they had crashed into a dock, instantly killing the two men. One of the farmers, Jake Henderson, lowered his voice as if the details were too grim to be overheard, but Mills still heard him say, "The two men were decapitated by the pier section of the dock."

Horrible! She refocused her thoughts on shopping and, when finished, she went to the cash register. The farmers had departed, leaving Mr. Dawkins alone at the front counter. "Did you hear about the boating accident?" he asked.

"Just what I heard you all talking about when I came inside."

"Yes, too bad about those folks. Boating and excessive alcohol can make a lethal combination. They haven't found either of the women yet." He spoke as if he was sharing a secret, "I hear that it's doubtful that either of them could have survived the crash."

Please no more grisly details. Mills thanked Mr. Dawkins and left the market. She started her Beetle and headed into Charleston on Highway 17. Her first stop of the day was the Low Country Gourmet. Melea Butler had left her a message that a donation to her scholarship program was at the front counter.

When she entered the store, Ford Butler was operating the cash register and he waved her inside. "A local man was in over the weekend and after he read about your scholarship program, he wanted to make a donation. Here you are," he said, handing her an envelope.

"Thank you, Mr. Butler. Is Paul around?"

"No, he's not. I've given him time off to help his ill friend." Without being asked, he wrote down Paul's address and handed it to her. "I expect he'll be there if you want to go by."

After her appointments, she walked to Paul's address, which was on Queen Street. His residence was located in an area of nice townhomes, and when she rang the doorbell, Paul answered the door.

He smiled as soon as he saw her. "Audrey, what brings you to my home?"

"I've missed you the last two times I've been to the Low Country Gourmet and I wanted to see how you are."

"I'm fine, Audrey."

"Mr. Butler said that you were taking care of a sick friend. Is there anything I can do to help?"

He paused as if he was considering her offer and then invited her inside. "Mills, I could use some help. My friend Max is ill, and I don't think I should leave him right now. Would you go to the grocery store for me?"

"Absolutely."

"I believe we are friends and I'd like for you to meet Max."

He led her into the living room and her eyes immediately focused on a magnificent grand piano.

"Max, we have a visitor. My friend, Audrey, who is the director of the Heath Foundation, has come by to see us."

Mills turned to one corner of the room where a man sat on a couch. The smell of rubbing alcohol permeated the air. Wrapped in a blanket, Max was the unhealthiest person she had ever seen in her life. *Poor thing—he's the shell of a man in a state of living decay.*

Paul took her hand and led her to the couch where Max sat.

"Miss Taylor, I know your real first name is Mills. I've heard so many nice things about you from Paul and I'm pleased to make your acquaintance." His voice quavered as he spoke, but he managed a smile, despite his illness.

Mills reached out to him and took his hand in hers. "I'm so happy to meet you, Max. That's a beautiful piano; is it yours?"

"Yes, it was a gift to me many years ago—a Bösendorfer—would you like to play it?"

"Oh, no, I never learned how, but my employer is a marvelous pianist."

"I have heard this before. Perhaps Cooper Heath will play for us sometime." On the piano was the sheet music of Claude Debussy, "Clair de Lune de la Suite bergamasque"; underneath the Debussy sheet music was a composition by Erik Satie.

"I was a professor of music before I became too ill," Max somberly added. "Audrey, we could use your help, if you don't mind visiting the grocery store for us."

Paul made a list of the items they needed and she drove to the Harris Teeter food market to purchase them. When she returned, she brought the groceries into their kitchen and handed the change to Paul.

"Is there anything else I can help you with?"

"No, Audrey, but I think I'll start calling you 'Angel' instead." He paused as he studied her face. "Have you ever seen the movie *Roman Holiday*, with Audrey Hepburn and Gregory Peck?"

"Yes, I have."

"Do you remember how she cuts her hair short? I think you would be stunning with your hair styled like that."

"Do you think so?"

"All the men of Charleston would be at your feet."

She felt herself blush. "Oh Paul, thank you. I'll ask Cooper—I mean Mr. Heath—if he'll come and play the piano for you." Max smiled at her gesture and held her hand tightly as they said goodbye.

When she returned to Edisto, Cooper and Charles had just come in from working in the fields. As soon as she parked her car, they called to her to join them on the porch and both men rose from their seats as she entered. They were drinking beer. Cooper sat his bottle on a table. "What can I get you to drink?" he asked.

"A glass of ice water, please."

"I'll be right back." Cooper went to the kitchen to retrieve her drink, and Mills sat down in a rocking chair.

"What did you and Cooper do on the farm today?" she asked Charles.

"We worked on Cooper's dove field. We're going to be planting sunflowers, sorghum, millet, corn, and wheat. He has an annual dove shoot on the opening day of dove season—it's a big social event for Cooper's friends." He cleared his throat. "Last year, Cooper canceled the shoot—we were too busy trying to find Miss Elise. A terrible thing." He shook his head. "We're also increasing the amount of acreage we farm each year, and Cooper has been restoring the fruit orchards . . . years ago, this property was known as 'The Orchards' for its abundance of fruit trees, but they gradually died out due to neglect and disease."

"I've noticed that Cooper works almost all the time."

"I think he was born industrious, but if you're working, there's less time for thinking."

"What do you—" Before she finished the question, Cooper returned with her glass of ice water. As she sipped it, she listened to the men discuss their plans for the next day. *What did Charles mean by less time for thinking?* Mills listened to Cooper's voice—it was smooth and calming to her, and she found herself at peace in the rocking chair. She was suddenly aware that Charles was speaking to her.

"Miss Mills, good night. I'll see you tomorrow.

"Oh, Charles. I didn't mean to ignore you. I was so relaxed."

"Have a good evening," Charles said as he left the porch. Within a few minutes, his truck passed by as he drove home.

Dusk approached. The gas lights on either side of the front door warmly lit the porch. Mills turned to Cooper and asked, "Why don't you have a southern accent?"

"I do. It's just not as pronounced as it used to be. The years that I was away in the Air Force caused me to lose most of it."

"I like to listen to your voice. It comforts me."

"No one has ever told me that."

As she took another sip of her water, she thought of Max and Paul. "Do you know the works of Claude Debussy and Erik Satie?"

"I've played Debussy before, but not Satie."

"Would you do me a favor? Would you play for Paul and his friend, Max? I'm afraid that Max is very ill and homebound."

"I can't do it tomorrow. Charles and I are working on the farm."

"I can't go tomorrow either. I'm meeting Britton for lunch."

Cooper gazed at her for a moment. "See if Thursday will work for Paul and his friend."

"I'll phone Paul—have you ever seen the movie *Roman Holiday*?"

"Audrey Hepburn and Gregory Peck?"

"Yes. Do you remember how she cuts her hair extremely short in the movie?"

Cooper nodded, and Mills continued, "Paul said that I would look good with my hair cut like that."

"You're lovely. Don't change the way you wear your hair."

"Thank you, Cooper."

She gently rocked back and forth and brought up an issue that was bothering her. "I'm worried about something."

"What's that, Mills?"

"I think someone is following you and canvassing this house. Saturday night, that man came out of nowhere, and there have been a few instances when I was supposed to be alone that I thought there may have been an intruder on this property."

"Are you afraid to be out here? You can move into the townhouse on Tradd Street."

"It's you that I'm worried about."

"Please, don't worry. If there's someone following me, they'll eventually make a mistake."

"I don't want to move into town. This is my home."

The next morning, there were details of the boating accident on the Edisto in the *Charleston Dispatch*. The body of one of the women had been recovered by fishermen the day before. When the boat hit the dock, the men—who were taller than their wives—had been hit across the neck by the pier section of the dock, while the woman whose body had been recovered was struck in the forehead.

As she started out for the day, there was an invitation on her screen door to go fishing Friday morning with Cooper and Williston. Mills wrote a note back to Cooper and left it on his kitchen door that she had no appointments on Friday morning and that she would meet them at the dock.

Britton was waiting for her when she reached the Baker's Café at noon. He already had a table, and he stood as soon as she entered the restaurant. Helping her with her chair, he smiled, saying, "I'm so glad that you could join me for lunch, Mills."

"Thank you for the invitation." She sat across from him. "I'd like to know more about your job."

"I assist the ships' masters in navigation in and out of the port of Charleston."

"How did you learn a skill like that?"

"I was in the US Navy, but I've been around ships my entire life. Most of my ancestors made their living off the sea, and my father had me on the deck of a ship before I could walk."

"How did you get to know Cooper and Jeff?"

"I was Beau's best friend all the way through school." He paused then added, "I still can't believe that he's gone, and I remember exactly what I was doing when I learned of the accident. Cooper was able to save Jeff's life, thank God. For someone as nice as Cooper, bad luck seems to follow him around. I feel terrible about Elise. Cooper adores her—what a beautiful woman. We searched for her for months, put up missing person posters all over the Low Country. If someone knows anything about her disappearance, they haven't come forward. People who don't know Cooper have made terrible accusations about him, but if I was in trouble, and I could only make one phone call, it would be to him. I know he'd come to my rescue."

Mills nodded. *If I was in trouble, Cooper would be the one I'd call too.*

The luncheon date was pleasant, and Mills found that, after Britton got over his nervousness, he was talkative and very nice. He explained that he had been married while in the Navy, but the long-term separations had been overwhelming for his wife and she had found another love interest. Britton also told her that he expected Jeff to remain a bachelor—he found too much excitement from having several different girlfriends at the same time.

CHAPTER 14

The Bösendorfer

Mills and Cooper arrived at Paul's residence on Thursday afternoon at two. During their walk to the Queen Street townhome, Cooper said, "I have a surprise for you after we visit with Paul and Max."

"Can I have a clue?"

"Nope—no clues," he responded with a smile.

Mills rang the doorbell at the townhome, and Paul answered the door, inviting them inside. He looked at Mills and then at Cooper. "Thank you for your kind gesture. Max is waiting for us in the living room."

Seated on the couch, Max made an effort to rise when they entered the room, but he did not get up. Cooper introduced himself and shook Max's hand.

"Mills has told us that you're a marvelous pianist, but I've heard that from others. Thank you for coming here to play for us."

"You're welcome." Cooper walked over to the piano and raised the keyboard cover. "Bösendorfer—a beautiful instrument, Max."

"My mother gave me the piano when I graduated from college, years ago."

"Mills said that you enjoy the music of Claude Debussy and Erik Satie. Is that what you'd like to hear me play?"

"Yes, the sheet music is on the piano."

Cooper sat down on the piano bench and looked through the sheet music before asking Mills if she'd turn the pages for him. He indicated that a nod of his head was the signal to turn the pages, and she joined him on the bench. He played the first composition. *Unbelievable—he sight reads as if he'd practiced the song a thousand times.*

She watched his strong hands on the keyboard, and as a tree outside the window rustled in the wind, intermittent waves of lights entered the room.

Cooper's wedding ring caught the light dancing on the keyboard and glistened on his finger. As he continued to play, Mills was captivated by the works of Debussy, especially the composition, "Reverie." Mills looked at Max as he wiped tears from his face.

Cooper completed the songs and there was silence in the room. As he composed himself, Max said, "Debussy and Satie were mavericks for their time. Besides being friends, they were often referred to as impressionist artists, although Debussy disliked the description." Max's voice trailed off as he continued, "Some of their works have strange but beautiful harmonies." Then his attention focused on Cooper. "Debussy himself could not have sight read any better than you."

"Thank you, Max," Cooper responded.

Mills gazed at Max. *He has a look of peace on his face.*

"I assure you that I will never forget this. Thank you, again," Max said.

Before they left, Cooper and Mills shook both men's hands, and Paul showed them to the door. Cooper descended the steps to the sidewalk, leaving Mills alone with Paul. He took her hand before saying, "You and Mr. Heath are exceptional people. I'm afraid that Max and I are present-day lepers. I'll never forget your kindness. God bless both of you."

As they walked back to Heath Brothers, Cooper said, "I'm afraid that Max is very ill."

"Thank you for playing for them this afternoon."

"I was glad to, Mills."

"What is the surprise you were going to show me?"

"I wanted to give you a tour of one of our container ships. The *Mary B. Chesnut* is in port this afternoon, and I'm going to see her captain."

"Yes, I'd like to go with you. Who was Mary B. Chesnut?"

"A well-connected Civil War diarist and South Carolina resident, also an early feminist. Julia named most of our ships and I'm sure that's what got her attention."

When they reached the Columbus Street Terminal, the last container was being loaded onto the deck of the massive ship. Cooper handed Mills a hard hat and then placed one on his own head before they boarded. As soon as Cooper came on deck, the crew members greeted him as "Mr. Heath." Cooper showed Mills around inside the bridge and introduced her to Captain Van Dyke.

The captain was a burly man with a barrel chest, but he gently led her around the bridge, explaining the operation of the mechanical equipment. After he kissed her hand, he excused himself and started a conversation with Cooper. Mills noticed a familiar face approaching the container ship. Britton was coming on board, and when he came on deck, he greeted Mills and said he would be the harbor pilot guiding the *Mary B. Chesnut* out to sea.

After several minutes, Cooper rejoined her and spoke to Britton before departing the ship. Mills turned around and noticed that several crewmen were staring at her. Feeling self-conscious, she asked Cooper, "Is there something wrong with my attire? Some of the men are staring at me." *My face is getting hot.*

"No, Mills, there's nothing wrong with your appearance." He noticed her blush, and said, "Rosy cheeks and all."

That night before she fell asleep, Mills thought of Paul and his statement, "Max and I are present-day lepers." *Is he sick as well?*

Friday morning, Mills arrived at Cooper's dock at six-thirty. Williston and Cooper were already on board, and the fishing poles were rigged. Cooper handed her a life jacket. "You should wear it; it will help you to stay warm."

Once away from the dock, Cooper pushed up the power on the engines and they motored downriver toward the Atlantic. On the way, Cooper pointed out trunk systems used for regulating the flow of water onto land. "You've seen them at the old house ruins," he reminded Mills.

Cooper anchored the boat near a grassy area and shut off the engines. "Redfish get into the marsh grass, so cast just outside of it." Numerous oyster banks were exposed that morning and Cooper explained that the lunar phase was the cause of the extremely low tide.

As they sat in the marsh area, an eerie sound of laughter interrupted the silence.

"What's that noise?" Mills inquired.

"Those are marsh hens—they sound like they're laughing at you. They're in season in the fall and easier to hunt during spring tides."

"Spring tides?"

"Yes, unusually high tides. They occur in September."

"Mills, you'll have to try Cooper's marsh hens prepared on the grill. They're a delicacy."

Williston's cork went under water and she jerked the line before reeling in a fish. "Not a keeper—too small."

"What kind of fish is that, Williston?"

"That's a redfish. See the spot on its tail? It almost looks like an eye. That's to fool predators."

There was a blowing sound nearby and Mills looked around the marsh for the origin of the noise. Several dolphins came toward their boat and, as they exhaled, water was released from their bodies.

"My goodness, there are several of them."

"They're chasing fish, could be redfish."

Wow—I've never seen dolphin up close before! Mills watched them until they disappeared from sight.

The next time Williston hooked a fish, it was a large redfish, and she excitedly said, "This one's a keeper!"

As the fishing trip continued, Cooper reeled in a Spanish mackerel, and Mills kept reeling in small sharks. Cooper would remove them from her hook and toss them back into the water. "Sorry you keep catching the sharks—they're nuisance fish."

"I keep getting duds." *I feel like Charlie Brown on Halloween. He kept getting rocks instead of candy.*

"Here let me cast your rod for you," Cooper said. Mills handed him her rod and he cast the line right beside the grass.

The marsh area was extremely quiet except for the flyover of a jet formation that Cooper identified as C-141s from the Charleston Air Force Base.

As Mills looked into the tea-hued waters of the river, she asked, "Where does the name Edisto come from?"

"It's from the tribe who inhabited this area before the arrival of Europeans. In the early 1700s, the Edisto population declined from diseases and wars. Some of the remaining natives may have joined other tribes, but gradually, they disappeared," Cooper explained.

"That's very sad," Mills replied.

Williston cast her line next to the marsh grass and began to quietly talk. "Eula and her children are coming to the opening of the Freedom School on Sunday. They've moved back into the trailer from the women's shelter. She's doing much better and there has been no further contact from Lee Roy.

I understand from Reverend Smalls that she has returned to work and to her studies."

"That's wonderful," said Mills.

Williston jerked her line and reeled it in a couple of feet. "I think she did the right thing for herself—thank God, she still had a legal alternative. I pray that the day never returns that poverty-stricken women like Eula have to return to the back alley."

"Julia felt that way too."

"I know."

Before they returned to Cooper's dock, Williston invited them both to her home that evening, saying that she would prepare the fish they caught for dinner.

That afternoon, Mills placed phone calls to the parents of children who wanted to participate in the Heath scholarship program. In between calls, her phone rang and a woman who identified herself as Lucille Simmons explained that she lived in adjacent Colleton County and wanted to make an appointment with Mr. Heath in regard to the scholarship program. She had read about the program in one of the news releases that Mills had written for the *Charleston Dispatch*; Lucille wished to learn if her son, Barry, would qualify for the scholarship. Mills told her that she would speak with Mr. Heath about her son and call her back. Before their conversation ended, Ms. Simmons said that Barry was at the top of his class academically, but that financial issues might prevent him from attending college.

At a quarter to seven, Mills walked to Cooper's to ride with him to Williston's home. The evening was warm and she wore a pair of navy shorts and a linen blouse. Cooper had just come out of the shower and his hair was damp. Mills could not help but notice how handsome he was in khaki shorts and a white shirt with sleeves rolled up to the elbows. Cooper carried a bottle of wine from the house and as he opened her car door, he said, "You and I are in for a treat. Williston is a fabulous cook."

The delicious aromas of tomatoes and garlic filled the air when Williston invited them into her home. Cooper handed her the chilled bottle of wine and said, "Our contribution to dinner."

She opened the wine and poured each of them a glass. "About ten more minutes on the fish and then we'll be ready to eat."

When the dish was served, the baked fish was succulent in a tomato sauce with garlic, capers, and peppers. "This is delicious," Mills told Williston after her first bite.

As they dined, Williston mentioned that a blood drive would be held at her clinic the following week. "I hope you two can come out and donate blood again."

"I can come—what about you, Mills?"

"Yes, I'll come too."

"Mills, did you get a card in the mail from the Red Cross identifying your blood type?"

"Yes, ma'am. I am O positive."

"How about that? You two have the same blood type. While an individual with an O positive blood type can donate to people with other blood types, you can only receive blood from another O donor. Doesn't seem fair does it?"

"No, ma'am," Cooper replied.

Mills remembered about the phone call from Lucille Simmons. "Cooper, I forgot to tell you: a lady from Colleton County called about the Heath scholarship program and would like to make an appointment with you about her son."

"You can make the appointment for next Wednesday after we give blood."

After dinner, the trio talked for over an hour before they thanked Williston for the wonderful meal and told her good night. Mills was the first into the foyer and she noticed photos of Williston's family. There were pictures of a young Williston with an olive-skinned man on a fishing excursion. On the way home, Mills asked, "Cooper, I saw photos of a man with Williston. Was that her husband?"

"Yes."

"What happened to him?"

"When we get home, come up on the porch, and I'll tell you."

They arrived at Cooper's home and went to the front porch. They sat down in rocking chairs and he began to explain, "Williston's husband, Alan, was from Martinique and his parents owned a resort on the island. His father was French and Portuguese, and his mother was of West Indian descent. Alan and Williston met while they were at Princeton. When they finished school, they both took jobs in Charleston, Alan at the Medical University and Williston at Roper Hospital. He was chosen to attend a doctors' conference at Duke University, due to his contributions to research in the field of oncology. On his return trip to Charleston, a truck ran a stop sign and hit him on the driver's side of the vehicle. While he was waiting for an ambulance, a passerby robbed him of his wallet, watch, and wedding band. He was hemorrhaging from a severe laceration and could have been saved if the bleeding had been controlled, but this individual chose to steal from him instead. He died on the way to the hospital."

"That's horrible."

"Obscenely so. When Alan passed away, their children were ages three and one. Williston raised them by herself, and I think I told you that Julia had met her at the emergency room at Roper Hospital when I broke my arm. Julia liked her so much that she backed her practice at Alston Station and the clinic was started. Williston's daughters have followed in their parents' footsteps, and both are in medical residency."

Mills sat silently in her rocking chair, stunned by what Cooper had shared with her before saying, "I hope you haven't been having any more nightmares."

"Not since the weekend of my birthday."

They rocked slightly in their chairs before Cooper said, "You told me that you had nightmares. Do you want to discuss them with me?"

She was quiet for a moment. "They're about my father and the day he died."

"Please tell me about them."

"In my dreams, snow is falling, and I'm excited because I associate it with having fun—sledding and snowball fights. In the middle of a snowball fight, an ambulance arrives with flashing red lights. The driver tells Vivien and me that he's come for our father. When we go inside, my father is on the floor and my mother is holding his hand. She doesn't want to let go. I shake my father telling him to get up, but he doesn't. His body is getting colder as I touch him. Then the ambulance takes him away, and I stand frozen in place looking at the red lights—and I hear that sound."

"What sound?"

"The sound of the siren from the ambulance." *I must have heard that dreadful noise ten times a day in New York.* "Then, I wake up."

"Did it snow the day your father died?"

"Yes, the most beautiful, fluffy snow you've ever seen."

"I'm sorry, Mills. How old were you?"

"I was ten and Vivien was twelve."

"That's a terrible age to lose a parent."

Mills felt tears start to well in her eyes and she wiped them with her fingertips. "After he was dressed in his best suit for burial, I went to the attic and searched for a tiny angel that I placed on the Christmas tree each year. She had golden hair, blue eyes, and ruby-colored lips. I put her in my father's suit pocket, and she was buried with him."

Tears rolled down her cheeks and Cooper took her hand in his.

"I'm sorry, Mills," he said, as he wiped her tears with his handkerchief.

CHAPTER 15

Gesture of Kindness

Just after noon on Saturday, Mills was at the stables with Cooper and his neighbors when Dr. Susan Mitchell from the Charleston Children's Hospital arrived at the Heath farm. Cooper introduced Mills to the doctor, who appeared to be in her late thirties and had sandy-brown hair pulled back in a ponytail. She was almost as tall as Cooper and, wearing blue jeans and a barn jacket, she looked at home on the farm.

"Mr. Heath, I hope you don't mind, but I contacted the newsroom at Channel Two and the Metro editor at the *Charleston Dispatch* about today's event. We need media exposure to report the plight these children and their parents face every day."

"That's fine, doctor. I understand that from my work on a scholarship program that my mother founded."

Two vans approached the stables and, when they parked, the drivers helped the children and their parents from the vehicles. A number of children were bald; they had lost their hair from medical treatments. Cooper and his neighbors passed out cowboy hats to all the children, and they took turns riding the horses. *Their laughter is a pleasure to listen to.*

Dr. Mitchell stood beside Mills and said, "Last year was the first time that I helped with this event and it was held at the Caldwell's farm. I met Mr. Heath's wife there."

She was silent as she watched the children, and then she volunteered, "It's a shame about her disappearance. But there's always hope."

Representatives from the newspaper and television station arrived and Mills recognized Lee Mencken from the *Charleston Dispatch*. Dressed in his signature navy suit and a red bow tie, he approached Cooper to shake his hand.

"Mr. Heath, I hope you are well today. I'm here to report on the children's event."

"Thank you, Lee," Cooper responded.

The reporter recognized Mills, saying, "Miss Taylor, nice to see you again."

"Mr. Mencken—you, as well."

"Call me Lee, please."

He smiled as he shook Mills's hand and then joined Dr. Mitchell who stood nearby.

A little girl sat on Ginger's back, the same horse that Mills had ridden, and she was in tears. Her mother took the child off the horse's back and attempted to calm her. Cooper joined the pair and crouched down on one knee speaking to the girl. Mills could not hear what he said, but after a few minutes, the girl was willing to try again. Cooper placed her back on Ginger and held the reins as he led the horse around.

Mills stepped closer. She heard the mother say, "Thank you, Mr. Heath. I think Amy was nervous—you're very kind."

There's no way this man hurt his wife.

After the children were served refreshments, they got back in the vans for the return trip to Charleston. Mills noticed that one of the horses that Mr. Caldwell had brought to the event was not loaded up.

"Cooper, why is Mr. Caldwell leaving a horse behind?"

"You said that Vivien would like to explore while she's here, so I thought she might like to ride horses with us."

"Thank you, I know she'll be thrilled!"

When everyone had departed the Heath farm, Mills joined Cooper in his kitchen to make Marian's crab casserole to take to the opening of the Freedom School Community Center. He instructed her on the mixing of the ingredients.

While the casserole baked in the oven, they went onto the porch to talk. "Dr. Warren and I are going to visit the homes of students who want to participate in the scholarship program next week."

"Good, you'll have to let me know how it goes."

"I will."

Mills rocked back and forth slowly in the rocker. Her head rested against the back of the chair. *I am so relaxed—I could just stay here for the rest of the day.*

When the casserole was ready, Cooper removed the dish from the oven and the aroma of fresh-baked crab filled the room. They both took a small sample. It was delicious.

"Mills, would you like to join me for dinner?"

"I would like to, but I told Jeff that I would attend a party he's having at his house in Charleston."

A frown crossed Cooper's brow. "If you don't feel like driving back to the country tonight, you can stay in my townhouse. Just a minute."

He excused himself briefly and returned with the keys to his home and placed them in her hand. "Please be careful."

"I will. Thank you."

When she arrived at Jeff's townhouse, a couple answered the door, invited her inside, and introduced themselves. "I'd like to let Jeff know I'm here," Mills told them.

"He's in the courtyard." The man pointed to a French door across the room.

Mills walked to the door and looked out into a courtyard behind the townhome. Jeff was speaking on the phone, and a black Labrador was at his side. Opening the door, she went outside. Mills could hear Jeff in a heated discussion. As she approached, he said to the person on the line, "Okay, if you want to sue me, go right ahead and do it. I don't give a damn."

With that, Jeff hung up the phone and threw a cigarette to the ground, squashing it out with his shoe. He stood silently for a moment before he turned to join his guests. As soon as he saw Mills in front of him, his worried countenance transformed into a smile.

"I hope you didn't hear too much of that conversation. The worst part of the real estate business is dealing with unreasonable people—please forgive me. Can I get you something to drink?"

"White wine?"

"Come into my kitchen, young lady," he said, giving her a hug and a kiss. The black Lab rubbed against Jeff's legs. "Mills, this is Brutus. He's a champ in the dove field."

The dog followed them into the home and Jeff poured Mills a glass of wine. The kitchen was becoming crowded with guests. "Always seems like parties take place in the kitchen," Jeff said to Mills.

Madge and Cassie arrived, and Jeff excused himself from Mills to greet them. Music by The Who was playing at an almost unbearable volume on the stereo.

When Jeff rejoined her, he told her to make herself at home, and he continued to mingle with his other guests. Mills walked outside into his courtyard and a man followed her to where she sat. After a few moments of conversation, he stunned her by saying, "I believe you'd be great in bed—want to go upstairs and lock ourselves in a bedroom?"

"No—excuse me," she said, returning to the kitchen.

The party in the kitchen had also become racy. One of the women, who had arrived with Cassie and Madge, removed her top and was shaking her 44DDs, as she called them, in other peoples' faces. *Oh my God!*

Madge moved next to Mills and stared at the topless woman before commenting, "Naomi Peppers. Now I know how she gets so many real estate listings. What a sauce box."

Mills looked around the room for Jeff, but he was not in sight, and like Cooper, she determined that Jeff's crowd was too fast-paced for her. Putting on her coat, she exited onto the cobblestone street and walked to Washington Square. The obelisk monument in the park was illuminated in the moonlight, and she took deep breaths as she circled the memorial. *I should have known better than to come here. I want to go home.*

On the drive back to the Heath farm, Mills listened to a soothing recording of Ella Fitzgerald's music. She couldn't help but think what a nice evening she would have had if she had stayed at home to dine with Cooper. When she parked the car near her cottage, someone stepped out of the shadows in front of her. She nearly screamed, but recognizing the man, she gasped, "Cooper, you–you frightened me."

"I'm sorry, Mills. I saw the car's lights and I wasn't expecting anyone. I thought you were going to stay at my townhouse."

"I was very uncomfortable at Jeff's party and I wanted to come home."

"Did something happen?"

"I was propositioned by a man that I had met ten minutes before, and one woman proudly showed the way she was endowed—without her top . . . I should have known I didn't fit in with Jeff and his friends."

"Why do you say that?"

"I went sailing one afternoon in Charleston Harbor with Jeff and two of his friends. They were inhaling lines of coke on the boat."

"Why didn't you tell me this before now?"

"He's your cousin. I didn't want to say anything."

"Never mind if he's my cousin."

When she gazed up at Cooper, she could see his face in the landscape lighting. His expression was one of anger mixed with disgust. "I don't want you placed in a position like that, ever again."

As he walked her to her cottage, Mills confessed, "I wish I had stayed here and had dinner with you."

She placed the keys to his townhouse in his hand and he responded, "There will be plenty of occasions for us to dine together. I'll give you a ride tomorrow to the opening of the Freedom School."

The Freedom School gleamed with the freshness of renewed youth. A large number of volunteers had assembled to celebrate the restoration of the school and the dedication of the building as a new community center for young people. Mills placed the crab casserole on a picnic table that was already filled with a variety of dishes. A bluegrass band tuned their instruments and the first person who Mills spoke to was Eula Mullinax. She was with her children and she approached Mills and smiled brightly. Her teeth had been repaired and she beamed with new confidence.

"Miss Taylor, I'm so glad to see you today." She paused as she smiled again. "Reverend Smalls's son-in-law is a dentist, and he fixed my teeth. He said I could pay him something when I got my education completed and started work. Reverend Smalls says this is an investment in my future."

"What job are you training for?"

"I'm going to be a nurse's assistant. Maybe I can save up enough money to put myself through college and be a registered nurse one day. With Mr. Heath's help, I have a new life, me and my children—I have hope. Thank you for what you, Dr. Will, and Mr. Heath did for me the last time Lee Roy was at home. I pray he doesn't come back."

"If he returns, don't let him inside, and call the police—and Eula, when you're ready to begin studying for your nursing degree, don't forget there are scholarships available. I know someone who likes to help people achieve their educational goals."

Eula understood what Mills meant, and she smiled. "Thank you, Miss Taylor. I won't forget."

Mr. Caldwell went up the steps of the schoolhouse and thanked the group of volunteers who restored the old building. When he finished, Mr. Camp, the oldest member of the community, spoke to the group. "I've seen many events in my years, some good and some that touched my heart and soul with sadness, but opening this old schoolhouse as a community center is a wonderful thing for our young people. It's a place for gathering in friendship—it's a fresh start for all of us."

He then led the group in a prayer and thanked the volunteers, also noting the financial contribution that had been made by Mr. Caldwell, his son Edmund, and Cooper. When he said "Amen," the bluegrass band began to play and people prepared their plates from the covered dishes.

One of the first songs the band played was a song Mills knew the Rolling Stones had made famous, "Wild Horses," but she had never heard it performed in a bluegrass style. Mills noticed that Cooper listened intently to the song. *I seem to recall "Wild Horses" is about lovers who hurt each other. What is he thinking? He has an odd expression on his face.* He looked into her eyes and asked, "May I have this dance?"

She nodded and he placed his left arm behind her and took her right hand in his. He held her tightly and she felt like she was swept up in rapture as he moved them rhythmically to the music. He was so smooth and strong and she allowed him to take her in his powerful lead.

After their dance, Mills watched as Cooper danced with Williston and then with Susan Caldwell. She had not been to a community dinner like this since she was a child on a visit to her grandmother's in Georgia. As the afternoon went by, Mills was having such a nice time that she didn't realize that it was almost five-thirty and people were gathering their empty dishes to take home.

Approaching Cooper, Mills said, "I've had the best time. I could have danced all afternoon." *I know it's wrong, but I could have danced with you all afternoon.*

"I'm glad you enjoyed yourself. I've had a nice time as well. We're going to give Williston a ride home. She came with the Davenports and they've already departed."

On the trip home to Alston Station, Mills left the window down on the Suburban to inhale the fragrances of newly opened perennials that filled the evening air. When Cooper, Mills, and Williston arrived in town, there was a commotion at the landing; several police cars and an ambulance were parked near the boat ramp.

"I'll see what's happening," Williston told them as she got out of the vehicle.

She showed her credentials to a police officer and they walked to the waterfront together. After several minutes passed, Williston returned and explained that fishermen had found the fourth victim of last Sunday's boating accident and the body was about to be removed.

"Not a pretty sight, having been in the water for a week," Williston commented. "I'll walk the rest of the way to my house—see you both later."

As the corpse was being loaded into an emergency vehicle, the sheet over the body was caught on a tree branch and jerked to the side. The dead woman was exposed, revealing a horribly bloated face and blond hair about the color of Elise Heath's. *Jesus!*

Cooper took a deep breath at the sight of the corpse and Mills said, "Let's go home."

He didn't say a word, but drove Mills back to his farm. They reached his home and she accompanied him inside, stopping in the kitchen to pour him a glass of water. When she turned to give him the drink, he was gone. *Where is he?*

"Cooper?" she called out.

There was no response.

She walked to the front foyer and peered into the study. Cooper was seated at his desk—his back to her—and in his hands was the photo of his wife. He softly said, "'And this maiden, she lived with no other thought than to love and be loved by me'—I'm lying to myself."

She called his name, but he continued to stare at the photo—looks that her grandmother called the thousand-yard stare. She touched him on the shoulder, startling him, and some of the water spilled to the floor.

"I'm sorry, I was deep in thought. Please forgive me."

Cooper bent down and wiped the water off the floor with his handkerchief. Then, taking the glass from Mills, he took several large sips.

"Would you like to talk?" she asked.

"I think I need to be alone for a while."

"If you need me, I'll be next door."

"Thank you, Mills. I'm grateful for your friendship."

As she walked to her cottage, his words resonated in her ears, "I'm lying to myself." *What does he mean?*

———

One Monday morning, Mills placed her first phone call to Lucille Simmons to make an appointment with Cooper concerning Lucille's son's education. The meeting was set for late Wednesday afternoon and Mills could hear the joy in her voice.

When she left her cottage, she found the farm bustling with workers who were beginning the spring planting. As she passed by Cooper and Charles, she heard both men converse in Spanish with the workers. As the men began to disperse into the fields, Cooper joined Mills as she passed by.

"The farm is very busy this morning," she observed.

"Yes, there will be workers here through the planting season. Hopefully, we'll have a successful crop."

"I hope so too."

He cleared his throat. "Thank you for being so understanding last night."

"I can't imagine what you've been through—if you want to talk, I'll be glad to listen."

"Thank you, Mills. Give Dr. Warren my regards."

"I will. I want to remind you that Vivien is going to be here on Friday."

"And your birthday is on Saturday. Don't forget that I'd like to entertain you and your sister over the weekend."

"I can't wait!"

He walked her to her Volkswagen and opened the driver's side door. As she drove away, she could see him in the rearview mirror, watching.

———

Mills met Dr. Warren at Williston's clinic in Alston Station and they decided to ride together in Dr. Warren's car. The first house they visited was on a sandy road a few miles away, and when Mills knocked on the door, an elderly woman opened it.

"You must be Miss Taylor and Dr. Warren. Come inside, please. I'll call my daughter. Mary? Miss Taylor and Dr. Warren are here. Come and talk to them."

After a few moments, her daughter, who Mills thought to be in her late fifties, emerged from the hallway. She smiled brightly as she shook their hands. "Thank you for the visit. I'm Diana's grandmother and she stays with me. Diana's mother—my daughter—works in Philadelphia and visits when she's able. Please sit down."

She motioned for them to sit at her dining table. The aroma of freshly cooked gumbo was in the air and Mills took a seat opposite from Mary and Dr. Warren. An old RCA television was turned on and the volume was unbearably loud.

"Mama, will you turn down that TV while Miss Taylor and Dr. Warren are here?"

She turned back to them and said, "Mama can't hear too well, and she says her hearing aids hurt her, so the TV is usually turned up to where it deafens me. I have to work in another part of the house. I sew for a living."

Mary stopped for a moment before saying, "I hope Diana will qualify for Mr. Heath's scholarship. She is a nice girl, works hard, and don't hang out with troublemakers. Her grades are good and she wants to become a teacher—she would be the first member of our family to go to college. I've been saving for her, but I don't have enough money, and she wants this real bad."

Dr. Warren took papers from her briefcase and handed them to the woman. "This is the criteria for the Heath Scholarship, and I have included information on other programs that Diana can apply for as well. I've looked at Diana's grades and she's doing well."

Mary looked at the paperwork and said, "I am a widow. When my daughter had Diana, the father of the baby took off right before her birth, and we haven't seen him since. He is no longer welcome in Diana's life."

Mills nodded sympathetically and Mary continued.

"I have tried to instill a proper work ethic in Diana by setting an example for her. When I sew, I do the very best job I can for my customers, and she understands this. I want her to get an education and have a career—make something of herself. Diana and I will work on this paperwork and get it back to you. Thank you for your help."

As they continued to meet with families, Mills noticed a similar pattern; women were the heads of households and, often, grandchildren lived with their grandparents.

One home they visited would forever be etched into Mills's mind. She and Dr. Warren were invited inside by the grandmother of Jerome Watson and they sat on a couch beside a coffee table. Mills began to assemble the scholarship paperwork, but noticed that small cockroaches were crawling on the table. Jerome's grandmother spoke, "Dr. Warren, my daughter is at work right now. If you'll leave me the paperwork, I'll see that she gets it. Jerome wants to become a mechanical engineer."

Jerome was one of only eight boys who had expressed an interest in the scholarship, while there were more than thirty girls. When they left the house, Mills had to take a deep breath. *I've never seen such poverty—their living conditions are shocking.* There was no foundation wall around the house, which was built on piers, and Mills could see small children playing behind the house. One of the children pulled down his pants and defecated in the yard. *How pitiful!*

"Dr. Warren, I hope that Jerome will qualify for the scholarship," Mills declared.

"I hope so, as well."

For the next several days, they continued to call on the homes of students. In the afternoons, Mills would visit the school district office to review the applications for students who would attend college in the fall. All of the youths who had applied were qualified for the program, but Mills was surprised that more students weren't involved. Dr. Warren pointed out that many students who could have financially qualified had not worked hard enough on their studies to meet the academic criteria.

"I don't think some young people realize the opportunity being presented to them. A good education starts at home—we have to keep educating them and their parents."

On Wednesday afternoon, Mills went with Cooper to Williston's clinic to donate blood. She made it a special point to eat well before going. When they returned to Cooper's home, there was a 1960s Oldsmobile parked in front of the house. As Cooper pulled in, a middle-aged woman and a teenage boy got out of the Oldsmobile.

"Are you Mr. Heath and Miss Taylor?" the woman asked.

"Yes, ma'am."

"I'm Lucille Simmons and this is my son, Barry. Thank you for seeing us this afternoon. The lady inside invited us in, but I thought we should wait for you out here."

"Come in, Mrs. Simmons, Barry. Miss Taylor and I just finished donating blood."

They entered the house through the front door and Cooper called out to Marian that they were home. Cooper invited Barry and his mother to join him and Mills in his study and they sat down in front of his desk.

Barry wore wire-rimmed glasses on his rounded face. His hair was cut short and he was smartly dressed in khaki dress pants and a short-sleeved shirt with a tie.

"Mr. Heath, Barry wants to attend the University of South Carolina. We have already applied for scholarships, but we haven't received any responses yet. I read in the *Charleston Dispatch* that you run a scholarship program for young people who are willing to work hard and mind their behavior. Barry wants to be a journalist and we investigated the journalism program at Carolina. I work in the cafeteria at his high school and I don't make enough money to send him to college. I read that you help young people in Charleston County, and we're next door in Colleton. I was hoping that you'd make an exception for him."

"Barry, how are your grades?"

"Mr. Heath, I have a 4.0. I've been able to maintain that GPA since I started high school."

"That's outstanding. Why do you want to be a journalist?"

"I want to be an investigative journalist like Bob Woodward."

"I know an investigative reporter who works for the *Charleston Dispatch*."

"Yes, sir, Lee Mencken. I've read his articles about you."

Cooper smiled at the young man. "I'll tell Mr. Mencken about you the next time I see him. He strikes me as the type of person who would be glad to give a fellow journalist some pointers. Are you writing for your school newspaper?"

"Yes, sir, I'm the editor."

"I think that's wonderful. Mrs. Simmons, why don't you have the administrator of his high school send his transcript to Miss Taylor? This is the application for the Heath Scholarship," he told her, as he handed her the paperwork. "Please return this to Miss Taylor."

"Thank you, sir. Mr. Heath, what encouraged you to set up a program like this for young people?"

"My mother, Julia, started the program."

"Is she still involved in the program?"

"No, I'm afraid she passed away a few years ago."

"I'm sorry, Mr. Heath."

"Thank you, Mrs. Simmons, but her illness had debilitated her and her death was deliverance."

"I understand."

"Barry, Miss Taylor and I will look forward to receiving your application and transcript. I've enjoyed meeting both of you, and Mrs. Simmons, I know that you went to some trouble to come over here."

"We appreciate you taking the time to see us and give my son your consideration for the scholarship program. Barry, would you thank Mr. Heath for meeting with us? Wait for me in the car. I'll be there in a few minutes."

Barry shook Cooper's hand, and then excused himself, exiting through the front door. As soon as the door closed, Barry's mother said, "Mr. Heath, it is Barry's dream to be a college graduate and my dream for him. He works hard to keep good grades and he behaves. I'm afraid that some of his peers ridicule him and tell him that he's trying to be something he's not. I fear the sacrifices of men like Dr. King have been lost on some people. I want to see Barry achieve his goals. Anything you can do to help would be appreciated. He'll pass it on when he's in a position to do so."

Cooper and Mills accompanied Mrs. Simmons outside and she waved as she drove away from Cooper's property. Dust and exhaust surrounded the Oldsmobile as she departed.

"That young man is going to be a success. He's very precocious. Mills, as soon as you verify his grades and qualifications, you can call Barry's mother and let her know we'll help him."

That's wonderful!

CHAPTER 16

The Barbadoes Room

Vivien's flight arrived on schedule on Friday afternoon and Mills hugged her as she came off the jetway into the terminal. "God, you look great!" Vivien exclaimed.

"How was the flight?"

"Uneventful, which is fine with me."

"Cooper made arrangements for us to go out to dinner tonight and he has plans for us while you're visiting. I told him you want to explore."

"Cooper is being very gracious."

"He's always like this. Oh, you said that you had two surprises for me."

"I'll share one with you now, and save the other for later."

She held out her left hand in front of Mills. A diamond ring was on her left ring finger, and she enthusiastically announced, "Tim has asked me to marry him!"

Mills hugged her again. "That's wonderful! Have you set a date?"

"We're still talking about it, but I think, next spring."

"I'm so happy for you."

They put down the top on her car and drove around Charleston's downtown. "My goodness, it's beautiful here!"

"Cooper gave me the keys to his townhome. We're almost there."

Within a few moments, Mills had turned onto Tradd Street and she parked her VW near his home. "Cooper wants to meet us at five-thirty at the Mills House Hotel for a cocktail and I told him we'd be there."

"The Mills House. Interesting name, besides being your name."

"The hotel is very elegant. We'd better dress if we're going to be on time."

They went in the townhome and changed their clothes. Mills wore her favorite little black dress and Vivien put on a tea-length deep navy dress; they could have passed as twins as they walked together on Meeting Street.

"Are we going to see Jeff Radcliffe?"

"I don't think so, unless we call him. I went to a party at his home recently, and I was uncomfortable. I'm more conservative than him and his friends."

"Was it a wild party?"

"To me, it was."

"I think with you being the director of the Heath Foundation, you should avoid events like that. You don't want your name associated with outrageous parties and behavior."

"I haven't heard from Jeff since. When I told Cooper about it, he seemed angry."

Vivien remarked that the lobby of the Mills House was one of the most sophisticated and classically designed hotel lobbies that she had ever seen.

"This is lovely. Where are we supposed to meet Cooper?"

"In the Barbadoes Room."

The Barbadoes Room was located in the lobby of the hotel and, as they got closer, the sound of a jazz piano emanated from the room. The French doors of the lounge were opened up to a courtyard that had a large fountain in the center. When they entered the room, Mills immediately noticed Cooper waiting at the bar. She smiled at him, telling Vivien, "There he is."

Cooper came forward to greet them and Vivien said, "I'm thrilled to meet you. Mills has told me so much about you."

"I hope it was all favorable."

"Every word of it."

White wine was the drink of choice, and they went out into the courtyard to sit down.

"Vivien has a surprise."

"What's that?" Cooper asked.

She showed him her diamond ring and told Cooper about her engagement. "I'm very happy for you, Vivien," he said with a smile.

They were silent for a moment before Vivien asked, "Where did the name Barbadoes Room come from?"

"Many of the original settlers who established the permanent English settlement in Charles Town in the 1670s came from Barbados. My ancestors on my mother's side of the family came from Barbados during that time period. They started out as merchants, but later became planters."

"I think that Mills did mention that to me. So, your family has been in the Charleston area for over three hundred years?"

"Yes, Vivien."

"That, in itself, is amazing. Mills said that you left Charleston for several years while you were in the Air Force. What made you come back?"

"My mother was ill, but I always seemed to be drawn back here the years I was away. It's hard to explain, other than to say this is my home."

"Cooper, I'm sorry about your wife. Mills told me about her disappearance."

"I still hope for the best."

"We'll hope with you."

The courtyard and lounge began to get crowded, and Mills noticed that Jeff and his two real estate partners had just entered the Barbadoes Room. They were about to sit at a table when Jeff saw Cooper in the courtyard. All three of them—Jeff, Cassie, and Madge—came outside to speak. Cooper stood up when he realized they were approaching and took Jeff's hand.

"Jeff, Cassandra, Madge, I'd like for you to meet Mills's sister, Vivien. She's visiting for a few days."

Jeff took Vivien's hand in his and kissed it. "I think you two look enough alike to be twins." His intensely handsome face was accentuated by the beautiful smile that he gave Mills and Vivien. "It's a pleasure to meet you, and I hope you have a wonderful experience in Charleston. I know that Cooper will enjoy entertaining you and Mills."

He looked at Cooper again. "I think all the tables are about to be taken. I hope you'll excuse us, but we have some business to discuss."

Cooper replied, "Nice to see you three, enjoy your evening."

Jeff walked into the lounge with Cassandra behind him. Madge snuggled against Cooper and spoke to him softly. "I see what it takes to interest you in a threesome. You have to look like you stepped off the pages of *Vogue* to get your attention."

"Madge, you've said enough."

"Oh, Cooper, don't get testy with me. You know I'm crazy about you." Cooper looked at her with a firm expression on his face.

"I'll be going inside now. Goodnight, Cooper, ladies—have a lovely evening."

When she entered the lounge, Vivien asked Mills, "What was that?"

"Madge Sinclair, that's what."

Cooper cleared his throat, "I hope you like the restaurant that I've selected for dinner."

"I'm sure that your choice will be wonderful," Mills added.

Veneto's on Fulton was a diminutive Italian restaurant with fewer than twenty tables, but it was filled with character and ambiance. The maître d' seated them at the most private table in the establishment. "Mr. Heath, I haven't seen you in months. I'm so glad that you chose to dine with us tonight."

When the waiter came by for a drink order, Cooper ordered wine, "Brunello di Montalcino."

"Excellent choice—the nice, dark one," the waiter replied.

"Vivien, how do you like working in the Capitol building?"

"Most of my work is concentrated in the Senate office building, but I visit the Capitol often." She paused before saying, "Your South Carolina delegation knows you, Cooper."

"Yes, I'm notorious."

"No, they know you from your work in the shipping industry."

The waiter brought their wine and poured a sample for Cooper to taste. After he approved the wine, the waiter poured a glass for each of the Taylor sisters.

"Cooper, I received Barry Simmons's transcript from his high school. Just as he said, he has a 4.0 grade point average. The application has not been returned yet. I hope we can make that young man happy."

Mills then explained to Vivien about Barry Simmons and of their desire to help him through the foundation.

The Italian cuisine was fantastic, and when they finished their meals, Cooper asked, "Would you like for me to walk you back to the townhouse?"

"Yes. We thought we might put on casual clothes and explore town."

"I think you'll be safe. I'll get your coats."

The maître d' thanked Cooper and his guests for dining in the restaurant and then they went outside. Cooper stopped Mills and put his hands on her shoulders, turning her to face him. He attentively fixed the collar of her coat, which was bent under on one side, and then gazed into her eyes. "There, I've got you straightened out."

Continuing to look into her eyes, he said, "Thank you both for the wonderful evening and tomorrow—your birthday—is just a few hours away. Happy birthday! Can you two meet me at the dock tomorrow at eleven?"

"Yes!" Mills responded.

"Good, wear casual clothes and bring a jacket. It will be cool on the water during the morning. And Vivien, you should bring your things from the townhome with you to the farm. I have plans for you both in the evening as well."

She nodded and the group walked toward King Street. Suddenly, a man came out from behind several parked cars and approached them.

"Go back inside the restaurant," Cooper told Mills and Vivien while he stood his ground.

The man's voice sounded like a hiss as he yelled at Cooper. "You bluebeard! What are you doing with these women?"

Cooper calmly responded, "Carl, these two ladies are my guests. This is Miss Taylor, the director of the Heath Foundation, and her sister, Vivien. Would you please excuse us?"

"No, if I ever get the chance, I'm going to bash your brains in."

He walked away in a huff then turned around to say, "You're going to get what's coming to you, Heath."

"Good night, Carl," Cooper calmly said.

"Who was that?" Vivien asked in a shaken voice.

"I'm sorry, Vivien. He's my father-in-law, Carl Monroe. He has fighting in his blood. Once a Marine, always a Marine."

Cooper walked them back to his townhouse before apologizing again for Carl Monroe's outburst. "I have some paperwork I need to finish. If you need me, call the office and ask security to find me. I'll be there for the next couple of hours."

After they changed into casual clothes, Mills and Vivien walked around downtown, admiring the homes in the half-light. "Cooper is charming. I can understand why you like working for him." Vivien paused for a moment before adding, "I think he should be careful. His father-in-law seems to be obsessed with harming him."

In a concerned voice, Mills said, "He knew exactly where to find Cooper." *Is he having him followed?*

There was silence between them before Mills asked, "You said that you had a second surprise. What is it?"

"Mom is dating someone. They met at the Mozart Club, and they've been dining and listening to classical music."

"What's his name?"

"Blake Franklin. He's a retired English professor from George Washington University. They seem to be enjoying themselves."

"Why didn't she tell me?"

"This is all fairly recent. She probably hasn't had the chance."

"I think it's wonderful," Mills responded.

They reached the High Battery on East Bay Street, and as they climbed the steps, Mills asked, "What did you think of Jeff Radcliffe?"

"Like his cousin, he's very handsome, but there's something about him that disturbs me. He knows he's handsome—he does have a mirror after all—but the way he looks at you with those intense sea-colored eyes, it's as though he can see right into your soul."

"I like him, even though he's very different from me."

"Please be careful of him, though. And his friend, Madge—she strikes me as quite ruthless."

CHAPTER 17

The Best of Birthdays

The first words to escape Vivien's mouth when she saw Cooper's farm were, "Mills, it's like the Garden of Eden with all of the magnificent flowers and trees. I can't recall ever seeing a place so bountiful."

Mills parked her car in front of her cottage and proudly said, "This is my home."

Vivien smiled. "In that case, does Cooper need another assistant for his projects?"

Mills had a phone message from Joseph Cook, Mr. van der Wolf's assistant, asking her to call them about a luncheon appointment. When she returned the call, Mills explained that her sister was visiting and she would like to make an appointment for the following week. She wrote the date into her agenda and asked Mr. Cook to thank Mr. van der Wolf.

When they reached the boat dock, Cooper was already on board the *Miss Elise*.

"Happy birthday!" Cooper called out when he saw them.

"Thank you! What are we going to do?"

"Allow me to surprise you. Come on board."

They traveled down river in the motorboat and into the Atlantic Ocean, passing dolphins and even a massive sea turtle. Cooper slowed the boat in front of a lengthy white sand beach and said, "This is where we're going to have lunch."

"I don't think I've ever seen so many seashells before!" Mills exclaimed. Cooper eased himself out of the boat and waded in the surf as he pulled the *Miss Elise* onto the shore and anchored it on the beach.

He helped Mills and Vivien out of the boat and explained, "This property belongs to an old friend of my mother's, Mrs. Salter. She gave us permission to come here today."

"That was very gracious of her," Vivien said.

"This property is the combination of two former plantations; some of the ruins are still standing."

"Are the ruins similar to the old mansion that's on your property?"

"No—only a portion of a foundation remains here."

"Can we walk on the beach?"

"Sure, let's go."

They walked halfway down the beach when Cooper stopped them. "I'd like to show you something."

He motioned for them to enter a lush corridor formed between rows of palmetto trees. When they emerged on the other side, a bay was situated between the beach and the interior land—the beach was connected by a land bridge to the interior. Multitudes of white birds were in the marsh area of the bay. Cooper put his finger to his lips.

"They're a type of egret," he whispered.

Small groups of birds would take off and return to the marsh. They watched for several minutes before Cooper motioned for them to follow him back to the shoreline. As they continued their walk, they noticed the bare skeletons of dead trees protruded from the beach, gray in death, and a stark contrast to the golden beauty of the sand.

"There is a never-ending supply of seashells!" Vivien exclaimed.

Ahead was an inlet where the ocean had cut into the beachfront, causing a sand dune to crop up sharply from the sea. They watched in amazement as a group of dolphins chased baitfish into the inlet. When they cornered their prey, they caught the fish in their mouths, rolled up on the bank, and then descended back into the sea. After some time, the dolphins disappeared.

When they returned to the section of the beach where the *Miss Elise* was anchored, Cooper removed a large picnic basket from the boat and spread a blanket on the beach. He poured wine for the three of them and then proposed a toast to Mills. "Happy birthday, and I wish you many more!"

They clinked their wine glasses together and then opened the picnic basket, which was filled with chicken, salad, and a variety of fruits. Cooper explained that Marian had prepared the basket and had wished her the happiest of birthdays.

The afternoon was spent on the beach talking and enjoying the natural surroundings. Occasionally, a speedboat would pass, rocking on the waves with surf spraying in the air.

By the time they returned to the dock, it was late afternoon. When the engines were shut down, the first noise that they heard was the call of an animal that sounded like a crackling noise.

"What is that?" Vivien asked.

"An owl," Cooper answered.

"The cry is frightening," Vivien said.

"According to local lore, the cry of a screech owl foreshadows danger or death," Cooper added.

"That's scary," Mills said.

"No, it's just an ancient myth handed down from early Gullah people."

Within moments, another owl responded to the first call, and they began to communicate with each other.

"Cooper, thank you for the wonderful afternoon," Mills said.

"See you two at six in my kitchen?"

"Yes, we'll be there."

The sisters walked around the property until dusk, and then made their way to Cooper's house. When they entered through the screen door to the porch, both Jeff and Cooper were in the kitchen. The two men had their backs to them and appeared to be deeply involved in a conversation. Mills and Vivien went back into the courtyard and waited until they heard Jeff's Yukon pull away from the front of the house. Then they knocked on the door.

Cooper smiled and waved them inside. "Dinner will be ready shortly, and Williston will be here any minute."

"Is Jeff going to join us? We saw him when we came up from a walk."

"No, he can't. He has a commitment for the evening, but he said to tell you happy birthday."

Williston knocked on the kitchen door before entering and then declared with enthusiasm, "Mills, happy birthday!"

She held a beautifully wrapped gift. "This is for you, but why don't you wait until after dinner to open it?"

The formal dining table was set with exquisite place settings of china and silverware. "Who set the table?" Vivien inquired.

"I did," Cooper responded.

"Most of the men I know barely know the difference between a fork and a spoon," Vivien laughed.

"My mother insisted that my brother and I know how to do things like this. She wanted us to be cultured."

"I think she succeeded."

They all helped Cooper set the dishes on the buffet, and after a prayer led by Williston, they served their plates with the wonderful meal of tenderloin with mushroom sauce, mashed potatoes, and salad. Mills knew that the meat had to be venison, but she didn't mention it to Vivien. She would surprise her later with that information.

"Cooper, is this china a family heirloom?" Vivien asked.

"No, my father purchased the china and sterling silver in New York as a wedding gift to my mother."

"The silver even has an *H* monogramed into the handles."

"Our family heirlooms vanished during the Civil War."

"How did that happen?" Mills inquired.

"After Savannah, Georgia, surrendered to General Sherman around Christmas 1864, there was concern that he would make his next call on Charleston. My ancestors sent all their finest possessions to the home of an unmarried aunt who lived in Columbia. By early 1865, Charleston was deemed no longer of strategic importance, and a visit by the general would have been purely symbolic. He took his two columns of sixty thousand men from the Georgia coast and marched to Columbia where he annihilated the town, burning a large portion of it to the ground. Our heirlooms became the spoils of war, and the unmarried aunt in my family was burned out of her house and forced to sleep on the grounds of the lunatic asylum. She always said after her experiences with Sherman's men, she needed to take a room there."

"Did you ever recover any of your possessions?"

"Not one item."

"That's terrible."

After dinner, Mills and Vivien offered to clean up the dishes. As a trade, Cooper agreed to play the piano for them while they worked. The first two songs he played were Williston's favorites, two Chopin classics.

The sisters finished their work in the kitchen and came into the living room to listen to Cooper play. After playing a few songs, including music from Broadway musicals, he explained that he had a song for Mills. He proudly pointed out the painting that Mills had given to him for his birthday to Vivien and Williston, and then began a song that he had composed.

"This song is entitled 'Mills's Song.'"

The jazz composition was upbeat, with deep chord combinations and an inspirational melody. Mills sat in awe of his talent and gesture of kindness toward her. When the song was finished, he handed Mills the sheet music, which had written on the front: "To my dear friend, Mills Taylor, on the occasion of her 26th birthday. Cooper Heath."

What a lovely gift. I don't want this day to end. She felt herself blush.

Cooper rose from the piano bench and went into the foyer. He returned with a large box, wrapped in beautiful gift paper. He smiled as he handed it to her.

Carefully opening the package so as to not rip the paper, she gasped with excitement when she saw a pair of magnificent black leather riding boots inside the box. "Cooper, thank you—the boots are beautiful!"

"I'm glad you like them."

She slipped off the shoes she was wearing and put the boots on, tucking her pants inside. The fit was perfect and she walked across the room, enjoying the feel of the leather.

"I love them. How did you know my size?"

He winked at her and explained, "I know your size because I helped you carry in twenty boxes of shoes when you moved into your cottage."

"Open this one too!" Williston said and handed her gift to Mills. Inside was a silk scarf depicting a riding scene.

"Thank you both so much."

"One more to go," Vivien said, as she handed her a present.

"What wonderful surprises!"

Vivien's gift was a handsome leather riding satchel that could be placed on the saddle horn or worn over the rider's shoulder. It was made of black leather, the same as her new boots.

"You three know I like to ride Ginger! Did you plan this?"

Williston smiled at her. "Don't you know? Great minds think alike."

Mills hugged each one of them before Cooper added, "There's one more birthday gift for you." He went into the kitchen, and when he returned, he held a chocolate cake with lighted candles on the top.

They sang "Happy Birthday," and Mills made a wish and blew out the candles.

"Marian made this cake for you; I told her you like chocolate. What was it that my cousin Margaret called the dessert you enjoyed at my uncle's home, 'Death by Chocolate'?"

Mills smiled as she recalled the delicious torte. "I'm speechless. I've never had such a wonderful birthday."

After the cake was cut, Cooper told the sisters to meet him at the stables at eight the following morning and be ready for horseback riding.

That night, while Vivien and Mills talked in the living area of her cottage, Mills asked, "How did you like your steak at dinner?"

"I thought it was delicious."

"That was venison steak."

"You're kidding."

"No, I'm not."

"Well, I did want to try different things." Vivien said raising her eyebrows. "What did you wish for tonight?"

"You mean, when I blew out the candles?"

"Yes."

"I wished that Elise Heath could be found alive and unharmed."

The next morning, when the sisters arrived at the stables to ride, Cooper was there and the horses were saddled. "Good morning, Mills and Vivien. Mills, why don't you ride Ginger and Vivien can ride Blitzer?"

"Blitzer. Is she a calm horse?"

"Yes, despite her name."

"I'm proud of my boots," Mills told Cooper as he helped her mount Ginger. He smiled at her and then helped Vivien into the saddle.

The horses followed Mephisto out of the stables and into the pasture. A group of about ten deer ran across the trail in front of them and disappeared into the forest. "That was a big herd of deer! I believe even I could shoot one," Vivien exclaimed. "It would be like shooting into a crowd."

"They're hard on crops. Even an electric fence won't keep them out."

As they descended into the forest, the trees were leafy green with new growth and rays of sun shone through the boughs, illuminating the forest floor with gentle waves of light. In the near distance, the ruins of the old plantation appeared.

"Oh my God!" Vivien exclaimed.

They dismounted the horses and tied them to the remnants of the old brick entranceway.

"Snakes are out now, so be careful where you walk or put your hands," Cooper warned them.

They slowly explored the grounds, and Vivien said, "This must have been palatial when it was in its prime."

"Yes, I think it was," Cooper responded.

The daffodils in the meadow were past their peak, and while their greenery remained, the golden petals had dropped. The rosebush on the cabin had an abundance of new growth and was about to burst into a multitude of blossoms. At the top of the new growth was a single rose with rich, white petals. Cooper gently bent the limb of the bush down so they could smell the deeply scented bloom.

"We'll walk back this way after we visit the river."

Vivien had gone ahead of Cooper and Mills, and she walked onto the deteriorated dock.

"Vivien, we should stay off the dock," Cooper quickly warned as he moved in her direction.

Before he could reach her, her leg went down between some rotted boards and she lost her balance, falling backward. Within seconds, an occupant of the dock, a large snake, emerged from a missing plank.

"Cooper, Mills, come quick!"

Apparently, the serpent was as frightened of the situation as Vivien, and it slithered into the water and vanished from sight. When they reached her and began to pull her leg from the boards, she slowly asked, "What kind of snake was that?"

"You don't want to know."

"Poisonous?"

"I'm afraid so. Fortunately, it wasn't in the mood for a challenge."

Vivien had calmed down by the time they returned to the cabins, and she insisted that there was no pain in her leg from the accident. Cooper cut the first rose of spring from the bush and handed it to Mills.

"I want you to have this."

"Won't it wilt before we get back to the house?"

"No, it will be fine in the morning air."

After horseback riding, they took the *Miss Elise* to the Bohicket Marina. Cooper had arranged to take the sisters on a sailboat that belonged to Jeff and two other partners. As they passed by Rockville on Bohicket Creek, Mills noticed the Sea Island Yacht Club and remembered meeting Joshua White while exploring her first weekend in town.

As they entered the harbor, Cooper pointed out the *Theodosia*, which was a sleek navy-and-white sailboat with teak accents and clean lines.

"Jeff wants me to buy out his share in the boat partnership, but he knows that I don't purchase any type of property with partners."

Two young men were waiting on the deck of the *Theodosia* as Cooper docked his motorboat.

"Good afternoon!" one of the young men shouted.

Cooper introduced everyone and explained that the young men were from the Abbott family of Charleston and longtime friends of the Heath and Radcliffe families. Both young men were working on their captain's licenses and planned to crew a ship in the Bahamas during the summer.

Once under way on the *Theodosia*, one of the Abbott brothers acted as ship's captain, while Cooper and the other youth performed the duties of crew members.

The afternoon was unusually hot and humid, and both sisters took off their bathing suit cover-ups to bask in the warmth of the sun. As they sailed up the coast, Cooper pointed out the islands Seabrook and Kiawah. Mills noticed that Cooper would occasionally confer with the young man who acted as captain.

The winds were brisk, but by the midafternoon, both of the Abbott brothers had removed their shirts. Cooper was the last to follow suit and, when he removed his polo shirt, he revealed a chiseled chest and sculpted arms. *Oh my—he's gorgeous.*

"Mills, where did the name for this boat come from?" Vivien asked.

"Hmmm?"

Vivien shook her arm. "Mills, look at me. Where did the name for this sailboat come from?"

"I don't know. Cooper's busy right now; I'll ask him later."

"Shall I go tell Cooper to put his shirt back on?"

"Vivien, please don't embarrass me."

"I won't, Mills," Vivien said, smiling at her sister.

When the sailing trip was complete, the *Theodosia* was moored back at the dock and Cooper went inside the Bohicket Marina, leaving the others on board.

"I enjoyed sailing this afternoon," Mills told the brothers.

The boy who had served as captain said, "We had a good time ourselves. Cooper helped me with my sailing technique. He's the greatest."

The other brother added, "Jeff and Cooper won just about every race they competed in. They're sailing legends around Charleston. Cooper helped us get our jobs at the city marina and also the summer job sailing out of Harbour Island in the Bahamas. I can't wait for school to get out."

On the trip back to Cooper's property, Mills asked Cooper, "Where did the name *Theodosia* come from?"

"Theodosia Burr Alston."

"Who was she?"

"Theodosia was the daughter of Aaron Burr and wife of a former South Carolina governor, Joseph Alston. She was lost at sea during the War of 1812. Remember? Alston Station bears the name of the late governor."

"Don't you think it is bad luck to name a ship after someone who was lost at sea?"

"I don't believe I would have chosen that name, but Jeff and his partners must not be bothered by it."

When they returned to Cooper's home, the three of them made a quick dinner and Cooper showed them an itinerary he had drawn up but explained that these were just some suggestions. He planned to be away for several days to visit upstate shipping clients.

The weekend was capped by the viewing of Mills's favorite movie, *The Gods Must Be Crazy*. Cooper said that he had rented the film because he knew she enjoyed it. A Land Rover similar to Cooper's, called the "Anti-Christ," was a focal point of the humor in the film, and for the first time since Mills had known Cooper, she heard him laugh out loud. *He's laughing. I don't think I've really heard him laugh since I've been here.*

After the movie, Mills thanked Cooper for the wonderful weekend. "I don't think I've heard you laugh like you did tonight."

He smiled and responded, "I'm sorry, Mills, but I haven't had a lot to laugh about lately. I'll try to laugh more often."

"I didn't mean to—"

He patted her hand. "No, no, it's okay. Your observation is correct. I've had a wonderful weekend. Thank you for allowing me to entertain you and Vivien."

"Cooper, this was the best birthday I've ever had. Thank you!"

Before they all went to bed, Cooper discussed the itinerary he had made for Mills and Vivien. The trip included two canoe outings, one on the Edisto and the other on the Combahee River, which would conclude at a property owned by Cooper. He explained that a couple named Adams lived at the entrance to his property, and they helped him maintain his property in exchange for hunting privileges. They would drive the sisters upstream on the Combahee for their trip.

The next morning, after a large breakfast at Cooper's house, he asked Mills into his study. Cooper placed a revolver into a satchel and handed it to her. "I want you to take this with you. You can never be sure what you're going to encounter, and I'd much rather know you can defend yourself. And Mills—don't get too far off the waterways."

"Why do you say that?"

"You don't want to disturb someone's still or marijuana field. You never know how they might react." He smiled at her as he spoke. "Can you recognize this property from the Edisto? I don't want you to end up in the Atlantic."

"I think I can."

"You'll pass underneath an old bridge trestle that's no longer in use. It's still marked 'Patterson' on the side for its former owner, then you have about a mile to go."

"Cooper, do you think we could be in danger?"

"No, Mills, you could get robbed at Alston Station while buying a quart of milk. I just prefer that you have protection."

When they returned to the kitchen, Charles and Marian had just arrived for the day. Mills walked up and put her arms around Marian and thanked her for the cake and picnic basket.

"Baby, I hope you had a wonderful birthday," Marian told Mills, kissing her on the forehead. "Miss Vivien, I hope you're having a nice time."

"Oh, yes, ma'am."

Cooper told the sisters, "I'm leaving the Suburban for you to use, and Charles is ready to take you upstream. I'll see you Wednesday."

Charles drove them to Micah's Point and helped them put the red canoe into the tea-hued water. "Miss Mills, be very careful, and we'll see you this afternoon. Let us know when you get home."

"Thank you, Charles."

"My pleasure, Miss Mills. Miss Vivien."

He pushed the canoe off the bank, and within moments, the craft caught the current downstream. Mills sat in the rear of the canoe paddling with a j-stroke to steer.

"What makes the river look like the color of tea?"

"Cooper says the color is caused by the breakdown of leaves, especially cypress leaves." She pointed to a stand of trees along the bank. "Those are cypress trees and the stubs around them are called knees—they stabilize the root systems."

The current was swift with the outgoing tide and they floated by a camp site with rustic cabins. The aroma of cooking fish filled the air and a man waved to them from his place beside a roaring fire.

At a bend in the river, a large alligator sat in the sun on a sand bar. Completely still, he hardly seemed to notice the passing canoe. Two hours into the trip, the sisters stopped for lunch.

The picnic basket was packed with delicious foods, and as they started to eat, Vivien asked, "Does Cooper speak of his wife?"

Mills thought of the nightmares he had suffered, but she had promised to keep that information confidential. "No, not often," she responded.

"She could have been kidnapped and is a prisoner somewhere. What if she has amnesia?"

"Do you remember when May Harley disappeared in high school?" Mills asked.

"Yes, she attended a party at a club in Alexandria."

"And after the party, she left alone and was never seen again. That was ten years ago."

"I suppose it's harder to prosecute a suspect without physical evidence."

"Like a body. I don't believe Cooper had anything to do with Elise's disappearance."

"I believe in him too," Vivien concurred.

By the middle of the afternoon, they had reached the black-beamed trestle marked "Patterson," that crossed the river. Shade covered them as they passed underneath, and Mills's voice echoed when she said, "I think we have a mile to go."

"This trestle is spooky looking," Vivien called out.

"I agree."

At a bend in the river, they noticed a plume of black smoke rising from the waterway as they neared the old mansion ruins. "Something's on fire on Cooper's property!" Mills exclaimed.

They were relieved to see two men at the waterfront, burning the old dock that Vivien had put her leg through. Flames leapt toward the sky from the fire, with the old mansion ruins in the distance.

"It's scary, even in the daytime," Vivien said.

When they reached Cooper's home, they brought the canoe ashore and checked in with Charles and Marian to let them know they had returned. Charles told them that Cooper had ordered the old dock destroyed over safety concerns, and Marian gave both sisters a hug before excusing herself. "Cooper told me to phone him as soon as you returned. He's a worrier."

CHAPTER 18

The Sound of Dixie

*T*he following morning, the sisters left early for their drive to Cooper's property on the Combahee River. Marian had made certain they didn't leave hungry and had arrived at dawn to prepare a generous breakfast of eggs, bacon, grits, and biscuits. The canoe was loaded on Cooper's Suburban and, before departing, Mills phoned Mr. Vern Adams, the caretaker for the Combahee property. As they drove south on the Savannah Highway, Vivien said, "Mills, I think you're part of Cooper's family."

"They're gracious with everyone."

"I think you're different."

"What do you mean?"

"We'll talk about it later."

They crossed numerous waterways before reaching the Combahee River. After taking a drive down a sandy rural lane, they reached the Adams's house, which was near the gate to Cooper's property. Large ferns hung from the front porch, and the two-story farmhouse was situated in a shady area surrounded by live oaks.

Mills parked the Suburban in the driveway, and Mr. Adams and his wife came out of the house; she still had a dishcloth in her hands. They appeared to be in their sixties and Mr. Adams had deep wrinkles in his tanned skin, but a kind face and bright smile. His wife wore her salt-and-pepper hair in a tight bun and a solitary piece of jewelry around her neck, a cross on a silver chain.

"Good morning to you!" Mr. Adams said with enthusiasm. The sisters introduced themselves and Mr. Adams told them he would drive them to

Pinckney Landing whenever they were ready for their canoe trip down the river and back to Cooper's property. A dinner invitation offered by Mrs. Adams was promptly accepted.

Mrs. Adams spoke sparingly, but she offered one piece of advice. "Don't get too close to the trees along the bank of the river. You don't want any company to drop in on you."

"Why don't you follow me to Cooper's cabin and drop off your things?" Mr. Adams said. "When you finish canoeing, you'll be near his place—on our way down there, we're going to pass an old house and outbuildings. Please use caution if you decide to explore them. The last time I mowed the grass, I killed a five-foot water moccasin near the well house."

"We recently had an experience with a snake. We'll be careful."

The drive to Pinckney Landing was rough due to deep ruts from erosion in the back roads near the river. Mr. Adams assisted the sisters with the canoe before giving instructions. "You'll be on the river for about five hours before you see a white farmhouse on the right with a red metal roof. You can't miss it. Once you pass the house, you'll see horse stables and a grove of pecan trees. Cooper's dock will be the next one on the right. Oh—and girls? As you head downstream, you'll find the tide to be falling and the wind quartering from the right rear out of the northwest. Call us when you get to Cooper's!"

He smiled as he handed them the paddles and pushed the canoe away from the bank. They caught the current downstream and found the waterfront to be densely lined with cypress trees, with a quagmire of driftwood deposited along the banks.

In a large expanse of the river was an island with a stand of pine trees in a state of decay; some of the trees were broken white skeletons. A massive pine tree held a bird's nest, and as they passed the island, a bald eagle took wing, sounding like a helicopter producing lift. The eagle flew in the direction of an upcoming marsh area, which held scores of lily pads.

The current was still in the marsh and the sisters navigated between the aquatic plants. A growling noise echoed across the water and the sisters spotted alligators on a mud bank along the shore; the largest of the reptiles cocked his head back and bellowed a roar. They made quick use of their paddles and departed this section of the river. *Let's get out of here!*

By mid-afternoon, the red-roofed farmhouse came into view, and they began to watch for Cooper's dock. His cabin was set on a bluff away from the river and they pulled the canoe ashore. "That was great," Vivien said, bringing up the paddles from the river.

Mills carried the satchel that held the revolver into the cabin and showed it to Vivien. "Cooper wanted us to have protection."

"If a situation arises that we need it, you'll have to fire it. I'm afraid I might shoot myself. I hate to think about the kind of damage one of these can do."

They called Mr. Adams to let him know they had arrived at Cooper's cabin, and after a shower, they went to explore the old house and farm buildings.

The home was in superb condition. All of the windows were protected by hurricane shutters, which were held in place with seashell ornaments.

"Cooper says ornaments that hold hurricane shutters in place are called shutter dogs and are the jewelry of a house. At the Edisto house, the shutter dogs are sets of wrought-iron grapes."

They lifted a wooden latch and gave the front door a slight push. "The house is constructed of cypress, which is a resilient building material."

"How do you know?"

"Cooper told me. Peg construction was used and it's rare to find an example of a nineteenth-century home in such pristine condition."

Vivien nodded her head as Mills informed her about the home. The rooms were small, but the ceilings were at least twelve feet high. Behind the house, the kitchen was situated in a small brick building with a large fireplace in the rear; a short distance from the kitchen was a piece of metal covering an area of the ground. Mills slid the metal sheet back, revealing a deep hole.

"I think this is where the owner stored ice."

"Cooper didn't tell you?" Vivien teased.

"Quiet . . ."

The smokehouse still had its meat hooks and the well house had a rope wrapped around a wheel that held a bucket at the end, which could then be lowered into the well with a hand crank. Dipping gourds were hung around the housing and Mills took one down. She lowered the bucket into the well and allowed it to sink before cranking it back up. They drank from the gourd and found the taste of the water to be slightly metallic.

The sisters secured the doors to the buildings before walking to the Adams's house, where three cats guarded the front porch from their perches along the bannister rail. Unthreatened, they remained in their positions as the sisters rang the doorbell.

"Girls, come in, please!" Mrs. Adams enthusiastically said. "How was the river?"

"We had an excellent time."

"Vern let Cooper know as soon as you got back. I think he was worried about you."

Vivien looked at Mills before saying, "He is very conscientious."

Mrs. Adams led them into her dining room, which was sparsely decorated with one painting, *The Last Supper*, and on the opposite wall, a cross. "Girls, we're going to put dinner on the buffet after we say grace, and then, I want you to enjoy yourselves. We have plenty to eat."

Mr. and Mrs. Adams joined hands with the sisters at the table and Mr. Adams said a prayer over the meal. He also thanked the Lord for the safe return of Mills and Vivien from their trip on the river, Cooper's generosity, and, lastly, for Elise Heath.

Mrs. Adams had prepared a feast for them to dine on and the sisters filled their plates.

"I'm glad to see you girls have a healthy appetite," Mr. Adams said.

"The tenderloin is delicious," Mills declared.

"Cooper told us you like venison."

"Yes, ma'am. We explored the old farmhouse and the outbuildings before we came to dinner. All the buildings are in remarkable condition."

"The property was owned by one family for generations, but about eight years ago, a Mr. Rush Hawkins from upstate New York purchased the land for hunting. He and his friends stayed in the old house when they came down to hunt. One night, they showed up here and said there was a problem at the house and wanted to sleep on our screened porch. I told them they could come inside, but they preferred the porch."

"My goodness," Mills said.

"The next morning, several men in the hunting party left, and a few weeks later, Mr. Hawkins moved a mobile home onto the property as his new hunting base. He later built the cabin near the river. I don't think Mr. Hawkins's wife liked coming here. She said the mosquitoes were one thing, but the gnats were too much for her. When Cooper purchased the property, his cousin, Jeff Radcliffe, brokered the transaction, and Cooper and his friends use the property for hunting."

"Did you find out what the problem was at the old house that night?"

"Mr. Hawkins never spoke of it again, but one of those boys who was hunting with him said that, at night, there was the sound of a woman humming hymns, and they heard a noise like clothes being scrubbed on a washboard. The night they took off, she was humming 'Dixie,' and that was enough for those Yankee boys."

Mills laughed at the story, but Vivien sat wide-eyed across the table from her. "Have you ever heard the humming?" she asked.

"No, I haven't. I think the former mistress of the house was just getting even—one period of Northern occupation was enough for her."

Homemade ice cream was on the menu for dessert and, on their way to the screened porch, the sisters noticed a table set up like a shrine: there were photographs of a young man from childhood to adulthood. Several photos were of the young man in a Marine Corps uniform and with other soldiers. *He looks like Cooper.*

As they sat down on the porch, two whippoorwills cried their nighttime calls. Mr. Adams handed Mills a bowl of ice cream.

"Who is the handsome young man in the photos in the living room?" she asked.

No one spoke for a moment, and then, Mr. Adams said, "That's our son, Jeremy. He died in the Vietnam conflict."

"I'm sorry," Mills said.

There was silence before Mrs. Adams added, "One day, the reason for our loss will be revealed to us by our Heavenly Father. Until that time, I will rely on my faith in Christ to help me overcome the loneliness I feel from his loss." She was quiet for a moment. "He would be a few years older than Cooper if we still had him. It was almost twenty years ago. It seems like a long time, but it really isn't."

One of the whippoorwills had flown to a tree just behind the porch, and its call resonated over the other sounds of the night.

"While we were canoeing, we heard a growling noise made by alligators, but the echo was so strange. The noise sounded like it could have been made beside us or 100 feet away."

"Mating season is starting and what you heard was an alligator bellowing. They make strange noises. I leave them alone, and so far, they've left me alone."

After they finished their ice cream, Mills and Vivien thanked the couple for the wonderful meal and explained that they wished to walk home before dark. Mr. Adams followed them out into the yard. "Girls, don't hesitate to call us if you need us."

"I hope I didn't upset your wife by asking about your son."

"Oh, honey—don't worry about it. His passing is on her mind a lot lately. The anniversary of his—"

He stopped before finishing his sentence. "You girls have a good night, and we'll see you tomorrow."

They arrived at the cabin just before dark, and Mills lit a fire in the fireplace. Mr. Adams had thoughtfully prepared the firewood in advance, so they only had to light it. Vivien opened a bottle of wine, and the sisters sat down in front of the fire to relax.

"Mills, how do you feel about Cooper?"

"I admire him greatly and I love him like a brother."

"I've watched you two together for the last several days, and I've seen the way he looks at you. He gazes into your eyes the way a man looks into the eyes of his lover. I think he's fallen in love with you."

"That's nonsense."

"Mills, every other word out of your mouth pertains to Cooper." She was quiet for a few moments. "Do you remember when I graduated from college and was hired to be on the staff of Senator Leslie?"

"Yes, I do."

"I left that job two years later to accept another position, but I also took a cut in pay. I had to leave my job."

"Why?"

"I'm ashamed to admit this, but I became involved with the chief of staff who happened to be married. He said that he was in an unhappy relationship, but two years later, he was still in his unhappy marriage, and I knew it was time for me to go. After I found the new position, I gave notice and he begged me not to leave. He claimed he was filing for divorce, but he's still married."

"Why didn't you tell me about this?"

"I thought it was too personal."

"I'm your sister."

"Yes, and that's why I'm going to tell you this. Do not get involved with Cooper! I think I called him charming, but a better description would be 'exceptional.' I've never met anyone like him, and I could see you falling in love with him—but he's in trouble, and it could take years to resolve his problems."

"Vivien, no. I think you are reading into his kindness and consideration more than you should."

"I don't think so. He is speaking to you through his music. The song he wrote for you is one of the most beautiful songs I've ever heard, and if he'd penned a score, it would be a love song. I'm sorry to say it, but I only see heartbreak for the two of you if you become lovers."

"Vivien, I don't think Cooper feels that way about me."

"I think he is an honorable man, but he's human—with frailties and desires. Please think about what I've said."

Before returning to Cooper's home on the Edisto the next day, the sisters thanked Mr. and Mrs. Adams for their hospitality and started their drive home. Because Cooper had been so gracious to them, they decided they would prepare dinner for him that evening.

Marian met them at the kitchen door with hugs. "I hope you had a good time."

"Yes, ma'am, we did. I thought we would make dinner for Cooper this evening. He's been so good to us."

"I think that's a splendid idea. Cooper said he'd be home around seven."

"Are there any cookbooks we could look through?"

"Most of Miss Julia's cookbooks are in the attic. I'll get a flashlight, and we'll go take a look."

They went upstairs and Marian opened a door off the upstairs hallway. "I can never find the light switch—oh, yes, here it is." She turned on the light, revealing a room full of storage containers.

"I'm not sure which container they're in, so you might have to go through several to find the books. Do you want me to look with you?"

"Thank you, but we'll be all right."

She handed the sisters the flashlight and went downstairs.

"Let's start over here."

They opened the top of one of the containers and found it to be filled with awards and honors for Cooper and his brother. There were championship trophies in athletic competitions, which included swimming, diving, and football. Another container held awards for excellence in piano. "Look at this medal. Cooper Heath—it's a first place in the junior competition at the Juilliard School of Music."

One container was filled with sailing trophies; some included Jeff's name.

"Look at this gavel. It says: Cooper Heath, Student Body President, Porter-Gaud."

Mills noticed some hatboxes stored on top of a trunk; they contained formal wool chapeaus, and some contained several stylish straw hats. "Wow, I didn't see hats this sophisticated in New York."

"Well, these came from Paris," Vivien added, as she glanced at the labels. Mills opened the lid of a large trunk and inside were old letters, a wooden jewelry box, and what appeared to be daily journals. She looked inside one of the journals. "Years ago, people used such careful penmanship."

"They had more time to write."

"Come on; let's get back to finding the cookbooks."

The next container they opened was filled with cookbooks, and Mills looked through them. "This one looks interesting—Julia Child, *Mastering the Art of French Cooking*, Volume One."

As Mills looked through the cookbook, she saw a recipe that she knew Julia Child was famous for, "Coq au vin."

"We can purchase the items we need at Dawkins's Market, and Cooper will have the wine and cognac."

When they returned to the kitchen, Marian listened with keen interest to their dinner plans and smiled in approval. "I know Cooper will be thrilled by your gesture. I'm about to leave for the day, so I'll leave the kitchen door unlocked. The canoe equipment has been unloaded for you."

The sisters thanked Marian and prepared to drive to the market for the recipe items. There were just a few cars in the parking lot when they arrived, and Mills parked the Suburban near the base of the front steps. Mr. Dawkins greeted them when they came inside, and Mills introduced him to Vivien.

She showed him the recipe they planned to prepare for dinner, and he responded, "Julia Child. I'm sure you'll do a fine job. Fresh cut-up chicken is in the meat section, and let me know if you need help finding anything else."

They made quick work of collecting the required items, and after checking out, they walked toward the end of the porch, discussing their plans. They did not notice that someone had come around the corner of the building until they reached the bottom of the steps.

"Well, now," a nasal voice said.

Mills had heard that voice before. She had heard it on the day she witnessed legal documents for Cooper in his study. The voice belonged to Lee Roy Mullinax.

Lee Roy wore construction boots and dusty blue jeans. His unbuttoned shirt revealed a chest tattoo of a white-tailed deer holding a Confederate flag.

He had an offensive body odor of sweat, urine, and alcohol, and in a low, raspy voice he said, "I didn't know there was two of you. That Mr. Heath he is one lucky man . . . I'd like to have both of you at the same time, myself."

"Get away from us!" Vivien exclaimed.

Mr. Dawkins called out from the porch, "Lee Roy, I believe the police are looking for you. I'm on my way to call them right now!"

"I was just coming inside, and I thought I recognized one of these young ladies."

"Then you can wait for the police in here."

"I don't believe I will," he said, and returned to his car, his tires throwing sand and gravel into the air as he sped from the parking lot.

Mr. Dawkins walked down the steps to where the sisters were standing. "Girls, I'm sorry he bothered you. Please excuse me. I'm going to phone the police."

"Who was that?" Vivien asked.

"That was Lee Roy Mullinax. He's being sought by the police for assaulting his wife, and the people in this community have been helping her family."

Mills and Vivien went to Williston's clinic to advise her that Lee Roy was back in town. She was busy with a patient, but the receptionist said she'd give her the message.

When they returned from the market, the first item on the agenda was to pick out a bottle of wine to use in the recipe. "It says a full-bodied red wine such as Burgundy, Beaujolais, Côtes du Rhône, or Chianti."

They descended the stairwell into the cellar and Vivien was impressed by Cooper's collection. "How are we going to decide what wine to pick?"

"The wines are arranged by country and region."

"Cooper is the most organized man I've ever known."

"Jeff called him anal retentive."

"Sounds like someone's jealous."

Mills concentrated on the wines from France. "I hope I don't pick out a fifty-dollar bottle of wine." She removed one from the bin. "This one says Petrus, 1961, Cru Exceptional, Pomerol Grand Cru." She returned the bottle to the shelf, and took down a 1961 Chateau Margaux. "Something tells me that he's holding these."

After looking in another area of the French section, she picked a Côtes du Rhône, and they commenced dinner preparation. As they were browning the chicken, the phone rang and it was Williston. She had reached Eula and informed her that her estranged husband was in town.

"Did Lee Roy threaten you?"

"No, ma'am, but his language was vulgar."

"I hope the police find him."

After they finished the conversation, Mills returned to the stove to flame the pan with cognac. "I think we should cook like this more often."

"It's having the time to cook like this that's the problem."

When Cooper came home, they surprised him with their dinner preparation. He beamed with a radiant smile. "What's on the menu? It smells wonderful."

"Coq au vin. Julia Child's recipe. We went up to the attic and found the cookbook."

Mills held up the empty wine bottle and confessed, "I had a difficult time choosing the wine to go in the recipe. I saw a 1961 Chateau Margaux and a Petrus, but I thought you might be saving them."

"You did just fine."

Cooper quickly showered and returned in blue jeans and a linen shirt. He stood next to Mills while he sampled the sauce in the pan. *He smells so good—I can smell citrus.*

Over dinner, they discussed his business trip. He explained that a number of Heath Brothers' shipping clients were foreign-based and had operations in the upstate of South Carolina. "I prefer to visit our clients in person. There's no substitute for face-to-face meetings, but you both understand that from your work."

Cooper complimented them on their cooking skills and Mills brought up their trip to the Combahee. "Thank you for arranging for Vivien and me to visit your cabin. Mr. and Mrs. Adams were very kind to us and we had a wonderful time. Why didn't you tell us about the ghost that haunts the old house?"

He lifted an eyebrow. "A ghost haunts the old house?"

"Mr. Adams said the previous owner had an experience with a ghost that hums and washes clothes at night."

He laughed before saying, "Mr. Hawkins disclosed that before we settled on the transaction, but those fellows were probably indulging in bourbon. Anyone who indulges in bourbon can hear voices."

They laughed at his observation and then Mills thought to tell him about their encounter with Lee Roy. "We went to Dawkins's Market to purchase the ingredients for dinner. When we were leaving, we ran into Lee Roy Mullinax, and I'm afraid he recognized me. We went by the clinic to tell Williston and she spoke to Eula."

"Did he say anything to you?"

"Yes, he was vulgar."

"I'd like for you to tell me what he said."

"He insinuated that you were having relations with Vivien and me, and told us he'd like to have us both at the same time."

An expression of anger crossed Cooper's face and then he rose from the table, saying that he was going to open more wine. Mills followed him into the kitchen. "Cooper, should we have done anything different?"

"No, not you, Mills. I should have done something about him when I had the chance."

The final two days of Vivien's visit were spent in a whirlwind of activities. Cooper took them flying along the coast in his airplane and Mills sat in the right seat in the cockpit and listened with headphones to pilots speaking with air traffic controllers. Cooper even gave her instructions on how to fly the airplane.

They passed over rivers and marshes and he pointed out the blackness of the Edisto from the air. He circled the beachfront property of Mrs. Salter, where they had picnicked on Mills's birthday, and she marveled at the beauty of the late afternoon sky, the sunset, a gleaming shade of gold in the west, and the Atlantic Ocean, which turned a dark shade of blue-green with the fading light.

On Friday, Cooper's uncle arranged for the sisters to have private access to the gardens of his friends and neighbors. Several of the gardens were on Church Street, and they passed a home at 94 Church Street, which displayed a historical plaque. The home had belonged to Theodosia Burr Alston and her husband, Joseph. The plaque confirmed what Cooper had already told them; Theodosia had mysteriously vanished at sea.

"I don't understand Jeff naming his sailboat after a person that disappeared—it sounds like he's challenging the fates," Vivien remarked.

The sisters spent hours studying the magnificent garden designs and plants that composed them. A few people had left notes for them about the history of their properties, and the sisters learned that a landscape architect named Loutrel Briggs had designed several gardens.

"I'm inspired to create a beautiful garden around my cottage," Mills said.

"We've seen some fine examples today."

Saturday arrived and Mills hated to see Vivien leave. They had enjoyed a wonderful week together, and before she went down the jetway to the airplane, Vivien gave Mills a big hug and told her to thank Cooper again for his gracious hospitality. She wrapped her arms around Mills and kissed her. "Don't forget what I told you. I don't want you to get hurt."

Mills waved goodbye and watched from the terminal as the airliner took flight.

"I had a wonderful time too," Mills said aloud.

Before she returned to Edisto, she stopped at a plant shop on James Island and made selections of perennials and annuals to set out around her cottage. She filled her car with impatiens, ferns, lantana, and begonias. When Vivien said goodbye to Cooper, Mills told him she had been inspired by the gardens she had seen around Charleston and she wanted to plant flowers around her cottage that afternoon.

To her surprise, the beds around her cottage had been freshly tended with mushroom compost. She set out the plants and then stood back to admire her creation. At dusk, she heard the tractor shut down in the equipment barn and Cooper passed the corridor to her cottage.

"Come and look at my garden," she called to him. "Some very kind person tended the beds with fresh compost. Do you know who it might have been?"

"I know him personally, and he was glad to do it."

"You did it, didn't you?"

"Yes. I thought they could use some enrichment."

He sat down on the steps to her cottage and patted dirt off his pants. "When Vivien and I were in the attic looking for the cookbooks, we found treasures. Why don't you display your awards?"

"I suppose I don't like to look at them. They remind me of Beau."

"I'm sorry."

"What else interested you?"

"There were some old letters and journals in one of the trunks. They were over a hundred years old!"

"The correspondence in the trunk dates to the Civil War period. When we both have time, we'll read them."

"There were several stylish chapeaus. I especially liked the straw hats from Paris."

"Then, let me get a flashlight and we'll go retrieve them from the attic. They belonged to Julia, and I expect she'd like for you to have them."

I'm not sure I should take his mother's possessions.

"Are you sure you want me to take remembrances of your mother?"

"Yes, absolutely." Once they reached the attic, Cooper turned on the light and made his way to the stacks of hatboxes. One by one, they examined the hats, and Mills chose three for herself.

"Julia wore these hats for hunting and fishing, and you can put them to good use. Besides, you'll look lovely in her hats with your riding boots." When they returned downstairs, Cooper's Labrador, Sam, barked with determination. Mills carried the hatboxes to the front porch and listened to the dog. His bark intensified—it was now ferocious. *Sam's near the azalea bushes—must be barking at a wild animal.* When Cooper joined her on the porch, he stopped her from descending the steps any further. "I forgot something. Stay right here."

The floodlights on the front of the house came on and Cooper returned to the porch. She thought it odd that he did not offer to help with the hatboxes, but together they descended the steps and walked toward her cottage.

Suddenly, Cooper charged into the stand of azalea bushes and grabbed a man who hid among the vegetation. He ran the man headfirst into an oak tree and then turned him around for a face-to-face meeting. Mills watched in a state of shock, unable to speak, and the hatboxes fell from her hands to the ground. *Oh dear God!*

Cooper pushed him hard against the tree and then placed a handgun a few inches from his face and cocked the trigger. "Who are you and what are you doing on my property?"

The intruder did not speak. A look of confusion was on his face, and blood spilled from his nose.

"I'll give you to the count of three, and then I'm going to shoot you. One, two—"

"Stop," said the intruder. "I'm a private investigator. Let me show you my ID."

"Where is it?"

"In the front pocket of my coat. In my wallet."

"Turn around and spread your legs. Put your hands against the tree." Cooper patted him down and removed a gun that was in a holster inside his coat. He threw the gun into the bushes and then reached for the man's wallet.

He looked at his credentials. "Private investigator. Who are you working for?"

"That's confidential."

"If I were in your shoes, I think I'd forget about the confidentiality clause."

Cooper rammed his face into the tree again, and the man sank to his knees and begged him to stop. "I was hired by Carl Monroe. He thinks that you're going to make a mistake, and his daughter—whatever's left of her—will be recovered."

"You have exactly five minutes to get off my property. Tell your employer that whoever he hires next had better stay off my land. Don't come back here." The man was shaking with fear and pain, and he stumbled twice to the ground as he ran away from Cooper.

When he had vanished from sight, Cooper turned to Mills. Their eyes locked. She couldn't speak or move, and all she wanted to do was bury her face against Cooper's chest and feel his arms around her.

"Mills, I'm sorry, but he had no business here. You were right all along. There was someone shadowing me."

Cooper put his arm around her for a moment and then retrieved her hatboxes from the ground. "I would like for you to take one of the upstairs bedrooms tonight. I'll wait while you get your things."

She finally found her voice. "How did you know he was here?"

"I saw the movement of his shadow."

Cooper waited in the living room of her cottage while she collected her nightgown and robe, and then escorted her back to his house.

As the entered the screen porch Cooper said, "You're terrified, aren't you?"

"Yes, my hands won't stop shaking."

"Come in the house. I'm going to fix you something to eat."

Cooper made her a sandwich, but she ate very little of her meal. When he walked her to the base of the stairs, Cooper said, "You didn't eat very much."

"I'm too nervous."

"Take some deep breaths—let me see you do it."

She obliged him, and then he took her hand in his. "Are you going to be all right?"

"Yes, I think so."

"Mills, I have a commitment in Charleston in the morning, and I expect I'll be gone when you wake. Please don't be afraid."

She nodded and tried to find the courage not to be so frightened by what she had witnessed. The appearance of the intruder—and Cooper's aggression—had left her shaken. As she lay in bed, a screech owl made a haunting cry outside the home. Mills remembered that Cooper had told her that the nocturnal call of this creature was thought by ancient Low Country residents to foreshadow impending danger or death. She had difficulty falling asleep.

CHAPTER 19

Easter on the River

The next morning, Mills went to church services in West Ashley. Easter was celebrated with Pastor Rose's sermon that concentrated on the resurrection of Christ and the sacrifice that He made for mankind. The pastor brought up the need to be charitable to people in the community who required help and stressed that financial assistance was not the only way to aid individuals in trouble. He encouraged parishioners to get involved in organizations that helped the underprivileged.

When she left the church in West Ashley, dark gray clouds had moved into the area. As she passed over waterways on her drive back to Edisto, the wind-driven waves took on the color of the menacing sky.

Alston Station was busy with the Easter celebration and, near the river, she passed a large group of worshipers from Reverend Smalls's church. A number of young people were dressed in traditional white robes and headdresses to be baptized.

Mills parked her car and was welcomed into the congregation. She watched as Reverend Smalls baptized the youths in the waters of the Edisto, briefly leaning them back into the river. As soon as they were baptized, the young people were wrapped in blankets, and the group united in prayer and singing. The people joined hands as the pastor led them in a final prayer and, when the ceremony was finished, Reverend Smalls invited her to worship in his church.

This was the same church that she had avoided when she first moved to Alston Station because she felt she would not belong. Becoming acquainted with Reverend Smalls, and the kind deeds performed by his congregation for Eula Mullinax and her children, had enlightened her. She realized that her own lack of understanding about people of a different race had caused unfounded concerns.

———

When she got home, rain had not yet arrived, and Mills decided to ride Ginger to the old house ruins to cut roses. She wore her new riding boots, but due to the threat of precipitation, she did not wear one of Julia's hats. She placed the handles of a canvas tote around the saddle horn, mounted the horse, and rode into the pasture. Dark shadows fell underneath the live oaks and Ginger followed the path to the old mansion. The air was heavy with humidity and, in the warmth of the afternoon, tree frogs had emerged, filling the forest with their lively chant.

She tied Ginger to a brick column at the entrance to the ruin and crossed the meadow in the direction of the old slave row. Even from a distance, she could see the abundant blooms on the rosebush. Her breathing hitched at the sight of the rich, white flowers, and she withdrew her garden scissors from the saddlebag in order to cut stems. Leather riding gloves protected her hands from thorns and she filled her tote with roses.

The sound of thunder echoed in the distance and she decided that she should return to the stables. Mills crossed the perimeter of the old house foundation and saw Ginger patiently waiting for her.

As she began the ride home, the wind began to pick up. She tapped Ginger's sides with her heels to quicken the pace. When they reached the path through the forest, Ginger began to bray and cock her head from side to side. Mills had never seen the horse nervous and she patted Ginger on the neck to calm her.

The horse made an attempt to turn around and go back in the direction of the ruin, but Mills used the reins to direct her forward on the path. Suddenly, Ginger reared up, and Mills found herself rolling backward out of the saddle. The tote with the roses fell with her and the stems scattered to the ground.

Too shocked to feel pain from the fall, Mills quickly realized the reason for the horse's behavior. Staring at her from about six feet away was the pitted head of a rattlesnake, whose body was larger than her upper arm. The snake was coiled and moved in an aggressive motion. The deafening rattle of its tail was all she could hear. Her mouth was bone dry and she was too terrified to scream. *God help me!*

There were no sticks or rocks nearby, only the white blossoms of the rosebush. She slowly backed away from the snake on her hands and knees, then picked up a rose stem and hurled it at the snake. The rattler struck at the stem, and Mills rolled away in retreat, gaining her footing in a full running stride away from the snake.

Rain was beginning to fall, and she didn't slow down until she reached the pasture. She rubbed her glove across her cheek and blood smeared on the leather. As she slowed her pace, she took deep breaths and realized she had fallen into a briar patch. A vehicle was coming down into the pasture, and in the rain, she could not tell that it was Cooper's Suburban until he was very close. He stopped the vehicle in front of her and jumped out of the truck, putting his arm around her.

"I saw Ginger running back to the stables in a berserk manner; a riderless horse is frightening. Come and sit down in the truck."

He helped her into the vehicle, removed his handkerchief from his pocket, and placed it against the cuts on her cheek. "Tell me what happened."

Tears formed in her eyes and her voice cracked as she explained. "I went to pick roses, and when Ginger and I started back home she tried to warn me of danger, but I didn't understand. There was a rattlesnake on the pathway, and she became frightened. I struck my shoulder and hip when I fell, and I must have landed in some briars."

"I'll call Williston when we get to the house. You're completely soaked." He took his jacket and put it around her, then turned the Suburban toward home.

As Mills changed into dry clothes, Cooper phoned Williston, and she told him she'd meet them at the clinic. X-rays determined there were no broken bones, and as Williston cleaned the cuts on Mills's face, she teased her in a lighthearted way. "Have you ever heard the phrase, horse sense?"

Mills nodded.

"The next time Ginger tries to tell you something, you should pay attention."

Before they left the clinic, Williston gave Mills some medication for the pain in her hip and shoulder, and wrote a prescription for her.

"See that she rests," Williston told Cooper as they left the clinic. On the way home, Mills said, "Thank you for helping me."

He looked at her for a moment before responding, "You're my very good friend and friends look out for one another."

"Yes, they do," she replied.

They returned to Cooper's home, and he led her into his bedroom and turned down the covers for her to get inside. "I want you to rest while I tend to Ginger. I'll be back as soon as possible."

Cooper took rain gear from his closet and left the room. She heard the front door close as he went to the stables. The windows were raised in his bedroom, and the sound of rain on the metal roof and the wind chimes helped her relax. She could smell Cooper's fresh clean scent on the linens and she inhaled deeply as she fell asleep.

When she woke in the morning, she was still in Cooper's bed and the rain had stopped. The windows were open, which allowed the fragrances of rain and flowers to enter the room. She tried to rise up in the bed, but the pain in her hip and shoulder caused her to relax again. There was an aroma of cooked bacon in the air, and she was determined to make her way to the kitchen. She crawled out of bed and went into Cooper's bathroom to look at herself. She unbuttoned her shirt and there was a bruise on her shoulder; sliding her pants down, Mills discovered the same held true for her hip.

Cooper was in the middle of preparing breakfast when she entered the kitchen, and he smiled when he saw her. "I was going to serve you breakfast in bed. How are you this morning?"

"I'm so stiff. I'm sorry I took your bed last night."

"That's all right. I slept on the couch in the hunting room so I could be near you if you needed me. Come over here and sit down. I'll have your breakfast in just a minute. Mills, why don't you allow me to reschedule your appointments?"

"I have three important appointments this afternoon with companies that I've been calling on about donations to the foundation. Anyway, you gave me time off to spend with Vivien last week and I need to get to work."

"I admire your work ethic," he said with a smile, as he placed a large plate of eggs and bacon on the table in front of her.

"Do you think the scratches on my face will leave a scar?"

"No, they're not deep enough to scar. They'll heal in no time."

"When I fell yesterday, I dropped a tote on the horse path in the forested area. If anyone goes down there today, could you ask them to retrieve it? The roses I cut are scattered along the path."

"I'll make sure it's handled."

Marian and Charles entered the kitchen, and Cooper gave them details about the intruder and the fall that Mills had taken off Ginger's back. They were worried about the intruder, but even more concerned over her well-being. Marian bent down and gave her a gentle hug. "Please be more careful. I don't want my girl to get hurt," she said with a warm smile.

Mills ate every bite of her breakfast, and Cooper gently patted her on the back. "I'm glad to see that your appetite has returned."

Mills's first appointment was with Chicora Petroleum in North Charleston, and she was promptly shown into the president's office upon arrival.

His secretary, Mrs. Sinclair, noticed the Band-Aids on Mills's cheeks. "How did you get hurt, Miss Taylor?"

"I fell off a horse yesterday."

"I think you're brave to get on an animal of that size in the first place."

Within a few moments, the president, Press Reynolds, asked his secretary to send Mills into his office. He shook her hand and studied her face, then pointed to her cheeks. "What's this?"

"Mr. Reynolds, I had an accident while riding yesterday."

"I've been riding since I was seven years old, and when you get bucked off, you just get back on."

"There was a snake on the path, and it frightened my horse."

"Poisonous?"

"Yes, sir, a rattlesnake."

"Oh my!" He was quiet for a moment, and then said, "I admire your persistence in coming to see us so often about the Heath Foundation. I received a clearance from the Board of Directors to make a contribution." He handed her an envelope and continued, "I consider your educational work to be a worthy cause."

She stood up from her chair and held back a grimace of pain as she shook his hand and thanked him.

"Mills, take a bow of credit. If it weren't for your dedication to your program, the contribution would not have happened. Mr. Heath is fortunate to have such an intelligent person working for him. I know his uncle, Ian Heath, and I'm going to bring you up the next time I see him." Removing a manila envelope from his desk drawer, he said, "I made a list of companies and individuals that I thought you should visit. When you call on them, tell them that I gave you their name."

"Thank you."

He handed her the envelope. "I understand that Cooper's mother founded the program. It's a shame she's not here to see your success." He looked at his watch. "I apologize, but I have another appointment in ten minutes. I don't think I can get you another donation for several months, but come by any time that you're in the area."

As she sat down in her Beetle, she looked inside the envelope, and was thrilled by Chicora Petroleum's $10,000 donation.

The other two appointments were successful, and she received donations into the thousands from each one. The president of Black River Asphalt told her, "Some people would have given up months ago, but your determination caused me to make the gift to the foundation."

At her last appointment, Thomas Benet, president of Wescote, the pulpwood giant, offered her a job in his public relations department. Mills explained that she was happy with her present employer—he said that if her situation ever changed, to let him know.

When she arrived home, Mills stopped by the stables and went to Ginger's stall. The horse came to her instantly, and Mills patted her on the head. "It's all right, Ginger. It was my fault."

She said goodnight to the horse and drove to her cottage. There was an arrangement of white roses in a vase by her door, along with the tote that had fallen on the path. A note was not attached, but she knew who to thank.

The lights were off at Cooper's house, and she left him a note with the words, "Great success! I would like to tell you about my day, and the roses are beautiful!"

During the time that she waited to speak with Cooper, she phoned Paul to inquire about Max's health. Paul called her Audrey with his usual dry wit, and then explained that Max had been visited by his sister from New Orleans and that his health had improved after her stay.

"There's a lot to be said for what being with our loved ones can do for us." When Cooper knocked on her French doors, he was dirty from head to toe from working in the fields.

"This has been the best day yet," she said, handing him the donations.

He looked at the gifts and said, "I'm very proud of you." He started to shake her hand, but realized how dirty he was. "So, what's on the agenda for the rest of the week?"

"I have an appointment with Preston Jones at Rutledge House Bank and Trust, and I'm also meeting Piet van der Wolf at the East Bay Club for lunch."

"You'll enjoy that. Piet continues to impress me."

"Thank you for the roses and for retrieving my tote."

"You are most welcome," he said with a smile.

The maître d' led Mills into a cozy dining area that he called the back room at the East Bay Club. Piet rose from his seat as soon as he saw her enter the room and helped her with her chair.

"I trust you had a nice birthday."

"Yes, sir, I did. Cooper arranged for wonderful adventures for my sister and me."

"That doesn't surprise me at all," he said with a smile. "How did you hurt your face?"

"I fell from my horse. She got nervous because there was a snake on the path."

He looked at her with a concerned expression. "Mills, from now on, have your young man ride with you. Riding by yourself is not a good idea."

During the course of the meal, he asked her to recount the past week's adventures, and he listened intently for over two hours. When she told him about the humming ghost at Cooper's Combahee property, he laughed heartily about the northern men running out in the middle of the night because of the sound of Dixie.

She told him about the song that Cooper had written for her, and he replied, "I would love to hear him play it sometime. Did he pen a score?"

"No, sir, he didn't."

"Then, you can pen the score. You can write the lyrics. Decide how the song begins and ends."

Suddenly quiet, he took a sip from his vodka martini. "Mills, I have a birthday present for you, and another donation to the Heath Foundation. You will please me greatly by accepting both gifts."

He took an envelope out of his coat pocket and handed it to her. "You can open it now if you'd like."

She glanced inside the envelope and her mouth dropped open. He laughed at her reaction. "I didn't mean to shock you."

"Mr. van der Wolf, thank you so much for your donation. This is marvelous."

"And for you. I'd like to explain about this gift before I show it to you. I believe you are acquainted with the accident that took my daughter's life."

"Yes, sir."

"She was about to turn twenty-five years, and I had already purchased a gift for her birthday. There is something I want you to understand. When I pass away, my possessions will be auctioned off with the proceeds benefiting two charities, and the bulk of my estate will go to my alma mater, Yale University." He brought out a small box from inside his coat. "I purchased this ring for Lydia from Harry Winston's in New York, and I would like for you to have it." Due to the age of the case, Mills realized this was the original gift box from Harry Winston's, and when he opened it, a magnificent diamond-and-sapphire ring was revealed. A shaft of daylight from a nearby window illuminated the brilliant fire in the stones.

Her voice cracked as she spoke, "Mr. van der Wolf, I can't accept your ring."

"And why not?"

"It just wouldn't be appropriate."

"By whose standards? I want you to understand that you are the first friendly person to come into my life in many years. There is no one else that I would like to have it—but you. If you decide that you do not want it, feel free to sell the ring and donate the proceeds to the Heath Foundation."

Becoming somber at the end of the conversation, he said, "You will make me happy if you accept my gift and wear it." He took the ring from the case and slipped it on the ring finger of her right hand. "See? It fits perfectly. Your left ring finger is still available for the wedding band that you will wear, one day."

Mills waited on the rear steps of Cooper's back porch for him to get home from the fields. She could hear his tractor in the distance and the voices of men who were on the farm to help with planting.

Her second appointment of the day had been successful, and she felt good about the response she was receiving from donors, many of whom she had visited multiple times before they contributed to the Heath Foundation. When she called on Preston Jones at the Rutledge Bank and Trust, he had been unavailable, but his secretary gave Mills an envelope that contained a donation for $5,000. He had written her a note: "Keep up the good work, and stop by when you're downtown."

She continued to wait on the steps until dusk when she heard the tractor shut down and the voices of Cooper and Charles as they came up the path to the house. When they saw Mills waiting on the steps, Charles was the first to greet her. "Miss Mills, I hope you are well this evening?"

"Yes, Charles, and I hope you are."

"Doing well. Have a nice evening," he said, as he passed by.

Cooper sat down beside her on the steps. "I hope your day has not been difficult. How did your appointments go?"

She placed the donation from Rutledge Bank and Trust in his hand, and he smiled with approval. Then she gave him the check from Mr. van der Wolf, and his eyes grew large as he looked at the amount. "Whew! Maybe I should throw you in the briar patch before the start of each work week. Piet has been very generous."

"I have something else to show you, and I don't know what to do about it."

"What's wrong?"

She put her right hand out in front of her and showed him the magnificent ring that Piet had given her for her birthday.

He took her hand in his and closely inspected the ring before saying, "I think Piet is a little too old for you to marry. That's the wrong ring finger anyway."

"Marry? Would you please be serious?"

"Yes, ma'am. Now tell me about the ring."

"Mr. van der Wolf said he purchased the ring for his daughter, Lydia, before her accident, and he said that I am the first friendly person to come into his life in years. If I don't accept it, the ring will be auctioned with his other possessions when he passes away. I was also given the option of selling it and giving the proceeds to the Heath Foundation. Cooper, he said I would make him happy if I kept the ring."

"Do you want the ring?"

"Yes. I was flattered by his gift. I would like to keep it."

"Then, you should. I think it's very beautiful. I didn't know Piet had such good taste."

"Am I embarrassing the foundation by accepting it?"

"Mills, didn't he say that you would make him happy by accepting his gift?"

"Yes."

"Then keep the ring if you want to. This is up to you. You're not embarrassing me—I don't feel that way."

"He refers to you as my young man. I tell him that you're my employer, but he still does this, I think, unconsciously."

He smiled when she said this, and then added, "I hope that you will help me with a couple of things this weekend. Why don't you come inside? I'll make you dinner, and we can talk."

She nodded, and he held the door open for her as they went into his home.

Friday, on her way home from Charleston, Mills stopped by Dawkins's Market for groceries. The work week had been successful, but exhaustive, and she planned to go to bed early that evening. Cooper's cousins Blair and Zack would be visiting for the weekend, and she had been invited to participate in the activities.

After she made her purchase, she started down the steps of the market toward her car. Without warning, she was hit from behind by two boys. Her grocery bag was knocked from her arms, and she fell forward, scratching the palms of her hands and knees in the parking lot. She yelled loudly at the boys, but one of them grabbed her purse, and they disappeared around the corner of an antique store. Mr. Dawkins ran out of the market to help her up. Her eggs were smashed on the ground, and her groceries were scattered under cars in the parking lot.

"Mills, are you all right?"

"Yes, sir, but those boys—they must have been hiding underneath the steps. They stole my purse, and they have my car keys."

He helped her inside the market and then he phoned the sheriff and Cooper's house.

"The police are on the way, and Marian said that either Charles or Cooper would be here in a few minutes."

He offered her a Coke while she waited, and within a few minutes, she saw Cooper pull up in front of the market. He quickly came inside the store with a look of concern on his face. When he saw her, a hint of relief entered his eyes. "A couple of boys knocked Mills down and stole her purse. I've called the sheriff."

Cooper knelt beside her and looked into her eyes. "Are you all right?"

She showed him her abrasions and said, "I just skinned my hands and knees."

He pulled her to her feet. "I'd like for you to ride with me, and we'll try to find those boys."

As they began their drive around the village, Mills described the boys and their attire. They were both wearing yellow caps and black shirts. Cooper drove down a sandy lane that led away from Alston Station and stopped in front of two abandoned cotton warehouses. He spotted the boys behind some rusted-out machinery in the high grass between the buildings.

"Mills, are you up to walking to the main road and flagging down the deputy when he arrives in town?"

"Yes, I think so."

"Good. I'm going to retrieve your purse."

"Cooper, wait for the sheriff. Please."

"No. I can't let them get away." He parked the Suburban and went around the side of the building. As soon as the boys saw him coming, they split up, and Cooper chased the thief who ran with her handbag. Mills saw Cooper follow him into a forested area and she walked briskly to the intersection.

She flagged down the deputy as he came into town and explained about Cooper's pursuit of the thief. Mills got in the police car and they drove to the old warehouses, parking beside the Suburban. Cooper was coming out of the forest with the boy who had run with her purse and he was less than gentle with him.

When the deputy joined Cooper in restraining the youth, the boy began to scream obscenities at the top of his voice and attempted to kick the two men.

He was handcuffed, read his Miranda rights, and seated in the rear of the patrol car, but vulgarities continued to spew from his mouth.

Cooper was sweating from the chase, and he handed Mills her purse and asked her to see what was missing. He gave the deputy a description of the other boy and informed him that Miss Taylor would be pressing charges.

After taking the report, the deputy told them that an officer would be in touch with them and he drove away with the boy. "What's missing from your purse?"

"My money, makeup, and a small wooden charm that my mother gave me. My car keys are here."

They scoured the area where the boys had been hiding, but to no avail.

"Are you sure I should press charges against that boy? He looks so young."

"He may be young, but he has already resorted to assault and theft. Hopefully, some help can be provided to him and he has the courage to change."

When they returned to the market, Mr. Dawkins had replaced the damaged grocery items. Cooper lifted the bags for her and followed her home. He asked her to come inside his house so he could clean her abrasions.

When they entered the house, Cooper's cousins Blair and Zack had arrived, along with Cooper's Aunt Jennifer, and the boys immediately grabbed her hands and led her to a chair in the kitchen. "Miss Taylor, we want to take care of you," Blair told her. They watched intently as Cooper cleaned the scrapes on Mills's hands and knees with medication from the first-aid kit.

As Cooper put a Band-Aid on her knee, he asked, "Did anything ever happen like this back home — while you lived in New York?"

"Just once — a taxi came close to hitting me."

He looked worried until she said, "This is my home now."

"Boys — please take Miss Taylor's grocery items from the Suburban to her cottage."

"Yes sir," Blair responded. "We'll take care of it."

That afternoon, after Cooper's aunt returned to Charleston, the boys helped him make dinner and they refused to allow Mills to lift anything. She learned that the boys had been to New York with their grandmother to see Broadway plays and explore the city while their parents had gone to France on an antique-buying trip. The boys explained they had been forced to attend plays and wear suits and ties for afternoon tea. When Mills told them that attending Broadway plays was one of her favorite pastimes, the boys changed their attitude.

Cooper pulled Mills aside in the kitchen, "I think if you endorsed algebra homework for Blair, he would begin to like that too." They played cards after dinner, and the boys joined Cooper when he walked Mills to her cottage.

"Mills will join us for fishing tomorrow if she's up to it."

"That's great!" Zack exclaimed.

"Until tomorrow then," Cooper said as he took Zack by the hand and rubbed his other hand through Blair's hair.

"Good night," Mills said from the steps leading to her cottage.

The following day, the boys had success while fishing on new fly rods that Cooper had purchased for them. During the afternoon, Mills watched as Cooper played football with the boys on the green. They continued to pamper her for the remainder of the day, and after dinner and another round of cards, they joined Cooper to walk her home.

On Sunday afternoon, along with Jeff, Anne and her husband David came to shoot clays. A friend of Cooper's from the Air Force, James Burton, was also in attendance. When Cooper introduced Mills to him, he explained that James was also a friend of her former employer, Harry Foster, and they had met at the Air Force Academy.

Jeff gave her a hug on her sore shoulder and the pressure caused her to wince in pain.

"Have I lost my sex appeal?"

"Yes."

He laughed at her response and kissed her on the cheek.

Their eyes locked. "I fell off Ginger last Sunday after a snake encounter."

He was holding her hands, and when he turned her palms up, he noticed the abrasions inflicted during the robbery at the market. His eyes were intently focused on hers. "Snakes can be a problem, but is that how you hurt your hands?"

"No, two teenage boys knocked me down at the market on Friday and took my purse. Cooper was able to retrieve most of my possessions."

"Including your money?"

"No, they took it."

Jeff looked at Cooper, his faced tense with anger. "I bet those boys are from the group of individuals that you bend over backward to help." Before Cooper could respond, Jeff turned her palms down and noticed the ring that

Piet van der Wolf had given her. He looked at Cooper and then at her. "Where did you get this ring? It's exquisite."

"Piet van der Wolf gave it to me for my birthday. He purchased it for his daughter before she passed away."

In a challenge to Cooper, Jeff said, "You're not going to allow her to keep this, are you?"

"She makes her own decisions."

"Does she really? We'll talk about this later." He turned back to Mills and asked, "Are both hoodlums in jail?"

"No, Cooper could only catch one of the boys."

"I'm sorry that happened to you, but you'll never find the other crook. The boy who was arrested will not divulge the identity of his buddy."

"Jeff, Cooper, I thought we were going to shoot this afternoon," Anne interceded. She looked at Mills and said, "You've probably noticed that Jeff and Cooper enjoy verbal sparring."

Mills was wearing one of Julia's hunting hats, and Anne smiled at her. "I think I remember that hat."

"Cooper let me have three hats from the attic."

"You look as lovely in that hat as Julia did," Anne said.

Mills thanked her for her compliment and then helped Cooper operate the sporting clays stations. Jeff shot first and was flawless, and then the others took turns.

When James Burton shot, Mills noticed what a magnificent shotgun he owned. The side plate on his firearm was engraved with a hunting scene; neither Cooper nor any of his relatives possessed a gun with such handsome scrollwork. It was a shame that he was not as capable a marksman as his firearm suggested. Missing most of the clays, he made excuses as to why he missed his shots.

Jeff came to where Mills was stationed and said, "You have been given the honor of meeting the glorious aviator, James Burton. He'll be glad to tell you what an excellent pilot he is, but I suspect his flying skills are comparable to his shooting skills." Jeff laughed. "I'm not sure why Cooper ever liked him. It's a wonder that his back isn't permanently bent from carrying his flight kit in one hand and showing off his money with the other—that arrogant ass."

"Cooper seems to like him."

"Well, I can't figure out Cooper sometimes—by the way, Aunt Julia's hat looks lovely on you."

"Thank you," she said with a smile.

Cooper was the last to shoot, and when he finished, the group began to gather their gear and firearms to return to the house. Cooper was engaged in a conversation with James—Mills walked up behind them without their being aware of her presence. She heard James ask Cooper, "Mills is beautiful; how is she?"

Cooper replied, "What do you mean?"

"A girl that pretty, living out here alone with you."

"James, I think I understand your insinuation and I'll be nice about this. Miss Taylor is the director of the Heath Foundation and we have a professional relationship. I'd appreciate you showing her the respect she deserves." Cooper's voice became cold. "I think you have forgotten with whom you're speaking."

James Burton—what a sorry big mouth—I'm thankful I have Cooper as my friend and defender.

"Oh, come on, Ace, we're buddies from way back."

"James, I'll try to overlook this conversation. Let's go back to the house."

Cocktails and hors d'oeuvres were served on the porch. After drinking bourbon, James began to tell pilot stories about Cooper. "After Cooper and I left the Air Force, we both took jobs with the now-defunct Northern International Airlines. Cooper was copilot on a 727 from New York bound for Kansas City. It was his leg, and when the crew was executing landing procedures, it came to their attention that several ultralights were operating near the airport. One of those ultralights got in the wake turbulence of the 727 and plummeted a couple of thousand feet to the ground. For weeks, everyone teased Cooper about his confirmed kill and nicknamed him 'Ace.'"

"That's a marvelous story, James," Jeff told him.

"I think so too—I need more bourbon," James said, as he rose to fix another drink.

By late afternoon, all the guests had departed, and Mills sat with Cooper on the screened porch. "Thank you for taking up for me this afternoon with James."

"You heard him?"

"Yes."

"Mills, I'm sorry. I don't understand his coarse behavior. He wasn't always like this."

They were quiet for a moment and Mills asked, "What do you wish for?"

"What do you mean?"

"I mean, what do you want to accomplish in life that you haven't already done?"

He pondered her question, and then said, "What I want most in life is a wife who loves me and a family, my own children. I'm not sure if this is going to happen for me. What about you?"

"I want a husband who loves me."

"I hope your dream comes true."

Mills looked intently into Cooper's eyes. "Didn't Elise love you?"

"She did, for most of our marriage, but I think she ceased to love me. And I don't know why."

They were quiet until Mills said, "Thank you for including me in your plans during the weekend."

"You're welcome." He smiled and said, "I'll walk you to your cottage. I'm leaving for New Jersey in the morning and I'll be away for the next two weeks. We're beginning an expansion of the Newark terminal and my uncle wants me to supervise the project. I'll stay in touch while I'm away."

CHAPTER 20

Night Fires

Half asleep, Mills could not be certain if she was dreaming the knocking noise. As she began to wake, the sound became louder, and her name was called. "Mills, please come to the door. Let me in, honey!"

She rose from the bed and realized that Cooper was calling to her with alarm in his voice. When she opened the door, he took her in his arms and held her. "Thank God, you're all right. Where are your coat and slippers?"

Still half asleep, Mills responded, "My coat and slippers are in the closet. Cooper, what's wrong?"

"There's been an intruder on the property and the boathouse is on fire. I was so worried about you. The screen is off the window on your screened porch." He went to her closet and returned with her coat and slippers. Cooper helped her put on her coat and then buttoned it while she slid on her shoes. "Charles is on his way over here and the fire department should be here soon. Thank God for Sam; his barking woke me."

As she stepped onto her porch, the smell of smoke filled the air. Flames from the boathouse were leaping into the night sky. Cooper took her hand and led her to his house. "We're almost there," he said.

Once inside, they went into the hunting room, and Cooper removed the revolver that she had taken on the canoeing trips from the gun cabinet. "I'm going to the boathouse and this is for your self-defense."

"You're not leaving me here. I'm going with you."

He took her hand and together they went out the door into the rear courtyard. "I called the fire department as soon as I saw the flames. They told me there were two other calls that came in right before mine."

As they watched, gas cans inside the boathouse ignited in succession and burning debris exploded into the surrounding darkness. Charles arrived a few minutes later. He stared at the burning structure and then turned to Cooper. "Who would do this?" he asked.

"I have a good idea. A screen was off the window on Mills's cottage."

In the light from the flames, Mills saw a deep frown on Charles's face. *Someone was after me!*

The boathouse was engulfed in flames; due to the gas cans stored inside, they could do nothing to fight the fire. The roof began to collapse, but because of light winds, the fire was not spreading into the woods.

"Charles, I'm going to call Williston," Cooper said.

Mills tightly held his hand as they returned to his house. He let the phone ring several times at her residence before he replaced the receiver. "No answer. I'm going to check on her."

"I'm coming with you," Mills said emphatically.

"Let's go."

As they neared Alston Station, red lights from emergency vehicles glowed against the blackness of night, and Mills shuddered at the sight. "Oh my God, they're at Williston's clinic," Mills said, her voice unsteady with fear.

Cooper parked as close to the building as possible and said, "Mills, listen to me. I'm going to lock the doors. I want you to stay in the truck."

She nodded and watched apprehensively as Cooper walked toward a group of firefighters who sprayed the side of the building with water. Mills was relieved when she saw Williston step out of the group of men and put her arms around Cooper. *Thank God she's all right.*

The fire was extinguished and, in the beams of light provided by the firefighters, the damage appeared to be superficial to the exterior wall of the building. Several minutes passed before Cooper returned to the Suburban with Williston. The first rays of light were illuminating the eastern sky, and Mills could see the weariness in Williston's eyes as she got in the vehicle.

"We're going to drive to Eula's. I have a bad feeling about this," she said. When they arrived, all the lights were extinguished inside Eula's trailer. Cooper went to the door and knocked repeatedly, but there was no answer.

Mills had the window rolled down on the truck, and she could hear a faint voice calling for help.

She got out of the truck and started in the direction of the noise. "Cooper ... Williston, someone's calling for help."

Cooper grabbed her hand and stepped in front of her. "Mills, I want you to stay behind me." He held the revolver as he rounded the corner of the structure. A horrific scene awaited them; Eula's oldest son, Billy, was tied to a tree, and his mother lay motionless on the ground. Her burned schoolbooks rested near her.

As soon as he saw Williston, Billy cried pathetically, "Dr. Will, please help her. She hasn't moved in a long time."

As Cooper untied the boy from the tree, Williston examined Eula. The look on her face confirmed Mills's worst fears. Released from the bonds, Billy ran to his mother and took her in his arms. "She's so cold. We got to do something to get her warm."

Williston put her arms around Billy and said, "Son, I'm so sorry, but your mother has passed away."

A look of sheer terror gripped Billy, and he said, hysterically, "That bastard Lee Roy showed up here last night. He got inside our house and drug mama outside. I tried to fight him, but he smacked me and tied me to the tree." He sobbed as he continued, "Lee Roy asked me how I liked it, each time he hit her."

Williston took Billy's hand and led him away from her body. "Do you know where your sisters are?"

"I hope they're inside," he responded.

Mills looked with fear at Eula's body; her teeth had been knocked out, destroying her beautiful dental work. She had been so proud of her smile, and Mills quivered as she stared at the body. *That bastard Lee Roy.*

A strong arm went around Mills's shoulder and she looked up into Cooper's eyes. "Let's join Williston," he said as he led her away.

After the sheriff and emergency personnel concluded their interviews with Williston, Eula's children went with her to the clinic. In the daylight, their earlier observations were confirmed; there was only superficial fire damage to the clinic. Reverend Smalls and members of his church were there when they arrived. He explained that a third fire had been set at the Freedom School, but a local man returning from a trip noticed the flames on his way home. The fire department reached the building before it became engulfed.

When Cooper and Mills returned home, there were two vehicles parked outside the house. One car was from the sheriff's department and the other was an unmarked police vehicle driven by Lieutenant Barnes.

As soon as he saw Cooper and Mills arrive, Lieutenant Barnes walked to the Suburban and opened the truck door for Mills. "Cooper, I see you had some excitement out here last night."

"That's one way to put it. I didn't realize you took an interest in arson cases, Lieutenant."

"I asked to be involved. Why would a man of your stature get involved with a guy like Lee Roy?"

"Members of the community tried to help his wife and family improve their lives. I was one of them."

"I see." He turned and faced Mills. "Miss Taylor, I should have said good morning to you."

"Lieutenant Barnes, good morning."

Barnes refocused his attention on Cooper. "It appears that Lee Roy went on a rampage last night. You two are very fortunate . . . I'd like to show you something."

He led them to Mills's cottage and pushed aside an azalea bush; hidden underneath was a gas can and ropes. "Now, no one touch the gas can. I know this will frighten you, Miss Taylor, but there's a possibility that Lee Roy has plans for you."

The flowers she had planted in front of her cottage had been trampled, and as Cooper had discovered, a screen had been removed from a window that had been raised a few inches.

"He was interrupted before he completed his plans. Cooper, did you come and get Miss Taylor when you realized the boathouse was on fire?"

"Yes, my dog was barking and he woke me."

"There's a good reason dogs are called man's best friend. You were probably just in time to spare her from Lee Roy's plans. Nefarious individual, isn't he?"

The detective stepped out from the bushes. "I found out that your phone call was the third to come in for help. When there are two fire trucks and crews in the immediate area that means you wouldn't get assistance. I wonder if he was smart enough to plan it that way—probably not. I'm sorry about Mrs. Mullinax and her family. I wish she'd put that guy in jail a long time ago."

The three of them walked down to the smoldering ruins of the boathouse. The *Miss Elise* was on the boat lift covered with ashes, but otherwise unharmed.

Lieutenant Barnes looked at Cooper with a wry grin. "It looks like the boat named after your wife is unscathed. I keep hoping for the best on your wife, don't you?"

"Yes, Lieutenant, I do."

His grin faded and his face darkened. "I don't think you and Miss Taylor should stay out here until Lee Roy is apprehended. There's no way to know what else he might do."

After the policeman departed, Cooper put his hand on Mills's shoulder. "For once I agree with Lieutenant Barnes. I think you should move into town."

When they went inside Cooper's home, Marian was waiting for them in the kitchen. She hugged Mills and then Cooper. "Thank the Lord that wicked man didn't hurt either of you." Sam was at her feet and she patted the dog on the head. She looked into Cooper's eyes and said, "Charles told me that Sam woke you. Thank God. Labradors are the souls of good people who have returned to earth."

While Marian fixed breakfast, Cooper called Ian, his uncle, from the study. Charles had already informed Ian of the intruder and arson, and Ian asked to speak with Mills.

When she put the receiver to her ear, Ian said, "You're family to us, dear, and I want you to be safe. If you prefer, you can move into the upstairs of my home while Cooper is away."

After a brief discussion, Mills agreed to move into Cooper's townhome until Lee Roy was arrested and Ian told her he would check on her each day. They ate breakfast and then Cooper helped Mills pack her possessions. They were both stunned from the morning's events and they quietly loaded the Suburban.

When they finished packing, Mills spoke with Marian while Cooper prepared for his trip to Newark. He called out to Mills from the front of the house and she found him in his study. He was impeccably dressed in a deep navy business suit and was holding the photo of his wife, he said, "Mills, I have my failures in life—I fear Elise felt neglected by me." He placed Elise's photo on his desk and looked at Mills. Their eyes locked. "But—I will not fail you."

When they reached his townhome, Cooper helped her unpack her possessions. He then closed the door and put his arms around Mills. "Are you going to be all right here?"

She looked into his eyes and nodded. Mills felt at ease in his arms and she would have remained in his embrace, but after a moment, he put his hands on her shoulders and they faced one another. "I want you to call Ian if you need anything. He's just a few blocks away."

"Thank you, Cooper." *I wish you didn't have to go.*

He paused for a moment. "Mills, this construction project has been planned for months and my uncle believes that my presence is necessary. Please forgive me for leaving right now."

"I understand."

Cooper took a deep breath before saying, "I'll fly down for Eula's funeral."

He started to walk toward the door but turned around. "He was going to hurt you to get revenge on me for helping his wife. Thank God, he didn't touch you."

Mills could tell he was as nervous as she was and she took his hand in hers. "I'll be fine here. Don't worry."

"I can't help but worry."

"I'm going to be very busy with Dr. Warren. You know we have graduations coming up soon and we're finishing up the scholarship applications."

She walked with him to the door and he held both her hands before stepping outside. Fine lines of worry had emerged on his face, and as he went down the steps, he looked back at her as she stood in the open doorway.

Exhausted, Mills went upstairs and collapsed on a bed.

The next morning, the Edisto fires and the murder of Eula Mullinax were on the front page of the *Charleston Dispatch*. The article, written by Lee Mencken, went into complete detail of the circumstances surrounding her death. An arrest warrant was issued for Lee Roy, but his whereabouts were unknown.

Marian gave Mills's phone number to her friends as they called about her. All of Cooper's relatives contacted her and Joshua White called her from Washington, DC. Britton asked her to dinner that evening, and the last phone call of the morning came from Cooper, whose voice was still filled with anxiety.

They had been apart for one day, but already she missed him. She was beginning to realize that her feelings for him went much deeper than brotherly love and this frightened her. *I feel like I've cared about him for years.*

A Charleston County police officer phoned to let her know that the young man who stole her purse had been identified as Anthony Barre. He would not disclose the name of the other boy involved in the robbery, and as this was his first offense, he had been released into the custody of his grandmother. Mills also learned that a condition of his release was that Anthony was required to perform community service work and that Reverend Smalls would be his mentor.

Mills phoned her mother and Vivien to let them know of the events. They were both worried, but grateful to Cooper. When her mother asked her if she wanted to come home to Virginia, Mills responded, "Charleston is my home now."

That evening, she dined with Britton in a small outdoor café in Ansonborough. His shyness around her was diminishing and when they completed their meal, he showed her around the neighborhood and his home. He lived in a historical single house with a shade garden filled with an abundance of ferns, azaleas, and camellias. In awe of the beauty of his garden, she was impressed to discover that Britton had done the design work himself.

As they sat in a quiet corner of his yard, she glanced at the local newspaper that lay in the wrought-iron chair beside her. The front page article was about the shipwreck of the SS *Central America* and the treasure hunters who were recovering a fortune in gold off the Carolina coast.

Mills picked up the paper and asked, "Britton, how did the ship sink?"

"She went down in a hurricane in September 1857. The ship was laden with thirteen to fifteen tons of gold that had been prospected during the California gold rush."

Mills thought back to one of the conversations that had come up on Cooper's porch after shooting sporting clays. The discussion had centered on the rights of the salvage team versus the government and insurance companies.

"Britton, have you ever been in a hurricane?"

"The worst hurricanes to strike South Carolina during my lifetime were Hurricane Hazel in 1954 and Gracie in 1959. I was very young at the time, and my parents drove inland to Columbia. It's best to get out of the path of the storm and deal with the damage later. Entire communities have been wiped out by the storm surge that comes ashore during a hurricane. My advice is to evacuate inland if a hurricane is in the forecast."

Twice a day, Cooper called to check on Mills. The anxiety in his voice had lessened and he told Mills that he would like to accompany her to Eula's funeral. Williston had informed him that Eula's sister, who lived in Tennessee, would be taking Eula's children back with her after the service.

The funeral was held at the South Edisto All Saint's A.M.E. Church on Sunday afternoon. Reverend Smalls delivered a beautiful eulogy for Eula, pointing out how she had struggled against poverty and a difficult marriage to set goals for herself and her children. As he paid tribute to her, Mills looked at her children, who were in tears, except for her son, Billy.

Cooper sat beside Mills and stared straight ahead during the service. After the singing of "Amazing Grace," Reverend Smalls asked the gathering to join him for graveside services. Outside the church, Billy walked to where Cooper and Mills stood. He held his shoulders high, and when he reached Cooper, he said, "Mr. Heath, I want to thank you for what you did for our family. You gave my mother hope for the first time in her life." He started to walk away, but then turned back to face Cooper. "I intend to repay you for what you did for us."

After the graveside services, Eula's sister, Mae Reeves, approached Cooper and said, "Mr. Heath, thank you for what you did for Eula and her children. The last several months, she was the happiest I ever heard her. I ain't got no extra bedrooms for her children, but we're going to make do. Lee Roy's mean as a snake, and he's gonna rot in hell."

"Mrs. Reeves, I'd like to help you and the children." Cooper took an envelope from his inside his coat and tried to give it to her.

"Oh no, sir. My husband won't allow me to take money from you. You were generous to help with the funeral expenses. Mr. Heath, you are the most Christian gentleman I've ever met. Eula thought so too. God bless you."

She turned and walked away with Eula's children, along with three of her own.

Cooper returned the envelope to the inside of his coat, and Mills asked, "Did you pay for Eula's funeral?"

"Most of it . . . the church paid for some of the expenses." He looked toward Eula's gravesite and said, "I wanted her to succeed. She was going to better her life and that of her children."

Before they returned to Charleston, Cooper drove them to his Edisto property. Winds came off the river and the scent of charred wood lingered in the air. Cooper's dog ran in their direction when he realized they were home. They both petted the Lab, and as they passed her cottage, Mills noticed that the trampled flowers in front of her home had been replaced. "Cooper, you had my flowerbeds tended to."

He nodded in acknowledgment and asked her to come into the study with him. Behind a painting between the bookshelves was a wall safe. He opened it and placed the envelope he had attempted to give to Eula's sister inside.

"Are there any secret passageways in the house?"

"Not that I know of." Cooper smiled. "Is there anything you need from your cottage?"

"No . . . if I go inside, I might not want to leave."

That evening Cooper departed for Newark. He reminded Mills before he took her to his townhome that Susan Caldwell's wedding was the following Saturday night.

"Will you dance with me at the reception?" she asked.

"Yes, put my name down on your dance card."

Thankfully, the work week was very busy, and Mills kept her mind off Eula and Lee Roy. She spent much of the time at the school district office working with Dr. Warren on the scholarships.

One evening during a walk, she passed by Jeff's townhome on Chalmers Street. She was puzzled by his behavior. Jeff called her immediately after the fire to check on her, but then had not contacted her again.

After her walk, she returned to Cooper's townhome and tried on the dress she planned to wear to Susan Caldwell's wedding. Mills stood before the mirror and admired the sapphire-blue gown. The dress matched the ring that Piet van der Wolf had given her for her birthday.

Cooper arrived in Charleston on Saturday morning and spent the afternoon working on the farm. He asked Mills to meet him outside the chapel before the wedding so they could sit together.

When she arrived, Cooper was waiting for her in the parking lot, and he beamed with a bright smile as soon as he saw her.

He opened her car door and said, "You are lovely this evening."

She smiled warmly at him, and he kissed her on the cheek. Together, they walked to the building and were seated on the bride's side of the sanctuary. Mills studied the magnificent decor of the chapel, which Cooper explained had been created by slave artisans. Warmly illuminated with candles, shadows danced off the chapel's ceiling, while a pianist serenaded the wedding guests with music.

The organ sounded the wedding march and the guests stood while Susan walked down the aisle on her father's arm. She wore an exquisite wedding gown and it was as though a romantic spell had been cast over the chapel and all in attendance.

After the nuptials were complete, the wedding party remained at the church for photographs and Mills went outside with Cooper.

He walked her to her car and said, "I'll follow you to the River Bend Country Club." The country club was a short distance from the chapel and, when they arrived, a jazz ensemble was playing. The club was richly decorated for the reception and a hostess served them champagne as they entered the ballroom.

"I need to talk to you," Cooper said, as he led her onto the patio. The nighttime temperature was pleasant and several sets of French doors were open to the outside.

The volume of the jazz music softened as they moved to the far end of the terrace, and Cooper looked into her eyes. "I spoke with Williston before I came to the wedding. The sheriff's department called to let her know that Lee Roy Mullinax is no longer a threat."

She gasped with relief, "Did the police arrest him?"

"No, he attempted to rob a liquor store in Greenville this afternoon and the owner shot him dead . . . Mills, why don't you move back to your cottage? I don't have to go back to New Jersey for the time being and I could use your help at the farm."

She didn't have to think about his request for long. "Yes, I'd like to come back tonight and I can get my possessions from the townhouse later. I'll be glad to help you on the farm."

The jazz ensemble began to play a George Gershwin song, and Cooper said, "You promised to put my name on your dance card."

She smiled and nodded. He put one arm behind her back and led with his right hand. He was holding her tightly and she breathed in his clean, fresh scent. They were alone together on the terrace and they danced through a set of romantic songs. When the music stopped, Cooper touched her face and pushed her hair from her neck. Warmth surged through her body as he held her, but several couples came onto the patio and he released her.

"Could I get you another glass of champagne?"

She breathed in the evening air and said, "Yes, that would be nice."

By the time he returned with her wine, the terrace had become crowded with guests. "Williston is in the ballroom, and she'd like to see you."

As soon as Williston saw her, she hugged Mills and said, "I've heard from Eula's sister, Mrs. Reeves, and she said her children are getting along well. Lee Roy is finished hurting people." She looked up at Cooper and said, "I feel like dancing. Will you take a turn with me?"

"It would be my pleasure," he said, leading her onto the ballroom floor.

Cooper followed Mills home after the reception and they talked on the screened porch of his home until the early morning hours. He explained that he could use her help with farm management tasks. "Charles is overwhelmed with work since we increased planting, and if you could assist with deliveries and getting payroll checks to the workers, it would help tremendously."

"I'll be glad to help you, but please don't get angry if I make mistakes."

"I won't. We all make mistakes. Oh, and Mills—there will be additional compensation for your work."

She nodded.

Before they said good night for the evening, Cooper explained that a contractor would be at the property during the next week to begin rebuilding the boathouse. "Fritz Zimmermann. A brilliant fellow; he can speak seven languages and has lived all over the world. He renovated the kitchen several years ago. I think you'll enjoy meeting him."

On Sunday afternoon, Cooper and Mills sat down together in his study to go over a list of farm tasks. In the following days, she found herself immersed in her job of handling farm business in the morning and then working on foundation business for the remainder of the day.

One afternoon that week, Mills arrived at her cottage just before dark. There was a man with Cooper; he had thick, white hair and wore khaki work clothes. They were coming up the lane from the river and Cooper called to her to join them. The man was Fritz Zimmermann, the building contractor that Cooper had told her would reconstruct the boathouse. He was slightly shorter than she was, and when introduced, he bowed to her.

"Miss Taylor, Mr. Heath has told me that you are the director of the Heath Foundation and I congratulate you on your work." He spoke with a German accent. Turning to Cooper, he said, "Mr. Heath, it will be good to return to the Edisto and I look forward to working with you again. Until tomorrow, then."

He put a khaki bush hat on his crest of white hair and raised his chin to look into Mills's eyes. "I look forward to seeing you again, Miss Taylor."

After Fritz departed, they sat in the courtyard to discuss the business of the farm and the foundation. She was exhausted and, as she excused herself for the evening, Cooper told her that Fritz and his workers would be at the farm very early the following morning to begin work.

The crew arrived at the farm about the same time that Mills began her farm tasks. She heard Fritz speak Spanish to his workers when she passed by them and he tipped his hat to her. As his crew dispersed, he said, "Good morning, Miss Taylor, I promise we were not talking about you. Do you speak Spanish?"

"No, sir, I don't. Cooper said that you could speak seven languages."

"Yes, ma'am. My family was in the engineering business and we lived in South America, Africa, and, later, Southeast Asia."

One of the workers approached Fritz and they got into a lengthy conversation in Spanish. Mills excused herself and went to get the Land Rover out of the equipment barn. She drove into the fields to inform Charles that she had accepted the delivery of fertilizer he ordered. When she returned, she parked the Land Rover in front of her cottage and started to go inside to prepare for business meetings in Charleston. Fritz was on the way to his truck and he stopped to look at the Land Rover.

"My goodness, my family had a Land Rover when we lived in South America. I had my first date in one of these. My family considered motor cars to be for work purposes and I don't think my date's mother approved of our rustic lifestyle. It was our first rendezvous and our last. Oh well."

He ran his hand across the engine hood and said, "Miss Taylor, the fact that you are here lets me know that you do not believe that Mr. Heath had anything to do with his wife's disappearance. She is the most beautiful woman I have ever known and there is no possibility that he would have hurt her. If I thought he had, I would not be here myself."

Fritz excused himself and returned to work. *Why did he bring up Elise Heath?*

The heat and humidity of summer had descended on the Low Country, and after Mills performed her farm tasks, she had to take a shower before dressing for other business work. The construction on the boathouse was proceeding and, most evenings when she got home, Cooper and Fritz would be engaged in conversation on the screened porch. She was always invited to join them for refreshments and one afternoon their discussion was on land conservation and preservation of endangered animals.

"Miss Taylor, did you know that there used to be a native parakeet in South Carolina, but it is now extinct? When Cooper's ancestors arrived here from Barbados, there were thousands of them." Fritz paused as he took a sip of beer and then said, "Mr. Heath, do you still hunt?"

"Yes, I do."

"My wife attempts a garden each year, but the deer consume most of what she plants."

"Yes, even with an electric fence, they're hard on crops. I have a depredation permit and I donate the venison to the local churches."

Fritz glanced at his watch. "Mr. Heath, Miss Taylor. I must be going. My wife will be angry with me if I am not home soon."

He tipped his bush hat to them and exited out the screen door.

After his departure, Mills asked, "Why does Fritz address us by our surnames?"

"Years ago, I asked him to call me Cooper, but he said he was uncomfortable with the lack of propriety."

Two days later, while Mills was accepting a delivery of horse feed, she heard the crack of two rifle shots. Within a few moments, Cooper came down the driveway in an old Ford pickup used for farm work. In the truck bed were two deer that Cooper shot while they grazed in his fields. He waved to her and then went into the stables, returning with ice to put around the animals. "I'm going to take the deer to a member of Reverend Smalls's church for butchering. I'll be back in about thirty minutes."

She stood beside the truck and looked inside the cab. A rifle was propped against the passenger side of the vehicle. While she enjoyed shooting sporting clays, she was respectful of the power of a firearm.

That evening, Mills sat on her screened porch and listened to the sounds of the night. The humidity of the day had diminished with nightfall and whippoorwills made their piercing calls into the quietness of the evening.

As she came in for the night, her mother phoned from Virginia; she had read in *The New York Times* that Mozart's Requiem would be performed at the upcoming Spoleto Festival. Mills was aware that her mother was a fan of Mozart, an interest shared by her new friend, Blake. The two wanted to attend the performance and visit Mills.

The next day, when Mills told Cooper about her mother's plan, he told her he would like to help entertain them. "Your mother can use my townhouse, and I hope you'll allow me to take everyone to dinner while they're in Charleston."

"Cooper, why don't you join us for the performance?"

He thought for a moment before saying, "Thank you, I would like to join you."

In late May, the thirteenth annual Spoleto Festival began in Charleston, and Mills's mother Rebecca and her friend Blake arrived in town for the festivities. Mills met them at Cooper's townhome and she found Blake to be pleasant and attentive to her mother. They planned to stay in Charleston for a few days before continuing to St. Augustine where Blake had family.

The evening of the Mozart performance, Cooper met Mills, her mother, and Blake at the Barbadoes Room for cocktails at five-thirty. Mills introduced everyone as they sat down in the courtyard. Rebecca was trim, with the same dark, wavy hair as her daughter. She was a beautiful, middle-aged woman. Blake was of medium height with sandy blonde hair that had a touch of gray. Mills thought he had a nice smile that caused laugh lines all the way to his eyes.

"I am pleased to meet you, and thank you for being so kind to my daughter," she told Cooper.

"I'm sure you already know that Mills is an exceptional young lady, and I'm proud to have her as the director of the Heath Foundation. She works very hard."

The jazz pianist in the Barbadoes Room began to play, which prompted

Rebecca to say, "Cooper—Mills and Vivien have told me what a wonderful pianist you are. I hope to hear you play while I'm here."

"If you're not too tired after the Mozart performance, we can stop by my uncle's home and I'll play for you. He's out of town, so we won't be disturbing him."

Cooper took them to the East Bay Club for dinner. During their meal, Blake explained, "Mozart's Requiem was his last composition and he died before he was able to finish it. The artist's wife, Constanze, had the work completed by another composer, or composers, so that she could be paid for the music and ensure that Mozart received credit for the composition. While he was composing the arrangement, he told his wife that he was writing the Requiem for himself."

As they departed the club, Mills pulled Cooper aside. "I didn't know you belonged to the East Bay Club."

"Yes, but these days, I only come here for business meetings."

After the concert, they walked to Ian's home on Church Street. Rain had fallen while they attended the Mozart performance and a light mist hung in the air. Cooper opened the front door to his uncle's home and offered refreshments to his guests before inviting them into the living room where Ian's baby grand piano was situated.

The first composition he performed was Beethoven's "Für Elise," or "For Elise." He explained that his wife was fond of the song.

Mills listened to his interpretation of this hauntingly beautiful composition. *He's like a poet reading fine prose.*

Cooper next played two Mozart sonatas that she had never heard and he performed them flawlessly from memory.

"I have one last song that I would like to play, and I wrote it for a dear friend on the occasion of her twenty-sixth birthday. This is 'Mills's Song.'"

Cooper played the composition with such conviction that he appeared exhausted at the completion of the arrangement. He seemed oblivious to the applause that went through the room after his performance.

"That was brilliant," Blake told him. "Really, Cooper, I've never heard better."

After his recital, the group sat in the living room and talked. "Cooper, we had a wonderful evening," Rebecca said.

"I'm glad that you did," he responded.

"When Mills first expressed her interest in working for you, I was worried about the circumstances surrounding your wife's disappearance. Mills holds you in high regard and I think my original concerns were unfounded. I pray for your wife every day."

Cooper, still on the piano bench, said simply, "Thank you, Mrs. Taylor."

Before midnight, Cooper walked them to his townhouse and the group thanked him again for the wonderful evening. After her mother and Blake went inside, Mills said, "I didn't realize you knew those Mozart compositions."

"I started practicing them after you told me your mother was a Mozart fan, just in case I had the opportunity to play for her. I wanted to perform selections that would please her."

"You did. Thank you, Cooper."

Before bed, Mills and her mother sat together in the courtyard behind Cooper's townhome. Rebecca looked around the dimly lit courtyard before she said, "Cooper has a lovely garden here."

"Wait until you see his Edisto garden."

Her mother was quiet for a moment before she said, "Mills, I'm afraid that Cooper has a tortured heart. The first song he played, 'For Elise,' was a tribute to his wife, but the song he wrote for you was played with conviction; he poured his soul into your song. Mills, you've always exercised good judgment. Please continue to do so."

Her mother didn't say anything else, but kissed Mills on her forehead and said good night. Mills realized that her mother's last statement was a gentle warning in regard to affairs of the heart.

Before Rebecca and Blake departed for St. Augustine, Mills gave the two a tour of Cooper's Edisto property and introduced them to Charles and Marian. Rebecca told her that this was as close to paradise as she could imagine. When they stood at the construction site of the new boathouse, Rebecca took Mills's hand and said, "Thank God, Cooper was at home that night to protect you."

Graduation day for the students involved in the Heath Scholarship program arrived and Mills had the printer create parchment certificates that the students could frame in regard to their scholarships.

Cooper was to be a commencement speaker at both high schools where students were being awarded the scholarship, and when they arrived at Prospect High School, Dr. Warren was extremely flustered. She greeted Cooper and Mills with, "I'm trying to head off a disaster. Mr. Heath, I know you are an accomplished pianist and the lady who was going to play tonight has been involved in an accident. Would you consider playing for us?"

"I'll be glad to help you. Where's the sheet music?"

"It's on the piano."

Cooper played "Pomp and Circumstance," when the seniors marched into the auditorium and Mills performed her usual duty as page turner. When he reached a stopping point, he smiled and whispered in her ear, "Thank you, let's get to the stage."

Cooper gave an inspirational speech to the students, challenging them to excel at their chosen endeavors and then complimented the students who had received the Heath Scholarship. As the students were awarded their diplomas, Mills handed out certificates to the scholarship winners. Before the exercises were over, Cooper tugged at Mills's elbow and motioned for her to return to the piano.

As the students filed out, Cooper enthusiastically played the exit music of "Pomp and Circumstance," and when the commencement exercises were complete, Cooper and Mills joined the school administrators in conversation. As they said good night and started to leave, the voice of a woman called to Cooper from a darkened row in the auditorium.

"Mr. Heath, I know you won't recognize me, but I wanted to speak to you."

Cooper walked over to the woman, who appeared to be in her late thirties. As he approached, she rose from her seat and joined him in the aisle. "I enjoyed your performance of 'Pomp and Circumstance' this evening."

"Thank you, Miss—?"

"It's Mrs. Brown. Years ago, your mother and Dr. Devereux helped me during a desperate time of my life . . . I'm sorry, but I saw in the paper when your mother passed away. I went to her grave and placed flowers on it."

Cooper introduced Mills to her and admitted that he could not recall making her acquaintance.

"You were just about twelve or thirteen, and you were usually with your brother at Dr. Devereux's clinic. I wasn't quite eighteen, but I was in trouble and your mother turned my life around." Tears welled up in her eyes and she said, "My oldest son graduated tonight. I'm so proud of him."

"Did your son apply for the Heath Scholarship?"

"No, sir. My husband and I earn too much for my son to qualify, not that I'm complaining. My husband owns an engineering firm, and I'm a registered nurse. I chose a profession where I could help people, a repayment of sorts, I suppose."

"Mrs. Brown, thank you for speaking to me tonight."

"Please tell Dr. Devereux that Elaine Miller Brown said hello. I know she still operates her clinic."

"I will, and congratulations to your son."

As Cooper drove Mills home that evening, Mills asked, "How did your mother and Williston help Elaine Brown?"

"Julia believed that women should have safe medical services available to them when they were in trouble. Williston felt the same way."

Mills realized what he meant, and she was stunned after hearing Cooper's admission. *Abortions?*

"I trust your discretion; otherwise, it would have forever been left a secret."

"Cooper, Elaine Brown became a registered nurse. That was Eula's goal."

The next evening, the graduation ceremony at Washington High went smoothly and, after the awards, Cooper invited Mills to fly to Charlotte, North Carolina, at the end of the week to pick up Marian's great-granddaughters for a visit.

CHAPTER 21

Yellow Jackets

One morning, while Mills worked on orders for the farm, Cooper came into the study and said, "I'd like to show you something."

"What is it?"

"It's a surprise."

"Before we go, will you help me find a mistake in the farm checkbook?" Cooper sat down behind the desk and reviewed the financial inputs. "Here it is. I'll correct it for you." He changed the numbers inside the book. "Are you ready to go?"

"You did those calculations in your head."

"I was just fortunate to catch it."

He led her out of the house and they walked in the direction of the old barn. This was the site of Lee Roy's incendiary spray painting, months before. Cooper opened the barn's double doors and they stepped inside. Old farm equipment was stored at the rear of the building and bales of hay were stacked to the sides.

Cooper pointed to an open space between the bales of hay. In the straw, almost hidden from view, were a mother cat and two kittens. The mother's coat was a mix of gray and white, while the kittens were almost entirely white. "I thought you might want a kitten. They're too little to leave their mother now, but I'll feed her and see if she sticks around. She can always assist in keeping the mouse population down," he said, as he lightly petted the mother cat.

"They're adorable. Yes, I'd like to have a kitten."

Friday morning, Cooper and Mills flew his Baron from the John's Island Airport to Charlotte to pick up Marian's great-granddaughters. Mills flew the airplane from the right seat of the cockpit until they neared Charlotte. Then

Cooper took over the controls and Mills watched as he followed an airliner on the approach to Runway 36 Right. She noticed that he landed the airplane farther down the runway than where the airliner touched down.

He taxied the plane to a building where numerous airplanes were tied down, and after he shut the engines down, they went inside. Cooper spotted Charles's granddaughters and their mother; the girls ran to him and jumped into his arms.

"Thank you for coming to get us. We've been excited about flying again." Cooper introduced Mills to Charles's daughter, Ramona, and his granddaughters, Elizabeth and Jane. "Please call us Lizzie and Janie," they said, as they shook Mills's hand.

Cooper spoke with Ramona for several minutes before he loaded their suitcases in the Baron and they taxied for takeoff.

About one hour later, they landed at the John's Island Airport and drove to Cooper's farm. Marian and Charles came outside and hugged the girls. "I think you two have grown four inches since I last saw you," Charles said.

"Not that much, Granddaddy."

Marian had prepared a lunch of fresh fruits and vegetables from the garden. She told them as they sat down at the kitchen table, "I tasted the most delicious tomato. I think we're going to have a wonderful harvest."

"Let's hope so," Cooper responded.

After lunch, Cooper told Mills she could have the afternoon off to swim with the girls in the pool. Mills went to her cottage and changed into her bathing suit and met the girls at the pool. Lizzie and Janie were accomplished swimmers and also talented on the diving board.

"Where did you learn to swim like that?"

"We swim on the Charlotte YMCA team, and we dive as well."

"You're both very talented."

"Thank you, Miss Taylor."

The girls swam races against one another and then practiced their dives. In between dives, Mills clapped for them as they emerged from the water.

"What's your favorite subject in school?"

"I think my favorite class is science," Lizzie responded.

"Mine is algebra," Janie added.

"What do you want to be when you grow up?"

"We want to be like Dr. Will and her daughters and become doctors."

"Wow! Those are wonderful goals!"

"Yes, ma'am."

"That's outstanding. After we finish swimming, would you like to walk to the barn? A mother cat and her kittens are living there." Excitedly, the girls responded, "Oh, yes. We'd love to."

Mills changed into a pair of navy shorts and a blouse while the girls went to Cooper's house to put on dry clothes. They met in the front courtyard and started their walk to the barn. The afternoon heat and humidity were oppressive, and Mills was damp with beads of sweat that rolled down her chest and back.

They passed Cooper and Charles near the stable mending a fence, and both men waved as they passed by.

"How was your swim?"

"We had a wonderful time. Thank you for letting us swim," Lizzie replied.

"I'm going to show the girls the kittens. See you shortly," Mills said. When they reached the barn, Mills opened the double doors and found the air inside the building to be cooler than the outside. She was glad to get out of the sun.

They walked to the rear of the barn where the mother cat and kittens lived. Food and water were set out for the mother.

"They're adorable," Lizzie quietly said. The mother cat left her kittens and jumped up on a bale of hay. The girls started to pet her and Janie exclaimed, "She holds herself with pride; she looks like a queen. Does she have a name, Miss Taylor?"

"Girls, please call me Mills, and we haven't named them yet."

"I think she should be named Cleopatra, Queen of Egypt," Janie exclaimed. "We'll call her Cleo for short."

"What shall we name her kittens?"

"Oh, we better figure out if they're girls or boys," Janie said.

Mills lifted the kittens one at a time and Cleo watched her carefully while she held them.

"I believe they're both females," Mills observed.

"I think the cat that is almost white should be called Carmen, short for Lady Carmen Ashley, and the other kitten should be named Maya, after my favorite poet, Maya Angelou," Lizzie declared.

"Do you think Cooper would let us take the kittens home with us when we leave later this summer?" Janie asked.

"I don't see why not, but you'll have to ask your parents."

"We will. We're going to call them tonight."

"Mills, could we go back to Cooper's and get a drink of water? It's awfully hot."

"Sure, girls. Let's go."

They said goodbye to Cleo and her kittens, and Mills noticed a side door that was several steps closer than the double doors. The girls followed her, and she turned the doorknob, but found the door was stuck at the base. She gave the door a firm push and it opened. Mills held the barn door open as the girls exited in front of her.

Suddenly, she felt a sharp, intense pain on her right calf followed by another on her left thigh, and another. She looked down at her legs, and bees—or yellow jackets—were swarming out from the base of the barn door around her, dozens on her legs already. Mills yelled, "Run, girls!" as she was stung again and again.

The girls turned and, seeing the swarm, ran from the barn, Janie screaming, "Granddaddy, Cooper, come quick. Hurry!"

Mills swatted in vain at the yellow jackets that continued to swarm around her and sting her unmercifully, each sting like the blow of a hammer. She felt her legs give out under her; the intense heat of the afternoon sun and the pain in her limbs was too much to bear.

Then Cooper was there and he swiftly gathered her in his arms and ran away from the barn. Mills could barely speak and she was unable to lift her arms around his neck.

"Mills, I'm sorry, but the yellow jackets are inside your blouse," Cooper said anxiously.

He ripped her shirt open and began to pull them off her skin; several were removed from inside her bra. Mills tried to move, but couldn't, and the intense light of the afternoon sun went black.

The yellow jackets were still stinging her, or so she thought, as she sat up straight and found herself on an examination table. Confused and frightened, she started to swat at the insects again, but strong hands took hold of her own. Cooper's arms went around her and she listened to his soothing voice telling her to calm down.

"Shhh now, you're at Williston's clinic. You gave me a terrible fright," Cooper said.

"Are Janie and Lizzie all right?" were her first words.

"Neither girl was stung," Cooper told her. "Only you."

Williston came to the examination table. "Mills, are you allergic to insect stings?" she inquired.

"No, ma'am, not in the past," she replied, "but I've never been stung that many times either."

"Are you having trouble breathing?"

"No, ma'am."

"Your blood pressure is fine." She then addressed Cooper. "I think we'd better watch her for a couple of hours here at the clinic, and you should keep an eye on her tonight."

Williston paused as she handed Mills some medication and a cup of water. "This is Benadryl to reduce swelling and Ativan for anxiety."

After she took the medicine, Williston told Mills to lie back on the examination table. Cooper put ice on her stings.

Tears began to flow from her eyes. "Did you get all the stingers out?" Mills asked.

"Yellow jackets don't have the barb stinger of honeybees; they have a smooth stinger, so they usually don't leave their stingers behind."

She was in pain, and Cooper put a wet cloth on her forehead and then wiped the tears that were falling down her cheeks.

"I'm sorry I opened your blouse, but I had to get the yellow jackets out of your clothes."

"You saved me from being stung even more," she replied. "Oh, it hurts so much."

He patted her hand.

"Mills, I'm afraid you're going to feel these stings for a while. I've never seen anyone have a worse spell of misfortune than you. I hope you're finished with bad luck," Williston said. She turned to Cooper, "Fainting is a symptom of an allergic reaction to insect bites, but her blood pressure is normal and she's having no problems with her breathing. I want you to watch her carefully; allergic reactions can sometimes take hours to appear. Here's a list of symptoms to watch for, and I'll be at home tonight if you need me."

When Mills woke up next, she was in Cooper's bed and the ceiling fan above the bed rotated slowly. The pain in her limbs had not lessened and she felt weak as she tried to sit up.

"Take it easy now," Cooper's calming voice came from the corner of the room. He was reading by lamplight and then rose from his chair and came to the side of the bed. Sitting down beside her, he put his arm around her. "How's the patient feeling?" He leaned back so that he could look into her eyes.

"Like death warmed over."

"That bad. I hope you can eat some dinner," he said, leaving the room. Cooper brought her a bowl of chicken soup on a tray and told her that Marian had made it for her before she left for the day. "Everyone is worried about you, and I'm sorry about what happened this afternoon."

After she took a spoonful of the soup, she asked, "Do you think I'm not suited to be out here in the country?"

"The misfortunes you've encountered could happen to anyone; please don't think like that."

He rose from her bedside and phoned Williston and Charles to let them know that Mills was awake and was having supper. They were grateful for the news and asked to be updated in the morning.

Cooper removed her supper tray when she finished the soup and said, "I think you know how I got to know Williston. When I was twelve, I fell out of a tree and broke my arm. She looked after me in the emergency room and that night when I got home, I was in pain. My mother got into bed beside me and started to tell me stories of the Low Country. Of course, I thought I was too grown up to hear those tales, and I scoffed at them at first, but only at first. Julia was adamant that I would enjoy them if I just listened, and she was right. She recounted tales of mystery, pirates, and ghosts—Charleston is famous for its abundance of ghosts. I became absorbed in her tales and fell asleep in her arms. Would you like to hear a few of her stories?"

"Yes, I would. Cooper, would you put your arm around me?"

He nodded, and slid into the bed beside her. "Do you remember the name of the sailboat that we went out on when Vivien was here?"

"Yes, the *Theodosia*."

"The namesake of Jeff's sailboat disappeared at sea while sailing from Georgetown to New York. She was the daughter of Aaron Burr and you probably remember that while he served as Thomas Jefferson's vice president, he killed Alexander Hamilton in a duel."

"Yes, I do remember that from my high school American history class."

"After several years of exile in France, Burr returned to New York, and

Theodosia set out to see him. She was married to the governor of South Carolina, Joseph Alston."

"Alston Station is named after him."

"That's right. Theodosia was in poor health and the trip by sea should have taken four or five days, but the War of 1812 was under way, and British war ships were patrolling the Atlantic seaboard. The voyage began just before the new year of 1813, and when she set sail from Winyah Bay, she would never be seen again."

"What happened to the ship?"

"Desperate for news of Theodosia, Joseph Alston sent letters to Aaron Burr when the ship that transported her became overdue. Weeks passed, and there was no word on the ship, the *Patriot*, or her crew. Speculation that the *Patriot* was attacked by pirates was widespread."

"You mean they didn't know? The ship just vanished?" Mills asked.

"Well, there was one clue. Some years later, a Dr. Pool from Elizabeth City, North Carolina, came into possession of a portrait of a woman that was supposedly found on the Outer Banks. He received the portrait as payment for medical services from the aged widow of a ship wrecker. These scavengers, the ship wreckers, were known to lure ships aground off the Outer Banks of North Carolina and then kill the passengers and crew, looting the boat of its goods. According to the widow, the *Patriot* had been found adrift, and the wreckers boarded her to find the ship evacuated. Her husband removed the painting from the ship and gave it to his wife. The doctor tried, in vain, to authenticate the portrait, which became known as the Nag's Head Portrait, as being Theodosia, but too much time had transpired since her disappearance. Most of the people who knew Theodosia had passed away. Her fate remains a mystery to this day."

They were quiet for a moment and then Mills asked, "What happened to Joseph Alston?"

"The poor man died within a few years of her disappearance; he was just in his late thirties."

"What do you think happened to her?"

"Severe weather can come up on the ocean without warning, and it's possible that the *Patriot* encountered a catastrophic storm. I know that all too well." He paused and then continued, "I wonder if I'll ever know Elise's fate? I think I know how Joseph Alston felt."

The room was silent until Mills asked, "What do you mean you know about ocean storms all too well?"

He seemed deep in thought and then said, "The day of the accident that took the lives of my brother and father . . ." His face darkened in the dimly lit room, and he stopped speaking. "Mills, I don't think I can talk about it. Forgive me."

"It's all right."

After being silent for a few moments, he asked, "Would you like to hear the story of the Edisto Eight?"

"Yes, I would."

He started his second story and Mills rested her head against his chest.

High winds and rain awakened her during the night, but she nestled close to Cooper and wrapped her arm around him. When she woke in the morning, Cooper was no longer with her, and the aroma of fresh bread and bacon was in the air. The bedroom was dark and the rainfall continued.

Freshening up in the bathroom, she was shocked by the severity of the stings. There were red marks all over her legs. She was wearing a T-shirt and shorts. *How did I get these on?*

Mills entered the kitchen and Cooper's back was to her. She said softly, "Thank you for taking such good care of me."

He turned and looked into her eyes. "You're welcome. How are you feeling this morning?"

"The pain is not as bad as it was yesterday. How did I get to Williston's clinic?"

"You fainted, and I held you while Charles drove my Suburban."

"Oh, Cooper."

"Come and sit down. Your breakfast is ready."

He placed a plate of biscuits, eggs, and bacon in front of her, and she noticed multiple sting marks on Cooper's arms. "You didn't say anything about being stung," she said.

"I was too worried about you," he said as he joined her at the table. "It's going to rain all day. A few weeks ago, you expressed an interest in reading the letters that are upstairs in the attic. Would you like to do that today?"

"Yes. Will you read them with me?"

"After I clean up the breakfast dishes."

The rain was pounding on the metal roof and an occasional thunderclap rumbled nearby. Even with the lights turned on in the attic, they still needed flashlights to see inside the trunk. The flashlight beam illuminated the contents, and Cooper removed a stack of leather-bound letters, several books, and an ornately carved wooden box. "I haven't thought about these things in years. This is a jewelry box that belonged to my great-great-grandmother, Rachel Camp. Let's take everything downstairs into better light."

Once in the study, Cooper placed the jewelry box on his desk. There was a fragile latch on the box, and he lifted the lid to reveal the contents. There were a few yellowed letters, a music composition, and a daguerreotype portrait of a couple. Underneath the letters was a strand of pearls with a golden pendant, adorned with a sapphire. There were other mementoes of the past, including a small hand-carved doll with delicate facial features.

Cooper studied each piece and looking at Mills, he said, "I'd like for you to have the jewelry box and its contents. The pearls will match the ring that Piet gave you."

"I think they're beautiful, but shouldn't they stay in your family?"

"Elise always thought of these items as relics of the past. I would like for you to have them. They should be enjoyed—not sitting in the attic inside a jewelry box. Come here."

She walked to him and he turned her around, fastening the pearls. He lifted her hair, allowing the necklace to fall gently around her neck and then turned her to face him. "There. They're lovely on you."

"I feel honored to have your ancestor's treasures."

The phone rang and Cooper spoke with the individual on the line about the previous day's yellow jacket attack. "Ian would like to speak to you," he said, handing her the phone.

When she said hello, Ian said in a concerned voice, "Mills, please be more cautious out there on Cooper's property. This is your third or fourth mishap, and if Cooper is not more careful with you, I'm going to offer you a job at Heath Brothers and you can move into town."

"Thank you, Mr. Heath, but it could have happened to anybody. It just happened to be me."

Ian said, "You're like family, and we need to take better care of you."

When Cooper finished his conversation with Ian, he said to Mills, "Ian is angry with me. He's right. I should be taking more care to make certain the buildings are safe. Lizzie and Janie could have been hurt."

Mills went to the couch and viewed the items inside the jewelry box. A careful study of the daguerreotype revealed a handsome couple, the man with thick, dark hair, and his wife with raven-colored hair and the bright eyes of Jeff Radcliffe. Inscribed on the back of the portrait were their names, "Rachel and Grey Camp, 1870."

She placed the portrait back into the jewelry box and unfastened the leather strap that secured the letters. The letters were stacked in chronological order by date. Despite their age, they were in decent condition, and she carefully opened the first in the sequence.

28 August, 1864

Dear Mrs. Camp,

I am writing to you with a heavy heart. Last evening, I was summoned to the door by a young Negro, George Camp, who pleaded for help for his master, your son, Grey Camp. There was a downpour of rain and when I looked into the eyes of the young man who was on a horse's back, I knew that he could travel no further.

Our Dr. Butler has spent hours with him and is worried about his injuries. Two minié balls were removed from his chest and a third from his right leg. I am sorry to tell you that the doctor has told me that it is likely the leg cannot be saved. There is little medicine and pain killer, but we will do all that we can for your son.

Sara Cooper

The next letter was dated mid-September.

> 18 September, 1864
>
> Dear Mrs. Camp:
>
> My news about your son is hopeful, but guarded. Dr. Butler has saved your son's leg and while he is still weak, he is showing gradual signs of improvement. Grey has been disturbed by dreams of his father, who I understand was recently separated from your son in fighting to defend the Weldon Railroad. I have told him that these nightmares are a result of his fever, but he says that I do not understand about his dreams.
>
> For the first time in months, we have fresh game to eat. George hunted our fields and has harvested a young buck. We are thankful to have food in the house. George's devotion to Grey is inspirational to me.
>
> Sara Cooper

Mills read two more letters that discussed Grey Camp's gradual health improvements until she came to one from mid-October:

> ... I cannot help but eavesdrop on the conversations your son has with my four daughters. He recites Byron, Keats, Shelley, and Shakespeare's sonnets. I have not heard such poetry in years, but then, I have not been in the company of a young man like Grey since my own youth.
>
> This morning, I went into the pantry room where Grey sleeps and George was reading to him from the Bible. He is completely literate, and I have discovered he writes as well as I do. I asked him how this could be since it was illegal to teach slaves how to read, and he responded that Master Grey had taught him how to read and write and was proud of it ...

One week later, a letter addressed the disheartening news that Grey's father had been killed while protecting a widow's farmhouse, a mere fifteen miles away. She had taken in wounded Confederate and Federal soldiers alike, but a group of northern deserters had attempted to rob her—Grey's father was murdered while he defended her.

As Mills read the last portion of the letter, a strange sensation surged through her body. Sara Cooper had written: "Grey's dreams concerning the death of his father are strangely similar to the actual events surrounding his death. In his delirium, Grey foresaw the injustice that would befall his father." Mills drew a deep breath and thought of Cooper's psychic ability—he had foreseen the deaths of his own father and brother. She realized that his capability derived from deep within his ancestral roots.

When Cooper brought her lunch to her in the study, she asked him to recount the history of his ancestors mentioned in the letters.

"My ancestor, Grey Camp, his friend, Edward Goudelock, and his valet, George Camp, had joined Wade Hampton's forces in Virginia after serving in the defense of Charleston. Grey's father had already been serving with General Hampton, and the three had joined him near Petersburg, Virginia. Federal forces had attempted to cut the Weldon Railroad, which brought supplies from the south into Virginia. During a skirmish with Union soldiers, Edward Goudelock had been shot from his horse into a ravine. Grey had attempted to save his friend and went down the escarpment after him and was shot several times by concealed Federals." Cooper paused his retelling and said, "It's hard to defend against bushwhackers."

"No doubt," she replied. "Poor Edward and Grey!"

"But the valet hadn't been wounded. George had hidden to wait until after dark to attempt a rescue. It had been a hot August afternoon, and George said that the Union soldiers had made antagonizing calls for hours to the two wounded men in the ravine. It was only after darkness that George had descended into the gorge. Edward Goudelock had died at some point during the day and George had to pry Grey's hands off of him."

"And then?"

"Sara Cooper took them in, and after several months, Grey recovered. Both men eventually returned to the Confederate Army, but by then it was at the end of the war. Grey had married Sara's eldest daughter, Rachel, and remained in Virginia for years after the war."

Cooper paused at the end of his story, looking at her thoughtfully. "What happened to Grey's father?" Mills asked.

"The day that Grey was shot, he had been given a field command by General Hampton, and he and his father were separated. His father, Michael, was injured in fighting and, along with other wounded men from both sides of the war, they were given respite on a widow's front porch. A group of northern deserters attempted to rob the widow and Michael tried to stop them—Michael was murdered along with the rest of the Confederates on her farm."

"That's horrible," Mills responded.

"It was a brutal war and the suffering continued for years afterward."

Mills was quiet as she reflected on what he had told her and then she said, "I read that Grey Camp had foreseen the death of his father in his nightmares. Your psychic ability is an ancestral gift."

He looked out the window and softly replied, "Mills, it's not a gift. It's a curse."

That evening, Cooper sat beside the bed and told her more Low Country stories, but he did not sit on the bed with his arm around her as he had done the previous night. "Do you recall the trestle that you went underneath when you went canoeing on the Edisto?"

"Yes, the one marked 'Patterson.' I had an ominous feeling about it, even in the daytime."

"There's a good reason for you to feel that way. The owner of the bridge, James Patterson, came south from Pennsylvania after the Civil War. At that time, land could be purchased for a fraction of its pre-war value, and he invested in large tracts of Low Country property. The bridge was built to connect his properties in the adjacent counties of Charleston and Colleton, and he became a cotton planter. He also invested in the phosphate business, which had made large profits for some individuals."

"What was phosphate used for?"

"It was used as a type of fertilizer. In 1893, he was about to enjoy the fruits of his labor when a hurricane came ashore, not only wiping out his agricultural investments, but also taking a huge toll on the phosphate industry. Phosphate was mined in trenches, and the mines and equipment were swept away. He went into despair because he could not pay his creditors, and after days of soul-searching, he tied a rope to the trestle over the Edisto and hanged himself."

"Oh, that's awful," Mills exclaimed.

"Yes. Utter ruin is terrible. After Mr. Patterson committed suicide on the trestle, travelers on the river reported seeing the shape of a body hanging from the bridge, especially during a full moon. It was under the light of a harvest moon that he took his own life."

"Why didn't you tell me this before we went canoeing?"

"You weren't on the river after dark, and it wasn't during a full moon," he said with a smile.

"Don't tease me, Cooper."

She paused for a moment and then asked, "When did you see the lights at the old mansion ruin?"

He looked at her intently and responded, "Beau and I were fishing on the river one evening. The lights appeared near the old slave row and we watched them for about fifteen minutes before they vanished. This was a month before Beau and my father died." They both became quiet until Mills broke the silence by asking him to tell her another story. He thought for a minute before he began. "Ah, yes. The apparition of the Church Street garden . . ."

In the morning, she woke to a rich fragrance of roses. Glancing around the room, she saw a vase filled with the white blossoms of the flowers from the old cabin.

Cooper served her breakfast in bed.

"You're treating me so wonderfully, I'm not going to want to go back to my cottage."

"I care about you very much," Cooper responded, and their eyes locked. "I'll get the letters from the trunk so that you can continue to read them."

He turned to leave the room, and she relaxed her head on a pillow. *Cooper—I'm afraid of what I feel for you.*

Within a few minutes, he returned with the letters and her jewelry box. She opened a letter. As she read, Mills was amazed at the similarities between Grey Camp and Cooper. He was well educated, fluent in French, and well versed in Latin and the classics. He was also generous and self-sacrificing. For Christmas, he had written piano arrangements for each of Sara Cooper's daughters and then performed the compositions as his gift to them. During that same Christmas, George Camp gave each girl a figurine carved in her likeness and a jewelry box. Mills opened Rachel's jewelry box and admired the delicate features of the wooden doll. "Rachel, you were indeed lovely," she said out loud.

Carved underneath the box was the inscription, "G.C. 1864." Mills read that George had also created a cane for Grey Camp to help him walk after he was injured, with the handle carved in the shape of an African woman with her hair flowing. Mills rose from the bed and went into the living room. The walking cane was propped against the fireplace in its usual place, and upon examination, she read the inscription, "For G.C. 1864."

"For Grey Camp, 1864," Mills said quietly to herself.

In one of the letters, Sara Cooper mentioned that Grey and George resembled one another. Mills asked, "Cooper, didn't you tell me that George and Grey were related?"

"Yes, they shared the same grandfather, Amos Camp. Amos had a favorite mulatto slave with whom he fathered five children, in addition to the family he had with his wife."

That afternoon, Mills asked Cooper to play the sheet music that was inside the jewelry box. The composition had been recorded on what appeared to be stationery, and when he performed the arrangement, the song reminded Mills of Williston's favorite Chopin classics. "I think you might be the reincarnation of Grey Camp," Mills told him with a smile.

He laughed before responding, "Anything's possible. He did, at least, have a long and happy life."

"And your name?"

"It is a southern tradition to give sons their mother's maiden name. Grey and Rachel Camp had a son named Cooper who was my great-grandfather. I'm named after him."

Despite the pain from the yellow jacket stings, Mills had been thoroughly entertained the entire weekend. Sunday evening, when Cooper walked her back to her home, he told her to take the letters and journals from the trunk so she could finish reading them. The rain had stopped, and they stood at the bottom of her steps and looked at each other. They began to talk simultaneously, then stopped and laughed at each other.

"You go, first," Cooper said, still laughing.

"Thank you for helping me this weekend, and for the treasures from the attic."

"Mills, you are welcome."

They continued to look into each other's eyes and then Cooper broke the silence. "We're going to be very busy with the harvest in the weeks ahead. If you'd like, you can work with Marian and the girls in the kitchen for the next several days until those stings heal. They're going to be canning vegetables, and I know they could use another hand."

"Thank you. I will."

"Oh, Murphy notified me that I will finally be closing on the old Camp plantation that I've had under contract for about a year. You witnessed the contract extension in my office. Remember?"

"Yes, I do."

"Hopefully, by the end of the week, the property will be back in the family again. Well, goodnight."

She waved goodbye from the top of the steps and then thought about the day she had witnessed the contract extension. It was the day that Lee Roy Mullinax had come into their lives.

CHAPTER 22

The Harvest

Mills had taken deliveries from Camp Hardware and met with a representative of Edisto Tomato and Produce before seven the next morning. As Fritz and his crew arrived to work, Mills helped some of the farm workers move produce into the kitchen for the day's canning.

Fritz called to her, "Miss Taylor, stop and take a drink of water from Mr. Heath's well. You are going to become dehydrated if you don't slow down." As she walked to his side, he raised his chin up to look at the sting marks on her face. "I'm sorry about the yellow jackets. Mr. Heath told me about what happened to you on Friday."

Fritz went to his crew's supplies and removed a clean cup to obtain water for her. After he pumped the manual well handle several times, water began to flow from the spout and he filled her cup.

"I have noticed that you have an outstanding work ethic. Now you must pace yourself, and don't spend too much time in the heat. It is still early in the day, but it is already eighty-five degrees."

"After I finish this, I'll be inside the rest of the day," she responded.

"That is wise."

He took his handkerchief and pushed back his hat, wiping the sweat from his brow. "Miss Taylor, I will miss seeing you when we finish our work here. Do have a good morning."

Fritz turned and walked away toward the boathouse, and Mills responded, "I hope you have a good morning too." He continued to walk, but pulled his hat off and waved it in the air.

During the week after the yellow jacket attack, Mills helped Marian and the girls in the kitchen while they canned fruits and vegetables. She was impressed by how hard the girls worked. They required little instruction and had more knowledge of the canning process than she did. As their work continued, representatives from the local churches came by the house to pick up donations of goods.

In the afternoons, Mills took the girls swimming in the pool, which provided a lot of joy for all involved. On Friday afternoon, as they swam, she looked into the western sky and saw that it was obscured by a line of black thunderclouds. A jagged bolt of lightning erupted from the base of the clouds, and the sound of thunder followed.

"Janie, Lizzie, I think we'd better get out of the water."

As soon as she had spoken those words, a strong blast of wind came from the advancing storm and blew leaves into the pool. The gust was so powerful that deck chairs were overturned.

Marian met them at the rear courtyard with the news that a severe thunderstorm warning was in effect for Charleston County, and she hustled the girls into the house. Mills dashed to her cottage and watched large drops of rain hit the lane as Fritz and his crew ran past on the way to their trucks. There was another boom of thunder, and the lights went out in her cottage.

In the darkened room, she changed out of her wet bathing suit and examined the sting marks on her body. They were healing, but some of the marks were still sensitive and itched. She rubbed ointment into the stings and dressed in shorts and a polo shirt.

The phone began to ring and when she answered, Cooper's soothing voice said, "I hope you're all right out there on the farm. I understand there's a severe thunderstorm in the Edisto area right now. I hope we won't have much damage to the crops."

"Yes, several minutes ago, we lost electricity."

"Well—I called to let you know that I am now the owner of the old Camp Plantation, Crescent Hall. I met with Mr. Cusworth's heirs and legal counsels this afternoon at Murphy's office—they're a difficult group. Each of them brought their own attorney and heavily scrutinized the proceeds. There was no trust between them." He paused before continuing, "Fritz sent his crew to repair the fire damage at the Freedom School. Would you like to go with me this evening after the weather passes to take a look at it?"

"Yes, I would."

On the way to the Freedom School, they saw leaves and debris strewn all over the roadway. Dime-sized hail had been produced by the storm, and the outside air temperature had plunged. Before they left the farm, Cooper inspected the fields with Charles—while there had been some damage to the crops, he told her that it could have been much worse.

When they reached the school, an occasional echo of thunder could be heard from the storm, which had moved out to sea. The damage that Lee Roy had inflicted on the building had been repaired, and once again, the structure stood clean and white against the darkened sky.

"Fritz and his crew did a good job on the repairs," Cooper said.

"I didn't realize they were working on the building."

"Yes, this is the busiest time of year for many of us who worked on the restoration. With the harvest under way and my work at Heath Brothers, I just couldn't contribute my time right now. Insurance should handle most of the expenses, but any additional costs will be handled by a few of us in the community."

"I'm thankful that Lee Roy wasn't able to destroy the building."

"Me too."

Thoughts of Eula and her children went through her mind. *Poor Eula. Lee Roy has not destroyed the hope she instilled in her children—her dreams will live on through them.*

Cooper unlocked the front doors, and they walked inside the tiny building. Even in the fading light, the heart pine floors gleamed, but a slight smell of smoke still lingered near the front of the structure. Cooper ran his hand across the top of an oak desk and said, "I would like to ask you for your help on a Heath Brothers' project. Ian wants to do a direct mail to our clients about our business agreement with Perret International and the expansion of our Newark terminal. I was hoping that you would help me create a brochure."

"I'll be glad to help you. What if we work on it next week? I'll come by Heath Brothers after my farm responsibilities and we'll get started."

"Thank you."

After they locked the doors to the school building, they viewed the storm damage of downed limbs and debris that lay in the schoolyard. Cooper smiled and said, "The old Camp plantation returns to my family, and all hell breaks loose from the heavens." He laughed and opened the truck door for Mills.

⸻

One Monday morning, Mills assisted Charles with a delivery of a tractor implement and then dressed to go to Charleston. She wore a navy dress and put on Rachel Camp's pearls, admiring the necklace in the mirror. *Cooper said the pearls should be enjoyed.*

When she arrived at Heath Brothers, Cooper was in a meeting and she took a seat in the hallway outside his office. As she sipped a cup of coffee, she could hear his voice.

"Ms. Burris, I appreciate your taking your time to let me know about this property. My first cousin, Jeff Radcliffe, always helps me with my real estate purchases."

"Mr. Heath, I know Mr. Radcliffe and his partners, and I do not have a listing on the property. I was hoping to show it to you personally."

"I see. When you are able to secure an agreement that can include your company and Jeff's, I will be glad to look at it." Mills heard his chair move, and he continued, "Here's my cousin's business card."

"Mr. Heath, the seller will only agree for me to bring in prospective buyers, and you will probably pay more for the tract if two real estate companies are involved."

"There is one common element to all of my successful real estate purchases. As long as all parties involved in a transaction stay reasonable, then everyone can win."

"I admire your loyalty to Mr. Radcliffe, but I am acquainted with his partners, and I don't want information about this property floating around his office. You have an excellent reputation in the real estate community for being fair with agents, and that is why I came to see you."

"I would never do anything to hurt my cousin, so I suggest you speak to the seller of this property again and see if a reasonable solution can be found."

"I thought you wouldn't hesitate to look at this land since a large portion of it was formerly Sea Crest."

"Ms. Burris, my family comes first."

She heard Cooper rise from his chair and the two of them walk toward the doorway. When Ms. Burris reached the threshold, Mills observed that she was an attractive middle-aged woman.

Cooper smiled as soon as he saw Mills in the hallway and introduced her to the real estate agent. She firmly shook Mills's hand and said, "Miss Taylor, I follow your articles in the *Charleston Dispatch* on the Heath Foundation. I compliment you on your success. Good morning."

Mills entered his office and Cooper helped her with a chair. "The pearls look lovely on you."

"I love wearing them. I apologize, but I overheard you talking with Ms. Burris. Wasn't Sea Crest one of your family's properties?"

"Yes, at one time we owned eight plantations; two of them had houses. The rest of the properties, including Sea Crest, were strictly for agriculture and had only slaves' quarters and an overseer's house. I would like to take a look at the property, but I'm not going to omit Jeff from any of my transactions."

I admire his loyalty to Jeff.

"See if you like this," Cooper said as he handed her a rough draft for the brochure. They spent the rest of the morning working on the content. When Cooper and Mills finished, they showed their preliminary work-up to Ian. He smiled as he reviewed their efforts, and said, "I think this explains our expanded services quite well, and I look forward to seeing the brochure. Good work, you two."

That afternoon, Mills took the brochure copy and a number of photographs that illustrated Heath Brothers' business to the printer. She and Mr. Collins discussed the layout of the brochure. "I'll tell our graphics department what you are thinking of," Mr. Collins said. "We'll have samples for you to see, say Friday at two?"

The workweek was spent with a busy farm schedule. Mills was disappointed to see the amount of produce being discarded from storm damage, but Cooper accepted the losses with little comment and worked long hours in the fields, along with the other men.

On Friday, she planned to review the preliminary brochure for Heath Brothers, and Cooper told her that if she approved of it, to go ahead with the order. "I trust your opinion," he said.

When she arrived at Collins Printing, Mr. Collins placed a brochure on the counter. "We've done several proofs to test the color. I've read through the text, and I didn't see any mistakes. Please take a look."

Mills carefully reviewed the example. "Please tell your team that they've done an excellent job." She ordered the brochures on the spot.

The harvest continued, and by Sunday night, Mills was exhausted. Cooper prepared fresh vegetables for their dinner, but she was almost too tired to eat. She breathed deeply in an attempt to fight fatigue and said, "I'll come by your office tomorrow afternoon with the brochures from Collins Printing."

"Thank you. Henri Duchard with Perret International will be meeting with Ian and me in the morning, so that will be fine."

Monday morning, Mills received a phone call from the printer, and Mr. Collins explained that his wife was ill. He asked Mills if she would come in before lunch to pick up the brochures.

Dressing quickly, she phoned Heath Brothers to let Cooper know that she would be picking up the brochures at eleven. He told her he was about to go into a meeting, but she could leave a copy if they missed one another.

Mills accepted the brochures from Mr. Collins and then drove to Heath Brothers to show them to Cooper and his uncle. She was given clearance to enter the building and when she climbed the steps to the second story, Cooper was seated behind his desk, speaking on the telephone.

As soon as he saw Mills, he waved her into his office. She handed him a brochure and he glanced at it while he completed his conversation. After he hung up the phone, he gave his full attention to Mills and the brochure. "This looks good. I wish I had more time to read it, but I have to go back into my uncle's office in a minute—Mills, you've done an excellent job."

He rose from his chair and escorted her to the back steps. "You look lovely today."

She smiled with his kind words, but she had the sensation that she was being rushed out of the building. Just as she was about to take the stairs, Ian called her name.

"Wait just a minute. Cooper, you didn't let me know that Mills was in the building. I was just telling Henri about the brochure you two did to explain our expansion to our clients. Mills, I'd like for you to meet Henri Duchard with Perret International."

Ian took her by the hand and led her to meet the Frenchman. She glanced back at Cooper. *He looks frustrated. Why?*

"Henri, this is Mills Taylor, she and Cooper designed the brochure for our company. Mills is the director of the Heath Foundation that funds scholarships. Do you have a brochure with you?"

"Yes, sir, I just picked them up."

The Frenchman walked to Mills's side. *"Enchanté, mademoiselle."*

Henri was attractive, with black curly hair and a deep tan; he was slightly shorter than Cooper. He took her hand in his and kissed it while looking admiringly into her eyes. *"Je m'appelle Henri Duchard."*

"Henri has been working closely with Cooper for the last year, and we expect great success from our business arrangement."

Henri had not taken his eyes off Mills, and she gently removed her hand from his to retrieve a brochure from her briefcase.

She handed one to Ian, and he examined it closely. "Mills, this is exceptional work." He gave the brochure to Henri and as he studied it, he said, "Mademoiselle, this is outstanding."

"Mills, we were just about to go to the East Bay Club for lunch. I would like for you to join us, and I won't take no for an answer," Ian said.

Mills looked at Cooper, and he smiled slightly and nodded in approval. As they exited the second floor, Mills heard Henri say to Cooper, *"Elle est très jolie."*

They were seated in the cozy back room at the East Bay Club, and most of the luncheon conversation centered on the Newark terminal expansion, except when Mills asked, "Henri, are you a member of the Perret family?"

"No, mademoiselle. Like Heath Brothers, our shipping company has always been family owned. During World War II, the Nazi occupiers forced us to abandon operation, and with the Allied invasion of Normandy, our homeport, Le Havre, was virtually destroyed. My grandfather renamed our company to honor the architect, Auguste Perret, who rebuilt the city."

As Henri finished his story, the maître d' came to their table to tell Ian that he had a phone call.

Henri leaned toward Cooper and asked him a question she did not understand. *"Cooper, est-elle votre amante?"*

A darkened expression crossed Cooper's face and he responded, *"Henri, s'il vous plaît, votre question est trop personnelle."*

"*Oh, pardon, pardon.*"

Ian returned to the table with a concerned expression on his face. "Cooper, I'm afraid there's been an accident at the construction site at Newark. The supervisor didn't have details, but he said there are injuries involved. I'm going to make a phone call to the Newark office; why don't you three meet me outside in a few minutes?"

Cooper helped Mills with her chair and then went to sign the bill. Henri stood and said, "*Après vous, mademoiselle.*"

He opened the front door for her, and they stood outside in the shade of a veranda to wait for Cooper and his uncle. Henri drew close to her and said, "I must tell you that I have spent many hours with Cooper negotiating our business arrangement, and some of those hours were spent in leisure. I must confess I was worried about him."

"What do you mean, Mr. Duchard?"

"Henri—please call me Henri—I have never seen a man turn away the advances of more lovely women. I thought perhaps he was—well, you know—but now that I see you, his beautiful mistress, I completely understand his fidelity."

Cooper came out of the door, and Henri stepped toward the car. "Cooper, what did Henri ask you about me while we were dining?"

"What's the matter?"

"Henri thinks I'm your mistress. Don't you think I should have been allowed to speak for myself? It's not like we're—"

"It's not like we're what, Mills—lovers?"

She had never seen Cooper become angry, but he stepped close to her and removed his Wayfarer sunglasses. Mills moved backward against the outside of the building, and Cooper put his arm against the brick wall behind her and spoke to her within a few inches of her face.

"During the time that I have spent with Mr. Duchard, I have learned that he likes pretty little play things, but that's all they are—play things. He asked me if you were my lover, and I told him that his question was too personal. That's none of his business, but I thought he would leave you alone. You see, I can't bear the thought that he would consider you one of his play things."

He was clearly frustrated, and she was stunned by his behavior. "I can't help the way I feel about you," Cooper said.

Mr. Heath came out the door, and Cooper spoke quietly to Mills, *"Ma belle fille, j'ai très envie de ton amour."*

"I don't know what you said . . . speak to me in English."

Cooper turned away from her and walked toward Ian's car. Mills raised her voice, "Daniel, stop, I want to know what you said."

Cooper wheeled around and looked at her when she called him Daniel, but then kept walking. Ian had come outside and observed the interaction between Cooper and Mills. He took Mills by the hand. "It's quite warm outside . . . please allow me to walk you to the car."

Cooper told his uncle that he was going to stop by his tailor's shop on King Street; he would join them shortly at the office. He opened the car door for Mills, and when she was seated, he closed it and walked away.

They arrived back at the Heath Brothers' office, and Henri took Mills by the hand. *"Mademoiselle, je suis très heureux de faire votre connaissance aujourd'hui."*

"I'm sorry, Henri, but I don't understand."

Ian interjected, "He said, 'it was a pleasure to make your acquaintance today.'"

As Ian started toward the building, Henri drew close to Mills and quietly said, "Mademoiselle, I speak French when I want to, just like our friend, Cooper."

That afternoon, she mailed the brochures to Heath Brothers' clients from Alston Station. She couldn't get Cooper's actions off her mind. When she returned home, the phone was ringing and she dashed across the room to answer it. She hoped that it was Cooper, and she said hello with enthusiasm.

Cooper's uncle responded, "Mills, this is Ian Heath. Cooper asked me to phone you. He said for you to go ahead and mail the brochures. I'm afraid that the accident at our Newark terminal was serious, and one of the construction workers lost his life. Another worker was injured. Cooper has flown to Newark to meet with their families. I'm not sure when he'll be returning."

"Thank you for calling. I'm sorry to hear about the two workers."

"Yes, it's tragic." He paused before saying, "Mills—Cooper's behavior this afternoon was out of character for him, but he has been under severe stress for almost a year now. Please forgive him."

"He spoke to me in French as you were coming out of the East Bay Club. Did you understand what he said?"

"No, I'm afraid I was out of earshot. Mills, the work that you did on the brochure was excellent, and I know we'll have a tremendous response. I appreciate your efforts."

She thanked him for calling and hung up the phone. Feeling very sad, she began to read through the journals of Cooper's ancestors.

Mills rang the doorbell at Piet van der Wolf's home and Mr. Cook answered the door with a surprised look on his face. "Miss Taylor, how nice to see you. I'll let Mr. van der Wolf know you're here."

He invited her into the foyer and within moments she was shown into the living room. Piet greeted her with, "This is a marvelous surprise. What brings you here this morning?"

"I've been so busy with my work that I haven't been able to see any of my friends lately, and I wanted to see you."

"I am indeed flattered. If you don't have plans for this afternoon, why don't you join me at the Ocean Forest Club? I have a reservation at one, and I'd love to have your company."

"I'm not familiar with that club."

"It's in Summerville, which is a short distance from here. I think you'll enjoy the experience."

The drive to Summerville was about thirty minutes, and Mills sat comfortably in Piet's limousine. A tree-lined drive led to the club, which was housed in a restored plantation home.

They were seated in a lovely room situated next to a courtyard with a large fountain; water cascaded from the top tier to the bottom, sounding like a waterfall.

Piet looked at her closely and said, "Is there something wrong?"

She replied in a subdued tone, "What do you do if you care deeply for a person that you should not be with?"

He looked at her with caring warmth and responded, "I don't know if I'm the best person to give advice on relationships of the heart. I've been alone for years now, and my loneliness is mostly self-inflicted. I think you must look into your heart and decide what is right. You should base your decision on what you can live with, later in life, when your conscience talks to you every day and sometimes for hours on end. My dear, only you can decide what is right."

When they completed their meal, Piet said, "I'd like to show you something beautiful. Do you mind walking with me a short distance?"

"No, not at all."

They walked past the fountain and down a shady path that led to a rose garden. In the center of the garden was an area designated for growing herbs. The area had a sundial in the center.

"The Churchills who operate the Ocean Forest Club grow many of their herbs and vegetables in this garden. It's lovely, don't you think?"

"Yes, sir, it resembles Cooper's gardens."

That afternoon when they returned to Charleston, Piet dropped her off near her car, which was parked on Society Street. The rumblings of thunder prompted Mills to say, "It sounds like we could have another storm."

"With our humidity, it's common to have a storm almost every day during the summer," Piet replied.

She thanked him for the wonderful afternoon, and before she departed, he said, "I appreciate your confidence in me. I hold your friendship in the highest regard, and I would like to help you any time you need it."

He smiled at her, and as the limousine pulled away, Mills noticed a sign in the window of a dance club named Rembrandt's on Society. A Shag contest was scheduled for Saturday night. Mills had never learned the steps to the popular southern dance, but she hoped that Cooper would show her the Shag when he returned home.

Friday evening, Mills read through one of the journals of Cooper's ancestors, Ellen Camp. She discovered that Ellen essentially ran the eight Camp plantations and was a talented artist. Inside the pages where she kept receipts for purchases were also drawings of family members and caricatures of prominent men of the Civil War period. Mills was greatly amused by a caricature of General Sherman, which showed him with horns growing out of his forehead.

Mills put the book down and stepped onto her porch for fresh air. The lights were on in Cooper's living room, and she could hear the melodic sound of his piano. He was home at last; she wanted to see him. Mills went to his front door and began to knock. He continued to play the piano, and undeterred, she knocked louder until the music stopped. When he answered the door, Mills hugged him and could barely control the tears welling in her eyes.

He raised her face with his hand and said, "I don't want you to be unhappy. Please come into the living room."

He was still wearing his suit pants, his dress shirt was rolled up to the elbows, and he was sipping bourbon, which was rare for him.

"Please have a seat on the couch. Can I get you a refreshment?"

"No, I came to apologize to you. I've been upset about what happened on Monday at the East Bay Club."

"You don't owe me an apology. I owe you one."

He took out his handkerchief from his pocket and wiped the tears that had fallen down her cheeks. "I'm sorry for my behavior, and I hope you'll forgive me. I acted like a jealous adolescent. I couldn't stand the thought of Henri making a play for you, and I behaved like an ass."

"Jealous?"

"Yes, my dear. Don't think that I haven't thought a lot about us. I can't help how I feel, but our being intimate would be utterly unfair to you. We have worked well on a professional level, and I hope you will allow us to continue in that manner. Please accept my apology."

"Of course, I do, but why didn't you call me during the week?"

"There's more that I have to tell you. While I was in New Jersey, one of the contributors to the Heath Foundation, Thomas Benet, with Wescote, the pulpwood company, called our office to speak with me. Since I was unavailable, he spoke with Ian, and he explained that he gives a courtesy call to the employers of an individual that he wants to interview unless there's some compelling reason not to. He wants you to fly to Nashville and interview for the director's position for their public relations department. He said you'd be perfect for the job."

Cooper took a drink of his bourbon, and then continued, "I was too embarrassed to discuss this on the telephone so I planned to visit you tomorrow."

"I've been so worried."

"I have no desire to hurt you. If you only knew."

"What do you mean?"

He raised her chin up and smiled at her. "I think both of us have had a difficult week. I have a commitment in Charleston in the morning, but I was thinking you might join me for a boat trip to see the Camp property I just closed on. We'll leave before noon tomorrow."

"Yes, I'd like to go. Cooper, I'm sorry about the men who were involved in the accident."

"It's been hard." He stood and pulled her up from the couch. "I'll have a picnic basket for us. Please let me walk you to your cottage. We could both use a good night's sleep."

He escorted her back to her home, and when they reached the bottom of the steps, she asked, "You've thought about us being intimate?"

"Yes, Mills, I have." He raised an eyebrow in a question and she changed the subject.

"The job interview with Wescote—what do you want me to do?"

"My uncle says you're priceless. He's already received several positive responses from your brochure, and it's just been a few days since you mailed them."

"You didn't answer my question. Are you running for public office?"

He smiled at her joke and then stepped very close to her. "I don't want you to go. I'm proud of your work for the foundation, and I want you to stay with me."

As she undressed in her darkened bedroom, Mills could faintly hear the sound of Cooper's piano. She raised the window and listened to "Cast Your Fate to the Wind." When he finished playing the song, the lights went out in his living room and the only noises she could hear were the melodies of the wind chimes and the night sounds of the crickets.

CHAPTER 23

The Cast Net

As the *Miss Elise* entered Charleston Harbor, Cooper pointed out Morris Island and Fort Sumter. Mills had read in Ellen Camp's journal about the horrendous fighting that had occurred on the island in defense of Charleston during the Civil War. The Confederate defenders had been forced to abandon their fortifications because of a lack of potable water. She had been shocked to read that the decomposing bodies of soldiers in mass graves had contaminated the water supply.

They passed Fort Sumter and the ruins of an old fort named Castle Pinckney. The container cranes from the Columbus Street Terminal towered above the waterfront, and Cooper pointed out an enormous freight ship making its way out of the harbor.

Once on the Ashley River, Mills marveled at the waterside view of Middleton Place where the impressive grass terraces rose from the river to the hilltop home. Entering a section of the river that was pristine, Cooper pointed out survey tape that marked the boundaries of the Camp plantation. "I told the surveyors to open up a pathway from the river to the interior of the property." As they rounded a bend in the river, the cleared area came into view and Cooper maneuvered the *Miss Elise* to the bank. He handed insect repellent to Mills and told her to be liberal with its application.

Together they set off to explore the property on the pathway. Cooper pointed to his left and said, "The Camp mansion was in this direction."

They walked through an area of heavy forest and the air became cooler under the trees.

"This is beautiful. How old do you think these live oak trees are?"

"Maybe 150 years old."

"They're huge. Don't you think they could be older?"

"I don't think there's a first growth forest around here. Centuries ago, most of the original trees were harvested for ship building."

As they made their way through the forest, Mills ran into a spiderweb, coating her hair and clothes. Cooper brushed the former inhabitant of the web off of her shoulder.

"The spider was on me?"

"Yes, but they're harmless to humans. When I was a boy, some of the locals around Edisto used to say that if a writing spider wrote your name in its web, an unfortunate fate awaited you."

"But that's just an old wives' tale."

"Yes, ma'am," he said with a smile.

At one point, the forest became so dense that the sun was obscured and the ground was covered in a thick field of ferns. Two columns appeared in the near distance and a brick wall ran in either direction away from the structures. "This should be the riverside entry to where the house was situated."

As they passed the columns, the crumbling walls of an ancient home foundation were apparent within the forest growth. A large oak tree grew in the center of the foundation wall and Cooper said, "This is what's left of Crescent Hall."

"What happened to the house?"

"It burned down in 1917, destroying many pieces of George Camp's creations—I'd like to show you something."

They emerged onto a lane that suffered from neglect but was still navigable. A short distance away were a dozen small cabins surrounded by thick brush. "I think before we venture any closer to the cabins, I'll have a crew clear out the growth around them."

At the end of the lane was a large wrought-iron fence with ornately designed gates, which displayed crescents in the metalwork. The grounds around the fence were well manicured—ancient roses and camellias grew within the enclosure. Mills realized that a cemetery was inside. There was a pristine view of the Ashley River from this knoll of graves, and wilderness surrounded the enclave in a setting of peace.

"This is a Camp family cemetery. There was an easement to the graveyard, so, over the years, the grounds have never suffered from neglect."

"Cooper—the wrought-iron gates are magnificent, and look at the crescent designs."

"The crescent denotes peace, prosperity, and order; it has been a South Carolinian symbol for many years."

The gate squeaked as they entered the cemetery, and Mills noticed some of the markers dated to the eighteenth century. On the marker of Ellen and Michael Camp were the Latin words "Nex Mos Singulus Nos Pro Tantum A Brevis Dum."

"Can you read Latin?"

He studied the inscription before saying, "It reads, 'Death will separate us for only a short while.'"

The words gave her chills, and he said, "Grey and George moved Michael's body home from the widow's property in Virginia a few years after the Civil War. Ellen said she could not rest unless she spent eternity beside her beloved."

A large marker caught her attention and as she walked closer, the epitaph was arresting. There was an engraving of a man throwing a cast net and the words "Cast Out thy Net to All Men."

George and Grey Camp were buried side by side, and Mills began to read aloud the eroded inscription, "Family, Brothers, and the B—"

"—and the Best of Friends," Cooper finished. "All the talent in those two graves."

An iron cross designated the resting place of a Confederate veteran and graced the grave of Grey Camp, but not that of his cousin, George.

"What does the cross signify?"

"It's a replica of the Southern Cross of Honor Medals that can only be placed on the graves of Confederate veterans who served honorably. George was not officially a Confederate soldier, although he served with the Army—I think out of loyalty to Grey."

"What led them back to Charleston?"

"Both George and Grey married after the war. Grey remained in Virginia for a number of years until after his mother-in-law passed away. While George lived in Virginia, he sold his woodwork at a local mercantile for extra income. A businessman from Philadelphia noticed his craft and persuaded him to relocate and work full-time as a cabinetmaker.

"Grey and George decided at some point that they would be interred side by side and with George's successful business, he had the means to secure this marker. George and his wife didn't have any children who survived to adulthood, and some of their fortune was left to care for indigent youths of Philadelphia and Charleston."

Mills nodded, listening.

"By the time Grey passed away, our family had diminished wealth and our properties were sold to outsiders for subsistence."

Mills read the epitaph again, "'Cast Out Thy Net to All Men.' That's what the elder Mr. Camp told me one afternoon while we were restoring the Freedom School House."

"He said those words to my brother and me while he taught us to throw a cast net. It was good advice."

"But he changed the last word in the epitaph from 'men' to 'people.'"

On their way back to the *Miss Elise*, Cooper pointed out a brick structure off the pathway. "That's one of several wells on this property, and a good reason to be careful when we walk this land. They should be secure. I'll probably wait until after the first frost to have them inspected."

After they picnicked on the boat, Cooper told Mills he was going to shorten up the return trip by using the Intracoastal Waterway. They encountered several rain showers on the way home and the waterways were busy with weekend boat traffic. Mills was at the helm of the craft, and Cooper sat by her side. As they neared home, the sky was becoming dark in the west, and above the sound of the engines, thunder began to rumble.

By the time they reached his dock, strong winds whipped around them and the sky opened up with a deluge of rain. They secured his boat on the lift and then ran up the lane to his house. Drenched by rain, they removed their topsiders before entering the darkened house. Mills felt chilled, and she crossed her arms in front of her when she realized her body was reacting to the cold. Cooper turned on the light switch, but the electricity was off.

He retrieved a towel for her and said, "There's a pair of shorts and a T-shirt in the bathroom for you. I think you should get out of the wet clothes."

A hurricane lamp illuminated the bathroom, and Mills changed her clothes, hanging the wet garments to dry. She ran her fingers through her hair, and when she came out, there were hurricane lamps lighting the hallway and kitchen. Cooper had changed into dry clothes and was mopping up water puddles off the floor when she entered the room.

"Would you like a glass of wine?"

"I'd love one."

"Come with me to the cellar, and we'll pick out a bottle."

She held the hurricane light, and they descended the steps into the cellar. Cooper read several labels before making a choice. They were standing against one another, and Mills could feel the warmth of his body against hers. Looking into her eyes, he slowly said, "I think this will make a good accompaniment to the cuisine." They continued to look at each other until Cooper broke the silence, "Come on, let's go upstairs and make dinner."

They cut up vegetables from the garden, and Cooper removed a large frying pan from the rack above the island. He heated olive oil and sautéed the vegetables with some marinated venison before they sat down to dine.

"Have you forgiven my behavior on Monday?"

"Of course. Thank you for showing me the old Camp farm this afternoon."

"I enjoyed seeing it again myself."

"Do you know how to Shag?"

He laughed and said, "You mean the dance?"

"Yes, of course I mean the dance—while I was downtown this week, I saw that a Shag contest would be held tonight at Rembrandt's on Society."

"I don't think we'll go to Rembrandt's, but what if I show you the dance steps on the porch after dinner. I'm surprised that you, a Virginia girl, never learned to Shag."

When they finished dining, Cooper went into his hunting room, and Mills could hear him sorting through cassettes. He returned with a radio/cassette player and two tapes. "A true Shag enthusiast might argue that some of these songs aren't Shag music, but I think we can still dance to them."

He led her outside and placed a hurricane lamp on the screened porch.

The sun had set, and there was a light rain falling; the air was cool and damp. Cooper took her by the hands and showed her the dance steps while humming a song. Occasionally, he interjected a few lyrics from the Cornelius Brothers and Sister Rose song, "Too Late to Turn Back Now." *I wish I could read his thoughts.*

They moved together through the steps until Cooper asked, "Are you ready to try?"

She nodded, and he started the cassette player. The first song was by the Spiral Starecase, "More Today than Yesterday." They both sang along to the music. *Has he chosen these songs on purpose?*

Cooper was a smooth, athletic dancer, and Mills attempted to follow his lead but fumbled the maneuvers. He held her hands tightly, and despite her missteps, she had tremendous fun. One song played after another, and they all had one characteristic in common—they made her feel good.

When the tape finished, they were still in each other's arms swaying in the candlelight. He pulled her close to him, his fingers gently caressing her arms. She was mesmerized by his touch and he said, "I have a song I'd like to play for you. When I heard it for the first time, I was in a taxi in New Jersey. I could not stop thinking of you all week, and this song reminded me even more of you. I went to Manhattan to purchase it—it's a new release from Van Morrison from the album, *Avalon Sunsets*."

He spoke softly to her. "In the legend of King Arthur, Avalon was an island called the Island of Apples or the Fortunate Isle, because the fields needed no plows for cultivation; nature provided an abundance of grains and fruit. Avalon was a magical place—paradise."

He turned on the music and danced with her, holding her tightly in his arms. The song began with an instrumental overture and then the vocals started.

"What's the name of the song?" Mills softly asked.

"Have I Told You Lately," Cooper whispered in her ear. She felt flushed. *He loves me?*

The song continued to play, and as Cooper held her closely, she felt his first kiss on her throat. Captivated, she found herself breathless as his arm that was behind her was now inside her shirt, gently caressing her back. When the song finished, he turned off the cassette player and kissed her passionately on the mouth. Her entire existence was on fire.

She trembled in his arms and he softly whispered, "God help me, but I can't help the way I feel about you . . . my worst fear is that I might lose you. I want you to understand that I'm very much in love with you . . . *ma belle fille, j'ai très envie de ton amour.*"

"That's what you said to me at the East Bay Club. What does it mean?"

"It means: My beautiful girl, I long for your love."

After months of handshakes and pats on the back, she was stunned by his admission. She spoke quietly, "You had no reason to be jealous of Henri. You see, I wouldn't have been the least bit interested in him since I'm in love with someone else. Cooper, I feel like I've been in love with you my entire life."

When she said these words to him, he lifted her in his arms and carried her through the candlelit house into his bedroom. He placed her on his bed and she noticed a warming circle of light cast onto the ceiling by a hurricane lamp. She watched him remove his shirt before he embraced her in his arms. Gradually, they removed their clothes, and as he kissed and caressed her, she felt deep pleasures envelop her entire body, from head to toe. They were naked against one another, and when they became one for the first time, she cried for him to hold her closer. Stopping his caresses, he kissed her on the mouth and whispered, "I love you. I've got you, and I'm not going to let you go."

Mills never knew that such passion existed, and when she woke in the morning, they were still embracing each other, their bodies intertwined. They had loved one another until exhausted, then collapsed into each other's arms.

She gazed at the rotating ceiling fan above the bed. The electricity had been restored at some point during the night, and turning her face toward Cooper, she discovered that he was awake and looking at her.

When their eyes met he said, "You were so lovely asleep beside me, and I didn't want our time together to end. In my dreams, I've held you countless times, but loving you last night was more beautiful than I could have ever imagined."

He kissed her several times on her face and mouth, and then sat up on the bed, slipping on athletic shorts. She admired his well-chiseled physique as he did several sets of sit-ups and push-ups. Sweat moistened his chest, and he came back to her and stroked her hair. Curls had formed in her thick, brown hair, which had dried naturally after the rainstorm.

He looked at her naked body and stroked her hair. "You're so beautiful. I like your hair, untamed as it is this morning."

After he kissed her repeatedly on the face, he went into the bathroom. She heard the shower turn on, and she relaxed onto his bed. Her desire for him had overwhelmed her reasoning capabilities; she thought of their lovemaking and the way his hands felt on her body. What would the future hold?

He made breakfast for her and explained that he was meeting Ian to discuss Heath Brothers business, but would return in the afternoon. "I want you to save every dance for me tonight," he said, kissing her.

As he handed her a cup of coffee, she noticed that he had removed his wedding band.

Mills spent the morning sketching a waterfront scene, but found that she could not take her mind off Cooper. One realization would not leave her: he was perfect for her. Even when their energy was spent, they had touched and whispered words of love to one another. She had fought her emotions, but in the end, her love and desire for Cooper could not be subdued.

In the afternoon, she collected fresh herbs and tomatoes from the garden and made spaghetti sauce for their dinner. The aroma of the tomatoes and garlic lingered in the air, and she patiently waited for Cooper to return to her. She attempted to read from Ellen Camp's journal, but found that she was unable to concentrate. When she rose to stir the sauce, she saw that Cooper was in her doorway.

"Long before I got to your cottage, I could smell the aroma of your cooking."

"It's spaghetti sauce for our dinner."

He took her in his arms and said, "Ian told me to go home because I wasn't concentrating on my work. I've thought about you all day. I can still feel your arms around me. Mills, put your arms around me."

When she did, he backed her into the bedroom, disrobing her, while she unbuttoned his shirt. They fell together on her bed, and she could feel the hard muscles of his chest and thighs against her. He kissed her breasts and then slid his tongue down to her navel. As her excitement began to build, she wrapped herself around him, feeling his caresses deep within her body.

When they became still against one another, he held her tightly and kissed her gently on the forehead. He whispered to her, "I have something important to tell you."

"What is it?"

"I'm famished, let's eat."

"Oh, Cooper, don't tease me."

That evening after dinner, they danced to the soulful music of Ella Fitzgerald, and Cooper lifted her chin so that he could see into her eyes. "Mills, what are you going to do about the interview with Wescote?"

She remained in his embrace and replied, "I couldn't leave you if I tried."

He kissed her again on the forehead. "I'm glad to hear you say that."

"I've allowed my love for you to come before reason. I noticed you took off your wedding band."

He stroked her hair back and replied, "If Elise should come back, she can have everything I own. I told you that I thought she had ceased to love me." He looked at her intently and said, "The dreams I have about her in a dark confinement have not stopped. Before my father and brother were killed, I had a series of nightmares about the events that would take their lives. I didn't realize at the time the dreams foretold the future. You read yourself that this trait is ancestral—a curse of the Camp family men. Mills, I've given up hope of her return."

CHAPTER 24

The High and the Mighty

Before dawn, Cooper gently woke her with tender caresses. While in the throes of passion, Mills cried out his name and wept tears of pleasure until he became motionless against her. The first light of day barely illuminated the sky before he rose from bed to dress.

"I'll think of you today and look forward to seeing you this afternoon," he said.

She put on her robe and followed him to her French doors. They kissed one another before he descended the steps of her cottage.

Suddenly, the sound of a familiar voice interrupted the silence. "It's a little early in the morning for a report on the Heath Foundation, don't you think?"

Shocked, she watched as Jeff emerged from the side of her cottage and confronted Cooper. "I've been waiting for you. I looked for you in your house first, but I got a hint from Sam." Jeff petted Cooper's dog, and said, "When I saw the loyal dog waiting for his master on the top step of Mills's cottage, I knew where to look." He laughed and continued, "Cooper, do you have any idea how refreshing it is to see you have the same human frailties that I do?"

Cooper walked back and stood a few inches from Jeff's face. "You reek of alcohol."

Still laughing, Jeff said, "I need to see you in your office."

"About what?"

"I'll tell you when we get inside. Oh, my God, how the high and the mighty has crashed and burned. Well, Masser Amos, so you finally gave in to desire and decided to seduce the help?"

"Okay, that's enough. Let's go."

Anxiety overwhelmed Mills as she witnessed this scene between Cooper and Jeff. She quickly showered and dressed for her farm chores. Before leaving her cottage, she put on one of Julia's hats and descended the steps onto the path between the camellias. She walked only a few feet before Jeff stepped out from between the bushes and took her by the arms.

"I heard that Cooper has you working on the farm. It is harvest time, and I see Cooper's been busy." He drew her close and said, "I didn't want to disturb you this morning. I waited on Cooper for a long time outside your cottage. I heard your cries of passion, and I heard the way you said Cooper's name. I want to hear you say my name that way."

"Jeff, stop it."

"Didn't you realize you could have had either one of us? You should know that the Masser told me to stay away from you, and my current situation prevents me from telling him to go to hell. Cooper's been such a predictable bore, but this inspires me. I've discovered he's not that different from me. There is one thing I've figured out: beautiful women and farm labor are incompatible. When you get tired of Cooper and his gulag, you can come find me."

He smiled slightly; his facial muscles were tense and his normally clear sea-colored eyes were bloodshot. Jeff kissed her on the mouth, and she tasted and smelled the stench of alcohol.

Her hat fell to the ground, and she tried to push him away. "Let go of me! What's the matter with you?"

He slowly released her and bent over to retrieve her hat. He carefully placed it back on her head, tucking an errant curl inside the brim. "Cooper's too busy searching for his soul to pay attention to the most important things in his life." He smiled again. "Don't worry about my discussing your business. Why would I tell anyone else exclusive information that can be used to blackmail Cooper?"

Jeff grabbed her shoulders and kissed her forcefully on the forehead. When he released her, he turned and exited beyond the row of camellias. She felt her face become hot. *He's lost his mind.* Exasperated by the experience, Mills quickly walked to Cooper's home.

She knocked on the front door, and Cooper opened it standing before her. "Come in, Mills, I'm sorry about Jeff's behavior. Besides his overindulgence in alcohol, he's completely out of sorts over a problem."

Cooper helped her with a chair in the study and then walked to the window.

"Jeff came to see me after he left you. He was insulting toward you and overly forward with me. He said that you told him to stay away from me, and that his current situation prevented him from telling you to go to hell."

Cooper frowned. "I did tell him to stay away from you. Jeff's hedonistic pleasures take him from one woman to another. He and his friends hold pleasure as their highest priority, and you have too much potential to be associated with their cocaine-embraced lifestyle. I think his behavior this morning is due to the problems he's having."

"What problems?"

"I've been assisting Jeff with some of his investments. I had no intention of seeing my cousin hang himself from a bridge trestle because he's near ruin."

"I see."

Cooper moved away from the window and took her in his arms. "Calm down now. I love you. You've given me hope when I needed it the most."

The weekend after the Fourth of July, Cooper asked Mills to accompany him to his Combahee property. Prior to leaving, they did a final walk through the new boat house with Fritz. Beaming with satisfaction, Fritz pointed out the features of the new building—the mahogany and teak construction gleamed with perfection. Prior to his departure, he said with his usual formality, "Miss Taylor, stay away from yellow jackets and my best wishes with the foundation work." Then with a tip of his hat, Fritz said goodbye and left the Edisto.

After Fritz had gone, Cooper and Mills began their trip to his Combahee property. On the drive south on the Savannah Highway, Cooper was unusually quiet. *What's on his mind?*

Mills put her hand on top of his. "Is there something wrong?"

A slight smile came to his face. "I'm all right," he responded.

When they reached the Combahee property, Vern's truck was not in the driveway, but the cats were in their protective positions on the front porch. Cooper opened the gate to his property, and they drove down the lane to his cabin.

During the afternoon, they explored the old farmhouse and took a walk around the property. Cooper held her hand and kissed her palm several times, but said very little. After they made dinner, he played an oldies station out of Savannah on the radio, and they danced on the screened porch. He began to kiss her as they held one another, and he lifted her in his arms and carried her into the bedroom.

When she woke in the morning, Cooper was no longer with her. She put on a robe and left the bedroom to find him. He was standing on the porch, staring out to the river. She put her arms around his waist. "I'm worried about you. Why are you so quiet?"

He turned to face her. "My father and brother were killed twenty years ago today."

"Cooper, I'm so sorry. I had no idea. Do you want to talk about it?"

He led her to a couch and pulled her into a seat beside him. He took a deep breath and said, "We were two days at sea, having sailed from Harbour Island, Eleuthera. In the late afternoon, a storm began to build west of our position, and Jeff and I were on deck. The odd thing about the storm clouds was their appearance was nearly white, not the dark clouds you see with most thunderstorms. Then we began to see the strangest wall of white coming toward us. We realized that the wall was a wave, or in our case, a series of freak waves. My father told Jeff to put on a life jacket, but he was frozen in place. I guess he was too stunned to react."

"What happened then?"

"My father and Beau went in to the cabin to make a Mayday call, and I yelled to them about the wave—the wall was almost on us. The first wave knocked Jeff in the water, and I left the helm to save him. While I was in the ocean, another wall of water came across the bow and rolled the sailboat on her side. She began to take on water, and during the height of the storm, I could not get back to the cabin to save them."

Tears formed in his eyes and he continued, "We didn't realize it, but my father had made a successful Mayday call, and after several hours, help arrived. I felt so helpless while Jeff and I waited beside the capsized boat to be rescued." He wiped his face with the back of his hand. "I will never forget that wall of water bearing down on us."

As Mills took Cooper in her arms, she knew he was allowing her knowledge of his most deeply held secrets.

In the afternoon, Vern Adams came down to the cabin to check on the premises. Cooper invited him inside, and he initially had a look of astonishment, which changed to a smile when he saw Mills. "Miss Taylor, how nice to see you again. I saw the gate open, and I just wanted to make sure everything was all right."

"Vern, thanks for coming. I should have phoned to let you know we'd be here this weekend."

"Not to worry." Vern paused for a moment and then asked, "Cooper, why don't you and Miss Taylor join us for dinner tonight? My wife's not been feeling well lately, and I think your company would lift her spirits."

"That's a nice gesture. What time would you like for us to come?"

"How about seven?"

"Can we bring anything?"

"Just yourselves."

That evening, Mrs. Adams greeted Cooper and Mills at the door. As they walked into the living room, Mills noticed the shrine to their son was unchanged from her last visit. Mr. Adams rose from his seat to shake Cooper's hand and thanked them for coming to dinner.

"Cooper, have you been doing any fishing? It won't be long before the tarpon start running."

"We've mostly had success with redfish and sheepshead."

"Say—you ought to try the Broad and Chechessee Rivers near Beaufort for tarpon. I've done well there in the past."

Mrs. Adams came into the living room. "I've got dinner on the buffet; please join us for the blessing in the dining room."

They joined hands in prayer, and Mr. Adams led the prayer for the meal. Before he finished, he prayed for his son, killed long ago in Vietnam.

When Mr. Adams said, "Amen," Mills looked at Mrs. Adams, who seemed deep in thought. Her husband touched her arm. "Mrs. Adams, are you going to bring the fish in from the kitchen?"

"Oh, yes," she said rising from her chair.

When she returned, she managed a smile, and they filled their plates from the buffet. During the meal, Mrs. Adams contributed little to the conversation.

Homemade ice cream was served on the screened porch after dinner and Mills concluded this was a specialty of Vern's.

"Peach ice cream made with South Carolina peaches. I hope you enjoyed it," he said.

As they sat quietly on the porch, Mrs. Adams told them the reason for her quietness. "I hope I haven't been a terrible hostess this evening, but my mind is distracted. I've been so unhappy lately. Today is the anniversary of our son's death. I've missed him so much."

Cooper and Mills looked at one another, and then Cooper took Mrs. Adams' hand in his. "I'm sorry for your loss. We share an unfortunate anniversary. My brother and father were killed twenty years ago today."

Mrs. Adams rocked forward in her chair and stared into Cooper's eyes, as though his admission represented a revelation to her. "Cooper, I know we don't have blood roots, but I think there is a bond between us. There is a reason we have come to know one another."

Mr. Adams broke into the conversation, "It's a coincidence. You're going to scare Cooper with your superstitions."

"Oh, not at all," Cooper said. "I agree it's very odd."

She went to the living room and returned with a photograph of her son in his Marine Corps uniform. "This is my son, Jeremy. He would be a few years older than you, Cooper, if we still had him with us. There is a reason the Lord has permitted us to know one another. Like other events, this, too, will be revealed when the Heavenly Father sees fit to show us."

"I'm sorry, Mrs. Adams, but I'm not a religious person."

She looked into Cooper's eyes and then patted him on the hand.

When they finished dining, Mr. Adams walked with Cooper and Mills to the gate. The last light of day was in the evening sky, and the sounds of the night surrounded them.

"Cooper, Miss Taylor? Please don't worry about what my wife said this evening. The folks she comes from are Christian people, but they believe in signs and other notions that some folks might consider superstitious. It's just that her mourning for our son has never stopped and she looks for any hopeful indication that can help her deal with her loss."

"Vern, you don't need to offer any explanations. Please let me know if I can be of help to you and your wife."

"You're a good man, Cooper. Thank you for joining us this evening. Good night, folks."

When they returned to Edisto, Mills checked her answering machine for messages. Paul had phoned to let her know that Max had passed away. He explained that Max had one last request of Cooper. He wanted him to play the piano at his funeral and he had left a letter to that effect.

Mills went by their townhouse and picked up a letter that Max had written to both of them. That evening, Cooper read part of the note aloud:

> There are two songs that I'd like for you to play excerpts from at my funeral: Gershwin's *Rhapsody in Blue* and Peter de Rose's *Deep Purple*. The colors suit my disposition; they are not colors of despair, but are shades of deliverance. I cannot begin to thank you for the kindness you showed me, but there is one way you reached out to me for which I will always be grateful. Both of you were willing to touch me, to shake my hand. Thank you for your gentle and compassionate gesture.

The funeral was held at Watson's funeral Home on Ashley Avenue on what seemed the hottest day of the year. Cooper played the music that Max had requested and the room was filled with spiritual energy when he finished.

Mills noticed that the service was a celebration of Max's life and it was not intended to be a somber event. After hearing cheerful anecdotes about him from friends and former music students, Mills concluded that Max must have been an outgoing individual before disease had ravaged his body. At the end of the service, the attendees sang the only religious song chosen, "Let Us Break Bread Together."

During the service, Mills noticed that Paul did not sit with Max's family, but sat behind them with several friends. When the service was complete, Max's family sought Cooper.

"Young man, your playing was lovely. Were you one of Max's students?" Max's mother inquired.

"No, ma'am, Miss Taylor and I were friends with Max."

Cooper introduced himself and Mills, and Mrs. Oliver said, "Thank you for your gesture. Your music performance was like a reading of beautiful poetry."

CHAPTER 25

It is Nice to be Nice

The Rockville Regatta was held on the first weekend in August at the Sea Island Yacht Club. Jeff was competing in the event and Cooper invited Mills to travel with him by boat to watch him race. Both having received a written note from Jeff apologizing for his behavior the morning he had found them together, Mills and Cooper made the trek to support him during the race.

Maneuvering the *Miss Elise* into Bohicket Creek, Mills was astounded to see the number of boats tied together to watch the race and celebrate.

The grounds around the yacht club were filled with spectators and they walked through the crowd to gain a vantage point to view the race. Cooper was able to pick out Jeff's boat, and he said to Mills, "It looks like Jeff is going to have a hard time winning."

Jeff's sailboat was named *The Renegade*.

Cooper explained that Jeff's craft was termed a Sea Island One design, and the skipper with the best cumulative performance for the racing season won the Ellis Trophy. When the race was finished, they located Jeff and his sailing friends, Irving and Abigail Sellers.

Jeff saw Cooper and Mills approach, and he shook Cooper's hand and kissed Mills on the cheek. "No Ellis Trophy for me this year," Jeff said with a smile.

"You can't win them all," Abigail responded.

"I learned that a long time ago. Cooper, we were just about to have some drinks. Why don't you and Mills join us?"

"Thanks, Jeff, but we're going to start for home. I worry about the celebrating that occurs on the spectator boats. We just came to support you."

"Thank you, Cooper. I appreciate your telling me that."

When they arrived home, Cooper told Mills that he had a surprise for her. He left her on her screened porch and returned in several minutes with a colander of fruit. "Close your eyes and I'm going to give you something delicious."

His fingertips gently caressed her lips as he placed a piece of fruit in her mouth. "How do you like it?"

She felt a sensual pleasure with his touch and the taste of the fruit on her palate. "Mmmm, delicious. Fresh figs. Where's the tree?"

"It's on the other side of the equipment barn. The tree has almost finished bearing fruit for the season."

He picked up the book of poetry that was on her table and looked through the contents, then sat down beside her and began to read:

To Solitude

> O SOLITUDE! If I must with thee dwell,
> Let it not be among the jumbled heap
> Of murky buildings; - climb with me the steep,
> Nature's Observatory - whence the dell,
> Its flowery slopes – its rivers crystal swell,
> May seem a span: let me thy vigils keep
> 'Mongst boughs pavilioned; where the Deer's swift leap
> Startles the wild Bee from the Fox-glove bell.
> Ah! fain would I frequent such scenes with thee;
> But the sweet converse of an innocent mind,
> Whose words are images of thoughts refin'd
> Is my soul's pleasure; and it sure must be
> Almost the highest bliss of human kind,
> When to thy haunts two kindred spirits flee.

Closing the poetry book, he said, "John Keats." He paused and thoughtfully said, "Solitude. I am no longer alone. Mills—with you, I have another chance for love."

He put his arm around her and asked, "How would you like to go away with me for a few days?"

"Yes—where do you want to go?"

"St. John, in the US Virgin Islands. I stayed in a resort once that I think you'll like."

The Caneel Bay Resort was one of the most stunningly beautiful places that Mills had ever seen. On the ferry ride from St. Thomas, Mills admired the clear, blue-green waters of the Caribbean and the peaks of the volcanic islands of the American and British Virgin Islands. Cooper explained that Lawrence Rockefeller founded the resort in the 1950s as an ecofriendly escape.

Their room was at Hawk's Nest Beach and had a view of the ruins of a windmill on a nearby mountain. The young woman who showed them to their room pointed out the remains, saying, "When the Danes controlled these islands, they built windmills to aid in sugar production. There are several on the island."

Before she left the room, she asked, "Are you two on your honeymoon? Your eyes sparkle for one another."

Cooper smiled at her but did not respond.

The next morning, they walked around the acreage of the resort and marveled at the pristine beauty of the grounds. They encountered wild donkeys that brayed loudly when approached. When they reached a crest on a hillside, they sat down on a weathered teak bench that overlooked the ocean toward Tortola.

"When were you last here?"

"Jeff and I raced in the Springtime Regatta in the British Virgin Islands."

"Did you win?"

"The regatta is a series of races, and yes, we did win a few of the heats."

"Why did you give up competitive racing?"

"I just didn't have time for it anymore."

That afternoon they went snorkeling off Hawk's Nest Beach. Mills marveled at the abundance of colorful tropical fish, but hidden amongst the coral structures was a fish that Cooper prevented Mills from continuing toward. He took her hand, and they swam away from the area.

While they treaded water, Cooper explained that even in the beauty of such natural surroundings danger lurked. The fish among the coral formations was a barracuda.

After their swim, they sunbathed on Hawk's Nest Beach and watched the ferry boats pass by on their way to the British Virgin Islands.

"Cooper, I think you told me that you're open water certified for scuba diving. Do you want to dive while we're here?"

"No. I think I'm going to limit myself to snorkeling on this trip. The last time I went, I became ill during one of the dives."

"Where were you?"

"In the Turks and Caicos Islands. I rented a sailboat to take Elise, Jeff, and me on a diving and sailing excursion. The crew takes you to different locations in the islands, and you dive, eat, and sleep onboard the boat. I ended up in a hospital in Providenciales. I passed out underwater, and the dive master saved my life. Fortunately, we were on a shallow-water dive."

"Had you ever become sick while diving before that?"

"No, and the experience made a strong impression on me. I've written to the dive master, Erik Grootman, a couple of times to thank him for saving my life, but his return correspondence always says that no thanks are necessary."

Late that afternoon, they took a tour of the island by taxi. The front office had arranged the tour and they met their guide, Elias, at the taxi stand. "Greetings to you," he said with an island brogue. He smiled broadly, showing perfectly straight, white teeth.

They took the North Shore Road, and Elias pointed out Trunk Bay. "When the Danes controlled these islands, large sea turtles nested on the beach and the colonialists thought they looked like trunks." Elias pointed out the ruins of a sugar mill and they saw wild donkeys grazing within the stone structure.

On the side of a mountain, Elias parked the taxi at the ruins of the Annaberg Sugar Mill and accompanied them on a tour of the grounds. He led them to the crest of the mountain and pointed to a nearby island. "That is Tortola."

"It looks close enough to swim to," Mills responded.

"The distance is short; in fact, cows swim the channel. I have seen it myself."

Elias looked at where Mills was standing and said, "Ma'am, please step toward me. You are close to a plant that can sting you. It can be quite painful."

"I seem to attract things that sting and bite," Mills replied.

As they descended the mountain, Elias pointed out features of the ancient sugar mill and told them its history. When they left the ruins of the mill, Elias drove them to the highest peak of the island and pointed out a tranquil-looking bay in the distance. "That is Hurricane Hole. During hurricanes, mariners anchor their boats in the bay and tie them off to the mangroves. The natural topography that surrounds the inlet, plus the mangroves, have, for generations, spared boats from the violence of storms."

When they arrived in Cruz Bay, Elias dropped them off at an outdoor restaurant where the locals danced to Caribbean music. Elias volunteered, "That is called Quelbe. Slaves weren't allowed to play drums or dance African style by their colonial masters, so they originated this music, which has its roots in African and European folk music. Do you want me to pick you up later?"

"No, I think we'll walk back to Caneel Bay by the mountain trail."

"Do be careful. There are tarantulas along the paths, but ma'am, they will be more frightened of you than you are of them." *Tarantulas!?*

Cooper paid Elias for the tour, and he thanked them for allowing him to be their guide. He smiled broadly when he looked at Cooper's payment. "It is nice to be nice," he said.

"Elias, you have a beautiful smile," Mills said.

"Thank you, ma'am. It is in my family's blood roots."

The next morning, Cooper surprised Mills with a sailing excursion around the island. An adventurer, Marcel Renaud, an acquaintance of Jeff's, was the captain of the boat. There was one mate, named Josiah. They sailed to several diving locations, and Josiah went into the water with them each time. He brought an underwater writing tablet and wrote down the names of creatures that he could identify.

After snorkeling, Cooper and Mills enjoyed a variety of French dishes that Marcel had prepared for them.

"How do Marcel and Jeff know one another?"

"From yacht racing. Jeff said he travels from one exotic location to another and offers sailing excursions to earn a living. I think Jeff said he had been living in Costa Rica before he came here. He is a retired French military officer."

In the afternoon, Marcel returned them to the Caneel Bay dock and wished them well. As they departed the boat, he said, "Tell Mr. Radcliffe I look forward to racing against him in the future. He is a formidable opponent and a talented skipper."

Before the end of their summer vacation, Cooper's cousins, Zack and Blair, came for a visit to Edisto. He took Mills and the boys tarpon fishing, and she found Cooper's technique of catching bait fish to be very clever. He followed diving pelicans. Without failure, where the birds plunged into the river, bait fish congregated, causing the water to appear to shiver on the surface. He called the water "nervous," where the tiny, silvery menhaden fish teemed.

Cooper instructed Blair to throw the cast net to catch baitfish, but the net folded up on him each time. Blair began to get frustrated and Cooper told him they'd work on his technique that afternoon. Eventually, they caught enough baitfish to go for tarpon. They cast their lines and then sat in the intense heat of the August morning. Excitement broke loose when Blair's fishing rod completely bent over. He put on the fighting belt to hold his fishing rod, and a massive fish jumped out of the water; it seemed to walk across the surface on its tail before crashing into the river.

"Lower your pole when the tarpon jumps out of the water or it will break your line. Remember, bow to the king," Cooper said.

When Blair finally reeled the fish beside the boat, he was exhausted from the fight, but so was the fish. Cooper took photos of the boys with the fish in the background, and they beamed with delight. "Your fish must weigh a hundred pounds," Cooper said enthusiastically.

During the afternoon, Cooper worked with Blair on his technique for throwing the cast net. He was still having trouble keeping the net open and Mills listened as Cooper asked the boys to join him for a talk.

"Did we do something wrong?"

Cooper laughed at their response and said, "No, boys. When I learned to throw the cast net, I was taught the technique by a man who was already in his eighties."

"He must have been strong."

"No, he just understood that a proper technique can mean the difference between a successful cast or having the net close up on you. He taught my brother and me that this applied to people as well. When you successfully throw your cast net in life, you open yourself up to all kinds of people. You learn to respect and accept people who think differently from you. When you open your hearts to others, you'll feel better for your efforts. Boys, his name is James Camp, and he's now 105 years old and still lives in the Edisto area."

They were both quiet for a moment, and then they said, "Thank you for taking us fishing. We always have a great time when we're with you."

The boys hugged Cooper, and when Blair made another attempt at the net, he opened it up full circle as it landed in the water. He smiled with satisfaction.

Late that afternoon, Anne came to pick up her sons, and they were adamant that they didn't want to leave. They were dressed to visit their grandmother in Charleston, and when Anne looked at Blair's tennis shoes, she said, "I told you to wear your new shoes to your grandmother's."

"Mom, those shoes are fine if you're going to a funeral."

Cooper laughed at Blair's comment and hugged the boys. Before he got in the car, Blair kissed Mills on her cheek. "Thank you for driving the boat. I don't know when we'll visit again."

Anne drove away, and both boys waved goodbye from the rear window of the car.

As they watched Anne's car depart, they realized that another vehicle was approaching the house.

"It's Lieutenant Barnes. Mills, excuse me for a few minutes."

The policeman parked at the front of the house, and Cooper joined him for a conversation. Mills watched as they went inside. She waited for Cooper in the rear courtyard and after several minutes, the detective left the farm. Mills knocked on the front door, but when Cooper did not answer, she opened the door.

He was sitting at his desk in the study, and she heard him say, "You have my permission to show him any documents he wants to see. I don't think that's necessary. All right, goodbye."

She went to the study and tapped on the door. "Come in, Mills."

"Is everything all right?"

"Yes, the lieutenant asked me some questions about my most recent land purchase. He said that he just found out about the transaction from the land transfers, and I should have been more forthcoming. Mills, every property I own has been searched. He wants to look at Jeff's files on my real estate purchases." He was quiet for a moment. "Oddly, he asked me several questions about my diving accident in the Turks and Caicos Islands last summer. Jeff said that if Lieutenant Barnes wants information from him, he'll have to get a subpoena. His dislike for the lieutenant may have something to do with his refusal."

One evening in mid-August, Cooper took Mills onto the river to fish. They anchored the *Miss Elise* in a marsh area near the old mansion ruins. As the afternoon grew short, heat lightning was in the western sky, and over the ocean, lightning illuminated the vertical tops of thunderheads.

"How far away do you think those thunderclouds are?" Mills inquired.

"It's hard to tell. They could be twenty-five miles away."

When Mills turned around to face the mansion ruin, she was shocked to see lights moving about on the grounds. "Cooper. Look—the lights, they're at the ruins."

He turned and stared at the lights, and his face momentarily showed a deep frown. "It's probably a reflection from the thunderstorms at sea."

"They're moving about."

"You know . . .? We can solve this right now."

He pulled up the anchor, started the engines, and headed directly for the old house ruins.

"We're not going up there, are we?"

"Sure, why not? Maybe we can solve the mystery of the lights, once and for all. You're not afraid are you?"

"Yes."

"I'll hold your hand."

"Don't tease me."

Cooper anchored the boat at the bank, and they walked up the incline to the elevation of the ruin. When they reached the crest of the grade, they only saw multitudes of lightning bugs, perhaps as many as Mills had ever seen in one location.

"The lights are gone. There are only lightning bugs."

"The lights are probably a reflection, as I told you."

She looked up above her into the trees and in between the boughs of live oaks were the largest spiders that Mills had ever seen. They clustered together as if in a colony, and several of the spiders were as big as her hand.

"My God. Look at the size of those spiders."

"Golden silk orb weavers. You see them in the late summer. They've been known to catch small birds in the webs. Frightening-looking creatures, aren't they?"

Cooper took her hand, and they walked to the row of cabins. The grounds had been recently mowed, and he went to the rose bush to cut a single blossom for her. "This may be the last rose of summer, and I want you to have it."

When he cut the stem with his pocketknife, he severely pricked his finger on a thorn. Blood began to flow from the wound, and after handing her the rose, he wrapped his finger in his handkerchief.

"Are you all right?"

"Yes, it's just a prick."

As they walked back toward the boat, there were two magnificent butterflies meandering above the pathway toward the river. Abruptly, one of the butterflies flew up into the sky and was ensnared in the web of the spiders. The butterfly struggled for its freedom, but instantly, one of the orb weavers attacked the butterfly and sat on top of it, fingering it with its long legs.

Mills turned her head from the scene and Cooper led her to the boat. "I'm sorry, Mills; the processes in nature can seem cruel at times."

She held the rose in her hand and smelled its fragrance, but wished they had not come to the ruin at all. That night, as she lay beside him in bed, she felt an overwhelming sadness. She was in love with him; it was a love that she thought would never happen for her, but he was not hers, not really, not yet—and maybe not ever. For the first time since they became lovers, she was overcome by feelings of anxiety and guilt. Tears did not bring absolution.

In the early morning light, Mills noticed that the rose's petals were already beginning to fall.

CHAPTER 26

The Dove Shoot

The anniversary of Elise Heath's disappearance came and went. Cooper was quiet and at times withdrawn during the late days of August. He had had trouble sleeping during the night, and Mills attributed his insomnia to hurtful recollections of past memories.

One afternoon, Cooper drove her to the field where dove season would be opening in less than two weeks. The silence was broken by the beating wings of doves as they flew up from the millet and sunflowers, and then settled back down into a different location. Cooper walked to the fence and said, "Last year, I canceled the dove shoot. We were all out searching for Elise and putting up posters about her disappearance. It's been a year now. Mills, I want you to understand that I love you, but for all our sakes, I wish she could be found."

He took a deep breath and opened the truck door for her. When they returned to his home, they parked at the rear and Cooper led her to a bench in the courtyard.

"Mills, I need to talk to you." He took her hand and said, "I've had a nightmare at least a half dozen times."

"I noticed you were having trouble sleeping recently. Are you dreaming about Elise?"

"No, baby. I'm dreaming about you." He had a frighteningly somber expression on his face. "I'm worried, and I'm not sure what to do."

"Tell me about it."

"I'm with you and rain is falling. High winds are blowing through the trees near the river. You're drenched from the rainfall and as the dream continues, we're in the equipment barn. You have a shocked expression on your face. Mills, there's blood on your clothes and in your hair. Then you just stare at me."

Cooper took her in his arms and hugged her closely, kissing her on the forehead.

Just as he embraced her, Mills noticed a man walk around the side of Cooper's house toward them. "Britton is here."

Cooper released his embrace on Mills and stood to meet his friend. "Britton, I wasn't expecting you."

"That's obvious," Britton retorted. "I was on my way back to Charleston from Savannah, and I thought I'd stop and see you because I've hardly laid eyes on you in weeks. I now understand why. Cooper, I'm surprised at you. I've known you for over twenty years, and this is the first selfish thing I've ever seen you do. You kept Mills so busy with work that she didn't have time for anything—but you. Did you forget about Elise?"

"No. I didn't forget about Elise."

"And what about Mills? You can't give her what she deserves."

"My relationship with Mills is none of your concern."

"This farm may seem like Eden, but it takes very little to fall out of favor in Paradise."

Britton looked at both of them in disgust, and then walked away, disappearing around the corner of the house.

Cooper took a deep breath and sat back down beside Mills. "You've had two accidents on this farm, and now I'm having this dream. Am I not meant to love and be loved in return? I'll take you away from here if necessary."

"If I'm going to be hurt, it could happen anywhere. What if it's destiny?"

"And what if it's not? What if we can alter this premonition and we don't make an effort? We could go away together—Central America perhaps, and people would know you as my wife from the onset."

"I love you, but have you thought that if we leave right now, it will look like you're running away?"

"I've been putting up with false allegations for over a year now. Britton just accused me of not being able to give you the life you deserve. I can't fail you. I won't."

The opening day of dove season arrived in early September, but the summer heat had not yet left the Low Country. The farm had been prepared for Cooper's guests, and before the hunters began to arrive, Mills noticed Charles speaking with Cooper and then walking to his truck. He wiped the sweat from his brow with a handkerchief and then started to leave. Mills stopped him and asked, "Aren't you going to shoot with us?"

"No, Miss Mills. I'm not going to join in today. I'll shoot with you and Cooper later."

"Charles, I'm sure that Cooper would like for you to stay."

"I never hunt on opening day with this group. Cooper understands this."

"But I don't understand."

"Miss Mills, some of these folks make me uncomfortable. Cooper is a fine young man, but I'd just as soon shoot later on. Not to worry. There are plenty of doves this season." He smiled and gave his truck some gas. "Have a good time today."

Mills joined Cooper and said, "Why won't Charles shoot with us today?"

"He never shoots with me on opening day. He knows he's invited, but he says some members of the hunting group make him uncomfortable."

The caterers had set up refreshment tents around the house and as the hunters began to arrive, they congregated around the stands.

Cooper took Mills aside and said, "I have your hunting station set up. You won't be far from me, and as the afternoon comes on, you'll be in the shade." There was a large group of hunters, Cooper's neighbors, his relatives, and some people Mills had never met before. Just before noon, the hunters began to take their positions. At first, the birds arrived in sparse numbers, but by the middle of the afternoon, an abundance of doves began to flock to the field.

Jeff was not far from Cooper and Mills, and she watched as he shot with his usual perfection. His Labrador, Brutus, would immediately retrieve his birds from the field.

They called out inbound dove to each other, and Sam retrieved the downed birds for Cooper and Mills. The Labrador took the dove to the correct hunter each time.

Mills noticed that a number of guests had congregated underneath a live oak tree and were socializing, rather than hunting.

By four-thirty, Jeff had shot a limit of doves, and he stopped by to speak to Cooper. When they finished their conversation, on his way to the house, Jeff walked to where Mills was seated. "I see that Cooper picked a shady spot for you." He stepped close to her and quietly said, "You two have virtually disappeared all summer. I want you to show me firsthand what Cooper's been teaching you."

"Jeff, I thought you already knew how to throw a cast net."

He smiled at her, kissed her on the forehead, and then rubbed his sweaty cheek against hers.

"What are you doing?" *Yuck!*

"I'm just messing with you." He winked at her before heading toward the house, Brutus at his side.

Not long after Jeff's departure, Cooper asked Mills to gather her gear. He wanted to make sure his guests were being served properly.

Cooper requested refreshments for Mills and himself before his uncle Ian joined them. "Cooper, please allow me to borrow Mills for a few moments. There are some flowers in your garden I'd like to show her."

Cooper smiled, and Ian took her hand and led her away. "Mills, thank you for accommodating me. I'm very worried about Cooper. He came to me yesterday with this declaration that he was going to move to Central America and buy a cattle ranch—maybe he said Costa Rica. Needless to say, I was stunned."

"I know—I'm sorry you're worried."

"I'm not sure if you are aware of this, but in a few years, I plan to retire from Heath Brothers and arrangements are in place for Cooper to head the company. He practically runs the operation now. I also know that he would never let down my children who do not participate in the management of the company, but are dependent on Heath Brothers for their livelihoods."

He strolled close to a rose bush and bent a stem to inhale the fragrance of a blossom. "Cooper reminds me of King Edward VIII who abdicated the throne of England for an American divorcée, Wallis Simpson. He was unable to marry her and sit on the British throne, so he gave up his royal lineage to be her husband. I am only guessing at a relationship because Cooper is a private person and does not discuss his personal life. I realize that if he is in love, he cannot marry this lady because of his current situation, but going away right now would give his detractors more ammunition to accuse him of wrongdoing. All summer, I've noticed that Cooper has been thoughtful and, at times, preoccupied with an important issue. I also know that he has been under a terrible strain from Elise's disappearance, but I've never known him to make a poor decision." He took a deep breath and then asked, "I realize this is none of my business, but are you and Cooper expecting an infant?"

What? "No, Mr. Heath, Cooper and I are not expecting a baby." She felt herself blush.

"I'm sorry to have asked you that, but I'm just trying to understand his reasoning."

"Cooper has been having a nightmare about me, in which I am injured and bleeding. He thinks that if we go away from here, he can alter what he believes to be a premonition. In his dream, he sees me wet from the pouring rain of a raging storm. Before it's over, he envisions me with blood on my body, and I stare at him with a shocked expression. He thinks I'm going to be hurt if I stay here."

"Cooper has had these premonitions before. I remember him suffering a series of dreams before my brother and nephew were killed. I'm sorry; I'm frightening you."

She felt a chill run deep to her bones.

He put his hand on her shoulder and said, "I'll think about this. I hope I can think of a way to help you both. If I wasn't aware of Cooper's capability, I would think this too fantastic to believe—and Mills, I was not comparing you to Wallis Simpson. I related that story because it dealt with personal sacrifice. I don't want you two to go away and live in exile."

When they returned to the party, Mills noticed that Cooper's Air Force friend, James Burton, had joined the festivities, and he was becoming boisterous from alcohol consumption. Cooper took him aside and told him to go light on the bourbon, but James waved him off.

Mills went to Cooper's side.

"Britton didn't come to the hunt. I haven't heard from him since he—" Jeff and his father joined them before Cooper could finish his sentence. "Cooper, where have you been keeping yourself this summer?"

"Dad, Cooper's been extremely busy with his harvest. He's been very successful."

"Oh, good, Cooper, I'm so glad to hear that. I know you work very hard. Miss Taylor, I understand you've been pulling your weight around here too."

"I've tried to be helpful, sir."

"That's what I hear. Keep up the good work. Jeff, I'd like a scotch, son.

Let's go to the tent and then find your mother. We'll see you before we leave, Cooper."

As they walked away, Jeff turned and winked at Cooper and Mills.

The rest of the afternoon, Mills talked with guests and found herself comfortable in the company of Anne Jefferson and her husband. Jeff joined them and began to tell real estate stories. *Jeff has an excellent sense of humor—a side I haven't really seen.*

"I expected to do several real estate transactions with the Andersons, so after the closing, I called my florist and asked him to send them an arrangement. A couple of days later, Randolph Anderson phoned to thank me for the flowers, but he said that the florist had gotten my order confused with someone else's. He said, 'Jeff, the flowers that came to us had a note of sympathy for the loss of a loved one.' Well, I was furious with the florist because I had done so much business with him. When I got him on the telephone he said, 'You think the Andersons were upset—you should have heard from the folks at the funeral home. The note on the flowers that went to the family of the deceased read, 'welcome to your new home.'"

Mills laughed at his story and then went to find Cooper.

She located him inside the kitchen, retrieving a case of wine for his guests. As he came toward the front of the house, Mills offered to hold the front door open for him. She walked past the study, and James Burton called out to her, "Honey, would you get me bourbon, and see if you can find an ashtray?"

He was sitting in one of Cooper's leather chairs smoking a cigar. Cooper heard his request and put down the case of wine and entered the study. "James, I think you've had enough to drink, and if you need anything, I'd prefer that you ask me."

"Okay, okay, don't you think you're being a little testy?"

"No, James, I'm just tired of your asinine behavior."

"I'll get my own damn drink." He pushed past Cooper and went out the front door, ignoring Mills.

"Cooper, I didn't mean to cause a problem."

"You didn't cause a problem. James Burton's behavior caused a problem."

The party continued past night fall, and when the last of the guests departed, Mills sat on the porch with Cooper. "I thoroughly enjoyed myself today."

"I'm glad you did. We have one more task before we turn in for the evening. Come with me, and I'll show you how to clean the birds."

A few days after the dove shoot, Mills was handling farm chores when Cooper's attorney, Murphy Black, arrived at the property. He said it was urgent that he speak to Cooper. She drove the Land Rover into the fields to get him, and when they returned, Murphy was sitting on the front porch in a rocking chair. Cooper asked Mills to join him, and after he greeted Murphy, he said, "You can say anything you want to in front of her."

"All right, Cooper. I had a visit from Lieutenant Barnes, and he brought a subpoena, requiring me to turn over all documents dealing with your real estate purchases. Jeff has received a subpoena as well."

"I have no objection to you showing him the documents."

"I confess, I'm worried about you. Is there anything you want to tell me?"

"No, Murphy, there's nothing I have to tell you. It disappoints me that you ask."

"I'm just trying to help you, while I still can."

"I'm giving consideration to leaving here for an extended period of time. I still have my passport."

"If you leave here now, you'll be a marked man. Everyone will think you orchestrated Elise's disappearance and consider you a fugitive from justice."

"I have a reason for my decision, and it has nothing to do with Elise."

"Do you want to elaborate?"

"No, but I'll be asking you to help manage my affairs."

"I think you're making a mistake. Before Lieutenant Barnes left my office, he said that even those who demonstrate grace under pressure have their breaking point."

"He must have been a Hemingway fan."

"Cooper, don't joke around."

A few days later, Marian put her arm around Mills in the kitchen. "Miss Mills, Cooper has told me about his dreams. I'm sorry he's having these nightmares, but I do remember a premonition he had that turned out to be a reality. He has told me about his decision to take you away from here. I realized weeks ago that you two had become very close. Honey, I know it's none of my business, but I don't want to see either of you hurt. Lord knows he's been through enough already, and now these omens involve you." She paused for a moment and said, "All I know to do is pray. He has asked Charles and me to run the farm, and we'll help in any way we can."

"Marian, I love Cooper. He believes that I am going to be injured if I remain here. We've discussed moving to Central America, and I've agreed to go with him."

She put her arm around Mills and hugged her.

Before Cooper left the farm for work, he invited Mills to ride horses with him that afternoon. Before she met him at the stables, she took a walk to the river, and on her way back, she noticed his Suburban in the driveway. She saw that Cooper was in the rear courtyard, and she started to go to him. In her exuberance, she failed to realize that someone else was with him, a man whose position had been obscured by a camellia bush. She was almost to Cooper when he gently waved to her, and she halted in her tracks. The man with Cooper was Lieutenant Barnes.

"Well, Miss Taylor, how nice to see you again."

"Good afternoon, Lieutenant."

"Miss Taylor, forgive us, but I need to speak to Cooper alone."

Mills took a seat near the outdoor fireplace and waited for them to finish. After several minutes passed, Lieutenant Barnes called out to her, "Miss Taylor, I want to apologize for interrupting your meeting with Cooper. I hope you'll forgive me." He grinned at Cooper and said, "Is it possible that I've finally found a chink in your armor?"

Cooper did not respond to the question and with no change in his expression, he asked, "Lieutenant, if you don't have any more questions, would you please excuse us?"

"Yes. Miss Taylor, you look like you're dressed for riding. I hope you have a nice time."

She nodded to him, and they watched the detective depart. "What's wrong, Cooper?"

"He asked me questions about the Old Camp place that I just purchased. He wants to search the property again. I've told him repeatedly to search all he wants to, but I think he wants to see my reaction." He hugged her shoulder and said, "Uncle Ian has accepted what we're going to do. He told me he couldn't bear an accident befalling you if it could be prevented. Ian said I'm always welcome back at Heath Brothers. I think I've broken his heart. I have many jobs to complete at Heath Brothers before we go, but I think we can leave before the end of September."

"Cooper, I feel guilty."

"No, no." He hugged her again and said, "First, we'll look in Costa Rica."

CHAPTER 27

Death Knocks at the Door

A strong tropical disturbance formed off the coast of Africa around the ninth of September. In its earliest stages, it was more of a cluster of thunderstorms visible by satellite imagery. The thunderstorms were brought to Cooper's attention, but no Heath Brothers ships were operating in the proximity of the growing disturbance. By the tenth, the cluster of storms had formed into a tropical depression, and the National Hurricane Center began to track the system. On the eleventh, the depression became a tropical storm, and two days later, the storm was a full hurricane.

Cooper kept very busy with his work schedule, and he only mentioned the storm once to Mills, but over the Atlantic, it became the eighth named storm of the season and continued to gain strength as an intensifying hurricane named Hugo.

Early on the morning of the seventeenth, Cooper told Mills that the storm he had mentioned to her had become a powerful hurricane and was nearing the US Virgin Islands.

"I hate to be the bearer of bad news, but the islands we visited last month might be hit by a hurricane. Over the last couple of days, it tore through Montserrat and Guadeloupe, devastating those islands. If it takes a northwest path, the US and British Virgin Islands are going to take a beating. We don't have any ships in the area, but I'm worried about this hurricane. If it continues to travel at the speed and direction it's currently on, it will strike the eastern seaboard within the next several days."

The following morning, there was a front-page story in the newspaper about the hurricane devastation that had occurred on St. Croix. The public water system had been destroyed, leaving the inhabitants without drinking water. Looting was out of control on the island.

Over breakfast, Cooper said, "We have one ship, the *Rosa Parks*, at the Columbus Street Terminal. She came in yesterday and we're in the process of turning her around." He paused for a moment and said, "I think you should get some clothes together in case we have to evacuate."

"Do you think it could hit here?"

"I think it's a possibility. It's still a few days away from the eastern seaboard, but it bears watching. The National Hurricane Center has several different models predicting the path of the storm; no one can be sure at this point."

Early Monday morning, Cooper called Mills, waking her. He had stayed in Charleston overnight, maintaining an exhaustive work schedule. "The hurricane is over Puerto Rico today and will then move toward the Bahamas. I've called Reverend Smalls to see if anyone in the community can use some help. If the elderly residents of Alston Station wait until the end of the week to start preparing for the storm, it could be too late. I would like for you to go to Camp's Hardware in West Ashley and pick up items such as batteries, bottled water, and blankets and take them by Reverend Smalls's church this afternoon. Put the items on my account."

When Mills delivered the supplies from Camp's Hardware to All Saints A.M.E. Church, Reverend Smalls and a number of volunteers were in the fellowship hall, gathering emergency items to distribute to residents.

"Miss Taylor, how nice to see you . . . thank you for bringing us these supplies. Tell Cooper I said thank you."

"I will, Reverend. Is there anything else I can do?"

"As a matter of fact, there is. Several of us are going to start helping elderly residents in our community to prepare for the storm. We're going to board up windows. When you get old, you move slowly. I know firsthand."

All afternoon, Mills went with the other volunteers to the homes of the elderly, and Reverend Smalls explained why they were there. A few people weren't even aware of the hurricane. When they arrived at one lady's home, she stopped them before they could start. "Joseph, what do you think you're doing?"

"Miss Pearl, there's a possibility that a hurricane that's in the Caribbean right now is going to move in our direction."

"I've been through a number of these storms and I think I've pretty much seen it all."

"Miss Pearl, no disrespect intended, but this is a powerful storm, and where it's been, there's death and destruction. Please allow us to board up your windows today, and if the storm tracks away from here, we'll make you one of the first we visit to remove the plywood. You should think of where you are going to go if it comes here."

"I've never left Edisto during a storm, and I'm not going to start now. I'm eighty-five years old, and hurricanes don't bother me."

"Ma'am, I think this is a storm to worry about."

"Suit yourself, Joseph."

She sat down in a rocking chair on her porch and began to rock back and forth singing, "Swing low, sweet chariot, comin' for to carry me home. Swing low, sweet chariot, comin' for to carry me home."

Mills helped hold the plywood on the side of the house while another volunteer nailed the boards into the window frame.

The next morning, Cooper phoned her to let her know that the hurricane had passed the Bahamas, and unless it made a significant turn to the east, it was heading for the US mainland. "We have yet to get the *Rosa Parks* under way—the US Navy will be deploying their fleet no later than tomorrow, and the Air Force is relocating the C-141s from the Charleston Air Force Base. I hired a charter pilot to fly my Baron to Atlanta."

"This is making me nervous."

"Take deep breaths when you feel nervous. That will help you calm down. And this: I love you."

"I love you, too."

When she went outside to get in her Beetle, Charles was putting away the outdoor furniture and he told her that he would be closing the hurricane shutters on her cottage. Wiping sweat from his brow, he said, "If I finish securing the buildings on the farm, I'll join the volunteers in the community."

Mills was at the church by eight in the morning, and the group soon began calling on residents. One of the first residents they went to see was Miss India Lefaye Tate, the lady who drove a Model T. When she answered her door, she asked, "Joseph, what brings you to my home this morning?"

"Miss Tate, we're boarding up houses; there's a possibility that the hurricane in the Caribbean could make landfall along the South Carolina coast."

"I'm having guests this afternoon, but I would appreciate your securing my garage."

"Do you have a place to go if the storm heads in this direction?"

"Yes, our family has a retreat near Flat Rock. If it becomes necessary to leave, my niece from Charleston will pick me up."

"Yes, ma'am, we'll see to your garage."

The group secured the windows and garage doors, protecting Miss Tate's like-new Model T, before moving on to the next home. *Her lackadaisical attitude about this hurricane is amazing.*

Charles joined the group in the afternoon, and they continued their door-to-door campaign to help the neighbors. Some of the dwellings were in poor condition and might not withstand high winds to begin with. By late afternoon, Mills was exhausted and sat down on a bench at the church. Reverend Smalls thanked her for her efforts and then Charles joined her. "Cooper called and asked for us to take the horses to Aiken. He said that James Burton had offered to stable them, and we have all been offered accommodations on the Burton farm. Cooper said he'd join us as soon as he could."

"I'll let you know if I'm going to ride up with you."

"I'll be leaving around six tomorrow morning, but I'll be back to help in the community."

"I'd like to wait for Cooper."

When she returned home, the hurricane shutters had been closed on the dwellings, and the buildings had been secured. She walked to the barn and called for Cleo, the mother cat, but she did not appear. When she returned to her cottage, the closed shutters made the rooms dark, and she sat down to rest. She was about to doze off when the phone rang.

"I'd like for you to leave in the morning with Charles," Cooper said.

"I want to wait for you. I'm glad that you heard from James Burton."

"Yes, he called and apologized for his behavior at the dove shoot. Mills, there's much work to be done before I can leave. The *Rosa Parks* has a mechanical issue and isn't budging from the wharf. I've got to get that ship under way. I'll call you later."

That evening, Mills sat on her porch in the silence of the evening; she missed the familiar sound of the wind chimes and Cooper's piano playing. To take her thoughts off the hurricane, she read through Ellen Camp's journal.

The book had been on the shelf since she and Cooper had become lovers, and she opened the journal at her bookmark. The entry concerned the return of her husband's body to Charleston, several years after his death in Virginia:

> Despite the passage of time since my husband's death, Grey was able to locate the gravesite with little difficulty. A marker of heavy stones rested at his head along with a large rose bush that encompassed the fence line near the grave. The widow, whom he had attempted to defend, described it to me in her letter after Michael's death. We will bury his remains at the cemetery at Crescent Hall. I am thankful he has returned to me. *Nex mos singulus nos pro tantum a brevis dum.*

The last line, which was written in Latin, was familiar to her, but she put the book down and went inside to watch a weather bulletin. A hurricane watch had been issued from St. Augustine, Florida, to Cape Hatteras, North Carolina. The nervousness that had enveloped her earlier in the day had returned and she breathed deeply to control her anxiety.

Before five in the morning, Mills was up and dressed to meet Charles at the stables. He was already loading the horses into the trailer and Marian and Elizabeth were in the back seat of his truck. Cooper's dog was in the front seat to ride beside Charles.

"Mills, please come with us. Cooper isn't certain when he's going to get home, and we don't want you out here by yourself," Marian said.

"I'm going to help Reverend Smalls today, and I want to wait for Cooper. Please drive safely, and I'll see you all in Aiken."

"Be careful, child."

"Yes, ma'am."

Mills waved to them as they drove away, and nervous energy made her fidgety. She returned to her cottage and listened to the news. The hurricane watch had been upgraded to a warning for an area from Fernandina Beach, Florida, to Cape Lookout, North Carolina. Her phone rang and Cooper was on the line. "I take it you chose not to leave with Charles."

"I'm not going to leave until you do."

"We've finally gotten the *Rosa Parks* under way. I borrowed the parts we needed from my friends at the US Naval Base, but it took me hours to get in touch with the base commander. They were very helpful once I spoke with Admiral Wade. I'm going to be in Charleston all day, shutting down Heath Brothers, and several of the men and I are going to secure Ian's home and my townhouse, plus a few others. I'll be home as soon as I can." He paused for a moment and said, "How are you doing?"

"I'm nervous."

"Remember? Take deep breaths when you feel anxious."

All day long, Mills worked with volunteers to board up houses and help residents to hurricane shelters. She found by staying busy she could control her nervousness. The volunteers went into some areas of the Edisto region where, to her dismay, people were living in what she considered almost third-world conditions. Even though a hurricane warning had been issued for the coastal regions of South Carolina, some residents weren't aware of the approaching storm. By afternoon, sheriff's deputies were going door to door with the volunteers, encouraging people to leave. Mills heard one deputy tell a resident who refused to vacate his home that he should write his name and social security number with indelible ink on his arm, so that his body could be identified after the hurricane.

By late afternoon, Mills was exhausted and she drove home. There had been an increase in wind speed during the course of the day, and the sky was darkening with cloud cover. She returned to the barn to call for Cleo, but the cat did not respond.

Mills walked to the riverfront and gazed at the pristine condition of the natural surroundings. The *Miss Elise* was still on her boatlift and she assumed that Cooper would secure the boat when he returned home. As she watched the flow of the tea-hued Edisto, she wondered what would happen to this unspoiled area over the next few days. She felt weak by the thought of the destruction that might lie ahead.

At almost two in the morning, Cooper came through her door, disrobed, and got into the bed beside her. She kissed him and hugged him tightly.

"I can't remember ever being so tired. I'm thinking of moving the *Miss Elise* to a secure dry dock in Charleston. I'm afraid we could get the worst of the storm here." He was quiet for a moment, and then said, "I'm proud of you for helping people in the community prepare for the hurricane. I love you."

Cooper had only a few hours of sleep before they rose with the alarm clock before sunrise. Mills made a quick breakfast of fruits and bread, and over coffee, she noticed how tired Cooper looked. He had stubble on his face. He rubbed his chin and said, "I promise I'll shave when we get to Aiken. I'm going to sleep for at least a day." He took a sip of coffee. "Jeff is coming out here this morning. He's removing real estate signs from listings his company has out this way. They can become projectiles in high wind, and I think he wants to see me about some business."

"What kind of business?"

"He needs another cash influx on some investments. I told him to look for us in Alston Station if we're not here." Cooper picked up Ellen Camp's journal, which was sitting on her table. "Have you been reading more of her entries?"

"Yes, I needed to take my mind off the storm, and I read last night. There is a Latin phrase in her journal where she addresses the return of her husband's body to Charleston. I think I've seen it before."

She opened the book to the page and showed the expression to him. "You've seen this phrase. It's part of the inscription on Ellen and Michael's grave marker at Crescent Hall: *Nex mos singulus nos pro tantum a brevis dum* . . . death will separate us for only a short while."

"Why do you think she wrote it in Latin?"

"Perhaps intimate vows they shared?"

They were quiet as she finished cleaning up from breakfast. "I hope everything will be like we left it when we get back home after the storm."

"I do too."

They went to Cooper's house so he could change clothes, and after he showered and dressed, he joined Mills in his kitchen. Charles arrived at the house and as soon as he saw Cooper, he said, "Son, I think you are due some rest."

"You're right, but it will have to wait until we get to Aiken. There are still a few matters left to be handled."

The three of them drove to Alston Station and parked at the market. Mr. Dawkins was outside, boarding up his store. "Well, it looks like this could be a bad one, and I swear, it appears to be heading straight for the Edisto area. Cooper, have you got your place secure?"

"Just about—Jeff is going to be looking for me. We're going to board up Williston's clinic and help anyone else who could use a hand. We'll start with you."

"Thanks. That would be helpful. I have a few windows in the back left to board up."

As Charles and Cooper made quick work of boarding the rear windows, Mr. Dawkins asked, "Where are you all going to ride out the storm?"

"We're going to drive to Aiken. What about you?"

"I'm going to my daughter's house in Columbia. You know, I read in the paper this morning that the mayor of Charleston is discouraging hurricane parties on The Battery." He started to laugh. "Could you imagine anyone being foolish enough to throw a party in 140-mile-per-hour winds?"

Williston came out of her clinic and yelled, "I've just had a phone call from Miss India. She says the volunteers forgot to secure her house."

"Call her back and tell her we'll be there in a few minutes."

When they arrived at Miss Tate's home, she was sitting inside her parlor and she thanked the group for coming to her rescue. "I should have allowed Reverend Smalls to board up my house when he was here. I'm afraid I've been a bother to everyone, and I'm worried about my niece. She should have been here by now."

"Traffic could be heavy because of the evacuation. If she hasn't come to get you by the time we leave for Aiken, you can go with us."

"That's a considerate offer, Cooper. Come inside, I think it will be easier to close the shutters."

Miss Tate led them through her home, which was richly decorated with antiques and oriental rugs. The shutters were easily closed on the downstairs, but on the second story at the rear of the house, Cooper and Charles had to go on the metal roof. The work was treacherous, as rain was making the surface slick, and Charles almost lost his footing. Cooper grabbed his arm and prevented him from falling from the roof.

Charles took a deep breath and said, "That was a close call. Thank you, Cooper."

"You're welcome."

As they finished their work, Miss Tate's niece pulled into the driveway. She was flustered and she said, "Traffic congestion is terrible; I was stuck for two hours trying to travel five miles."

Cooper and Charles helped secure the house and loaded Miss Tate's bags into the trunk of her niece's Cadillac.

"I would like to properly thank you three, but it will have to wait until I get back. Take care of yourselves. And Cooper? Get some rest, young man."

When they returned to Alston Station, the town was almost deserted with most of the buildings boarded up. There were two cars in front of Williston's clinic, and when they went inside, she was conferring with a patient.

She stepped into the waiting room and said, "Cooper, the plywood for my windows is around back. Thank you."

The three of them began work and a familiar voice said, "Do you need another hand?"

Cooper turned and looked at his cousin, "Yes, Jeff—you can hold this sheet of plywood for me."

"Are you going for the rugged look, Cooper?"

"No, I've just been too busy to worry about shaving."

"I know what you mean about busy."

As they finished boarding up the windows, they noticed a truck was rapidly approaching the clinic. They recognized the driver as being a local farmer, Charlie Humphries. He had a woman and three children with him, and he called out, "Is Dr. Will here? These folks have been in a bad accident, and they need help right away."

Charles opened the truck door and helped the children from their seats. The woman held a small boy who had a severe laceration at his scalp. His eyes were closed, and Charles lifted the child in his arms and carried him inside.

The woman gasped with pain when Cooper assisted her into the clinic.

Williston examined the boy. "I'm going to dress his wound, but I need to get this young man to a hospital. What happened to them, Charlie?"

"The limb of a live oak came down on top of her car, and she ran off the road into the telephone exchange box before hitting the tree."

"Is the downed tree limb blocking our way out of town?" Charles asked.

"No, you can get around it."

Charles volunteered to drive the family and Williston to Charleston, and Cooper told him to take the Suburban.

Williston got inside the vehicle, and Charles handed her the boy, whom she cradled in her arms. "One of you put my medical bag in the truck. And Cooper? Will you bring my suitcase?"

"Yes, ma'am, and we'll make sure you're closed up tight."

"I'm going to take him to Roper Hospital. Why don't you meet us there? I don't want us to get separated."

"Yes, ma'am, we'll be there as soon as possible."

Charles pulled the Suburban away from the clinic and as he did, the rumblings of heavy thunder echoed through the community. Mills looked toward a nearby marsh, and she saw a white funnel cloud across the waterway. *Dear Jesus!* She could hardly get her words out. "Oh my, that's a water spout."

The funnel cloud was moving away from Alston Station in a northwest direction, and after a few moments in the river, it dissipated, withdrawing into the base of a thundercloud.

Mills took a deep breath, and Cooper put his arm around her. "It's gone. We'll go by the house and then travel to Charleston to join Williston."

Jeff looked at Cooper and said, "The latest report from the National Hurricane Center puts this hurricane making landfall between Beaufort and Charleston. That means it could come ashore right about here. I hate to tell you this, Cooper, but it's also increasing forward velocity and picking up strength."

"That's not what I wanted to hear."

"Sorry."

After they finished securing the clinic, they drove to Cooper's property in Jeff's Yukon. The men went inside his house, and Mills went to her cottage to put on dry clothes and get her suitcase. As she walked away from her home, she looked back, and as if speaking to an old friend, she said, "I hope you're here when I return."

When she went inside Cooper's home, he was writing Jeff a check in his study.

"Thank you, Cooper," Jeff said.

They had both changed into dry polo shirts and Cooper said, "Jeff is going to drive the *Miss Elise* to the dry dock at Yate's Marina. I'm not sure my boathouse can withstand 150-mile-per-hour winds."

"Joe Yates says he has the most secure storage facility in the Charleston area. I've stored my Hunter sailboat at his dry dock. I guess we'll find out if his claim is true."

"Where is the *Theodosia*?"

"My partners volunteered to move the boat, but I haven't been able to verify that they did."

Cooper stood up from his desk and said, "Jeff, I think it will take you a little over an hour to get to Bates Marina and we'll pick you up as soon as we can."

They finished securing the house, and as they started toward the river, they noticed a car coming down the drive in the pouring rain. "It must be the police making a round," Mills said.

Cooper looked at the car as it came closer. "It's Lieutenant Barnes, and he has someone with him. Whatever he's got to say, I'm sure it can wait."

He stopped the vehicle near them and yelled above the rain, "Good day, Cooper. I've been trying to phone you, but judging from the accident I saw up the road, I can understand why there's trouble on the line. This is Deputy Phil Parks. He's recently been assigned to my unit."

Cooper nodded to the deputy and said, "Lieutenant, can't this wait until after the storm passes?"

"No, it can't, and I'm glad to find you and your cousin together. Can we go inside the barn? We can get the rain out of our faces."

The inside of the barn was dark and damp, and it smelled of oil and gasoline. Jeff turned on the lights, and the group gathered near the Lieutenant.

Barnes began to speak, raising his voice to be heard over the rain pounding on the roof. "I've been waiting for this moment for months. I just couldn't understand how a beautiful, sophisticated woman like Elise Heath could disappear without a trace. She drives to Charleston to shop and just never returns. No one sees her. No one knows anything about her."

"What's this about, Lieutenant?"

"It turns out that those missing person's posters finally did some good, but not as we would have liked. I recently had a visit from a couple of fishermen who come to this area every year to fish for tarpon. When they're not fishing, they're exploring the area. They said they'd like to retire here." He walked to a railing and leaned against it. "Cooper, I believe you said your wife disappeared on August 26th of last year."

Cooper's face darkened as he listened to the detective.

"The two fishermen are certain that they saw your wife at Harry's Country Store outside Summerville that morning. They're sure of the date because they had a successful fishing excursion the day before."

He looked sternly at Cooper and Jeff before continuing, "Both men said they remembered her because she was so beautiful—driving a red Mercedes;

their description matches your wife's car. They said she was gracious to them when they asked her for directions. Imagine their shock when they saw her photo on a missing person's poster while they were here for their annual fishing trip."

"Lieutenant, what happened to Elise?" Cooper asked.

"The two men said that there was a man with her." Barnes looked intently into Cooper's eyes. "I was certain they would identify you, so I showed them your photograph first. They studied the photo, but said the man who was with her had lighter hair."

The detective turned to Jeff and said, "I next showed them your photograph, and guess what? They identified you as the man in the car with her that morning. That would have put you two near the Camp property on the Ashley River, which Cooper had just purchased back into your family."

"What were you doing with Elise, Jeff?"

Jeff did not respond.

Lieutenant Barnes walked toward the barn door and said, "I'd like for you two to come to police headquarters to answer more questions. There is new evidence that we need to discuss, and with this storm coming, a person could easily get displaced."

"What evidence?" Cooper demanded.

"I think it's hard to talk above the storm, and I'd prefer to have the rest of the discussion at headquarters."

Cooper grew agitated, and he raised his voice to the police officer, "I want to know what you're talking about—right now!"

The lieutenant calmly paused and said, "After your wife disappeared, I thought we did a thorough job of searching your properties. I was very impressed by your real estate holdings. When I recently subpoenaed the records from your transactions, I noticed that your cousin always acted as your broker."

He turned to Jeff and said, "You've made some handsome commissions while helping your cousin. It's nice to have loyal relatives. Cooper, I came to understand that you attempted to purchase the Camp property a year ago, but the owner died intestate, and his heirs fought each other until they finally agreed to settle with you just a few months ago." His expression became troubled. "I personally joined my men in searching the Camp property: we found a woman's remains at the bottom of an abandoned well. Dental records may be the only way to identify the individual."

The policeman's tone of voice was now threatening. "Jeff, my theory is that you would have been thrilled to see your lover, Elise, inherit her husband's estate. Cooper, did you ever conclude what happened to you during your diving accident in the Turks and Caicos Islands?"

"No. It was an accident. Nobody knows what happened. Not even me."

Lieutenant Barnes took a deep breath and said, "Jeff, you were having an affair with Elise Heath and I can prove it."

Mills looked at Jeff and Cooper. Jeff's face was drained of color and Cooper's face was contorted by rage.

"You know, Cooper, I really thought that you were behind your wife's disappearance, and I suppose I've made your life miserable at times. What a shame for you, your wife, and your closest friend, deeply involved. Jeff, cocaine and greed cause a calamitous combination."

"Jeff, what in the hell is he talking about?" Cooper asked.

"Something must have happened. Did you just kill her in a drug-induced rage?" Barnes paused. "Jeff?"

"I've never intentionally hurt anyone in my life," Jeff responded.

"You didn't answer the question."

"If you know so much, where's the warrant for my arrest?"

In shock, Mills watched as Cooper charged Jeff, grabbed him by his shirt collar, and shoved him. He then struck Jeff hard across the face, knocking him to the ground. Exhaustion and pent-up rage made Cooper insane with anger, and he stood above his cousin with his fists clenched.

"Get up, you Cassius!"

As Jeff rose from the ground, he signaled for surrender, but then charged into Cooper's torso and struck him in the right eye. The deputy tried to pull them apart, but they hit each other with severe blows until Jeff pushed Cooper away. As he wiped blood from the corner of his mouth, Jeff said to Cooper, "I ought to make you bleed!"

He then turned to look at Lieutenant Barnes and said, "You son of a bitch. I'm not admitting anything. You want to put me in jail? You'll have to arrest me first."

With those words, Jeff removed a handgun from the waistband at the back of his pants and strode toward the barn door that was closest to the river. In response, Lieutenant Barnes drew his weapon, and the deputy charged Jeff and began to struggle with him for control of the handgun. Cooper moved quickly in Mills's direction, and taking her hand, he positioned himself between her and the fight. He tried to get her out the door, but there were loud cracks that sounded almost like thunder.

A warm red spray settled onto Mills's hair and face. She wiped her hand across her cheek and there was blood on her palm, but she felt no pain. Her mouth dropped open.

Cooper turned to face her and she could see the anguish in his eyes. They stared at each other in disbelief. His vision had just become a reality. It was not Mills's blood that he saw stain her flesh during each nightmare, but his own.

She realized she was alone with Cooper. Jeff and the two policemen had run through the door closest to the river. As he sank to the floor, she tried to support him in her arms. He was bleeding from wounds to his arm and right side. Running to a workbench, she removed some clean cloths from the drawers and performed emergency first aid on Cooper's wounds. *Stop the bleeding, just stop the bleeding.*

He was unconscious on the concrete floor and after she finished binding his wounds, she ran outside into the pouring rain. There was no one in sight, and she went to Lieutenant Barnes's vehicle and attempted to open the doors. He had locked them. Without hesitation, she went back into the barn and removed a large wrench from its hook on the wall. The rain was almost blinding, but she returned to the vehicle and smashed the driver's side window with all her strength. When she got the car door open, she nervously fumbled with the radio mike to make a call to the police dispatcher to report the shooting and call for an ambulance. Her mouth was bone dry, and she could barely speak, but somehow, she gave the address to a police dispatcher and then threw down the microphone and ran back inside.

Cooper was still on the floor, and she returned, lifting his head gently into her arms. "Cooper, you've got to get up."

He didn't respond, and she began to shake him gently at first and then with more force. When he finally opened his eyes, she told him, "I'm going to get you in the Land Rover. Stay awake. Just stay awake!"

Mills cranked the vehicle and raised the garage door to the barn. Wind and rain blew into the structure, and she returned to Cooper to get him to his feet.

"Come on. Get up now." He didn't respond, and she raised her voice, "Cooper, listen to me. Get on your feet!"

He slowly rolled to his side and she assisted him into the Land Rover. She overapplied the accelerator and the vehicle lurched forward out of the barn.

Mills knew that she had a decision to make. Cooper was bleeding and she was frightened of getting stuck in evacuation traffic. She had requested an ambulance, so she decided to get him inside his house and take care of him until help arrived. The struggle to get him up the steps into his home turned out to be just as difficult as the fight to get him off the barn floor, but they made it. Once inside, he sank to his knees in the foyer and she collapsed beside him in exhaustion. When her energy returned, she went to the light switch to turn on the lights, but the power was out. In the center of the foyer was the mahogany table with the hurricane lamp. Mills lit the candle with matches on the table and a circle of light danced on the ceiling, illuminating the handsome workmanship of plaster designs. She went to his bedroom and returned with blankets, pillows, and the first aid kit.

He was unconscious, but trembling, and she feared he was suffering from hypothermia. She removed his wet clothes. What she couldn't pull off, she cut off. Then, removing her own wet garments, she slid under the blanket and held him until the heat from her body warmed him and he stopped shaking. Then she checked his wounds, which continued to bleed. With the palm of her hand, she pressed additional bandages into the wounds, in hopes that she could control the bleeding. For a few moments, she wrapped herself in a blanket and rested at his side. Her mind wandered to the events of the day, and she wondered what had happened to Jeff, Lieutenant Barnes, and his deputy. *Jesus, keep me strong.*

Tears began to well up in her eyes, but she fought them back, knowing that Cooper's life depended on her ability to keep her composure. She dressed in dry shorts and a T-shirt from his dresser and secured the hurricane shutters that banged against the front door. Mills remembered that the telephone junction box near Alston Station had been hit by the woman's car after the live oak limb fell on it. She decided to try it anyway. Lifting the receiver on the phone in Cooper's bedroom, she found it was dead.

As the hours passed, and night fell, her hopes of a rescue faded. She knew they would remain in Cooper's home for the duration of the storm. The winds roared and objects hit the house with a frightening frequency. She kept Cooper hydrated by squeezing water from a sports bottle into his mouth when he was conscious.

Around midnight, the winds died down for a few minutes but then returned with a fury from a different direction. Cooper began to talk to himself, and she held his hand and continued to assure him that he would be all right. She wasn't sure if he comprehended her words because he was conversing with people who were long deceased.

She realized that she had not said a prayer for Cooper during the entire ordeal. He had sacrificed himself to prevent her from being harmed. She started to pray, but as she did, her voice became louder, and she repeatedly asked the Lord to spare Cooper's life.

At first light, the rain still fell, but the winds had slowed. Cooper was asleep, the bleeding was under control, and his bloody clothes lay in a heap in a corner.

Her back ached as she rose from the floor, and when she opened the front door, the heavy scent of pine rushed into the house. The storm damage was shocking; trees were broken off halfway up and the ground was coated with pine needles and downed limbs. Near the front steps, a large black snake slithered in standing water around the house. She noticed Cooper's bloody handprint displayed on the front door. *My poor Cooper.*

When she reentered the house, she opened the hurricane shutters to allow more light inside. She was exhausted, but she would not permit her failing strength to overcome her. Cooper began to call to her and a look of desolation appeared in his eyes. "Mills, there's someone knocking at the door. Can you hear them?"

"There's no one here but us." *He's having a premonition. No!* He reached for her hand, and she took his and held it tightly. "I'm sorry, Mills, but I have to let go." *Don't leave me!*

His hand became lifeless, and she attempted to wake him, but to no avail. She quickly rose to her knees and as she did, the room became a strange color of amber, like the tea-hued Edisto. Dizzy and sick, she got down on her hands and knees to regain her strength before rising again.

There were footsteps on the front porch and as she looked toward the open door, two figures appeared in the threshold. Her eyes ached with pain, but she recognized the silhouettes of Williston and Charles against the light streaming into the doorway.

"Thank God you're here."

"Mills, what happened to you and Cooper?"

"He's been shot—he won't move. I tried to wake him."

Williston dropped to her knees, took a small flashlight, and pushed back his eyelid, looking into his eye. She then felt for a pulse. "He's alive. How long has he been like this?"

Mills's emotions could no longer be subdued, and she began to cry. "Thank God," she murmured over and over.

"Shhh, it's going to be all right."

"He was hurt right after you and Charles left. Lieutenant Barnes and a deputy showed up, and he accused Jeff of killing Elise Heath. Jeff had a handgun. Cooper stood in front of me to protect me, and the gun went off. Jeff disappeared into the storm along with the two police officers. I don't know what happened to them."

Williston looked at Mills as she removed a blood pressure cuff from her bag. "What has he had to eat and drink?"

"Just water."

Dr. Will looked up at Charles who had a deeply concerned expression on his face. "Can you please get the hurricane shutters open in the kitchen and get the gas back on to the cook top? I'm going to need you to help me lift him onto the kitchen table."

"Charles, I saw a snake outside the front door."

"I know, Miss Mills, these storms run animals out of their homes, just like it does people. I have hip waders outside the door."

He patted her on the shoulder and then went out the front door.

Williston fixed Mills a sandwich in the kitchen while explaining that she wanted to give Cooper a blood transfusion from her. "You have the same blood type—remember? Could your blood have been affected by any changes since your last donation?"

"No, ma'am."

"Then let's get started."

As Williston performed the transfusion, she explained that she and Charles had spent the night at Roper Hospital, but due to the condition of the roadways, they had to borrow a boat from Yates Marina to get back to Edisto. Williston said her fears increased when she found out that the *Miss Elise* had not been delivered to storage for protection.

Charles returned to the foyer and said, "Dr. Will, I've got the shutters open, and the gas is back on. Let me know when you're ready for me."

When she was finished with the transfusion, Williston put a bandage on Mills arm and she hugged her. "I'm very proud of you. Charles, I'm ready for you to help me now."

He lifted Cooper from the floor with little difficulty and carried him to the kitchen table. With the movement, Cooper woke. Confused, he began a feeble attempt to defend himself.

"No, no. Jeff."

Charles grabbed his hands, and pressed his arms to the table. "Cooper, calm down now. It's Charles, it's Charles."

Eventually Cooper relaxed, quietly repeating Charles's name.

Mills began to cry, but Williston quickly led her into the living room and to the couch. Williston left for a few moments and returned with a blanket and a glass of milk. "I want you to rest."

"Dr. Will, please save him."

"I'll do everything I can for him. Have faith, Mills."

She closed her eyes to rest and said another prayer, but the vows of Ellen and Michael Camp would not leave her: Death will separate us for only a short while.

Her dreams were filled with anxiety and cries of pain. She wasn't sure if she heard them or if they were part of her nightmares.

The air was full of tropical moisture and Mills woke feeling damp. Her shirt was wet from sweat. Dazed, she looked at her wristwatch and realized she had slept for hours.

As she rose from the couch, she felt battered, and her back ached from her all-night vigil of caring for Cooper. When she entered the foyer, the aroma of cooking tomatoes filled the air. Cooper's bedroom door was slightly ajar and she couldn't see inside. There were candles burning in the kitchen and Mills caught sight of Williston stirring a large steaming pot on the stove. Cooper was nowhere in sight.

When Williston saw Mills, she went to her and helped her to a seat. "How are you feeling?"

"I ache all over. Where's Cooper?"

"We put him to bed several hours ago. Go see for yourself."

"He's not going to die, is he?"

Williston patted her on the shoulder and in a reassuring manner said, "No, Mills, he's not going to die. He'll recover, in time."

She opened his door and saw two hurricane lamps lighting the room; their circles of light moving slightly on the ceiling. Cooper had an IV in his arm, and an IV bag was hanging from a makeshift support that ran between the posts of the Rice bed. An ice pack was on his right eye, and Charles was holding his hand and praying. When he heard Mills enter the room, he turned and she could see that he had been crying. As she approached, he placed Cooper's hand on the bed and helped her with a seat so she could come close to him.

Charles softly said, "Miss Mills, he's holding his own. Thank God."

She sat with him and studied Cooper's features. His face was pale from blood loss, and bruises were emerging from the fight with Jeff. Williston laid her hand on Mills's shoulder and motioned for her to join her. When they returned to the kitchen, there was a large bowl of soup on the island for Mills, and Williston asked her to sit down.

"I know you're tired, but while you eat, please tell me what the lieutenant had to say. As far as we know, the two policemen and Jeff are missing, and we need to protect Cooper from further false accusations."

"Lieutenant Barnes said that a woman's remains were found at the bottom of an abandoned well on the Camp property that Cooper just purchased. Two men—who make an annual fishing trip to this area—identified Jeff as being with Elise on the morning of her disappearance. Barnes said there was other evidence and claimed that he could prove that Jeff was having an affair with Elise. Dr. Will, he asked Jeff if he killed her in a drug-induced rage."

"My Lord," Williston responded.

"Jeff told him that he had never intentionally hurt anyone." Mills paused for a moment and said, "The lieutenant asked Cooper if he determined how he became ill while diving last summer in the Turks and Caicos Islands. Cooper was so tired, and he lost control and attacked Jeff. They beat each other unmercifully."

"I could tell by looking at Cooper. I'm afraid the lieutenant allowed the situation to get out of control." She patted Mills on the hand. "When you get enough to eat, I've placed water upstairs in one of the bathrooms for you. Charles has put your suitcase in one of the bedrooms and I think you should sleep. Charles and I will watch Cooper closely tonight, and we won't let anything happen to him, I promise."

"I'd like to sit with him for a while, if that's all right."

"I'm sure he'd like that."

Mills didn't wake until almost noon the next day. When she rose from her bed, she lit a hurricane lamp in her bathroom and washed her face. Her hair was matted from Cooper's blood and when she lifted her shirt, stains were on her chest. The water in the sink turned red as she rubbed her skin with a washcloth. She tried to scrub the dried blood out of her hair, but had little success. Instead, she pulled her hair back in a ponytail and decided not to think about it for the time being.

After she changed into fresh clothes, she went downstairs to check on Cooper. The shutters were closed in his bedroom and the IV bag still hung between the posts of the rice bed. Williston was sitting in a chair close to him and she spoke quietly to Mills when she became aware of her presence.

"He was restless for part of the night, but he's doing better this morning." Mills moved to the side of the bed and took his hand in hers. His warmth comforted her as she watched him sleep. The beard on his face was now thick and his right eye was swollen from the blow that Jeff had delivered.

"There's a pan on the stove with potatoes in it. Why don't you go fix yourself something to eat and then you can sit with Cooper."

As she started to leave the room, Mills asked, "How did you get the medical supplies?"

"Charles walked to my clinic and brought back what I needed in an ice chest. For the time being, my generator is refrigerating the medical supplies. Cooper donated the money to have an automatic transfer system installed a few years ago. When the electricity failed, the generator came online."

Mills ate some of the potatoes and then went into Cooper's bedroom to relieve Williston. As she rose from the chair, Williston stretched her muscles and said, "I'm going to lie down. I'll be upstairs. Come and get me if you need me."

After sitting with Cooper for a couple of hours, Mills found herself becoming drowsy. She began to hear a knocking sound. At first she thought it was part of a dream, but the sound persisted, and she rose from her chair to investigate. Charles passed her in the foyer. "Miss Mills, let me handle this."

She closed the door to Cooper's bedroom and stood with Charles in the foyer. Two Charleston County police officers were on the porch and they provided identification to Charles. They explained they were there to follow up on a frantic radio call for help and two missing policemen. The men looked exhausted and their uniforms were soiled with mud.

Charles invited them into the house and the officers asked to speak to Mills Taylor. Before Mills could respond, Williston descended the steps and introduced herself. She offered the officers a drink of water, which they gladly accepted. Once in the kitchen, Mills explained what had transpired at the farm before the storm and that Jeff, Lieutenant Barnes, and his deputy had vanished after the shooting.

Charles interjected, "Mr. Heath's boat, the *Miss Elise* has been taken."

"I'd like to see Cooper Heath," an officer named Gonzales insisted. "I can have you all evacuated by helicopter."

"Mr. Heath is in his room, and I would prefer he not be moved at this time."

Williston led the policeman to Cooper's bedroom. He attempted to step close to Cooper, but she blocked his path. "There are system failures at the local hospitals, and he's fine where he is. If you need him, you know where to find him," she said firmly.

Williston went to the kitchen and returned with a plastic bag that contained the bullet she had removed from Cooper's side. She asked the policeman to place several phone calls to let friends and relatives know they were all right, and handed him a list of phone numbers. He graciously agreed to do what he could, and then Charles accompanied them to Lieutenant Barnes's storm-ravaged police car.

In the late afternoon, Cooper was awake long enough to eat a bowl of soup, but he could not remember the hurricane or his fight with Jeff. After eating the warm food, he fell asleep almost immediately.

Mills pulled the covers up on his chest and then joined Williston on the front porch. As they stood together looking over the wind-damaged yard, Mills asked, "Are you worried that blame could be placed on Cooper for the altercation?"

"I know firsthand that in the wake of tragedy, there is often confusion over what is right or wrong. He was provoked. Eventually, we'll find out what happened to the others."

That night, when Mills took her turn sitting with Cooper, she laid her head on the side of his bed to rest her eyes. She had fought fatigue all day and she was having a difficult time staying awake. Tears came to her eyes as she thought of his suffering. While she rested, she began to feel his hand gently caress her head, and she looked up to see him awake. She hugged him as carefully as possible, and he whispered to her, "I love you. Please don't leave me until we can walk out together—promise me."

"I promise."

CHAPTER 28

The Choice

The next morning, when she entered Cooper's bedroom, he was flat on his back with his eyes closed. Empty breakfast plates were on a tray near the bed and he was clean shaven. She quietly walked to the bed and placed her hands near his. Without opening his eyes, his hand slid over and took hers.

"I recognized your footfalls," he quietly said. His eyes slowly opened, and he managed a slight smile.

Mills bent over and kissed him on the lips. "How are you feeling?"

"Like warmed over death."

Mills remembered she had described the way she felt after being stung by yellow jackets in a similar fashion. "That bad?"

"Yes, I'm afraid so."

"Can I get you anything?"

"No, I just had breakfast. Go get something to eat." She kissed him again.

"I've had a shave this morning, so I expect more kisses," he said, closing his eyes.

Williston had breakfast of grits and eggs on the stovetop, and she helped Mills with a plate. "We've moved as many perishable items as possible to the refrigerator in the barn. Charles has a generator powering it."

She ate breakfast, and realizing that over the last two days, the workload had been handled by Williston and Charles, she offered to wash the dishes.

"We've been using the manual well in the courtyard to get water," Williston told her.

Mills went outside and pumped the handle repeatedly until she filled a large cooking pot. She boiled the water on the stove and washed the dishes, stacking them on the side of the sink. As she cleaned them, she decided that she could use the well pump to wash her hair.

Returning to the courtyard with a rinsing pot, towel, and shampoo, she started to pump the handle until she filled the pot with water. She wet her hair and splashed water on her face before taking some in her mouth; it was cold and stimulating. When she finished washing the blood from her hair, she sat down in the courtyard to rest. She felt renewed; it was like being baptized, and she thanked God for looking after them.

As she combed her hair, she noticed an unusually loud volume of bird calls coming from the waterfront. She decided to investigate, and she walked in the direction of the noise, being careful to avoid downed tree branches. Numerous birds were circling and diving toward a target along the bank of the river.

As she got closer, she realized birds were sitting on top of the object that had been caught between the branches of a downed tree limb. A sickening odor permeated the air.

Suddenly, she realized that the shape intertwined in the tree branch was the body of a man. His arms were spread out from his torso, his legs pulled by the current, and his flesh seemed to be in motion. The birds were mutilating his face and insects were crawling on him. Horror-struck, she became uncontrollably nauseated and collapsed several times on her way back to the house.

When she reached the courtyard, she used the manual well pump to wash her face and get water. Williston saw her from the house and ran outside. Mills could barely speak, but eventually she was able to explain about the unfortunate man by the waterfront.

Williston hugged her and then summoned Charles to accompany her to the river. Before they left, Williston asked Mills to go and sit with Cooper. She felt sick and taking deep breaths was not helping. She went to Cooper's pantry and took a fifth of bourbon off the shelf and poured a shot. The effect of the alcohol was swift on her now-empty stomach, and she sat down at the kitchen table to calm down.

As her nervousness subsided, she went into Cooper's bedroom and sat down in the chair near the bed. Hopefully, she could regain her composure before he woke.

When Williston returned, she informed Mills that the body was that of the deputy who had accompanied Lieutenant Barnes on the day of the storm.

"Poor fellow, I fear he drowned," she said. "Bless Charles; he's retrieving his body from the river."

That afternoon, two policemen arrived, the same ones who had visited them the day before. Mills was sitting with Cooper when the kitchen door slammed and the sound of distressed voices came from the rear of the house. She went to the kitchen, and Williston was attending one of the men, who had become nauseated when he viewed the corpse. She put a damp cloth on the back of his neck, and he sipped a glass of water, but his face was white like snow.

The other officer, Gonzales, began to tell them the news they had come to report. "Lieutenant Barnes was found yesterday by a tree removal crew on Wadmalaw Island. He's hurt pretty bad and has a head injury. Cooper Heath's boat, the *Miss Elise*, was found partially submerged near Rockville in Bohicket Creek. Divers are going to search the area, but with all the strong currents we've had the last few days, who knows if they'll find anything."

"Have you found Jeff, my cousin?" Cooper inquired as he stood in the kitchen doorway using the frame for support.

Shocked, they all turned to look at him, and Charles was at his side within seconds.

"Cooper, what are you doing? That wall is not going to hold you up," Williston said.

Charles helped him to a chair, and he winced with pain as he sat down. Mills grabbed a quilt from the back of a chair and put it around his shoulders.

"Mr. Heath, there's no sign of Jeff Radcliffe. I'm sorry."

"Yes, and I'm sorry about the lieutenant. What about the other officer?" The two policemen looked at one another as they realized that the information about the deputy's death had not been shared with Cooper.

Williston put her arm on his shoulder and said, "Cooper, I'm sorry, but the deputy's remains were found this morning. We didn't want to upset you."

"Where did you find him?"

"His body was caught in a tree branch along the waterfront of your property."

Cooper leaned forward resting his head on his hand and said quietly, "I'm very sorry to hear that."

"Son—let us help you back to your bedroom," Charles said.

He looked up at Williston and Charles and nodded. They assisted him into the room, and he asked to sit in an armchair.

"Charles and I are going to help the policemen with the deputy's body, and we'll be back as soon as possible. Cooper, please stay seated until we return."

Cooper stared into space, and Mills pulled up a chair to sit beside him. Tears were beginning to well up in his eyes and he said, "That man's body washed up in front of my property and that's where it belongs."

"You didn't harm anyone."

"My cousin, whom I have considered my brother, betrayed me, along with my wife. I failed at the most important thing in my life—my marriage. How could I have been so blind?" His voice began to quiver. "Mills, when my father and brother were killed in the boating accident, I could have saved them. The first wave knocked Jeff into the water, and I went in after him. I made a decision to leave the helm and rescue Jeff. If I had stayed at the controls, I could have maneuvered the boat to counter the wave that capsized her. All I could do was watch as the boat took on water and my father and brother drowned. I should have saved them first. Don't you see? I'm responsible for their deaths."

"You had no way of knowing that the boat would be hit by another wave. You acted on instinct to save Jeff. I would have done the same."

"My father dove into shark-infested waters repeatedly to save the lives of men he didn't even know, but all I could do was cling to the side of the boat and watch. They died because of me. I've never told anyone this before."

"Stop blaming yourself for events and behavior that were beyond your control."

He struggled to get out of the chair and stood facing her, utter madness in his eyes.

"What are you doing?"

"Britton was correct. I had no right to take you as my lover. My behavior is no better than theirs."

"Cooper, I fell in love with you. We chose to be together."

His face became pale and he collapsed to the floor and continued to murmur to himself, "I failed."

Mills ran to the rear courtyard and yelled to Williston and Charles to come to the house. When they saw Cooper unconscious on the floor, Charles lifted him like a child back into this bed.

"Cooper, you're not helping yourself," Williston told him, as she looked at his side.

When Williston finished examining Cooper, she took Mills by the hand and led her to the front porch. They sat down together on the front steps and Williston put her arm around her.

"What happened to him?" she inquired.

"He thinks he's responsible for the deaths of his father and brother. He told me if he had remained at the helm of the sailboat instead of saving Jeff's life, he could have kept the boat from capsizing."

"There's no way to know if he could have saved them . . . my poor tortured boy."

"He also said he failed in his marriage to Elise."

"I don't like to see him tormenting himself. He's never failed anyone."

A heavy rainstorm on Monday brought more misery to Low Country residents who had already suffered from the hurricane. Mills sat on the screened porch watching the rain fall when she saw two figures approaching from the waterfront. At first, she thought they were the two policemen who had come twice to the house, but as they approached, she recognized Cooper's Uncle Ian and Britton Smith. They wore rain gear, and she held the door open when they reached the screened porch.

"Mills, where is Cooper?" Mr. Heath asked.

"He's in his bedroom."

"I had a visit from two policemen who told me that Cooper was injured in a shooting incident."

Both men removed their gear and went inside the house. Williston was sitting with Cooper, and she rose from her chair when they entered his room. Ian patted Williston on the back and then bent over Cooper, taking his hand. "It's your uncle. How are you?"

Cooper opened his eyes, which were glassy, and his speech was slurred when he spoke.

"Yesterday was very difficult for him, and I've given him medication to help him rest," Williston said.

Ian sat down in the chair beside Cooper's bed and asked to be alone with his nephew. He spent over an hour with Cooper, and when he came out, he asked Mills to join him on the porch. "Mills, the officer who gave me the details of the shooting was recounting your story. I have to ask you if you think Jeff shot Cooper on purpose."

"Jeff and the deputy were struggling for control of the weapon. I don't know."

Before he went back inside, he hugged her shoulder and said, "Thank you for what you did for Cooper."

"You're welcome, sir."

She continued to stand on the porch and watch the rain fall, and Britton brought her a glass of water. He cleared his throat and said, "Mills, I'm sorry about the way I behaved when I was last here. Please forgive me. I hope Cooper will allow me to make amends."

"Britton, he considers you his friend."

"I can't understand Jeff hurting Cooper like this. We both know Jeff is an expert marksman. I believe if he'd wanted Cooper dead, he'd be dead right now."

That evening, Williston grilled dove that had been shot on the opening day of dove season. She was trying to prepare perishable foods in case they lost generator power. When the meal was ready, Ian asked Mills if it would be all right if he took Cooper's tray in to him.

When he left the kitchen, Mills went to the cellar to choose wine for dinner. The brick floor was slightly damp, and she maneuvered carefully to avoid a fall. She looked at the labels with her flashlight and made a decision. While attempting to hold two bottles, plus her flashlight, she almost dropped one bottle of wine to the floor. As she regained her composure, she heard a noise in the cellar. Startled, she asked, "Is someone there?"

There was no answer and fear surged through her body. Hastily, she ran up the stairs and locked the door to the cellar. Williston had located a radio in the pantry and was playing classical music from a station in Savannah. She commented that she could find only one local station on the air in the Charleston area.

After he helped Cooper with his dinner, Ian asked Mills to step into the hallway. "I apologize to you, but I have monopolized his waking moments. Williston has told me about his feelings of failure, and I have done my best to make him understand he has not failed anyone; there are, however, some individuals who have failed him. I don't know how much longer he'll be awake, but he wants to see you."

She went into his bedroom and sat down in the chair beside his bed.

He reached for her hand and said, "I don't think I said thank you for saving my life."

"You're welcome, Cooper. In your premonition, I was the one hurt and bleeding. You stepped in front of me and saved me."

"I was granted a blessing—the opportunity to protect you."

She put her arms around him and kissed him as he fell asleep. "Please forgive yesterday's tirade. I intend to stop feeling sorry for myself, and I plan to feel much better tomorrow. I just hope my body cooperates."

After he went to sleep, Mills went to Charles and told him of the noise she had heard in the cellar. He took a flashlight and went down the steps. When he returned, he said, "I didn't see anything in the cellar, but the door to the outside was open. I put some of the furniture back out today, and I thought I locked that door. I must have made a mistake."

On Tuesday morning, the men moved a generator capable of powering the well pump and water heaters from the barn. Mills offered her assistance and was shocked to see the interior of the barn coated with leaves, even across the ceiling. Charles had not mentioned the damage, and she knew he had done so to spare her feelings. In her haste to get Cooper to safety, she had failed to close the garage door.

When she returned to the house, she was surprised to see Cleo sitting on the steps leading to the back porch. She petted the cat and said, "Did you make the noise in the basement last night?"

The cat rubbed against her legs and Mills went to the kitchen for food. Cleo ate as though famished and then disappeared into the bushes.

The men helped Cooper with a shower, and then Mills was offered a turn. The warmth of the water soothed her sore muscles, but she showered quickly to give others a chance. When she finished, she went into Cooper's bedroom. His hair was wet from his shower and his bed linens had been changed. Ian stood beside the bed, discussing some paperwork that he had brought in a briefcase.

"Please join us, Mills," Ian said. "Britton and I are going to return to Charleston, and I'll be back tomorrow for an extended stay. I've asked Cooper to help me review these legal documents. Could you please help him with the paperwork?"

"Yes, sir."

Before he departed, Ian said to Mills, "I want to keep Cooper busy, and when I return tomorrow, I'll have several business proposals for him to review." He patted her on the shoulder and said, "I think his premonition about you has been manifested."

Williston and Charles went to Alston Station that afternoon to reopen her clinic. Her last words to Cooper were, "Stay off your feet."

Once they were alone in the house, he asked, "Would you do something for me?"

"Yes."

"Would you bring me Grey Camp's walking cane from the living room?"

"Williston told you to stay off your feet."

"I want to go on the porch for fresh air. I'll put my feet up when we get outside."

She retrieved the cane for him, studying the intricate carving on the staff as she walked back into his bedroom. Cooper was sitting on the edge of the bed, and she put his robe around his shoulders and helped him to stand. He put his weight on the cane and shuffled out to the porch.

He sank into a seat on a couch and Mills put a quilt around him. "I feel like I'm about a hundred years old." He smiled slightly and sighed.

"Put your head in my lap," Mills told him.

He winced as he lay down, but then looked up into her eyes. "You are a beautiful sight."

She ran her fingers inside his robe, feeling his hard muscles, and then lightly massaged his scalp. With his eyes closed, he gently said, "I remember I was cold after I was hurt. You took off your wet clothes and held me until I was warm."

"You're starting to remember."

"Yes, but I'm not sure I want to remember everything."

"Do you recall Williston giving you a blood transfusion from me to you?" He opened his eyes, smiled and said, "I don't remember that, but now that some of your blood is flowing through my veins, does that mean I'm going to have an obsession with high-heeled shoes?"

She lightly tapped him with a rolled-up newspaper.

"Don't beat the wounded."

Mills smiled at him.

As he settled his head into her lap, he said, "You're a bossy little thing."

"Only when I have to be . . ."

CHAPTER 29

Good Neighbors

Cooper fell asleep in her arms, and this was the most serene time they had shared since the storm. The wind chimes had been re-hung on the porch and they tinkled with a peaceful melody of harmonious notes.

They had been together for over two hours when Mills heard the sound of two male voices coming closer to the porch. The men sounded like they were speaking a language other than English. Reverends Smalls and Johnson came into view in the rear courtyard. Mills quickly raised her index finger to her lips to signal for quiet, and they entered the screened porch carefully, closing the door behind them.

Even though they spoke quietly, Cooper woke at the sound of their voices and made an attempt to sit up.

"Hold on now. Let us help you. Williston told us what happened. Is there anything we can do?"

They assisted Cooper to an upright position on the couch. "I think we're getting along all right."

"We're preparing supper in the fellowship hall at church this evening. We'd like to bring you dinner."

"That's very gracious . . . when you come, I want you to take canned produce from my pantry and game meat that Charles has saved from spoiling."

"There are some people who can use the food," Reverend Johnson said. Reverend Smalls took Cooper by the hand and said, "You're going to get through this—everything's going to be all right."

When they left, Cooper again laid down. "They saw you with your head in my lap."

"They're friends. Don't worry."

"I could have sworn they were speaking a different dialect as they approached the porch."

"Both Reverends Smalls and Johnson are from the Sea Islands near Beaufort, and they were probably speaking Gullah."

As the news of Cooper's injury began to spread to his friends and neighbors, visitors began to arrive to express their concern. At times, there were more than a dozen cars parked around the house. Miss India LaFaye brought Cooper a basket of beignets in her Model T, which was unscathed by the storm, and James Burton drove Elizabeth and Marian back to Edisto from Aiken. After Marian saw Cooper, she went on the porch, and Mills found her in tears. They held each other without saying a word.

Murphy Black arrived by motorboat and anxiously requested to see Cooper. He breathed a sigh of relief when he saw Cooper sitting on the screened porch. Murphy approached him and took Cooper's hand in his. "I'm so glad to see you. You're looking a bit rough, but still good for a dead man."

"A dead man?"

"I heard a dreadful rumor that you had been fatally shot by Jeff. Thank God, it's not true. Where is Jeff?"

"We don't know. Jeff did shoot me."

"That's not possible."

"Lieutenant Barnes came to see me before the storm. He said that two witnesses saw Jeff with Elise the day of her disappearance near the Camp farm. The subpoena you received concerning my real estate documents was to see if Jeff had been my broker on that transaction, and was therefore, familiar with the property. Murphy, the police found a woman's remains at the bottom of an abandoned well."

"Do they know the woman's identity?"

"The lieutenant said dental records would be required to identify the body. I lost my head, and I attacked Jeff. There was a fight over a handgun and I—Mills saved my life."

"Is there anything I can do?"

"I'm sure there will be. You're my attorney, but I also consider you my friend. Thank you for visiting me."

"Wait until you get my bill."

"Thanks, Murphy."

There was no doubt that Ian dearly loved his nephew. Although he made himself scarce at times, he was always available when Cooper needed assistance. Mills had never seen Ian wear blue jeans; he wore a suit and tie whenever she was around him. These days, though, he was attired in jeans and button-down shirts that even had wrinkles in them. Cooper and his uncle spent hours discussing Heath Brothers' business, and Mills discovered that Ian was an excellent chef, as he prepared most of their meals. There was a relaxed atmosphere during these days of Cooper's recovery; they were taking it one day at a time.

Anne Jefferson and her sons came to see Cooper. They arrived by a boat that was captained by one of the Abbott brothers. When Blair and Zack saw Cooper, the expression on their faces became increasingly serious as they looked at him. They wrapped their arms around him for a hug, but their mother cautioned, "Don't squeeze him too hard right now."

Anne asked the boys to go out on the green and toss a football to each other. Taking Cooper's hand, she kissed him on the cheek. "I'm sorry, but my parents weren't able to come with us today. I'm worried my mother is having a nervous breakdown. We had a phone call from the Bohicket Marina. The *Theodosia* is missing. At first they thought she had been relocated to avoid the storm, but after making phone calls to Jeff's partners, they realized she had been taken." She paused as she looked at Cooper. "The *Miss Elise* was scuttled not far from the Bohicket Marina. Do you think Jeff took the *Theodosia*?"

"She's a large craft for a one-man operation, but Jeff is an exceptional sailor."

"He must have lost his mind," Anne said, as she began to cry. "The police have been to my parents' home a number of times, and there's a warrant for Jeff's arrest."

Mills left them alone on the porch and went out to the green to toss the football with the boys. Over an hour passed and the boys sat down under an oak tree.

"Whew, it's hot," Blair said.

"You boys wear me out," Mills said as she joined them.

They were quiet for a moment and Zack said, "We know what happened. We heard the police speaking with our grandfather, and Mom explained about Cooper and Uncle Jeff. I'm worried about both of them."

When they went back to the porch, Anne had regained her composure, and the boys sat down beside Cooper.

"We hope you feel better soon."

"Thank you, boys. Next time you're out here, maybe we can go fishing again."

"Can we stay with you?"

"Boys, when Cooper feels better, you can visit with him. Go wait for me in the courtyard, and I'll be there in a minute."

Anne kissed Mills and then sat beside Cooper. "You were Jeff's best friend, and I just can't understand about Elise. I'm sorry, Cooper."

They held hands and after she kissed his cheek, Anne left through the screen door.

One week after the storm, young people who were involved in the scholarship program arrived at Cooper's property and spent an entire day cleaning up downed tree limbs and debris. Reverend Smalls led the group, and he brought a young man with him to the back porch where Mills and Cooper sat.

"This is Anthony Barre, and he has something he would like to say to Miss Taylor."

Mills recognized him immediately and stiffened. *That's the boy that robbed me!*

He spoke with hesitation, "Miss Taylor, I want to apologize for hurting you and stealing your purse. I was doing wrong. I know that now."

The boy handed Mills an envelope. "This is forty dollars. It's the amount of money that me and my friend stole from you. I earned this money mowing grass." He then removed from his pocket her small wooden doll that had been stolen. "I had to buy this back, but I wanted to return it."

"I accept your apology. Thank you for returning my money and my doll."

"Anthony, it takes courage to admit you were wrong, and I admire you for making restitution to Miss Taylor," Cooper said.

The boy nodded to them and left the porch.

In the afternoon, an old truck pulled up to the rear courtyard and Mills recognized Mr. and Mrs. Adams from Cooper's Combahee property. Cooper was asleep on the porch, and Mills went into the courtyard to greet them.

"Miss Taylor, we saw an article in the *Charleston Dispatch* about an incident at this farm before the hurricane. We tried to phone, but we couldn't get through. Is Cooper all right?"

"He is getting better; he was hurt in a shooting."

"A hunting accident?"

"No, sir."

Cooper woke and called to them, and Mr. Adams went on the porch to help him sit up. The couple stared at Cooper's injuries in disbelief, and Mrs. Adams got down on her knees and prayed, holding Cooper's hand in hers.

When she finished, she looked at him. "I think the reason we have come to know one another is that I am the friend who can help you with spiritual guidance."

She sat down beside Cooper, and Mr. Adams asked Mills to help him with items in the truck. They brought an abundance of baked foods and she helped him bring the baskets into the kitchen. Mr. Adams asked, "Miss Taylor, the article in the paper was toward the back page of the Metro section, but it said that police were involved, along with Cooper's cousin, Jeff Radcliffe. Can this be true?"

"Yes, sir, I'm afraid so."

When Mills and Mr. Adams went back to the porch, Cooper explained to them what had occurred, and they both were aghast by the events. Mrs. Adams took Cooper's hand again and said, "We've been through painful experiences in our lives, but I don't believe God sends His people heartache and tragedy. You do a great deal of investing in real estate, but please don't forget to invest in your soul. The doors are always open to the Lord's house."

Mr. and Mrs. Adams visited with Cooper and Mills for over an hour until Mr. Adams told his wife they needed to be going. She had a difficult time leaving Cooper, and she wiped tears from her eyes as they departed. "If we can do anything for you, let us know," Mr. Adams said as he closed the screen door.

When Mills was alone with Cooper, she went down to her knees and wrapped her arms around him. He rested his chin on her shoulder and kissed her on the neck.

"Cooper? Your nightmares about Elise? In the dark enclosure? Lieutenant Barnes said the woman's remains were in an abandoned well."

"I know, Mills. It frightens me to think about my dreams. At times, I feel like I'm going mad."

"You're not going insane. The lieutenant said there was additional evidence."

"I'm sure we'll find out soon enough. One thing's for certain: they know where to find me."

The next afternoon, Lee Mencken, with the *Charleston Dispatch*, arrived at Cooper's house. Mills met him at the front door and he re-introduced himself, but she remembered meeting him.

He went straight to the point. "I would like to speak with Mr. Heath. I've obtained a police report that states there was a shooting at this property before the hurricane. I've already written a brief article on the incident, but I've been busy with storm-related stories. I know that a policeman died here."

"Cooper is asleep. Wait just a minute."

She went to Cooper's desk and retrieved Murphy Black's business card. When she handed it to him he said, "Yes, Mr. Black, I'm acquainted with him, but he's not been at his office. Miss Taylor, I just want to know the truth."

"Lee, I'm not at liberty to discuss Mr. Heath."

As he descended the steps, he pushed his blond hair back and said, "I know Jeff Radcliffe is missing, and I also know there was a love triangle—a deadly one."

"Good-bye Lee."

"Miss Taylor, good afternoon."

Mills went back to Cooper's bedroom and sat with him until he woke. "You had a visitor. Lee Mencken came to see you."

"H.L.?"

"Yes, I gave him Murphy's business card."

"You did the right thing."

"He told me he had been preoccupied with events from the hurricane, but he's concentrating on you now."

"I'm not surprised."

⎯⎯

Several days later, Cooper reviewed a business proposal at his desk while Mills read a book on the couch in the study. A car pulled up to the front of the house, and Cooper looked out the window. "I'm going to need your help. We have visitors."

When she opened the front door, Lieutenant Barnes and another officer, named Clancy, were on the porch. She invited them inside and showed them into the study.

"Lieutenant, forgive me if I don't get up. Please sit down," Cooper said. Mills noticed that Lieutenant Barnes was pale and his arm was in a sling.

He appeared to have lost weight and was not as fit looking as she'd seen him in the past.

The detective sat down in a chair in front of Cooper and said, "I'm sorry you were hurt before the hurricane. I apologize that it's taken me longer than expected to get back to you. The medical examiner's office has not been fully operational, due to storm damage."

The usually zealous policeman spoke in a subdued tone and continued, "I have bad news for you, but it's what I expected. There was a dental records match between your wife, Elise, and the woman's remains in the well."

Cooper appeared suddenly exhausted and he rested his head on his hand, leaning over his desk.

"There was a handbag in the well, one that you described as being in her possession at the time of her disappearance. It was in decent condition, considering the moisture that surrounded it. Inside I found a letter to your wife from Jeff Radcliffe. A handwriting expert has confirmed its authenticity. This is a copy," he said, handing Cooper the document.

As he read the words, Cooper's face turned white as snow and he looked faint.

"Lieutenant? In the barn, Jeff said that he had never intentionally hurt anyone in his life."

"She had a fractured skull."

"I see," Cooper responded.

"There was a chemical compound called GHB, or gamma-hydroxybutyrate, in her handbag. When ingested, it can cause an individual to lose consciousness rapidly, and in forensic investigation, it's hard to detect. High doses can lead to respiratory and heart failure. Your cousin had a drug dealer, Troy Whitley, with whom he dealt with on a regular basis, usually to purchase cocaine. Troy's under arrest for drug-related charges, but you can imagine how quickly adding attempted murder to a set of charges will loosen someone's tongue. He said that Jeff had purchased GHB from him on more than one occasion—about the time you nearly drowned while diving in the Turks and Caicos Islands, and then right before your dove shoot that was canceled after your wife vanished."

"Oh, no," Cooper said. Mills and Cooper exchanged glances.

"I spoke to Erik Grootman, the dive master on the sailboat on the day that you nearly died. He said he changed the dive site at the last moment from a deep-water dive to a nondecompression dive, due to weather conditions. Elise was your dive partner. Where was she while you were drowning? You were fortunate that Mr. Grootman noticed you were in trouble. Being blindsided by someone you trust is virtually impossible to defend against."

"Lieutenant, when you came to my house on the eve of the hurricane, were you already aware of the contents of her purse?"

"I was, but I had to wait on a dental records comparison to verify her identity."

"While I was lying on the floor of the barn with two gunshot wounds, I wanted to get my hands on Jeff and then on you. Do you feel any remorse for the deputy that died?"

"Yes."

"What was it you said to Murphy Black? Even those who exhibit grace under pressure have their breaking point. You got what you were looking for."

"It wasn't just you. Can you imagine what it must have been like for Jeff—concealing these terrible secrets month after month, borrowing large sums of money from you and hiding his betrayal? The punishment that our own guilt imposes on us can be far worse than any penitence that society might decree."

"How do you know about my financial assistance to Jeff?"

"We've been monitoring your bank accounts and Jeff Radcliffe's since your wife's disappearance."

"Let's see. You knew I was innocent when you came out here, but you manipulated the two of us in an attempt to extract a confession. Barnes, you have a unique approach to law enforcement: sacrifice the innocent."

"Really, Heath, if I'd known you were injured, I would not have pursued your cousin."

"Where were you during the storm, Lieutenant?"

"I don't know. I must have spent the night in someone's house."

"In the future, I would prefer to come to police headquarters if you have questions for me. You are acquainted with my attorney, Murphy Black, and I'd appreciate any future discussions be arranged through him. In fact, unless you have a warrant for my arrest, don't come here at all."

"The coroner's office will be in touch with you, and I'm sorry for what you've been through."

"You're sorry for what I've been through? I've been harassed and vilified, and you're just going to say, 'Sorry, Cooper?'" He looked at Mills and then at Lieutenant Barnes. "If she had not been with me, I would have died. You don't appear to be in any better shape than I am right now. Are you afraid that someone might make an arrest and deprive you of your glory? I usually show my guests to the door, but in your case, you can show yourself out!"

Cooper was livid, and he sat back in his desk chair with his eyes closed. The policemen looked at Cooper and then rose from their seats and left through the front door. Calmly, Cooper turned and picked up the photograph of his wife on the shelf behind him. He studied her face for a few moments and then abruptly rose from his seat and hurled her picture into the fireplace.

He collapsed back into the chair as Ian entered the room. "Mills, could I talk to Cooper alone, please?"

She nodded and left the two men in the study.

Cooper would have one more visitor that afternoon. When Mills answered the door, an attractive woman with red-rimmed eyes stood on the porch. She explained to Mills that she was Lana Monroe, Elise's mother, and she wanted to speak to Cooper. "I've tried to phone out here, but your telephone is out of order."

When Cooper joined her in the living room, they hugged each other, and Mrs. Monroe wept as he held her. He asked her to sit down and she said, "I've had a visit from Lieutenant Barnes."

"Yes. I have as well."

"I'm sorry about what has happened." She was silent for a moment. "I noticed a change in Elise's behavior over the last few years, but I didn't do anything about it. I first noticed it while your mother was ill, when you were devoting a great deal of your time to her care. Elise must have become involved with Jeff then. There were times that she told you she was visiting with Carl and me. When you'd call, I wasn't sure what to do, so I told you she was with her friends, Cassie and Madge. I confronted her about it once and she told me to mind my own affairs. I should have told you the truth. Carl is bitter and is blaming you. He keeps saying that if you had paid attention to what was happening in your own household, this would not have occurred. He was aware of her change in behavior, but he's not willing to accept that Elise had a role in this. Lieutenant Barnes said that Jeff and Elise were heavy users of cocaine. He also told me about the drug that was found in her purse—and the letter. Cooper, I just can't believe they would hurt you. This is devastating for me."

Cooper took her hand in his, but said nothing.

"I would like to handle the funeral arrangements," Lana said.

With this statement, she began to cry, and Mills went to the pantry to get her a glass of water. When Mrs. Monroe regained composure, she stood up and said, "Thank you for seeing me. I didn't realize you were hurt until I saw an article in the newspaper."

As she made her way to the door, she said, "I hope you feel better soon. I know you are innocent, and Carl will eventually realize this, but it's going to take some time."

After she departed, Ian made the suggestion that they move to his house on Church Street. "Electrical power has been restored to the Charleston peninsula, and I think we will have an easier time of it."

As Mills got their possessions together, Ian spoke to her privately. "I'm very worried about Cooper, and I think he should not be sitting out here in the dark. I want to see if he will accompany me to work a few hours each day, and I would appreciate your assisting him. It would be good for both of you."

When they arrived at Ian's home, Mills called her mother and sister. Williston had phoned them to keep them informed, but they were anxious to speak with Mills and very concerned about Cooper.

Ian gave up his downstairs bedroom for his nephew, and that evening, Mills read to him. She thought Cooper had fallen asleep, but when she closed the book, he spoke, "We walked out of the house together. Thank you for standing by me."

"You know I love you."

"Would you please hold me?"

She put the book down and slid under the covers with Cooper.

The following morning, the *Charleston Dispatch* had a front-page article on Elise Heath and the facts about the case. As Cooper read the article, he said, "My private hell is no longer private. You've got to hand it to him. Mr. Mencken has done a thorough investigation."

When Ian read the article, he said, "This will not be the end of it." He paused as he sipped his coffee. "Williston suggested that you might want to see a doctor, someone to help you sort through the events of this last year."

"You mean a psychiatrist?"

"I think you could benefit from just talking to someone."

"I'll think about it."

The employees at Heath Brothers were ecstatic when Cooper came to work that morning. As she glanced around the office, Mills noticed the newspaper article about Elise Heath was on several desks, but they quickly disappeared from view.

Cooper was still using Grey Camp's cane to help with balance, but Mills realized that, each day, he got stronger and used the staff less. When Ian and Cooper engaged in a business conversation, she was always included, and Cooper told her she'd be running Heath Brothers in no time.

That afternoon, while Cooper rested, Mills sat outside on the patio at Ian's home. A tree crew had already been to his house, and she was saddened to see several of his live oaks had suffered broken limbs that had to be cut back. There was the sound of someone clearing their throat, and Mills turned to see Lee Mencken standing at the brick wall that surrounded the rear garden.

"Good afternoon, Miss Taylor."

"Hello, Lee," she responded.

"Is Mr. Heath available?"

"No, he's resting right now."

"I seem to always come at the wrong time," he said, pushing his hair back. "Miss Taylor, have you heard from Jeff Radcliffe?"

"Lee—why do you ask such a question?"

"Someone tried to cash a check for nine thousand dollars that was made out to Jeff Radcliffe from Cooper Heath. The teller questioned the authenticity of the check, and while she went to get the supervisor, the man left. He had light hair, but unfortunately the bank's security cameras have been malfunctioning since the storm, and his image is distorted." He handed Mills a business card over the brick wall and said goodbye, his blond hair blowing in the wind as he walked down the sidewalk.

Lieutenant Barnes phoned Cooper that afternoon and confirmed what Lee Mencken had already disclosed. The man who had attempted to cash the check bore a resemblance to Jeff Radcliffe. There was another odd turn of events; several residential listings of Jeff's real estate company had been recently robbed, but there was no sign of forced entry at any of them. When he finished the conversation with the detective, Cooper put a stop payment on the check.

"I wonder how Lee Mencken got that information."

"You said he was a thorough investigator."

"Yes, I did," Cooper said with a smile.

A few days later, Celeste, Cooper's aunt, returned home. She had delayed her trip due to the conditions in Charleston, but she wanted to help care for Cooper. The evening of her return, Jeff's father, Robert Radcliffe, came to see them.

"I have just returned from police headquarters. A man tried to cash a check made out to Jeff from you, Cooper. He resembled my son. When he attempted to cash the check, he was detained by a bank security guard. The police have charged him with an assortment of crimes, including grand larceny."

Mr. Radcliffe rubbed his temples and said, "He found the check and keys to several of Jeffrey's residential listings in a floatation container near Rockville. The container was in the marsh grass and instead of turning over the contents to the police, he took advantage of others. Apparently, he used the keys to the listings to break inside while homeowners were away. Cooper, I didn't realize Jeff was borrowing money from you. I don't understand why he didn't speak to me about a loan if he needed it."

Cooper took his uncle's hand, and Mr. Radcliffe continued, "I'm at a loss about this whole ordeal. I can't understand Jeff's behavior. Please forgive us, Cooper."

As he rose from his seat to leave, he wiped tears from his face and said, "I will repay every cent that is owed to you."

"Thank you, Uncle Robert."

Mr. Radcliffe hugged Cooper before he went out the door.

CHAPTER 30

Dark and Stormy

On the morning of Elise Heath's funeral, rain fell gently as Cooper's closest friends and family rode with him to St. Thomas Church in Charleston. Elise was to be buried near Moncks Corner, but there would be no graveside service because of the still-hazardous condition of some of the roadways. Visitation was one hour prior to the service, and Cooper stood in line to greet the steady stream of mourners as they came through the church. He asked Mills to stand beside him, and she noticed that Carl Monroe gave Cooper evil looks from time to time.

An older gentleman took Cooper's hand and told him he was sorry about Elise, but then said, "We heard that you'd been—well, never mind. I'm glad to see you here."

Piet van der Wolf hugged Mills and shook Cooper's hand. He quietly said to Cooper, "I know you're a man of your own means, but I would be honored to help you if you need anything."

Cooper thanked him for his graciousness. In line behind Piet were Madge and Cassie. They had both been in tears as their red-rimmed eyes showed. This did not stop Madge from verbally sparring with Cooper.

"I heard that you passed away—that you were fatally shot in a fight with Jeffrey over Elise. You've made a magnificent resurrection."

Cooper did not respond to her, and her expression changed to one of sadness. "I am sorry, Cooper. I'm sorry for all of us."

As Madge and Cassie walked away, Mills noticed Lieutenant Barnes and two other plain clothes policemen standing with him near the entrance to the church. An organ began to play, and Cooper and Mills took their seats.

The pastor who led the services had come from North Carolina, where he'd known Elise as a child. He spoke of her exceptional beauty and how everyone adored her. There was no mention of Jeff Radcliffe or Cooper for that matter; he chose to speak only of fond remembrances that he had of Elise. On top of her casket were several beautiful photographs, including a copy of the one that had sat behind Cooper's desk.

Mills was still having a difficult time believing that Jeff could have done what he was accused of. Elise's car had been located on the Camp property. It had been sunk into a deep pond, and the police had towed it from the murky waters. The thought of Cooper's premonitions about Elise gave Mills chills whenever she thought about the accuracy of his dreams. The dark chasm where she was trapped was an abandoned well—her sepulcher—and the sound of moving water came from the nearby Ashley River.

After the funeral, Mills lost sight of Cooper in the crowd of mourners, but she saw him as he walked out of the church with his father-in-law. She followed them outside but could not see them because of the height of the grave markers. When she heard their voices, she moved quickly and located them just as Carl Monroe shoved Cooper. Mills ran to Cooper's side to stop the altercation.

"Do you have women fighting for you now, you son of a bitch?"

He looked at Mills and said, "Young woman, how long did it take this bastard to charm his way into your bed?"

"Leave him alone!"

She looked at Cooper, who was calm despite the situation. "Carl, I have no intentions of fighting you."

"It's been a long time since I heard you play the piano. You've played your last composition. I'm going to break every bone in both your hands."

"Carl, go back inside the church," Cooper said, trying to reason with him.

"Like hell I will!"

He came toward Cooper, but Cooper held his ground and pushed Carl away. Mills started to scream for help, and she placed herself in front of Carl Monroe in an attempt to stop the attack. He shoved her aside.

"Carl, keep your hands off her!"

"Or what?"

Carl picked up a small marble urn off a marker and raised it to strike Cooper. He connected with a blow across Cooper's forearm and Cooper backed away slightly. As Carl attempted to strike Cooper again, Cooper tripped over a rain-slicked stone and fell amongst the graves. Carl was on him immediately and pulled Cooper's right hand across a marker. As he raised the urn to hit Cooper, a hand grabbed his arm and Carl Monroe was run head first into a large gravestone. Blood began to spill from his nose, and a police officer pinned him to the ground.

"Carl, you didn't really think we would allow you to do something like this, did you? Cooper, I let you out of my sight for one minute and this happens," said Lieutenant Barnes.

He gave Cooper his hand and pulled him up from the graves. "Do you need a doctor?"

"No, I think I'll be all right. Thank you, Lieutenant."

He looked thoughtfully at Cooper and said, "It's nice to hear you say those words to me. Officer Walters, will you read Mr. Monroe his Miranda rights and take him to the patrol car?"

"I don't want to press charges. There's been enough pain already."

Lana Monroe had been informed of what was happening, and she ran to her husband's side. She came close to him and gestured toward Cooper with her hand. "It's not his fault. It was Elise and Jeff. Why can't you accept this, Carl?"

Mills looked toward the entrance gate to the cemetery and caught sight of Madge Sinclair, who was fixated on Cooper and crying. When Mills looked in her direction again, Madge was gone.

Lieutenant Barnes stepped close to Carl Monroe and said, "I was a Marine Corps officer just like you, but I don't recall the men I served with preying on an adversary that wasn't fit."

Carl jerked his arm away from the policeman, and his wife grabbed his hand, pulling him away from the scene.

"Thank you again, Lieutenant," Cooper said, as he walked away with Mills to the limousine.

Williston checked Cooper's side and declared that he was fortunate that the police arrived when they did. Charles was troubled that he had not prevented the attack in the first place, but Cooper assured him that he was all right.

That evening, a number of Cooper's friends and relatives came by Ian's home to visit. After everyone left, Cooper began to play songs on his uncle's piano. He performed beautiful compositions from memory. Then he began to play the song that he had written for Mills. After completing it the first time, he played it again, but before he finished the work, he lifted his hands from the keyboard. His hands trembled, and he stared at them before he slid from the piano seat to the floor in one fluid motion. Burying his head in his forearms, he cried until his body began to shake. Mills and Ian were immediately beside him and tried to lift him from the floor, but he remained there until his pent-up emotions were released.

Eventually, they were able to get him to his bed. Ian spoke to Mills in the hallway, "Don't hesitate to come and get me if you need anything during the night."

She got in the bed beside Cooper and held him tightly as he went to sleep. In the middle of the night, she was awakened by coldness inside the bedroom. Cooper was no longer beside her: he was standing undressed in front of an open window. He stared into the garden, his impressive physique illuminated in the dim lights of the outside street lamps.

Quietly, she rose from the bed and went to his side. "Cooper, come to bed, the room is cold and you're going to get chilled."

Mills feared he was sleepwalking and she gently led him back to the bed. After he was settled under the covers, she closed the window and got in bed beside him. He quietly said to her, "Jeff is alive. I was on the *Miss Elise* alone. I looked into the water, and just below the surface was his face, laughing at me. His hand came out of the water to pull me in."

"Shhh. I've got you. Try to go back to sleep." *I fear he's on the verge of an emotional breakdown.*

When morning came, Mills went to Ian and told him of the events of the night. Ian looked thoughtfully at Mills before saying, "I think you and Cooper could use a change in scenery. My wife owns a home in Bermuda, and I'm going to find a doctor for Cooper to talk with while you're there. I know you'll look after him, and apparently he still needs care, more than I realized."

Before the airliner landed in Bermuda, Mills could see the clear blue-green waters that surrounded the island, and she thought of Jeff. When they went through immigration, the officer who attended them was acquainted with the Heath family. He knew the story of the torpedoed American transport and the bravery of the men who had rescued some of the crew in waters off Bermuda during World War II.

"When I was a child, my father took me to the Maritime Museum in Sandy's Parish. I was fascinated by the courage of your father and his crew, going into shark-infested waters to get those men out—your father was a true hero."

Cooper thanked him for his kindness and then the officer asked Cooper if he was visiting for business or pleasure.

He responded, "Relaxation. I'm trying to calm my nerves."

The officer thought he was joking and told him to have a wonderful vacation.

The morning after their arrival, a diminutive man with white, wispy hair came to their door at nine o'clock. He introduced himself as Dr. Bakker. "My old friend, Williston Devereux, has explained that you might want to talk about some issues that have been bothering you. I'd like to help," he said with a smile.

Cooper spent the next two hours speaking with Dr. Bakker on a screened porch. When the doctor left, he made a request of Mills.

"I'll be here tomorrow at nine o'clock, and if you don't mind—I like to drink iced tea while I talk with patients. Thank you, Miss Taylor."

He reminded her of Fritz with his white hair and the formality in his tone of voice.

When she joined Cooper on the porch, he took her hand. "Dr. Bakker says that I'm depressed and wants to help me. I suppose I didn't need him to tell me that. He says that he would like to speak with you as well, if you don't mind."

"I don't mind."

He rose from his seat and led her inside. "I'm going to take you to lunch and then we'll explore the island."

For the next few weeks, mornings were spent with Dr. Bakker, and Mills always had his glass of iced tea ready when he arrived. Occasionally, he questioned Mills about Cooper and Jeff, and her thoughts about both of them. Cooper joked that his uncle must be paying Dr. Bakker handsomely because he was making house calls. "Williston makes house calls out of friendship," he added.

Each afternoon, they spent time exploring the island; it was beautiful like St. John and perhaps the cleanest place she had ever visited. The most fascinating aspects of the island were water-filled caves with stalagmites and stalactites. The ocean water surrounding the island was almost sapphire-blue with a hint of light green and, at times, the clouds in the sky took on the same coloration as the ocean. The sea was the color of Jeff Radcliffe's eyes.

Some afternoons, they went to the Princess Hotel in Hamilton for a Dark and Stormy, the cocktail that had been introduced to her at Ian's party months before. The weather was like an Indian summer with warm days and cool nights. They spent some early evenings looking out over the Atlantic from the porch. Cooper had been quiet when they first arrived, but as the days went by, he talked to Mills for hours at a time. Their passionate lovemaking of the summer had been replaced by an intimacy of gentle caresses and kisses.

One afternoon, they took the ferry from Hamilton to Sandy's Parish and toured the Maritime Museum. On a wall that featured exhibits from World War II was a series of photographs honoring the crew of the Heath Brothers' ship that rescued the men off the stricken American transport. A photograph of Cooper's father was included in the display, and the resemblance between father and son was remarkable.

"He would have been about twenty-five in that photograph," Cooper said.

"You look just like him. No wonder your mother mistook you for him when she had Alzheimer's."

"How did you know that?"

"Marian told me."

Cooper smiled and put his arm around her. "Let's take the ferry back to Hamilton. I want to show you something and then we'll go to the Princess for a Dark and Stormy."

When they disembarked the ferry, Cooper led her across Front Street to a goldsmith that had exotic, beautiful jewelry displayed in the windows. A cruise ship was in town, and the area bustled with tourists. Cooper opened the door to the jewelry store and led Mills to a glass case with unique wedding bands. They were engraved with what appeared to be ancient Greek designs and were a brilliant shade of gold, at least eighteen carat.

Cooper asked the jeweler to show them the rings, and he asked Mills, "Which one do you like the best?"

She tried on several and then picked one as her favorite. She showed it to him and said, "I think this ring is beautiful."

As she handed the ring back to the jeweler, Cooper said, "That's all I wanted to know. Tomorrow, I have a place I'd like to show you, so be ready to go after Dr. Bakker and I finish talking."

The next afternoon, Cooper took Mills to lunch in St. George's Parish. They drove past the airport to get to this area of the island, and Cooper pointed out abandoned railway trestles that had formerly supported a working train system that had traversed the island. Only the trestles remained; the rails had been sold, long ago, to another country.

"We're going to St. George. This area was one of the first portions to be settled by Europeans after a shipwreck in the early 1600s. The ship was on its way to Jamestown, Virginia, but it met its fate on the reefs."

"How can you remember things like that?"

"I came here with my parents a number of times, and I raced in regattas with Jeff."

He bought Mills a lunch of conch fritters and then led her through the village. In front of the plaza at King's Square were sets of stocks, and Mills put her head and arms through the wooden devices. "I think this form of punishment could have been quite miserable . . . especially during the summer months," she said.

As they walked through the town, Cooper led her to a whitewashed church that stood on Duke of York Street. "This is St. Peter's Church. I remember touring it when I was a boy. Let's go inside."

Mills marveled at the roughhewn cedar beams in the church, and Cooper said, "It's amazing, but this church was built in the early 1600s and some of the original pews are still used today."

He led her to the altar, and then got down on his knees in front of her and took her hand in his. "Mills, I can't begin to tell you how much you mean to me. When I was lonely, you gave me hope, and when I was hurt, I don't know what I would have done without you. I love you, and I want you to be my wife."

He took a ring box out of his jacket pocket and opened the case, which held two magnificent wedding bands that Cooper had showed her in the jewelry store on Front Street. He slipped her favorite ring on her left ring finger. She took the other ring from the box and then joined him on her knees, placing the ring on his finger.

"The answer is yes—I want to be your wife."

They repeated marriage vows to one another. A clergyman entered the sanctuary and smiled at them with approval, but then continued his business, leaving them alone. Cooper kissed her, and they held each other tightly, until he whispered, "I have another place I'd like to show you."

Driving to a secluded beach on the south shore, Cooper brought out a bottle of champagne and two glasses. He opened the bottle, and they sat down together, looking at the pink sand and the waves that kissed the beach.

"How did you get the rings and the champagne without my knowing?"

"Dr. Bakker was kind enough to pick them up for me. He says that he's a romantic at heart and was glad to help."

As they sat quietly together, Mills asked, "Are you feeling better?"

"I needed to rest, more than I realized. I have been told that deep emotional wounds can take a long time to heal."

When they returned to the house, Cooper led Mills into the bedroom and passionately took her in his arms. After weeks of gentle caresses, this was a return to the deeply romantic way he had loved her during the summer. They fell asleep in each other's arms, feeling secure in the love they shared for one another.

The next morning, Dr. Bakker thanked Mills for her hospitality during the weeks that he visited with Cooper. "I have enjoyed meeting you and Mr. Heath. If I can be of help in the future, don't hesitate to phone me. Mr. Heath has told me he is ready to return to Charleston. Thanksgiving is now several days away, and he says he would like to go home."

He took her right hand in his, first studying her sapphire-and-diamond ring, and then took her left hand and examined her new gold ring. "Your rings are lovely, and they complement your pearls nicely." He paused for a moment and said, "You make excellent iced tea, Miss Taylor. I hope you have enjoyed your stay in Bermuda. It's a beautiful place, is it not?"

"Yes, sir, it is."

"My best wishes to you and Mr. Heath, and happy Thanksgiving."

When Dr. Bakker left the house, Mills joined Cooper on the screened porch. She put her hand on his shoulder and sat down beside him. He turned toward her, and asked, "Are you ready to go home?"

"Yes."

"When we repeat our wedding vows, what type of wedding would you like?"

"I'd like an intimate wedding with our friends and family in attendance. I love your surprises. Why don't you surprise me?"

He smiled at her and then kissed the palm of her hand.

CHAPTER 31

The Beauty in White

When they returned to Charleston, there were several letters waiting for Cooper from Mrs. Adams. She had included spiritual passages in her writings that were meant to be supportive of Cooper. He wrote her back and told her he was touched by her thoughtfulness.

Just before Thanksgiving, Cooper asked Mills to meet him at Heath Brothers, saying that he wanted her to go with him to make a purchase. When she asked what the purchase was, he responded, "Let it be a surprise."

They drove to the courthouse where Cooper took out a marriage license. "Do you think there could be sentiment against our marrying so soon after Elise's funeral?"

"I've grieved for over a year now. I want to be your husband, although Carl Monroe might shoot me when he finds out."

"Don't even joke about that."

He smiled, putting his arm around her, and then placed the license in his wallet.

Thanksgiving arrived a few days later, and Cooper told Mills they would dine with his uncle in Charleston later in the day. He wanted to take her out on the river, and they walked to the waterfront.

At the dock was a new fishing boat, a Grady-White, named *Mills*. "This is my wedding gift to you," he said.

She put her arms around his neck and thanked him for the wonderful present. "I like the boat, and I love you, Cooper," Mills declared, as she hugged his neck.

"You shall be her first captain."

Cooper assisted her with starting the engines, and they took the boat toward the ocean in the cool morning air. They anchored the boat at Mrs. Salter's beach property and gathered seashells to take home. After a long walk, he looked at his watch and suggested they return home to dress for the trip into Charleston. The last words he spoke before starting the engines were, "I have much to be thankful for."

When they arrived at his dock, Mills was astounded to see her mother and sister and their boyfriends waiting at the riverfront. They hugged one another and Cooper whispered, "I forgot to mention that we're going to have a few folks join us for Thanksgiving. This is part of my gift to you."

As they made their way to his home, Mills realized that all the parking spots were full and a large gathering of family and friends waited for them inside. Piet van der Wolf smiled at her with adoration, and Mr. and Mrs. Adams hugged them. Mrs. Adams had a beautiful smile that Mills had never before noticed. Cooper's Uncle Ian stepped forward and said, "Joseph is ready when you two are."

"We'll be back in a few minutes," Cooper told his guests.

He led Mills into the master bedroom; pressed and lying on the bed was a magnificent tea-length wedding gown with pearls woven into the lace. White high heels were on the floor in front of the bed.

"Are you ready to repeat your wedding vows?"

She jumped into his arms and excitedly said, "You've made me so happy. I had no idea you had planned this."

"What, and ruin your surprise?"

While dressing, Mill tried to put her pearls on, but her hands were trembling so much that she could not close the clasp.

"Come here. I'll help you." He fastened the necklace and then turned her around to face him. "You're my beautiful bride."

Mills went to the mirror. The dress fit perfectly, and she gazed at herself from different angles. *I couldn't possibly be any more excited!*

When they left the bedroom, the first person they met was Blair. He stopped them and said, "Cooper, Mom says that you and Mills are going to get married today. I wanted to be one of the first to welcome her into the family. Since I'm too young to get married, I think it's great that you will be her husband. At least we get to keep her in the family."

Mills bent down and kissed him on the cheek, and Cooper shook his hand. "Thank you, Blair; one day, there will be a wonderful girl for you to love and marry."

When they entered the living room, Reverend Smalls called the wedding guests together. Anne Jefferson gave Mills a bouquet of small pink roses. Her hands trembled as she accepted it, and Vivien came to her side as maid of honor. Cooper's uncle stood with him as best man. Mills's mother, Rebecca, beamed at her daughters from the front row of chairs in the living room.

When they completed their vows, Reverend Smalls told Cooper that he could kiss his bride, and Cooper put his arms around her. The afternoon was spent in joyous merriment. The wedding guests congratulated the bride and groom, and then partook in an outstanding Thanksgiving dinner. The guests had brought a dish for the feast, and Marian had roasted an exceptionally large turkey. When Mills finally settled down, tears came to her eyes and she wept with joy. Cooper removed a handkerchief from his suit pocket and wiped her tears. Looking down at her white high heels, he whispered, "How did I do on picking out your shoes?"

"This is the pair I would have chosen."

"I've got your blood in my veins now, Mills, but I'll try and control my shoe fetish and let you wear the high heels in the family—you look better in them anyway."

"Oh, Cooper," she smiled and cried at the same time.

The next several weeks were times of excitement, full of shopping for Christmas and attending gatherings and dinners. As Christmas neared, they often spent the night in Cooper's townhouse on Tradd Street. The hurricane had caused little damage to this home, but the intrusion of salt water into his garden had killed many plants and would have to be tended in the spring. While they lay in bed one night, there was a late phone call.

Jeff's father was on the line and he had some shocking news. The *Theodosia* had been located in St. John in the US Virgin Islands, moored to the mangroves in the Hurricane Hole. When no one moved it after several weeks, the authorities checked the ship's registry and found that it belonged to Jeff Radcliffe and two other partners. "There is no evidence to support that Jeffrey sailed the *Theodosia* to St. John, but I have hope, Cooper. God help me, I have hope."

When he hung up the receiver, Cooper held Mills close to him and said, "I wonder if Marcel Renaud is still in St. John?" He kissed her on the forehead and asked her to pray with him for Jeff.

Mills was excited to spend her first Christmas as Cooper's wife. They planned to join his Uncle Ian for Christmas day, but they wanted to spend Christmas Eve at the townhouse and make dinner together. Amazingly, a snowstorm moved along the coast two days before Christmas, and by Christmas Eve, a magnificent blanket of snow lay across the Low Country. The entire day, Mills and Cooper walked and played in the snow like teenagers. They threw snowballs and held hands as they made their way through the city streets. There were still areas where damage from the hurricane was obvious, and some debris lay in heaps, coated by the pure white of the driven snow.

From the promenade at The Battery, Mills grasped the metal railing and gazed toward Fort Sumter, which was occasionally obscured by passing low-level clouds. She looked at Cooper and said, "It's as though the city is being reborn by the cleansing beauty of the snow." She thought for only a moment about the dreams she had endured about her father's death, and the snow that had fallen on the day he died. She considered it for just a moment, and then her thoughts came back to the present and the happiness she felt with Cooper.

Late in the afternoon, they passed by St. Michael's, which was having a Christmas Eve service; despite the snowstorm, the church was filled with worshippers. Mills and Cooper shook the snow from their boots and clothes, and went inside. They sat near the back and listened to the pastor speak about the birth of the Christ Child and the sacrifices he would make for mankind. He then spoke of the sacrifices that many people in the Charleston area had made to help others in the wake of the hurricane, and how sacrifices were still being made. "Goodness and mercy can come from the hearts of all men and women when the community gathers together to overcome the worst of situations. I believe our Lord would say, cast out thy net to all people and help those in need—and find forgiveness in your hearts for those who have trespassed against you."

The pastor closed his service with a prayer, and Cooper sat motionless for just a moment before he said, "Cast out thy net to all men."

Mills looked back into his eyes and said, "That's the inscription on the grave marker of George and Grey Camp."

"Yes, that's right. They were exceptional men, and ahead of their time." Cooper helped Mills with her coat, and they walked outside into the cold evening air. The sky was beginning to darken, but the beauty of the snow that blanketed the city was virtually perfect. They walked to the bandstand in White Point Gardens, and Cooper took her by the hand and led her up the steps. He held her tightly, and they slowly rotated in the center of the stage, away from snow drifts that covered the edges of the structure. He whispered in her ear, "I love you, I've got you, and I'll never let you go."

The End